Miss Ellerby and the Ferryman

Tales of Aylfenhame, Book 2

Charlotte E. English

CHAPTER ONE

Now, halt just a moment if ye'd be so kind! There's a toll to pay, if ye wish to pass over the Tilby bridge, an' I'm the toll-keeper. Balligumph's my name! I may be a troll but I'll not be hurtin' ye. No, I'll not ask ye to step out o' yer fine carriage, but yer coachman won't do. I need a toll from ye. Nowt o' any particular importance, mind. Just a bit of information. Yer name, an' yer business in Tilby; that'll do. An' one little tidbit o' somethin' else — somethin' secret-like. That'll do nicely. An' on ye go!

Or, no! Stay a while. I fancy I've heard yer name before. Maybe I'm mistaken — I'm no young troll, ye may notice, an' I sometimes forget things. Remind me. Was it yer good self to whom I told the tale o' Miss Sophy Landon an' her husband, Aubranael? It's tales I like. I like to hear 'em, an' I like to tell 'em. Ye'll remember, perhaps, about Miss Sophy, an' what a fix she was in. No home, no money, an' no one to look after her! But she's well an' settled in Grenlowe now — that bein' a town in Aylfenhame, ye'll recall — an' mighty happy she is.

But she's not the only young lady o' Tilby to get 'erself entangled wi' the faerie realm. She 'as a friend, Miss Isabel — oh, she's one o' the kindest young ladies in these parts, no doubt o' that! Perhaps ye'd like t' hear her story? It's a jolly tale, for all tha' she came to — well, no, I'll no give away the ending! Come, sit wi' me a while an' I'll start from the beginnin'!

'Isabel, my love, do come and look! The shoe-roses have arrived. Now, these will do very well with your lavender gown, do you not think?'

Mrs. Ellerby's voice, penetrating in its enthusiasm, carried easily over the sounds made by the Ellerby household brownie as she vigorously swept the parlour hearth. Isabel's mother chattered on, holding up handfuls of ribbons, shoe roses and other trifles for her daughter's perusal and approval. With an inward sigh, Isabel set aside her needlework, and went to the parlour table.

'They are beautiful, Mama,' she said in a mild tone, 'but I had thought we had decided upon my gown for tomorrow? Is it not to be the blue?'

Mrs Ellerby nodded absently, her attention fixed, apparently irrevocably, on the ribbons in her hands. 'It is what we agreed upon, but think, my love, how much the lavender becomes you! It is the very thing to go with your hair. If you had been light-haired I should not venture to recommend it, for it can be a trifle insipid! But with your colouring I should think it the very thing!' Mrs Ellerby continued on in this style for some time while her daughter listened dutifully, playing about with a piece of gold ribbon which had fallen from the box.

In due course came the inevitable. 'And I am persuaded, you know, that it is the very thing which Mr. Thompson would like.'

'Mama,' said Isabel gently, 'we must not allow Mr. Thompson's supposed preferences to rule us entirely. I should prefer the blue.'

'Yes, yes, I am sure you are right.' Mrs. Ellerby paused, and bent her attention to a fresh pair of shoe-roses she had at that moment pulled from the box.

Isabel waited.

'But I am persuaded you might reconsider, if only you were to think —'

'Mama! Please! It is decided: I shall wear the blue.' Isabel dropped her ribbon and stood up. 'It is time for my walk, now that the rain has cleared. Please, put the shoe-roses away.'

Mrs. Ellerby subsided with only one more faint protest, and Isabel made her escape.

It was early in July, and the morning was warm. Isabel regretted the bonnet and spencer jacket that propriety insisted she should wear, though the former was of straw and the latter of the lightest sarsenet. A breeze ruffled her dark brown locks as she turned in the direction of Tilton Wood, and for a wistful moment she considered removing her bonnet entirely, and tucking it under her arm. After all, there was no one to see her.

But no, it would not do. A passerby may happen upon her at any moment, and even were it but a farmer, Miss Ellerby of Ferndeane must not be seen to commit so great an impropriety as to wander the fields of Tilby without a hat. Her Mama would be appalled.

Resigned, Isabel heaved a great sigh and walked on, turning into Tilton Wood with relief. The great oak trees offered cooling shade, and the sunlight filtered through the green, green leaves cast pleasing dapples over the earthen floor. Isabel slowed her pace to a stroll, and her tumbling thoughts slowed to match it.

Mr. Thompson was the son of an old friend of her Mama's — at least, Mrs. Ellerby chose to claim Mrs. Thompson as a friend. In truth, they had merely been at school together, and Isabel could not find out that they had ever been close. But her schoolfellow had married well. The Thompsons were a family of consequence, settled some fifteen or twenty miles south of York, and Mr. Thompson was, as yet, unmarried.

By some means beyond Isabel's comprehension, her mother had re-established contact with Mrs. Thompson, coaxed her into renewing their acquaintance and had at last persuaded her to attend an assembly in Lincolnshire — with her son. That assembly was due to take place tomorrow night, hence all Mrs. Ellerby's anxious preparations today.

Nothing had been said to Isabel in so many words, but she understood that she was to be offered to the young man as an eligible bride. Her family was not wealthy, but they were respectably endowed with a genteel fortune, and Isabel could expect to inherit some twelve thousand pounds someday. Mama hoped that this, together with Isabel's person, manners and accomplishments, might be sufficient to tempt the young man.

Isabel's own feelings upon the matter were undecided. She had long known that she was expected to raise the credit and position of her family through her marriage, and now that her brother Charles had engaged himself to Miss Jane Ellis — a very pleasant, unobjectionable girl, but one who brought neither money nor connection to her marriage — the obligation had fallen more heavily upon Isabel herself. She had rejected the advances of Mr. Reed, Tilby's new parson, not long since. He was neither rich enough nor important enough to satisfy her parents, and he had not been congenial enough to satisfy her. But having failed to accept one proposal of marriage, her parents were beginning to grow anxious that she should soon receive another.

She was ready to perform her duty, and willing to be directed by her parents if it must be so. Their ambitions were not such as to lead them to bestow her upon anyone unworthy, or to give her in marriage to anyone she had taken in dislike. But she felt all the pressure of their hopes and expectations keenly, and she knew very well that Mama especially had set her heart upon Isabel's liking Mr. Thompson well enough to marry him.

Of course, since his marriage with Isabel would bring him little by way of connection or standing and only a moderate fortune, it fell upon her to try to capture his heart. This she was not at all certain she was equal to. Mrs. Ellerby sensed this, and had tried to make up for Isabel's reluctance with a fever of preparation over her dress, hair and ornaments. If Mr. Thompson did not instantly fall in love with her daughter's beauty, it would not be for lack of trying.

These reflections weighed heavily upon Isabel's mind as she strolled and sighed through Tilton Wood, paying only the barest attention to the route she took. Her abstraction was such that she wandered deeper into the wilder parts than she would normally choose to do, and soon began to feel that she had lost her way.

She walked about for some minutes, attempting with all of her natural good sense to calm the flutter of worry which began to intrude upon her peace. But it would not do. She could not convince herself that she recognised any of the several winding pathways which presented themselves to her searching gaze, and the flutter of alarm grew. Tilton Wood was not known for being especially expansive, but it was fully large enough to detain her some hours should she lose her way. Severe would be Mama's alarm should she fail to reappear within an hour.

Schooling herself to calmness, she paused to consider that walking about aimlessly was as likely to render her situation worse, as to bring about any solution. She stopped instead, reposed herself upon a great branch which had fallen nearby, and applied herself to the question of how best to extricate herself from her predicament.

She had not been about this for more than a few moments before it occurred to her that the cluster of leaves at which she had been vacantly staring was not a cluster of leaves at all, but something living. Its limbs were as slender and gnarled as twigs, its head a shade too large for its body, and it sported a great pot-belly which strained against the ragged leaf-brown dress it wore. The creature's nose was as knotted as a whorl of wood, its ears long and twisted, its eyes bright, azure blue — and fixed upon her.

Isabel started, but before she could speak a word, the creature said in a high, lisping voice, 'Goodest of mornings to you, Mistress! What is your bidding?' She — for Isabel felt, by some instinct, that the creature was female — bowed low as she spoke, and offered Isabel a tiny violet flower.

Isabel opened her mouth; found, in her surprise, that she had nothing to say; and closed it again.

'Mistress?' prompted the little fae creature, staring fixedly up into Isabel's face.

'I think there must be some mistake,' said Isabel. 'I am not your mistress! Indeed, I do not think we have ever before met.'

'This is our first meeting,' agreed the fae, 'but without doubt, my mistress you are! For did you not summon me?'

'I assure you, I did not!' cried Isabel. 'I do not know how I could have done so! I am sorry, if you have been put to any trouble.'

The fae creature considered this in silence, her tiny lips pursed. 'Then you are not lost?' she said at last.

'I am lost,' Isabel admitted. 'But I feel sure I shall find my way at any moment; pray do not be put to any trouble on my account.'

'It is that way,' said the fae, pointing out the direction with a finger as thin and delicate as a new shoot.

Isabel glanced in the direction indicated. A pathway opened up through the thick undergrowth, clear and inviting. It was odd, but in beholding it now, it was perfectly evident that therein lay her route home.

Isabel came to her feet and shook out her skirt. 'Thank you,' she said, and curtseyed.

The little fae bobbed an ungainly curtsey in response and smiled with sunny enthusiasm, revealing a mouthful of green teeth.

'I am Tiltager,' she offered. 'This is my wood.' With that, she vanished. Isabel found herself staring at a cluster of leaves which so nearly resembled Tiltager, she wondered whether she had imagined the whole.

No; she had not. She paused a moment in indecision. Should she trust Tiltager? Fae were a common enough sight in England, but while some of them devoted themselves to aiding their human counterparts and sometimes formed the deepest friendships, others were equally dedicated to causing harm. Tiltager's path may not lead back to Tilby at all, but to somewhere else entirely; somewhere Isabel could have no wish to go.

But the little fae had seemed friendly. Nothing in her behaviour or her manner had led Isabel to suppose that she intended any harm. Isabel began walking in the direction Tiltager had indicated, tentatively at first and then with growing confidence as the pathway soon took on proportions that were familiar to her. It even seemed, as she walked, that the tranquil oaks sped by a little faster than was entirely reasonable, and she found herself restored to the outskirts of Tilby sooner than she had imagined possible.

CHAPTER TWO

If Isabel had entertained hopes that her mother's preparations for the assembly might, by nightfall, be considered completed, she was obliged to banish all such comforting thoughts almost as soon as she arose the following morning. She was woken at an intolerably early hour by her mother's sudden appearance in her room, apparently for the sole purpose of expressing her renewed concerns about Isabel's choice of gown — and shoes — and ornaments. Though Isabel succeeded in banishing her within a very few minutes, the attack was renewed at the breakfast table.

The onslaught continued throughout the day, and by the time the hour approached to step into the family carriage and depart, Isabel's nerves were torn to ragged shreds. She was, therefore, in no fit state to bear with equanimity the speech her father saw fit to address to her before she left the house.

Mr. Ellerby was typically of a congenial disposition, and inclined to be an indulgent parent. But once in a great while, when some matter struck him as bearing particular importance, he became grave and dignified, and spoke at great length in a style bordering upon forbidding. He was in just such a humour when Isabel, answering his summons, arrived at the door to his book-room. He gazed at his daughter with such pride that Isabel's heart softened even as she quailed at what she must inevitably hear.

'My dear Isabel,' he said gravely, as he indicated the chair in which she was to sit. 'You do the family great honour today.'

Isabel blinked, and wondered, with brief anxiety, whether he referred to her appearance in some obscure fashion or whether her hand had already been bestowed upon Mr. Thompson without her knowledge. She took the chair without speaking, taking great care not to crush the silken skirts of the lavender gown she had been at last persuaded into wearing.

'Your mother and I are both keen that this alliance with the Thompson family should take place,' he continued, 'and in view of the success of her diligent efforts I am sanguine indeed! For nothing could be more attaching than your appearance this evening. No man of sense, I am sure, could remain indifferent.'

Taking this to mean that she was expected to captivate the mysterious Mr. Thompson by the close of the assembly, Isabel could not feel much flattered by this tribute to her looks. Instead, a tight knot of anxiety formed in her stomach. Would Mr. Thompson find her appearance agreeable? Did she truly wish him to? How did he feel about the proposed alliance? She said none of these things, however, replying merely with a murmur of suitably modest gratitude for his confidence in her.

Mr. Ellerby's manner swiftly developed its deepest gravity and he said, 'I need not inform you, Isabel, of how important it is that you make a creditable appearance before the Thompsons. You are well aware of the desirability of this connection — the more so, following your brother's engagement to Miss Ellis. Indeed, I would not have sanctioned such a marriage had I not been possessed of the fullest confidence in your ability to improve the family's consequence with your own.'

'Yes, father.' Isabel, listening to this with a sinking heart, could find nothing more to say. It was his appalling confidence which silenced her; he could not conceive of a scenario where his daughter might fail in an object to which she had been assigned, or decline to do her duty.

Mr. Ellerby smiled upon his daughter with paralysing affection and said, more kindly, 'You will make us very proud, my dear. I have not the smallest doubt of it. And when Mr. Thompson sees you this evening, I know he cannot fail of being extremely pleased with you.'

Isabel murmured something else appropriate, and tried to ignore the deepening sense of foreboding she suffered in the wake of it. But an hour later, as she stepped down from her family's carriage and entered the Assembly Rooms at Alford, her spirits were so much affected that she struggled to muster even the appearance of enjoyment and anticipation that would satisfy her mother. Her cloak was taken, her shoes exchanged for the slippers suitable for dancing, and the assembly began; in such a whirl of colour and heat and noise that Isabel, in her troubled state, soon began to feel severely discomposed. In the mass of faces both familiar and strange which passed before her, she failed to distinguish the features which had been described to her as Mr. Thompson's. Finally her mother, impatient to achieve the sole object of the evening's excursion, caught her arm and propelled her towards a knot of particularly finely-dressed people who had taken up a station on the farthest side of the room from the door.

Isabel saw at once the reason for her mother's extreme anxiety about her choice of attire. The Thompson family bore every appearance of both considerable wealth and a value for the latest and highest fashions which far exceeded Isabel's own. They resembled a group of peacocks which had strayed into a farmyard; their clothes were in the best possible taste, and not at all garish, but the quality of their silks and velvets and the superiority of their jewels and ornaments cast even the best of Alford's society into the shade.

Mr. and Mrs. Thompson had both attended their son to the assembly. The elder Mr. Thompson was tall, his wife of a height perfectly matched to his. All three possessed smooth, curling locks in similar chestnut shades, and dark eyes. They more nearly resembled a work of art than a family of flesh and blood.

The younger Mr. Thompson was as tall as his father, with the same burnished curls. He was dressed in a pair of superb pale knee-breeches with a dark coat and waistcoat. This was all that Isabel was able to discern with the brief glance she dared to direct at him before introductions were made, and the curtsey she offered directed her eyes back to the floor.

'It is a pleasure to make your acquaintance, Miss Ellerby,' said Mr. Thompson. She raised her eyes to his face, and saw, to her relief, that he was smiling. His countenance was boyish, though she gathered him to be of some eight-and-twenty years of age, and his dark green eyes bore an expression of friendliness and good humour which she found reassuring. They rested upon her, moreover, with an air of mild approval, and she guessed him to be ready to be pleased by her. Isabel took a breath, and as she let it out much of her nervousness dissipated along with it.

He solicited her hand for the first dances in a very proper style, and with modesty which further recommended him to her; for he must be well aware that she had no power of refusal. He led her into the set, and as they awaited the beginning of the music he talked to her in an agreeable way about the dance, and the number of couples, and the roads, in a fashion exactly calculated to soothe. She found him to be an excellent partner. He danced with a little reserve, but with grace and perfect correctness. When the two dances were over, she was conscious of having enjoyed them more than she had expected to.

Afterwards, he led her to a sofa, bowed over her hand as he settled her upon it, and retreated for a few moments. He returned shortly, bearing a glass of punch for her, and seated himself beside her with a smile.

'I hope the circumstances of this meeting have not left you feeling too uncomfortable,' he said. 'Our families have been a little high-handed, I fear.'

Isabel was surprised into a genuine smile, though she felt it incumbent upon her to make a polite demurral.

'Oh, come now,' he said, laughing. 'To introduce us like this and expect that we should dutifully take to one another! It cannot have been easy for you, and I am sorry for it.'

'It has been unusual,' Isabel conceded, though she smiled as she spoke.

Mr. Thompson nodded. 'I did want to assure you that I shan't press any suit upon you unless we should both genuinely wish it,' he continued. 'And regardless of the wishes of your mother — or mine — I do not expect that any such conclusion can be arrived at under so short an acquaintance as this evening allows. Several more meetings, at least, will be necessary to determine our feelings.'

Isabel had not expected to receive such plain-speaking, and it briefly disconcerted her. But she was also reassured by it, and a moment's reflection allowed her to say, 'I am pleased to find that I can view the prospect of further meetings with pleasure.'

It was spoken with sincerity, for she found in Mr. Thompson a congenial young man, not at all the self-important high-stickler she had been picturing under the onslaught of her Mama's panic. It was far too early to imagine with equanimity the prospect of a lifetime spent as his wife, but the idea did not actively repel her.

Mr. Thompson smiled upon this cautious praise, looking, Isabel thought, rather relieved. Had his mother been as urgent with him as Mrs. Ellerby had with Isabel? Surely not, for the Thompsons enjoyed undoubtedly the stronger social position as well as being far wealthier.

Mr. Thompson began to talk of his family in a manner designed, Isabel felt, to introduce to her some idea of the company she would be keeping if she married him. She watched the dancers as he spoke of his three sisters, for she could see them all, suitably partnered and whirling about the floor. The picture he painted agreed but little with what she saw, for he spoke of amiable, unpretending young women, and they did not, to her eye, appear much pleased with their company.

She saw her brother Charles as well, dancing with Jane Ellis. Charles was smiling, and Jane was in high bloom. The match was not what her parents had hoped for, but that it made him happy, none could deny. Her friend Anne had also married the man of her choice, as had Sophy Landon. Isabel could only hope that her parents had chosen as well for her, as Anne, Charles and Sophy had chosen for themselves.

Mr. Thompson had progressed to speaking of his horses. She turned her attention back to him, watching his face as he talked. Amiable he might be, and well-looking, but he seemed well-pleased to talk at great length upon his own topics without requiring much response from her. Conscious of a feeling of boredom, it occurred to her that she had made little effort to speak, and she sought in her mind for a suitable topic.

But then the orchestra began to play a lively reel, which instantly inspired Mr. Thompson to bring an end to his disclosures and to say instead, 'May I solicit you as a partner for a second time, Miss Ellerby?'

Grateful for the interruption and not at all disinclined to dance, Isabel smiled upon him and allowed him to lead her back onto the floor. But as she waited for the couples to form and the dance to begin, she became aware of an alteration in the music. It began as a subtle change in the tone, as though one of the instruments had wandered off to play a slightly different part. Then it began to seem as though the instruments themselves had undergone some indescribable change; that what had once been a fiddle had transformed into something similar, but not quite the same — like the difference between a pianoforte and a harpsichord.

Isabel was obliged to turn about entirely in order to see the orchestra, and thus risk missing the beginning of the dance. But as the tones and the tune grew rapidly stranger, she could not refrain from satisfying herself that all was well. She turned.

The orchestra was not clearly visible from the dance floor, for they were raised up upon a square balcony which overlooked the hall some way above the dancers' heads. At first, all she could discern was the white, full sleeve of a fiddler billowing as he played, and a becurled head bobbing in time to the music. But then one of the players leaned over the rail to survey the dancers, affording Isabel a clear view of his countenance.

He was not human; that much she discerned at a glance. His skin was too white, and it shimmered in an odd way, like mother-of-pearl. His hair was pale too, long and straight and bound back in a fashion no gentleman would ever think proper. His eyes glittered like chips of ice and his smile stretched a fraction too wide.

Isabel stared. She now saw that not one of the four-piece orchestra was human, for beside the pale fiddler stood another man, taller than the first, whose golden skin and green-streaked hair were every bit as wild and strange. There were two others besides these, both dark of skin and hair and eye. All four wore clothes of outlandish style, and their ears curled at the tips.

Isabel had spent little time beyond the shores of England, but she had thrice travelled beyond the walls which separated her homeland from the realm of the fae. Aylfenhame, it was called, and its principle denizens were the Ayliri. In face and form and feature they resembled humans, and yet they were not like at all.

These musicians were Ayliri, but how they came to be playing for a country assembly in England she could not guess. Lesser denizens of Aylfenhame often wandered into England; indeed many, such as the household brownies and Balligumph the bridge-keeper, settled in England entirely. But to her knowledge, the Ayliri visited but rarely, and never without good reason.

Her thoughts flew to Sophy. Her dearest friend in the world, Miss Sophy Landon, had — by a series of strange events — come to marry one of the Ayliri, and had settled in Aylfenhame. Had she somehow contrived to send these musicians?

But Isabel could not conceive of how Sophy could have known of the assembly at all, nor why she might have chosen to interfere in such a way. Besides, Isabel felt sure that until a few minutes ago, both the music and its players had been human indeed.

The dancers were in shambles and the steps forgotten as the music grew stranger, and the ball guests more uneasy. Mr. Thompson was at Isabel's elbow, a picture of gentlemanly concern as he tried to steer her away from the confusion. 'I do not know what can be amiss with the musicians,' he was saying in a placid way, 'but I trust it will soon be put right. In the meantime, please come and sit out of the way, and I will procure you some refreshment.'

Isabel stared at him in confusion. His smile was tranquil enough, and he betrayed no sign that he was other than mildly puzzled. Had he not observed how badly amiss the musicians were?

Rising over the strains of the music came a dull, hollow boom, and then another: the main doors had been thrown open. Whirling to observe this new disturbance, Isabel saw streaming into the assembly room the strangest procession of people she had ever beheld.

At their head strode a tall, thin man, taller than anyone else in the room. He wore knee-breeches, waistcoat and cutaway coat in the fashion of the English gentry, but his were cut from strange, shimmering fabrics dyed in the colours of spring flowers. His hair was indigo in hue and fell in a tangled mess around his face, and at his lips he held a strangely curling pipe. The music he played upon this enchanting instrument rippled like water, and melded perfectly with the lively melody the orchestra played.

Behind him danced a lady only slightly shorter than he, her figure as wispy and fragile as a blade of grass. Her golden hair was swept up upon her head and bound with long pins, at the ends of which rested living butterflies — Isabel's startled gaze discerned the slow movement of wings. Her dress mimicked the style of Isabel's own, but hers was as light and silky as flower petals. Its colour was some hue between purple, blue and pink that Isabel had never seen before, and shockingly vibrant. She wore clusters of glass bells upon her wrists; these she shook in time with the piper's song, setting them ringing with an eerie music.

Behind these two came six more couples, all dressed in the same manner of familiar, yet strange fashions. Their hair was long and flowing, straight and heavy or curling like wisps of smoke. Some wore their sumptuous locks loose, while others had bound their hair up with jewels and combs. Their eyes flashed with merriment and anticipation and something else — mischief, perhaps.

Isabel's mind flew back to the visits she had paid to Sophy in the fae town of Grenlowe. Being a skilled seamstress, Sophy had set up a shop there. She now sold fashions for both men and women, wondrous garments which mixed English styles with the strange and beautiful materials available in Aylfenhame and a glimmer of fae magic. These Ayliri were wearing Sophy's clothes!

Did that mean that Sophy had sent them? But why would she do such a thing? Isabel watched in a daze as the Ayliri dancers streamed through to the centre of the room, the assembly's displaced guests falling back as one to make way for them. Even the Thompsons' finery paled to nothing against the riot of colour and light and magic the fae brought with them, and the Alford assembly guests were silent in awe.

The Ayliri formed themselves into a set and began a whirling, laughing dance that was as alien as their music. They dominated the space with their flamboyant movements, and the people of Alford and Tilby were forced back against the walls.

Isabel couldn't see who first began, but in the blink of an eye she realised that the eight Ayliri were no longer alone in their dance. A young Englishman and his fair partner were whirling along with them. Rapidly, the lines of silent people ringing the walls melted into the set, and it grew bigger and more encompassing.

Isabel watched, mesmerised, and aware of a growing longing to join them — a longing which swiftly deepened into a kind of compulsion. Soon her desire to whirl into the merry dance outweighed her hesitance and her inhibitions and in the next instant she was caught up in the flow, Mr. Thompson swept in alongside her.

No dance in Isabel's life could have prepared her for the sensations she now felt. She was caught up in a fever of energy, activity and colour so intense she could barely comprehend what she did. The steps were wholly strange to her, yet she knew their patterns instinctively and kept pace with the intricacy of the dance without any

effort. Her skirts twirled and swayed around her legs with the vigour of her movements and her cheeks flushed as she was swept along. And the music grew ever stranger.

Moreover, she felt a sense of wild, almost violent joy which had never been hers to experience before; and a sensation of perfect belonging, as though she had always been intended for such a dance as this. Had she but had leisure enough to observe her companions, she would have seen that the same sensations affected all around her. But she had attention for nothing but her own place in the circle, and the lithe, strange, bright figures of the Ayliri who led the dance.

Only one moment amongst this blur of activity particularly impressed itself upon her memory. There came the briefest of pauses in the dance, when, for an instant, the breathless whirl ceased and the dancers waited, suspended, as in the grip of some strange enchantment. And as she waited, among the others, for the dance to continue, Isabel found herself observed.

It was the tall piper's gaze which rested upon her. His tangled indigo hair was swept back from his face, revealing violet eyes. These eyes were fixed upon Isabel, intent and questioning, though she had no way of knowing what questions he asked of her in the silence of his own mind.

This scrutiny lasted but a moment. Then he lifted his curious pipe to his lips once more, and blew three rippling notes. The fiddlers took up the tune, and the dance resumed. Isabel lost sight of the piper.

The evening passed by in a blur of colour and sound, and the assembly did not break up until the small hours of the morning. Isabel came to herself at last, deposited upon the step of her own home without the smallest recollection of how she came to be there.

CHAPTER THREE

Ye may be thinkin' these are mighty strange goin's-on fer a quiet place like Tilby. Ye'd be right enough. Oh, there's brownies an' sprites and the like in these parts — as well as my good self, o' course! — but in the common way o' things the county o' Lincolnshire's a proper human place, wi' less o' the fae-begotten antics.

'Tis not normal, indeed, fer the likes o' Tiltager to appear out o' nowhere an' offer service to a human woman. An' fer the Ayliri to descend in force upon a mere country assembly, well! Thas far out o' the ordinary.

An' there was stranger t' come. Fer instance, when I woke on th' morning a few days after tha' strangest of assemblies, the most unexpected sight met my eyes. Have ye ever seen a creature resemblin' some kind o' feline crossed wi' a bear and wi' more than a little o' the bat about its features? I'll reckon ye 'ave not. No more had I. An' what's more, it was o' the strangest colours. All striped wi' brown an' gold, an' some kind o' scarlet tassel on the tip of its tail.

An' it — she, I should say, as it was a lady — was grumblin' and whinin' fit to burst as she crossed over my bridge. Crankiest beast I 'ave encountered in many a long year! An' when I stopped her t' ask fer my toll, 'twas Miss Isabel's name she were bandyin' about. Walked all the way from the wilds o' Aylfenhame to find Miss Ellerby! It were a while before I learned the truth o' the reason why.

On the morning of the seventh of July, Isabel breakfasted very early with her mother. Her trunk had already gone outside and she was soon to follow, for a visit to her aunt in York was to occupy her for the next few weeks.

Mrs. Ellerby's reasons for proposing the visit had been twofold. In the first instance, she wished for Isabel to be nearer to the Thompsons, and Mrs. Grey had promised to shepherd Isabel around all of the public functions which might be supposed to include the son of the house.

In the second instance, all of Tilby had been shocked by the intrusion of the Ayliri into the Alford Assembly, and even more shocked by their own behaviour under it. Though unusual events typically spurred a flurry of gossip and chatter which might last weeks or even months, the town had entered into a grim, unspoken pact never to mention it at all. Though her mother never said it in so many words, Isabel knew that her motive in sending her daughter to York was partly to remove her from the environs of Lincolnshire which had, so suddenly and unexpectedly, descended into a state bordering on degeneracy — at least in the minds of some.

To send her daughter away from disturbing fae magics and towards the delights promised by her marriage into the Thompson family seemed the best combination of motives to Mrs. Ellerby. It mattered not that the Ayliri had faded out of Lincolnshire the moment the assembly had ended, and that nothing more had been seen or heard of them since. Once such a thing had occurred, no dependence whatsoever could be placed upon its never occurring again.

Isabel was hustled outside by her mother the moment she could fairly be supposed to have finished her breakfast. Neither was expecting to find that a most curious-looking creature had taken possession of the doorstep.

'What manner of being is this?' cried Mrs. Ellerby, upon finding a furred and striped animal curled up around itself just a little to the left of her front door.

Isabel stared at it in wonder. It was a cat, or something like, though its ears more nearly resembled those of a bear and its face was curiously reminiscent of a bat. It was handsomely striped in shades of brown with glittering flickers of gold, and its tail bore a lively tuft of crimson.

'It is some kind of stray cat, perhaps,' said Isabel in some doubt. 'Perhaps it is hungry? I shall ask Cook to find some scraps for it to eat.'

'You will do no such thing, for you are to depart at once,' said Mrs. Ellerby firmly. 'And if it is fed, you know it will only linger and we will never be rid of the odd thing.'

'It will take only a moment, Mama!' said Isabel. 'If it is a stray it is surely hungry, and it would be cruelty to turn it away.' She turned and went back inside the house as she spoke, before her mother could detain her further. Cook was obliging, and soon Isabel was able to bear a saucer with assorted morsels out to the curious creature at the doorstep. It had occurred to her halfway down to the kitchens that she had no notion what such an animal might be inclined to eat, so she had arranged a variety of treats upon the plate: meat scraps, a handful of summer berries from the garden, and a pool of honey.

The cat — or whatever it may be — uncurled itself as Isabel approached, its sensitive nose twitching as it scented the delights she carried. She placed the saucer down upon the floor before it, and watched as it ate, with apparent relish, everything but the meat.

'Very well, my love, and now it is time to go,' said Mrs. Ellerby with ill-concealed impatience. Isabel allowed herself to be shepherded into the carriage, casting only a single look back at the strange cat. She was not concerned about its immediate future, for she had left word with Cook to watch for it, and ensure that it was fed again should it require further sustenance. But she was left with the strange impression that the creature had spoken to her as she had put down the food. She had heard, she thought, an irritable "thank you" as she had stooped down. But that could not be, for her Mama must surely have heard it as well, and apparently she had not.

But as she climbed into the carriage and the door was shut upon her, the creature abruptly darted up, and cast after the departing vehicle a look which Isabel could only interpret as dismay. This smote her a little, but she heartened herself with the reflection that the creature had come to think of her as a source of food, and now feared that the food as well as Isabel had gone away. Soon enough Cook, or one of the kitchen maids, would appear with more, and the creature would be reassured.

Isabel sat back as the carriage began upon the six-hour journey to York, and tried to put the matter from her mind. It would not do to trouble herself any more about the little animal, though it had borne a woeful look about it. After all, she had ensured that it would be provided for.

Arriving at her aunt's handsome townhouse at four o'clock, Isabel was grateful to alight from the sweltering carriage. The day had been hotter than she liked, and she was sorely in need of refreshment and rest.

Her aunt, a sensible woman some few years older than her sister Mrs. Ellerby, had anticipated such a need and her arrangements were everything that Isabel could wish. Isabel was directly conducted upstairs to her bedchamber, where a basin of water and a maid both awaited her requirements. When Isabel descended the stairs again some little time later she felt considerably refreshed, and the tea and tarts which Mrs. Grey immediately ordered laid out in the parlour were of significant benefit in reviving her further. She was able to speak to Mrs. Grey with composure, and the first hour soon passed away as Isabel conveyed all of her family's news.

'Now, my dear,' said Mrs. Grey, as Isabel finished recounting Charles's wedding plans. 'I understand something of a most unusual character has lately occurred.'

Isabel's heart sank a little. She had hoped that news of the Alford Assembly could not have travelled so far, considering the neighbourhood's reluctance to speak of it. Her mother had not precisely forbidden her to mention the subject, for that would have necessitated her raising it herself in the first place. But it had been tacitly forbidden, and Isabel felt some discomfort under her aunt's scrutiny.

For Mrs. Grey was displaying far more interest in this topic than she had in every other particle of the news Isabel had already shared. She was a tall, elegant woman, somewhere above forty years of age; still handsome, and well-dressed. Isabel had never known her to be anything less than impeccably groomed and attired, and she was typically serene of countenance and composed in her manner. But now she regarded Isabel with an expression of intense interest which seemed wholly at odds with her usual placid demeanour, and her eyes were oddly alight.

'Well, aunt, I scarcely know what to tell you!' Isabel began. 'You must know, it is not much to be talked of…' She allowed her words to tail off, for Mrs. Grey clearly knew no such thing. 'How came you to hear of it, if I may enquire?' Isabel said instead.

Mrs. Grey sat back a little, and tapped the tip of one long finger against her lips. 'That would be telling, my dear.'

Isabel regarded her aunt in silent thought. The expression the older lady now wore was one Isabel had never before seen. It comprised a degree of interest bordering upon avidity, together with a hint of smugness and something else harder to classify – something eager, even rapacious. It was most puzzling.

'Ayliri, were they not?' Mrs. Grey offered, apparently tiring of her niece's silence. 'Ayliri! In England! But how came they to be there?'

Isabel set down her tea cup and took a calming breath. 'I do not know,' she said gravely. 'No explanation for their presence has been discovered. They were not expected, of course, and how they came to be aware that such an assembly was planned, or to feel the smallest interest in attending so modest an affair, is beyond anybody's power to account for.'

Mrs. Grey leaned forward a little. 'My dear Isabel. I will not keep you to this topic for very long, if it troubles you, but I must ask you to tell me just one thing more.'

Isabel nodded once.

Mrs. Grey took a deep breath and let it out slowly, as though she were trying to calm some tumult of spirit. At last she said: 'What were they like?'

Isabel blinked, a little surprised. This had not been the question she might have expected. 'Like?' she repeated. 'Why, they were wild and strange, as you may imagine.'

Mrs. Grey nodded impatiently. 'That much I do imagine, indeed. It is details I require. Humour me in this one request, my dear, if you please.'

Isabel could not resist such an entreaty. With a silent apology to her mother, she recounted everything that had occurred at the assembly, from the moment that the music had changed. She described those melodies as best she could, though words failed her in the attempt, for it was far too wild and strange to admit of easy representation in words. Her accounts of the dancers were more successful, for their curious appearances, the magnificent and beauteous oddity of their garb and the dizzying strangeness of their behaviour had lodged themselves in her memory with peculiar exactness. Mrs. Grey listened to all of these particularities with breathless eagerness, and did not interrupt by so much as a syllable while Isabel spoke.

Then she came to the piper, and that moment when he had seemed to see Isabel, and she alone, out of all the company. Her voice softened near to a whisper as she recounted this, for she had been tempted to omit the incident altogether. But the intensity of her aunt's interest urged her on to greater confidences than she might otherwise have been inclined to offer. She could not begin to imagine the source of Mrs. Grey's eagerness to hear of the affair, but it was evident that it mattered greatly to her. This being the case, having once begun her account, Isabel could not bring herself to leave out anything of note.

'A piper,' mused Mrs. Grey, when Isabel at last fell silent. She had ended with her confusion at waking up at home on the following morning, with no recollection of having travelled there. But Mrs. Grey's thoughts seemed to be fixed upon the piper.

'He was the leader, we must assume,' Mrs. Grey continued. 'He brought the dancers to the assembly. The lady with the butterflies. His consort, perhaps?'

Mrs. Grey paused, her eyebrows raised. Isabel realised this was a question, not mere musing on her aunt's part, but she could only shake her head. 'I do not know. I detected no symptom of particular regard for her, but I cannot say that I received more than occasional glimpses of either of them during the evening.'

Mrs. Grey was silent for some time. Isabel returned to the quiet contemplation of her tea, allowing her aunt time to indulge in her reflections. At length, Mrs. Grey opened her lips to say, in a tone of deep reverie, 'I once knew a piper.'

Isabel set down her cup. 'In England, you mean, aunt?'

Mrs. Grey's only response was a considering look which swept over Isabel from her curled hair to the tips of her shoes. 'Hmm,' she said impenetrably, and sat back in her chair. 'I thought we might pay a visit to the library this afternoon. You will wish for some reading, perhaps, to while away those hours we are not spending in pursuit of Mr. Thompson.'

Isabel cast a shocked look at her aunt, whose blue eyes twinkled back at her with irrepressible humour. Managing a laugh, she protested, 'We are not in pursuit of Mr. Thompson, I hope! How lowering a thought.'

Mrs. Grey's smile widened. 'But of course, we are. I have the strictest instructions from your mother about it. If I do not send you home avowedly engaged, I shall be declared the wretchedest person alive.'

'Wretchedest?' repeated Isabel faintly.

Mrs. Grey nodded. 'Her word. And underlined! Twice!'

Isabel sighed. 'Aunt—' she began.

Mrs. Grey did not wait for her to complete her remonstrance. 'Do you wish to marry this Mr. Thompson?' she said, in a serious tone.

Isabel hesitated. 'My mother and father wish it very much.'

'That is not what I asked.'

Isabel looked at her hands. 'I can have no objection. He is an agreeable man, not ill-looking, and it will be a suitable establishment for me.'

Mrs. Grey sighed softly. 'How drear it all sounds.'

Isabel cast her a suspicious look. 'Are these not the reasons why you married my uncle?'

'Why, yes,' said her aunt. 'So they were.'

'And were you not contented with your choice?'

Mrs. Grey's gaze wandered over Isabel's face, and she said nothing for several moments. 'My dear niece,' she finally said, and softly. 'All I wish to know is what you want for yourself.'

Isabel stared, bewildered, and tried to recall when she had ever been asked such a question before. 'I… I am fully aware of the importance of seeking a suitable establishment. My fortune is not such that I can expect to secure the necessities of life without marrying, and it will be a pleasure to me to please my family as well as myself.'

Mrs. Grey's eyes narrowed. 'A pretty speech, my love. But is it what you want?'

Isabel had no answer to give. Gentlewomen were not raised to think of such questions as wants; or at least, she certainly had not been. Her duty had been clearly marked out for her since her birth, and she had never imagined that she might prefer to deviate from the ascribed course of an arranged marriage, and all the happiness that a well-chosen alliance could bring. 'Then… then you are not in favour of the match?'

'As far as my sister is concerned, I am fully in favour of it,' said Mrs. Grey. 'We shall do our appointed duty, and attend all the necessary social engagements. But I shall not scruple to present you with alternatives to marriage with Mr. Thompson. I see you consider this a sacred duty, and one which you have no power to avoid. That, my love, is taking entirely the wrong view of the case.'

Isabel sat a little straighter. 'I am not aware of any alternatives, ma'am.'

'Because you have not been given any. And really, the wretched selfishness of your brother — I could throttle him for it, if I were not much more inclined to applaud him.'

Isabel blinked at that. 'Charles is happy,' she said. 'I cannot accuse him of selfishness, in having contracted an engagement that is so clearly of benefit to himself.'

Mrs. Grey merely looked at her, and smiled.

'An engagement to Mr. Thompson would be of considerable benefit to me!' Isabel insisted. 'Mama only has my happiness in view.'

'That is a wilful misunderstanding,' said Mrs. Grey. 'She has a great deal more in view than your happiness, as you are well aware.'

'Mama would not wish for me to be unhappy.'

'No, indeed. I can acquit her of ruthlessness, but perhaps not of carelessness.'

Isabel opened her mouth, and closed it again with a short sigh. 'This cannot be a proper way of talking, aunt! My poor Mama.'

'Not at all dutiful, is it?' said Mrs. Grey cheerfully. 'I have had my fill of duty, as you will discover before many days have passed. But I shall not discomfort you further. Let us instead consider all the many delights we are to enjoy in the coming weeks! What heights of tea-drinking and small conversations! What promenades! And we shall talk over every evening engagement exhaustively, upon each succeeding morning.'

Her aunt's sarcastic tone troubled Isabel a little, as to her mind these delights sounded reassuringly familiar. But she did not say so. Instead, she nodded her acquiescence to these plans and rose from her chair. 'If you will excuse me, aunt—' she began, but an interruption unluckily occurred to prevent her immediate departure.

Mrs. Grey, inattentive, had rung the bell, and a servant entered the room immediately afterwards; so promptly that Isabel could not help suspecting that the girl had been hovering outside the door. 'Ah, Jane! Please remove the tray,' said Mrs. Grey, and the girl complied at once.

Entering the parlour in her wake was a household brownie. To Isabel, this was no unusual sight, for it was common enough for Tilby households to house one or two of the creatures — or more than that, in some cases. It was not so common in York. Some speculated that the beings of Aylfenhame disliked the bustle of human cities, which might very well be true, though Isabel had never enquired into the matter. Perhaps Sophy would know.

What struck her more than the brownie's appearance was the way in which the little creature reacted to Isabel's presence. The brownie was a female, Isabel judged from the ragged dress she was wearing. Her hair was a mop of black curls, her eyes wide and dark. Those eyes were fixed upon Isabel with an arrested expression; so intent was she in her scrutiny that she stopped in the doorway, her errand forgotten.

Isabel looked away, confused. Did she present so very odd an appearance? Discreet examination assured her that there was nothing amiss with her gown, but perhaps something untoward had happened to her hair. She caught her aunt's eye, questioning her with a silent look as to the respectability of her appearance.

Mrs. Grey merely looked intrigued. 'What is it, Rossan?' she said.

The brownie, Rossan, inched closer to Mrs. Grey and said to her in a hoarse whisper: 'Is it she? Is that the one?'

Mrs. Grey's eyes twinkled at Isabel. 'My niece, Miss Ellerby.'

Rossan stared at Isabel. She appeared to reach no particular conclusion, for she finally turned away without comment and offered something to Mrs. Grey in her two small hands. This offering was accepted with care, and the object tucked into Mrs. Grey's reticule. Isabel could not see what it was, but she heard Rossan say in a low voice, 'Well fed, and fast asleep.'

Mrs. Grey nodded, and murmured her thanks. Isabel watched these proceedings in utter mystification, but her aunt did not see fit to explain. She merely rose from her chair with enviable grace and gestured Isabel out of the room. 'You will wish to rest, I imagine? We will enjoy some cosy outing together tomorrow.'

Isabel was too well brought-up to display a vulgar curiosity where none was either expected or wanted. She left her questions unvoiced, and allowed herself to be gently shepherded back to her room. Mrs. Grey had always been among Isabel's favourites of her relatives, but her habits and behaviours did sometimes puzzle her niece — particularly since the death of Isabel's uncle two years before. Her aunt had settled into her solitary state with alacrity, and though nothing about her life had undergone any significant change in the intervening years, the woman herself had certainly changed. It had happened by such slow degrees that for some time Isabel had barely noticed. Reflecting upon it now, she was aware that the respectable, dutiful aunt she had known in her first youth had faded away. Standing in her place was the woman who could speak slightingly of matters which meant a great deal to her family; could disparage the social niceties around which their worlds revolved; and who could display an inordinate degree of interest in matters magical, when all those around her strove to hide or explain them away.

Isabel loved her aunt as much as ever, but the alteration puzzled her, and sometimes left her feeling lamentably out of step. She did not know what her aunt intended from this visit, but it was evident that her mother's expectations of her sister were somewhat misplaced.

Isabel withdrew to her room, settled herself in an armchair, and took up an improving book. She intended to focus her mind upon the text, and thus to banish all the disquieting thoughts that disturbed her peace of mind. In this she was unsuccessful. Her mind turned upon its pressing questions without cease; and by the time the dinner hour arrived, Isabel had been thinking with little interruption upon such curiosities as Rossan the brownie, the obliging Tiltager and the Ayliri assembly for almost two hours.

She went down to dinner with the piper's face before her, his indigo hair swept back and his violet eyes fixed upon her as he played.

CHAPTER FOUR

The next morning was so mundane in character that Isabel felt reassured. She accompanied her aunt in paying some morning calls upon various of their acquaintance, and nothing untoward occurred. Isabel did not glimpse so much as a brownie wandering the drawing-rooms of her aunt's friends. They were universally respectable, and the conversation turned upon such well-trodden topics as the recent marriage of Mr. George Barnes to Miss Mary Blackwell; some hazy conjecture as to the progress of Bonaparte in Russia (or perhaps it had not been Russia, perhaps it was rather another place entirely; Mrs. Spender could not precisely recollect); and the newest fashions from Paris.

Isabel listened placidly, and rarely interjected any comments of her own. It was her habit to listen a great deal more than she talked, though perhaps it was not considered becoming to be so quiet.

But upon their return to Castlegate, Isabel's tranquil mood abruptly evaporated. As she followed her aunt out of the carriage and back onto the street, shading her eyes against the glare of the noon sun, an irate voice reached her ears.

'At very last!' it said crossly. 'And how very dare thee! Didst thou think I enjoyed the journey to find thee the first time? I did not! I most very indeed did not! And what must thou do the very moment I find thee at long last but step into thy fancy-fine carriage and sail away!

'Not,' continued the voice, 'that I am ungrateful for the eatin's. That was suitable. But what happened after the eatin's! That was most very surely not!'

Isabel had been casting about throughout this speech for the source of the irritable tirade, but the street appeared to her to be virtually unoccupied save for their two selves. A carriage was turning in at the end of the street, but the voice could not possibly be emanating from so far away.

'Down, my girl!' said the voice. 'Look thee down, by thy daintily-shod paws! Aye, there. Here I am.'

Isabel blinked. Lying flat to the ground by the wheels of Mrs. Grey's carriage was the strange cat-like creature with the striped fur that had appeared on the doorstep at Ferndeane. The creature appeared to be exhausted, for it — she? — lay in a spent huddle, though her head was raised to stare at Isabel with no friendly demeanour. Knowing herself to have secured Isabel's attention at last, she slowly toppled over to lie stretched and inert upon the pavement, her long tail drooping.

'My very goodness,' said the creature. 'I will have some more of those fine eatin's before the mornin' is very much advanced! Make no mistake about that.' One long ear twitched.

Isabel found her voice. 'I…' she began. 'I did not know that you were… are you looking for me?'

The ear twitched again, twice, and the creature said in a faint voice, 'Why, 'tis rare to encounter a companion with such ready wit.'

Isabel felt her cheeks warm, and she gazed helplessly at her aunt. 'But truly, it seems so very odd. And I am not accustomed to being addressed by… well, by such a being as you.'

'The nature of thy duties seems to be escapin' thee,' replied the creature, 'so I'll explain. What thou must do is bend down a ways, take up the poor exhausted bein' lyin' at thy feet, and convey her into thy humble abode. Once done, thou must find some comfortable spot for said bein' to occupy an' ply her with the choicest of eatin's, without the smallest delay. An' then, perhaps thy new companion will not track thee down only to expire at thy uncarin' feet.'

'I will call Rossan,' said Mrs. Grey smoothly. 'Perhaps she can help.'

Mrs. Grey disappeared inside the house, her composure unruffled by this untoward event. Isabel watched helplessly. Did she encounter talking animals so often as to make such an occurrence commonplace?

'Immediately, would be best,' added the creature, her tail swishing once with displeasure.

Isabel secured her reticule upon her arm and bent down. The creature's fur was silky-soft under her hands as she gently lifted her up and settled her in her arms. 'There, now, is that better?' Isabel said in a soft tone.

'No,' replied the creature.

Isabel blinked. 'Eatings,' she said hastily. 'Without delay.'

The creature nodded once, her fur bristling. 'And lots of it.'

Ten minutes later, Isabel and her aunt sat in the parlour, watching with some amazement as the striped creature devoured a heroic portion of food. Mrs. Grey, guided in part by Isabel's prior experience of her visitor's tastes, had requested of her cook every delight a garden in high summer could afford, together with an array of sweet things. The cook had, with impressive promptitude, produced an enormous platter spread about with raspberries, strawberries, currants, cherries, apricots, chunks of courgette and carrot and piles of crisp green leaves. She had also provided tiny porcelain bowls filled with honey, milk, cream and weak tea. The little beast worked her way down the mountain of food upon the platter, methodically and without pause, until not a scrap of food was left. She then proceeded to slurp noisily through the contents of each bowl, delicately licking up the residue until each porcelain dish was scrupulously clean.

Having completed this magnificent repast, the creature tucked herself into a neat ball upon the parlour carpet and, to all appearances, went to sleep.

While all of this was going forward, Mrs. Grey had been quietly tatting lace. Her whole manner was one of placid acceptance of these untoward occurrences. Even more strangely, there was something in her face when she glanced at Isabel that suggested smug satisfaction. Isabel could not understand it.

'She will sleep for at least a day,' Mrs. Grey said at last. 'She has undertaken a long journey.'

'From where, aunt?' said Isabel cautiously. 'And how can you know anything of this?'

Mrs. Grey carefully set aside her tatting and regarded Isabel in silent thought for some moments. At last she said: 'Do you trust me, my dear?'

'Yes, of course, but—' began Isabel.

'Excellent!' This word was spoken with a delighted, cat-like smile which made Isabel faintly nervous. 'In that case.' Mrs. Grey reached a hand into her sleeve and withdrew something from within. The object was tiny, whatever it was; Isabel could discern nothing about it from her station across the room.

Mrs. Grey reached down and opened her hand. Something tiny, green and furred tiptoed delicately off her her palm and set off across the floor towards Isabel, who watched its approach with mounting amazement. It resembled a vole in size and shape, but in no other respect. Its colour was that of spring grass mingled with velvet woodland moss, and its ears were long and pointed. It scurried up to Isabel's feet, its long claws sinking into the elegantly pale carpet, and began to climb her leg.

Isabel flinched, for the claws scratched a little. She dared not display any objection to this intrusion, however; she had said she trusted her aunt, and she did. She held herself still while the strange vole clambered up to her left leg to her knee, and there stopped, its snout lifted to inhale whatever assortment of scents met its long nose from this vantage point.

'Smells sweetlish,' it pronounced, startling Isabel. 'Leerwise she be, but soundish enough in the toploft.'

Having delivered itself of this strange speech, the vole sniffed the air twice more, nodded in a decisive manner, and ran lightly down Isabel's leg to the floor. From there it ambled back to Mrs. Grey and was received back into her sleeve. Isabel watched until the tip of its green tail had vanished inside the soft muslin of her aunt's gown, speechless.

'My companion,' said Mrs. Grey. 'His name is Vershibat.'

Connections snapped together in Isabel's mind. 'You...' she began, though her voice failed her. She cleared her throat and tried again. 'You said you knew a piper,' she managed.

Mrs. Grey beamed. 'Soundish in the toploft, indeed!' she said. 'Yes, my dear, I did. Oh, more than twenty years ago now.'

'You have some connection with Aylfenhame.'

'Had,' corrected Mrs. Grey. 'Vershibat is the only link I have retained.'

'He is a fae beast,' Isabel said. 'So is...' she stopped, unsure by

what name to refer to the striped, furred creature still asleep on the carpet.

'They are here for a reason.'

'What reason?' Isabel watched her aunt's face, puzzled. 'And how came you to visit Aylfenhame? Who is the piper?'

'My grandmother was the belle of Tilby,' said Mrs. Grey, apparently at random. 'She was the most beautiful woman ever seen in those parts — or so I understand. But her beauty was of a peculiar kind. Her hair was a shade of red never before seen in England, and her eyes of an unusual hue: brown, but shaded with gold. Everything about her was uncommon, and unlikely. It mesmerised.'

Isabel nodded, uncertain as to the direction of her aunt's reflections.

'There is one in Tilby who remembers her,' continued Mrs. Grey. 'The bridge-keeper. He told me a tale of her, once. She was said to take a striking pet about with her everywhere. Some kind of weasel, it was said to be, only smaller, and strangely coloured.'

'My great-grandmother,' said Isabel.

'Indeed. Years later, similar things were said of her daughter — my mother.'

Isabel's thoughts flew to the Ayliri who had danced at the Alford Assembly. They, too, had been beautiful and strange; their faces and bodies were human enough, but their eyes and hair and colouring were quite unlike.

Mrs. Grey saw the realisation dawn on Isabel's face, for her smile grew wider. 'You understand,' she said.

'The piper…?' Isabel said faintly.

'No, it was not he. But your great-grandmother's father was most certainly Aylir.' Mrs. Grey paused, allowing Isabel a moment to absorb this information.

Isabel swallowed. 'I am part Aylir?' she said at last.

'A small part, by this time,' said Mrs. Grey. 'But a little of the blood of Aylenhame is yours, and it appears to have bred true in your case. There is one in every generation, you see. It was always my regret that Mr. Grey and I were not blessed with children. Your mother never showed the slightest signs of her Aylir heritage. She is human, body and soul. I feared perhaps that the blood had died out with us, for it seemed unlikely that she and Mr. Ellerby could produce such a child. But so they have.'

Isabel's thoughts whirled. 'But—' she said faintly. 'But I am not remarkable! My hair is of the most commonplace, merely brown, and my eyes naught but brown as well, and—'

'Yes, yes,' said Mrs. Grey, cutting short this outburst with a wave of one elegant hand. 'But generations have passed, and the blood has thinned with time. It does not show in your appearance, perhaps, but it is very apparent in your abilities. And in mine.'

'What abilities?' said Isabel.

'Aylfenlike,' said a voice from the carpet.

Isabel looked down. The being who proclaimed herself Isabel's new companion stretched out one of her long, slender forelegs, spreading her paw wide, and yawned hugely. 'More likely thou wouldst know it as witchery.'

Isabel silently repeated the word to herself, disturbed at the way her stomach fluttered in response. Witchery. 'That cannot be,' she said. She spoke impulsively, but from her heart. In her mind she held two visions: one of herself as she had always been, the Miss Ellerby of Ferndeane whose duties were clear, and whose future was all but decided. Whether she married Mr. Thompson or someone else of similar eligibility, her path in life was settled: she would marry, she would be mistress of a house and a mother. And with such a destiny, she was content. There was no room in this vision for Ayliri heritage, witchery or a fae companion. She struggled to reconcile the two contrasting ideas, and failed.

In this second vision of herself, how would her life progress? Isabel the witch, part Aylir, and enjoying a close acquaintance with denizens of Aylfenhame! None of it registered as plausible. She could not imagine the path of her life under these conditions. Even remembering Sophy, happily settled in Grenlowe with an Aylir husband, offered her little comfort. She was delighted for Sophy's happiness, but never for an instant had she imagined that any part of Sophy's life could be hers as well.

'It can be,' said the creature sleepily. 'It is.' This was said in a bored tone.

'But—' Isabel faltered.

The creature roused herself from slumber with a growl and stood up, turning on Isabel. 'How very feeble!' she said, the growl still rumbling behind her words. 'I have walked and walked to find thee, followed thee all the way to this nethersome backway of a place, and this is my welcome! Witch! I say that of thee, and it is the truth. I am thy companion. My name is Tafferty.'

'I am sorry,' said Isabel at once. 'It is not that I do not appreciate your efforts. It is merely that I do not understand. How is it that you came to venture here?'

'I felt the call.' This appeared to conclude Tafferty's interest in conversing, for she turned her back on Isabel once more and curled up with her tail over her nose.

Isabel looked at her aunt.

'I cannot precisely explain it,' said Mrs. Grey, a hint of amusement lighting her eyes. 'Vershibat was the same. He arrived one morning, out of breath and very weary. He announced that he had been summoned, and promptly fell asleep. Since then he has scarcely left my side.'

'Did you summon him?'

Mrs. Grey shook her head. 'Not intentionally. Whatever brings our companions to us is involuntary, I believe, but they feel it powerfully.'

'How long ago did Vershibat arrive?'

'Twenty-three years ago. He is beginning to feel his age a little, but he is sprightly still.'

Isabel nodded. She wanted to ask a great many questions, most of them pertaining to the witchery she was purported to be capable of. But she was also afraid to delve into this mystery. Her mind clung to the safe, familiar image of Miss Ellerby of Ferndeane and refused to relinquish it.

'Tafferty will sleep until tomorrow,' predicted Mrs. Grey. She added in a kindly tone, 'Perhaps further discussion of this matter will wait until she wakes?'

Isabel gratefully accepted this offer of deferral, and soon afterwards excused herself to wander in her aunt's rose garden. Her mind turned upon the strange developments in her life, but without bringing her any nearer to understanding. It was too sudden, and too surprising. She was numb with shock, and her mind was as often blank as filled with confused reflection.

She did not doubt anything that she had been told; her aunt would not lie to her, and she had received considerable evidence in support. Nonetheless, her mind shied away from acceptance. How was it that her mother had never told her of her heritage, or considered the possibility that Isabel might, in adulthood, come to follow her great-grandmother's path?

With a soft sigh, she resolved to put all thoughts of Aylfenhame, witchery, the Ayliri or the fae from her mind until Tafferty should wake, for she was merely distressing herself with her confusion of ideas. But with the best of intentions behind this praiseworthy resolution, she failed, for her mind continued to turn upon these forbidden topics for the whole of the morning, through dinner with her aunt, and well into the night. It was long indeed before sleep finally put an end to the turmoil of her thoughts.

CHAPTER FIVE

Isabel woke upon the following morning to find herself somewhat less than alone. She opened her eyes to a blur of brown, gold-flecked fur filling her vision entirely, and the sound of a deep, rumbling purr resonating throughout the room. Isabel lay still for some moments, suffering under considerable confusion until her sleepy mind recollected the identity of the bundle of fur upon her pillow. 'Good morning, Tafferty.'

As soon as she spoke, the purring abruptly stopped. Tafferty sat bolt upright, blinking, and proceeded to address — apparently — the drawn curtains. 'That it is! Mornin' entirely, and sunny in the world, and she lies slugabed!' Tafferty hooked a claw into the fabric of Isabel's blanket and, with a swish of her paw, drew it back. 'Whishawist, and up with thee! Time's a fair grouch, and she's waitin' for none of ye.' Tafferty stuck her nose into Isabel's ear, then whirled about and hurled herself off the bed. She was gone in the blink of an eye, darting out through the bedroom door — which Isabel did not remember leaving open.

'Whishawist,' she repeated to herself, blinking, and hastened to dress.

Upon her descent of the stairs, she found her aunt already at the breakfast table. Vershibat sat upon the table-cloth to her right; he had taken up a station adjacent to Mrs. Grey's freshly-poured cup of tea, with a small feast of toast-crumbs laid out upon the cloth before him. Of Tafferty there was no sign.

'Good morning, my dear,' said Mrs. Grey cheerfully as Isabel took her seat. 'I hope you slept well, for there is much to do today! You must form an acquaintance with Tafferty, as a matter of urgency, for a good relationship with one's companion is simply vital. The art of glamour, or illusion, is to be your initial study, for it is useful, and the centre of a witch's arts! I have not kept up the practice as I ought to have, to my regret, but I have found it convenient on more than one occasion. There is a great deal one may accomplish with the subtle use of glamour, from altering the colour of one's gown to something considerably more significant. Now, is that not an alluring prospect!' Mrs. Grey paused to drink a little tea. 'Then there is the matter of boons, and curses. I have never had cause to employ a curse, myself. I do not advise it, all told, for it is a dangerous and unpleasant art. But something of it must be learned, at the very least so that you may protect yourself in case of any ill-natured attack. And tomorrow—'

Isabel felt a flash of panic, and took a deep breath. 'Aunt,' she said. 'I dare say you are perfectly right, and I shall be guided by you. But what of my mother's plans? I had understood there is to be an assembly this evening, which the Thompsons are expected to attend. Some portion of the day must, I think, be given over to preparations for that?'

Mrs. Grey looked at her niece for a long moment. In the silence, Isabel became aware of a faint slurping sound emanating from somewhere underneath the table. Lifting the edge of the snowy table-cloth, she discovered Tafferty crouched near her aunt's feet with a vast platter of fruits, vegetables and sweet delicacies at her disposal. She was at that moment availing herself of the contents of a bowl of cream, some of which had become deposited upon her whiskers.

'Yes, of course,' said Mrs. Grey. 'The assembly! I had not forgotten, I assure you. Your mother's excellent arrangements are every bit as important as your career in witchery.'

This was said in a cool tone which caused Isabel some doubt as to its sincerity, but she nodded. 'It is important to Mama,' she said quietly.

Mrs. Grey's mouth twisted, but she said nothing, preferring instead to devote herself to the fullest appreciation of her tea.

Conscious of an air of disapproval in Mrs. Grey's manner and posture, Isabel felt a sinking in her stomach. 'It is not that I do not appreciate the importance of — of —' She could not quite bring herself to repeat the word witchery, the whole notion still striking her as strange and ludicrous beyond words.

Mrs. Grey set down her tea cup once more and gazed at Isabel. 'Indeed, I am sure it is not that,' she said, and then added in a brisk tone, 'There is an acquaintance I wish you to meet, prior to the assembly. Perhaps you will drive out with me later this morning?'

Isabel assented to this graciously, and in the spirit of compromise she permitted Tafferty to commandeer her company as soon as breakfast was finished. Four long hours followed, during which Tafferty endeavoured to explain to her the nature of the art of Glamour.

'Glamour,' said her companion with a pompous air, 'is the art of makin' somethin' seem in the fashion of some other thing, which it is not.'

Isabel blinked. 'I see.'

'Glamour,' continued Tafferty, 'is also called the art of Seemin'. With it, I may adopt the Seemin' of some other thing, which I am not. Make it so.'

Tafferty tucked herself up into a ball, her paws folded beneath herself, and waited expectantly.

'I may make you appear to be another type of creature?' Isabel queried, rather hesitantly, for the explanation shed little light.

Tafferty gave an affirmative nod, and offered no further comment at all.

'How do I accomplish this?' Isabel said.

Tafferty opened her eyes and fixed them upon Isabel with a disbelieving air. 'Why, it is the very clearest thing!' she said disgustedly. 'If thou wert born to it, thou must understand it.'

'I am very sorry,' said Isabel apologetically, 'but I do not at all understand it. How is it done?'

Tafferty sighed, uncurled herself and stretched. 'I will explain,' she pronounced. But this did not proceed very successfully, for Tafferty's explanations were as outlandish as the art she was attempting to convey, and the peculiar patterns of her speech sometimes confused Isabel still further.

She was to understand that it was as simple as breathing, and yet the art was as unfathomable as the stars; a baby could grasp its intricacies, and yet its complexities knew no bounds. Isabel passed her hands back and forth over a plump raspberry from the garden, without succeeding in making it resemble a strawberry in the smallest degree. Her head began, at last, to ache, and she felt with a hint of bitterness that the whole exercise had been devised for her humiliation.

It was a relief, later in the day, to don her bonnet and spencer and step into her aunt's carriage. She felt that she was leaving witchery and all its attendant absurdities behind her, and returning to the familiar world of York and its comfortingly mundane activities. To pay a social call at such an advanced hour of the day was unusual, to be sure, but she was ready to believe that some of Mrs. Grey's acquaintances kept unusual hours.

She was more perplexed when the carriage bowled out of York and into the fields, leaving the town far behind, yet without delivering her to any of the villages she had expected they were to visit. Half an hour's journey passed away and still they did not stop. Isabel began to glance at her aunt, uncertain of whether she should raise a question. Mrs. Grey did not look at her; her attention was directed out of the window.

Isabel contented herself with silence. Fully an hour had passed by the time the carriage at last began to slow, and finally stopped.

'Quickly, now,' said Mrs. Grey as they stepped down. She consulted a pocket-watch, a slight frown creasing her brow.

Isabel looked around in utter confusion. They had stopped in the midst of an expanse of fields. Tall rows of flourishing wheat met her gaze in every direction, with nothing else to be observed save for the strip of narrow, uneven road running through the middle. Besides herself, her aunt, and her aunt's coachman and footmen, not another soul did she see.

Tafferty jumped down from the carriage behind Isabel and took up a station near her feet. This surprised Isabel, as she had been unaware of her companion's presence upon the journey. Where had Tafferty hidden herself? She, too, appeared to feel no disorientation at the peculiarity of their excursion, for she sat down and began, in the calmest fashion, to wash her paws.

'Five minutes, perhaps?' murmured Mrs. Grey.

Tafferty made an assenting noise, and continued to groom her toes.

Isabel began to feel a sensation of mild pique at this treatment. Was she not to be informed as to the nature of their errand out here in this remote place? She pushed such feelings away, for they were unworthy, and stood her ground. Her aunt and Tafferty were both facing the same way, out into the fields, and watched the horizon with an expectant air. Isabel could understand nothing of this behaviour, but she followed the line of their gaze and waited alongside them, fiddling with the ribbon of her reticule.

It seemed to her, after some minutes, that the sky was growing fractionally lighter. She blinked, and looked a little closer. Was she, in her impatience, imagining the almost imperceptible fading of the azure sky into a paler hue? No; for there followed an unmistakeable brightening of the light, until it grew so dazzling Isabel was obliged, briefly, to close her eyes.

When she opened them, a dark shape had appeared in the sky, starkly outlined against the blazing light. It began as a small object barely larger than her fist, but grew rapidly. Isabel realised that it was something airborne, and coming closer.

It was a boat. It was shaped like one, at least, with a mast and a sail and all the usual features; the fact that it was sailing through the sky instead of the sea appeared not to matter one whit. The boat soared out of nothing and descended until it landed atop a low rise some distance away.

'Quickly, now!' said Mrs. Grey, and to Isabel's amazement, her aunt began to run.

'Whishawist!' bawled Tafferty, and sprang after Mrs. Grey.

Isabel stood stock still, dumbfounded.

Tafferty turned and galloped back. 'Hurry, foolish little witch! The Ferryman will not wait for such as thee, mark my words!' She barrelled into Isabel's legs and propelled her forward. Isabel dutifully set off at a fast walk, but at Tafferty's renewed cries of "Wist, whishawist!' and the sight of her aunt running at speed towards the boat, a sense of urgency took hold of her and she, too, began to run.

If she had expected the boat to be made out of something familiar — wood, for example — she was destined to be further surprised. As she neared the strange craft, she discerned that it shone in odd colours. The body of the boat was constructed from a substance resembling wood mingled, in some odd fashion, with clouds; the sail was bright with colour and looked painted upon the sky. The boat rose up high in the front and at the back, forming graceful, curled-over points at each end, and the mast was silvery-pale and deeply graven with complex images Isabel could not make out.

In the prow stood a man Isabel had never before seen. He was tall and lean, and dressed in the fashions of the previous century: tall boots, a frock coat and waistcoat, and a cocked hat with three corners. The style of the clothing was familiar, but its materials and colours were not. His frock coat was rich blue and sewn from velvet as soft and plush as moss; his waistcoat was as light as insect's wings and glimmered with silvery iridescence.

He was golden-skinned, bronze-eyed and dark-haired, his features human but with that faint, odd cast which proclaimed him Other. He was, in short, Aylir.

Mrs. Grey reached the boat some way ahead of her niece. Isabel drew level with her aunt, somewhat out of breath and, she feared, unbecomingly flushed in the face. She took a moment to regain her breath, averting her gaze from the dazzling vision of the boatman.

'You wish to embark?' said the Ferryman. His voice was deep and melodic. He would sing well, Isabel thought irrelevantly.

'This lady wishes to embark,' said Mrs. Grey, gently pushing Isabel forward.

Alarmed, Isabel cried, 'No! I do not wish to embark! My dear aunt, what can be the meaning of this?'

Mrs. Grey clutched Isabel's hand. All trace of the playful attitude she sometimes adopted had vanished; her face, her manner, her tone were all serious as she said: 'You have some notion, I think, that you may live as I have done; choose the life of an Englishwoman and manage your abilities alongside it. I wish you will not! For I have long regretted the choice that I made.'

Isabel's mouth opened in surprise. 'But — my uncle — were you not happy?'

Mrs. Grey's mouth twisted with some emotion Isabel could not name. 'I chose safety,' she said. 'If that is the choice you, too, wish to make, then you shall. But I beg you: please, explore the alternative! I have arranged everything. The Ferryman will take you to your Miss Landon, and she will help you.'

'But—' said Isabel, shocked. 'But the assembly — Mr. Thompson —'

'Think nothing of them,' said Mrs. Grey. 'Assemblies, and such men as Mr. Thompson, are easily come by!'

'My mother—'

'Your mother shall know nothing of this,' said Mrs. Grey

earnestly. 'Trust me to manage my sister, and do as I ask. Please.'

Isabel glanced at the boat and the Aylir man who stood, silent and impassive, in its prow. A knot of fear had taken root in her stomach and she felt its effects in every part of her being. To step into this boat and allow it to bear her away to Aylfenhame seemed an irreversible step. 'I cannot,' she said softly.

'You can,' said Mrs. Grey with quiet confidence. 'Tafferty will be with you. You are not alone.' She squeezed Isabel's hand and added, 'It is not forever.'

Not forever. Isabel looked again at the boat, and, to her infinite surprise, a tiny spark of excitement unfurled somewhere inside. It was feeble, and almost drowned by the weight of her doubt, her uncertainty and her fear; but it lived, and she felt it. To see Aylfenhame as Sophy did! Not as a brief, and wholly other, visitor, but as one who enjoyed some right to be there; who might, in some small way, belong.

She squeezed her aunt's hand in return. 'Thank you,' she said. A vision of Mr. Thompson at the coming assembly flashed through her mind. Would he notice her absence? Would it be any source of regret to him? Perhaps he would withdraw his interest in her. Her mother's dismay — her father's disappointment — the loss to her family. All this passed through her mind in an instant, and her steps faltered.

But she looked again at the Ferryman, and her resolve hardened.

'I cannot wait,' said he. He spoke gravely, but Isabel thought she detected a twinkle in his dark eyes.

'I am coming,' Isabel replied. He held out his hand to her; she took it, and with his help climbed aboard the boat. Tafferty leapt in after her with a flick of her tasselled tail.

She had no time to bid her aunt farewell, for the boat began immediately to rise. All she could do was wave to her aunt's rapidly shrinking figure as she was borne upwards, conscious of a forlorn feeling.

CHAPTER SIX

Isabel had expected the ascent to be alarming, perhaps even dangerous, but it was not. The boat's progress was steady and smooth, and though the rising winds buffeted her with growing ferocity as they climbed into the skies, she never felt in danger of being blown out of the boat.

The vision of England she was thus afforded staggered and thrilled her. Vast expanses of fields lay spread before her, painted in various colours and fitted edge-to-edge like scraps of fabric in a blanket. Here and there she saw a village or a town, mere clusters of blocky protrusions in grey or red or white; they were tiny and toy-like from her vantage point aloft. At length her view was obscured as white mist billowed into being around her, thickening rapidly until she could see nothing beyond the edges of the boat. With a small sigh of regret, she turned her back upon the vanished panorama and sought some place where she could seat herself.

The Ferryman sat three feet away, his eyes upon her. She jumped at seeing him, for in her wonder at the view she had all but forgotten him. She swallowed her surprise, smitten abruptly with remorse.

'I am very sorry,' she said with a smile. 'I was so enchanted with our ascent, I have sent courtesy to the winds. How do you do? My aunt ought, perhaps, to have introduced us, but there was not time. I am Miss Ellerby.' She made him a curtsey. He ought to have stood to receive this honour, and it felt strange to her to curtsey to a seated gentleman. But things were different in Aylfenhame, no doubt.

The Ferryman's answering smile was crooked; twisted, she

suspected, with some form of hidden amusement, though the expression of his eyes was congenial enough. 'Missellerby,' he mused. 'No name I ever heard before. 'Tis a privilege to be unique, and I hope ye make fine use of it.' He got to his feet and bowed fluidly to her in return, sweeping his three-cornered hat from his head. She saw that his hair was black and long, and tied back with a plain red ribbon. He soon regained his seat, and indicated that she should avail herself of one opposite. They were chairs in truth, soft and comfortable, and upholstered in a shimmering silk Isabel eyed with covetous envy, so beautiful a gown would it make.

She reposed herself gracefully upon the indicated chair, and smiled. 'No indeed, I am not at all unique. It is two words: Miss — Ellerby — the first being a title, you see.'

His smile widened, and the twinkle in his eyes grew more pronounced. 'I thank ye for yer explanation,' he said gravely.

Isabel laughed, her cheeks warming. 'Oh, I see. You are teasing me.'

'An' I should not, I know,' he said with a note of apology. 'It's the matter o' having company that's done the mischief. Goes to my 'ead more'n a little.'

His manner of speaking reminded Isabel of Balligumph, the bridge-keeper, though his accent was neither so thick nor so pronounced as his; more of a lilt. 'Are you so short of company?' said she. 'I would think a Ferryman would meet a great many people.'

'The Ferry,' he said, 'is not often used, for few seek passage between my world an' yours.'

Isabel felt a creeping sensation of discomfort, for it did not do to be alone with a gentleman like this. Did Tafferty qualify as chaperone? Her companion had taken up a station on one of the other chairs, and sat there straight-backed and wholly inattentive. Isabel looked down at her hands. 'I did not precisely seek passage,' she admitted.

'I saw that.' The Ferryman lounged against the side of the boat, idly flipping his hat in his hands.

Isabel flushed with embarrassment. 'My aunt had given me no warning,' she said. 'It was not discussed between us.'

'An' ye were reluctant t' trade the delights of England fer the stiflin' mundanity of Aylfenhame,' said he wisely, with an affirmative nod. ''Tis natural enough.'

'No, indeed!' Isabel protested. 'It is only that—' She stopped, uncertain. It was absurd to imagine that this Aylir would feel in the smallest degree interested in her turmoil. 'You have not told me your name,' she said instead. 'May I know whom I am addressing?'

'Ye are addressin' the Ferryman,' he said with a lazy smile. ''Tis the only name ye need know.'

Isabel nodded, a little stung by the rebuff. After a moment, she asked: 'Are we among the clouds?'

The Ferryman laughed at that. 'Not nearly so high. What ye're seein' is but mist, not clouds. We are somewhere In Between.'

He spoke the latter two words with a peculiar emphasis, which aroused Isabel's curiosity. 'In Between?' she repeated.

'Betwixt my world an' yours. We will be sailin' that road a while yet, so I hope ye are comfortable.'

Isabel was very comfortable, somewhat to her own surprise. The air was cool, but not cold; a pleasure after the summer heat she had left behind below. The wind was mild, the light moderate. Her only discomfort came from within, for the gnawing sensation of doubt had not left her. What madness had seized her, to send her sailing away from everything she knew in pursuit of an unfathomable adventure? She would be outright petrified, were it not for the promise of Sophy's guidance once she reached Aylfenhame.

A sudden stab of trepidation led her to ask, 'Where are we to alight?' If she was to be deposited at some unknown ferry-point in the Aylir world, how was she to find her way to Grenlowe, and Sophy? Would Tafferty's guidance be sufficient? Would they be obliged to travel a long way?

The Ferryman grinned. 'Fear not, for ye are to be set down in the town o' Grenlowe, an' with all the care I might bestow upon some tender, newborn thing.'

'Oh.' Isabel considered that.

'Someone 'as paid a great deal fer it,' he added, tossing up his hat once more before settling it back on his head. 'Ye are a woman o' privilege.'

Paid? To her shame, it had not occurred to Isabel that passage between England and Grenlowe most likely incurred a fee. But it had been paid already. By whom? Her aunt? What manner of currency might the Ferryman require for his services? She had no notion, and felt too much embarrassment to ask.

'Whither in Grenlowe are ye bound?' he said.

'I am to visit a friend, Miss Landon,' said Isabel. Then she stopped, frowning. 'At least, Miss Landon is what she was called, in England. She has married since, after the fashion of your kind, and I do not know how she is now addressed.'

'Married an Aylir, did she?' said the Ferryman, one of his dark brows lifting. 'Uncommon.'

'Is it?' faltered Isabel, conscious of her own ignorance. 'Perhaps it is. It came about in a strange way.'

That grin flashed again, and Isabel once more received the impression that he was laughing at her. 'Such an oddity could hardly come about in any normal kind o' way,' he said. 'In point o' fact, I cannot remember it ever happenin' before. To my knowledge, that is.'

Isabel's thoughts flew to the Aylir ancestor her aunt had spoken of. 'Sometimes it happens the other way around, I think?' she ventured.

His brows snapped down. 'Ye mean an Aylir marryin' one o' your kind, an' settlin' in your world. I've heard o' such a time or two, but it's no common thing either.' For a moment his thoughts seemed turned inwards, as though he had forgotten her presence entirely. Then his attention shifted to focus upon her, and his gaze grew intent. 'I see,' he said.

'You see… what?' Isabel said, self-conscious under his scrutiny.

'What it is about ye that had me wonderin'.' The twinkle was back in his eyes. 'Human — an' yet not, entirely. There's a flicker o' somethin' else there.'

Isabel nodded. 'That is why I am bound for Grenlowe,' she said. 'Sophy — Miss Landon, I mean — will assist me.'

'Ye just take some care,' he said warningly. 'A little flower like yerself? Ye'll attract a deal of attention in Grenlowe. Tis good fortune that ye've a friend t' go to.'

These words disturbed Isabel. She had expected to feel disoriented, out of place, and confused, but it had not occurred to her that she might attract any particular attention — nor that such attention might prove dangerous.

Her trepidation perhaps showed upon her face, for he added, 'Ye will be safe enough.' He nodded to Tafferty, who still sat upright and alert with her back to Isabel. 'Ye've the right sort o' guide in yon catterdandy there.'

'Catterdandy?' repeated Isabel. Tafferty twitched, and her tail lashed once.

The Ferryman grinned widely. ''Tis what some call the likes o' yer friend there.'

'I do not think Tafferty appreciates the name,' Isabel said with a smile. 'But I find it charming.'

Tafferty growled something inaudible, and the Ferryman laughed. 'I beg yer pardon, Tafferty-tail,' he said.

Tafferty sniffed.

'We 'ave a ways t' go, yet,' said the Ferryman. 'An' I like a tale. Tell me what manner o' circumstance could bring yer friend t' Grenlowe.'

Isabel told him of Sophy's predicament as the only daughter of a poor clergyman, and the lack of prospects which had overshadowed her life. With Balligumph's help, she had wandered into Aylfenhame — to Grenlowe — and there met Aubranael, an Aylir as lonely and beset with troubles as Sophy had been herself. Their story had been unusual, for the involvement of a witch, a brownie and the Goblin King had complicated matters considerably. At length, Sophy had settled in Grenlowe and opened the shop, Silverling, wherein she stitched and sold wondrous creations of her own designing. Such an enterprise would have lowered her standing to an intolerable degree, had it been undertaken in England. In Grenlowe, her creativity exalted her.

Isabel was proud of her friend's success, and awed by her bravery. But she remained silent on the topic of one of Sophy's exploits: Lihyaen, princess of Aylfenhame, had been extricated from a grievous curse and now resided in Grenlowe under Sophy and Aubranael's protection. The princess had been presumed dead for many years, and her survival was a secret. Isabel had no intention of sharing it with this stranger.

His eyes, though, bored into hers with an intentness which she found disturbing. 'I 'ave rarely come across such strange tales,' he said slowly. 'An' I think ye 'ave told only some of it.'

'There is more,' admitted Isabel. 'But it is not all mine to tell.'

The Ferryman inclined his head at that and looked away, over the prow of the boat into the dense mist which still obscured everything that lay beyond its confines. Colours had begun to drift into the white expanse: the pale blue of summer skies, the golden-yellow of sunlight, and soft pink like the wild roses which grew near Ferndeane. Isabel watched the ebb and flow of these gentle hues for some minutes, expecting the Ferryman to make some further remark as to her tale. But he did not. At length she said: 'Is it really so strange, for an Aylir to marry an Englishwoman? You speak of it as very far out of the common way, but to me it does not seem so very unlikely.'

The Ferryman blinked, as though he had been so lost in reverie as to forget her presence — again. His head turned and he regarded her impassively. 'Ye are curious,' he said.

Isabel bowed her head. 'Forgive me, if I was rude.'

'Rude, no,' he said in a livelier tone. 'Not that. Ye 'ave told me a fine tale, 'tis fair that I should tell ye somethin' in return. Listen, then.' He took off his hat again, and threw it upwards. It did not sail away into the mists to be lost forever, as Isabel had expected. Instead it began to float, drifting dreamily upon the soft currents of air. The Ferryman rested his head against the side of the boat, face tipped up to watch the strange progress of his hat.

'Once,' he began, 'far back in the mists o' time — ye know how this part goes in a tale — there was freer passage betwixt an' between yer own world an' mine. Such marriages as ye describe were not so uncommon, in those days. Many folk travelled back an' forth, an' there were many ways t' make the crossin'. This ferry was but one o' many, sailin' travellers from England an' Scotland an' the rest into Aylfenhame.

'Some folk, though, are never 'appy with what they 'ave. Ye'll 'ave noticed that fer yer own self, I'll wager. An' one such was a lanky type, name o'… well in fact, no one alive remembers what 'is true name was. We remember 'im as Kostigern, which means somethin' like traitor in an old tongue. Betrayer. Ye get the idea.

'Naught would do fer this paragon o' virtue but t' reign over every last bit of Aylfenhame. Ye'll recognise that well enough; yer own world's 'ad its share o' such fine folk, 'as it not?'

Thinking of Bonaparte, Isabel nodded her assent to this point.

'I won't bore ye with all the long, long tale. 'Tis sufficient to tell ye that Kostigern was overthrown an' destroyed. Some say he came out o' your world, an' perhaps that's why the borders between our two lands were closed. Whatever the reason fer that, they were closed, an' most o' the routes between were closed likewise. Now, gates only open on the solstices, an' 'tis said there is but one ferry left. Ye're on it.'

The Ferryman paused, eyes upon Isabel, expression considering. She coloured, and looked away. His close scrutiny made her uncomfortable, and she could not account for it. None of his thoughts were ever visible to her.

'I do understand the difficulty of travel,' Isabel offered. 'Sophy departed for Grenlowe a year ago, or more, and I have been able to visit her but rarely in that time.' Her parents' disapprobation for the idea had also been an obstacle, but there could be no cause to mention that. 'I do not ever remember hearing of a ferry.'

'There's sense enough in that, on account o' there not bein' one.'

Isabel blinked. 'I cannot understand you.'

'Many long years 'ave passed since that time, an' travel 'as only become more difficult. Well, in Aylfenhame, those things which nobody wants or needs can… fade. An' that's what 'appened to the ferry.'

He said this with an air of finality, as though it concluded the tale. Isabel frowned, questions awhirl in her mind. 'The ferry was gone?' she said.

He nodded. 'Fer many years.'

'Why has it returned?'

The Ferryman shrugged. 'Somethin'… called me back. An' before ye ask, I 'ave no notion as t' what that was. I found meself awake, I resumed my duty, an' that is that. Though near as I can tell, of the lot of us remainin' 'tis jest me that's awoken. Mayhap that will change.'

'Us?'

He nodded once. 'The ferries all 'ad a guide. More than a navigator — their souls an' will were bound up with the boats. 'Tis powerful magic t' bring such a thing from one world t'another, on any day o' the year, an' at any time. 'Tis a voluntary post.' His mouth twisted and he added, 'Most of the time.'

'You are the last Ferry-guide, then?'

'I believe I am, but I cannot be certain.'

'But where were you, when the ferry was lost?'

'Don't ask me where I was, for I know naught of it. I only know I woke as from a long slumber, an' there I was, ferry an' all, an' with passengers t' convey. An' off we went again.' He ran a hand gently over the boat's silvery, misty wood and smiled. 'She is called Mirisane, if ye were wonderin'.'

'She is beautiful,' said Isabel sincerely.

He nodded, but said nothing.

A thought flashed through Isabel's mind, and she sat up straighter. 'Passengers! Was this many days ago?'

The Ferryman raised one black brow. 'Not so very many as all that, I reckon, no. Why do ye ask?'

'Was there a piper?'

'There was.'

'And a fiddler, and other musicians besides? And ladies dressed very fine.'

'All those, an' more,' said the Ferryman with a nod. 'Mirisane 'as scarcely ever carried such a deal o' people in one go. 'Twas into England I took 'em.' He cocked his head at Isabel. 'Happen ye saw 'em there?'

'I did. They attended an assembly in Alford, and…' she hesitated. 'It was very strange. They played music and danced, and — and it was like nothing we had ever seen or heard before. Did they say why they came?'

'Nay,' said the Ferryman. 'But 'tis not the custom o' most folk t' talk to me. I am but a lowly Ferryman, an' the circumstances of my bein' here are such as to discourage most folk from makin' the attempt.' He grinned at her. 'Tis why I am enjoyin' yer presence. Ye're a different sort.'

Isabel frowned. 'But what circumstances could produce such an unpleasant, and unkind, result? How is it that you came to be a Ferryman? And the last of them, too!'

His eyes flicked back to hers, and narrowed. 'That is a tale fer some other day,' he said, after a short pause. 'I 'ave told ye enough. Besides, we shall soon be settin' ye down in Grenlowe.'

'It is a long journey,' Isabel commented. 'I have been through twice before, on the solstice, and it was but a short distance. I thought that Tilby and Grenlowe were not so very far apart.'

The Ferryman grinned. 'Truth be told, they are not. I 'ave been indulgin' in a little mischief, an' have kept ye aboard longer than I should 'ave. We 'ave been goin' in circles a while.'

Isabel's mouth opened in surprise. 'But why should you do that?'

'Because the pleasure o' talkin' t' anyone at all is more'n I expected ever t' have again,' he said, his grin fading. 'An' when my passenger is a pretty maid o' England, with wit an' brains an' more besides, I am loathe t' let her leave.' His eyes twinkled at Isabel, and he laughed at her blush. 'Fear not, for leave ye shall, an' I will not keep ye very much longer. But I will be lookin' forward to takin' ye home once again, when ye should be ready t' return.' He held out his hand: Isabel saw a tiny silver whistle nestled in the palm. 'Take it,' he urged her. 'When ye wish t' go home, ye must simply blow a tiny toot upon this shiny thing, an' I'll be able t' find ye.'

Isabel took the whistle carefully, and tucked it into her reticule. 'Thank you,' she said cautiously.

He nodded. 'I cannot promise not t' keep ye longer'n I should on that day, but I will see ye safely home. That I do promise.'

Isabel murmured her thanks. She said no more, for she was struggling with a variety of feelings, none of which she could express. The startling realisation that he had, via magics beyond her comprehension or control, kept her trapped in his boat for above an hour was no welcome news, for it reminded her how powerless she was. Could she trust him to keep to his word, and release her?

And there was the matter of his compliments. A pretty maid o' England, with wit an' brains an' more besides. She ought to be offended at such freely-expressed admiration; these were not the words of a gentleman, and nor was his manner such. But she was not offended. On the contrary, the knowledge that her journey was almost at an end left her feeling curiously dismayed. If he did not choose to release her just yet, would she be sorry?

Her mother's long-ago admonition drifted through her mind. If you are ever in doubt as to what to say to a gentleman, my love, say something gracious, and remember your manners. 'I thank you for your kind care,' she said.

'Aye,' he said, his frank gaze running over her from her hair to her boots. 'Ye are all in one piece, to be sure. I 'ave not permitted ye t' fall over the side.'

Isabel glanced up at his hat, still soaring some way above their heads. 'That does not appear to have been a danger, if I may judge by the behaviour of your hat.'

'Ye may, in point o' fact. Would ye like t' try it?'

Isabel looked at him, startled. 'Your hat?'

'No! Would ye like t' fly like my hat, up there?'

Isabel stared up at the silky sail rippling gently in the breeze. The

hat hovered just before it, bobbing in the air like a feather.

For a moment, she was tempted to accept his offer. To fly like that! Such felicity! Her lips parted on the word yes, but she left it unspoken. She was no feather. There would be no protecting her modesty under such circumstances — the winds would play havoc with her light muslin gown — and it would end with her hair and attire in such a state of disorder as could not be put to rights without significant attention. Such a flight was incompatible with the decorum expected of her; her mother would be shocked that she could even consider such an offer.

'I thank you, but I cannot,' she said quietly, folding her hands in her lap.

'No? An' why not, if I may ask?'

Isabel attempted to explain her reasons, in as few words as possible. She felt an unsettling degree of embarrassment on recounting them, perhaps from the realisation that such scruples could only seem absurd to him.

The Ferryman looked at her with disbelief, and shook his head. 'Strange notions ye 'ave, in England,' he said.

She coloured, and looked away. 'They are of importance to us.'

He bowed gravely, reclaimed his hat, and returned it to his head. 'Then I'll not speak further against them. Mind yerself, now, for we are goin' t' land.'

The mist streamed away as he spoke, leaving a clear vista spread before Isabel. Aylfenhame looked as wondrous and strange from above as from below: meadows of bronzed-golden grass covered the ground almost as far as she could see, melding into a thick, vast forest to the north. Trees with silvery bark were dotted here and thereabout, their leaves shining in shades of cerulean, indigo, sage and moss-green. Colourful birds and enormous butterflies flitted lazily from tree to tree, wings glinting in the sunlight. In the midst of all this stood the town of Grenlowe, a haphazard knot of grey stone-and-wood buildings, riotously thatched and cheerfully painted. The ferry came down a little way to the south of the town. As soon as it had ceased to move, the Ferryman vaulted easily out and offered his hand to Isabel.

'Thank you,' she murmured, taking the proffered hand with, she feared, heightened colour in her cheeks. She managed the descent gracefully, and curtseyed to her guide. 'You have been very kind.'

He surveyed her frankly, and with scepticism. 'I 'ave not been kind,' he corrected her. 'I 'ave merely performed my assigned duty, an' I found a way t' be selfish about it, at that.'

Isabel bowed her head, feeling chastened. 'My thanks, nonetheless.' She hesitated, and added, 'It was a pleasure to meet you.' And it had been, in spite of his directness and his odd manners. She had met no one even half so interesting in Tilby.

He stared at her, and blinked. 'Was it indeed?'

He seemed surprised, and Isabel felt uncomfortable. Nonetheless, she smiled. 'Very much so.'

The Ferryman smiled back. An ironic tilt to his lips suggested that he found something amusing, but she thought that he smiled with real pleasure. 'I did not find it entirely displeasin', my own self,' he said with a twinkle, and Isabel's smile grew. She hesitated. His tale had afflicted her, for a lonelier life she could scarcely imagine. She wished to offer more than thanks, but she was uncertain as to the nature or degree of her acquaintance with him. Could she properly term him an acquaintance at all?

'The house of my friend is not far,' she said, with some diffidence. 'It would please them to meet you, I have no doubt. May I invite you to call upon us there?'

The Ferryman merely blinked and stared, his whole expression one of such surprise that Isabel felt deeply uncomfortable. 'I am sorry,' she said quickly. 'It was presumptuous of me.'

He opened his mouth, closed it again, and then shook his head. 'It was… kind o' ye,' he said softly. 'An' it's been many a year since I was offered kindness.' He tipped his hat to her and smiled with a deep warmth. 'I'd be delighted t' accept yer offer, only fer the fact that I can't.'

'You cannot?' Isabel said with a frown. 'It is true that we are barely acquainted, but I assure you—'

He cut her off with a wave of his hand, his eyes glinting with amusement. ''Tis not that. Such niceties are of no matter in Aylfenhame. I cannot, because of somethin' in the nature of a curse. I may not leave the boat.'

It was Isabel's turn to stare, aghast. 'Never?' she said in a choked voice. 'But whyever not?'

The Ferryman's amusement faded and his face turned grim. 'That, as I 'ave said, is more than I wish t' share.'

Recalling his earlier words, Isabel surmised that the circumstances of his becoming a Ferry Keeper and the curse that kept him from relinquishing the post were the same tale, and she nodded. 'Forgive me, it was not my intention to pry. But then… shall you be bound forever?'

'Mayhap,' he said. 'Most like.'

Isabel thought back to her first excursion into Aylfenhame, and the peculiar enchantment that had entrapped the princess Lihyaen. She had been cursed to remain as hostess of the Teapot Society, a party which never ended, and which no one was ever permitted to leave — unless someone consented to take her place.

'Can you not be released?' she ventured. 'What if someone were to take your place here?'

He laughed. 'I could hardly expect anyone t' agree t' that, now could I?' he said. 'For who would be so foolish? An' there's the fact that I 'ave been gone so long, there's none as remembers me now.' He paused, and added, 'Though there is a way.'

'What is it?' Isabel said eagerly. 'For truly, if there is some way I can help you, I will.'

He looked at her oddly. 'Ye 'ave but just met me, an' ye freely make such promises?'

Isabel hesitated, taken aback. 'But of course,' she said. 'How can I but feel for such a plight as yours? I am free, and I will help you.'

His brows lifted. 'Ye cannot, I think. 'Tis my name. It is held hostage, lost entirely t' time, an' I must remain until it is found.' Isabel felt a flicker of excitement, for this seemed no impossible task! But he smiled ruefully and shook his head at her. 'Tis not so easy as I see ye fancy,' he cautioned. 'My name is long-lost, and well hid. An' many o' my memories are gone along with it. I can remember little that'd be of use t' ye in yer search.'

The words poured from Isabel's lips without pause to consider. 'I will find it,' she said. 'I promise it.' She did not fully understand why she had made such a profound promise, and to a stranger, but it felt right to say it.

Something gathered in the air as she spoke; a sense of pressure, or expectation. The Ferryman's eyes narrowed. 'Ye 'ave committed yerself,' he said softly. 'An' there is no goin' back on it now. I only hope ye may not come t' regret it.'

Isabel merely curtseyed by way of answer, but as she rose she found both her hands taken, and lightly squeezed, and then kissed. She looked up into the Ferryman's face in surprise, and found him gazing at her with warm regard.

'Ye are fair unusual,' he said. 'Did I ever meet such a vast heart as ye seem t' possess? I think not.'

Isabel coloured, and looked away. 'You do me too much honour, sir,' she said gravely. 'Anybody must feel for you, and act as I have acted.'

He shook his head, still holding her hands in his own. 'Tis t' yer credit that ye can believe that, but there's not so much as a flicker o' truth in it. That ye must know. Few would even listen t' my tale — I 'ave told ye as much already. Fewer still would feel fer me, and no one else, I think, would 'ave promised t' help.'

'When I have carried out my promise,' said Isabel, 'then you may thank me, but do not do so too soon! For I am not at all sure of my power to perform it.'

He nodded. 'That's wise enough, but I do thank ye. Fer carin'.' He released her hands and swept her a bow. 'I'll be seein' ye when ye're ready t' return.'

'Will you be far away?'

He shrugged. 'Who knows? Duty calls, an' I answer.'

Tafferty growled impatiently and swatted Isabel's legs with her lashing tail. 'Time waits for no one, least of all thee!'

Isabel nodded, curtseyed to the Ferryman and hastened after her companion. She looked back, once, to see the Ferryman already aboard his boat and the craft rising rapidly into the sky; borne, apparently, on waves of white mist.

'I hope you know the way to Sophy's house,' Isabel called after Tafferty. 'For I am all turned about. I do not know this part of the town at all.'

Tafferty's tail lashed. 'Thou must trust thy companion in all things,' she said crossly. 'That's the first lesson I must teach thee.' She paused, bounded a few more steps away, and then added, 'Twas a fine piece o' foolery, that.'

'How could I have done otherwise?' Isabel protested. 'I could not consent to leave anyone in such an intolerable situation!'

Tafferty's tail whipped with irritation. 'Cease thy protestin', an' keep up.'

Isabel subsided, and hurried after. Tafferty's pace was not

designed to cater to her convenience, and she risked being left behind if she lingered too long to look about herself. Her companion — the catterdandy, as the Ferryman had called her — navigated the twisting streets without an instant's hesitation, and so Isabel trusted and followed along.

CHAPTER SEVEN

Now, I'm not sayin' as I had owt to do wi' the callin' o' the Ferry. An' I'm not sayin' as I didn't, neitherwise. I'll only say as I've known Eliza Grey fer many years, an' she's a woman wi' a head on 'er shoulders.

Poor Miss Ellerby! I felt fer 'er. Such a deal o' strangeness t' fall upon 'er all together-like, an' she not at all prepared. It's perhaps a help tha' she was never the excitable kind, or she might 'ave lost her good sense there awhile. But not Miss Isabel! Oh, no! Took it in 'er stride, she did, more or less, an' it's very much t' her credit tha' she did.

The Ferryman, now. There's a strange tale, an' no mistake. I knew a thing or two about him, an' the Kostigern besides, as ye'll soon hear. Isabel's meetin' wi' that gentleman — if I may call 'im such, I'm not rightly certain — was important in more ways than she knew, or he either. The tale grows stranger and darker from here; do ye wish t' hear more? Are ye certain? Then I will continue.

Sophy's shop, Silverling, was housed in an odd building near the centre of Grenlowe. It stood alone, surrounded on all sides by circling roads of haphazardly-placed cobblestones. It was three storeys high, built from the same dreamy-grey, silver-touched wood as many other buildings in Grenlowe, and its roof was a spectacular riot of sloping corners and sharp angles all covered over in sleek, dark thatch. The shop occupied much of the ground floor, though on Isabel's previous visits she had seen a kitchen at the back. Sophy, her husband Aubranael and the princess Lihyaen lived in rooms above-stairs; Sophy's friend and erstwhile servant, Mary, resided on the third floor, together with the brownie, Thundigle. It was a snug establishment, and a happy one. Isabel had always cherished the brief, sparse visits she had been able to make before, when the barriers between England and Aylfenhame fell on the solstice days.

On such days she was always expected, and welcomed promptly. But to arrive unannounced, with no warning given of her visit, was the very height of rudeness. A dear friend Sophy may be, but Isabel would never have presumed so far if she had been given any choice. She followed Tafferty until the streets began to look familiar to her, and she realised she was within a minute or two of Sophy's house and shop. Despite her pleasure at the prospect of seeing her friends, she also suffered some feelings of dismay.

She paused for a moment at Silverling's front door, looking up at the sign with some indecision. Ought she to repair to an inn, if such a thing existed here, and send word ahead of her arrival? It would be the courteous thing to do. But she knew of no such establishment, and when she ventured to suggest the idea to Tafferty, she received only a growl of irritation in response. To her horror, Tafferty turned her back on Isabel and trotted through the open door of the shop. Isabel could only follow, clutching nervously at her reticule.

Sophy was engaged with a customer. A young goblin, with lank black hair and features not wholly repellent, stood near the window, attired in a gown which, Isabel assumed, had just been completed for her. Reams of the lightest, airiest gauze floated around her in a silvery cloud, winking with wisp-lit gems and fluttering with rose-hued ribbons of pure fae silk. The effect of these luscious hues set against the goblin's yellow complexion could only be termed unfortunate. The lady herself was blissfully unaware of this, however, and twisted and turned on the spot in pure delight, her crooked teeth bared in a smile as she observed the drape of the gown.

'My informants did not exaggerate,' said the goblin. 'Are all Englishwomen so talented with a needle?'

Sophy, on her knees as she adjusted some small detail near the hem of the gown, laughed and shook her head. 'You flatter me, Miss Tramble. The materials of Aylfenhame are of a quality far beyond those of England. Only here could I produce such fantastic creations.'

Miss Tramble's grin broadened alarmingly. 'Then it was a good day for Aylfenhame fashion when you came to Grenlowe, Mrs.

Sophy.'

Tafferty stalked into the midst of this exchange without ceremony, her tasselled tail raised like a flag. She strolled up to the goblin, sniffed the hem of her luscious gown in a desultory fashion, and sat down.

'Good morning!' said Sophy brightly to the catterdandy. Finished with her adjustments, she stood up; her back was turned, so she did not see Isabel standing diffidently in the doorway. 'If you are satisfied, Miss Tramble, then I will fetch your bonnet and shoes. Perhaps you will wish to wear your new ensemble home?'

Miss Tramble's eyes flicked over Isabel with faint curiosity, but she said nothing, and directed another wide smile at Sophy. 'To be sure!' she said promptly, and handed over a bulging pouch of coins. Sophy took this, and after a little discussion with her customer on the topic of overpayment, disappeared into the back.

'A fine confection t' be stompin' about the countryside in,' observed Tafferty to the goblin.

Miss Tramble sniffed. 'Mind your business, catterdandy, and I will mind mine.'

Tafferty's tail twitched with derision. She leapt up onto the shop's counter and began to wash one tufted paw.

Sophy reappeared an instant later, her hands full of shoes, bonnet, reticules and other fripperies, and at once noticed Isabel standing in the doorway. Her face lit up. 'Isabel! And in excellent time, too. Just the briefest of moments, my dear, and I will show you to your room. I am sure you are very tired after such an unusual journey!'

She turned at once to Miss Tramble, leaving Isabel to blink in confusion at this speech. Had her aunt sent word of Isabel's visit? How had she contrived it? Isabel was grateful to discover that her concerns had been misplaced, but she was puzzled as well — and a little awed. The aunt she had known her whole life through — the pleasant, courteous, respectable Mrs. Grey with whom she had always enjoyed a friendship — receded further and further. In her place stood a new Mrs. Grey, one who wielded powers Isabel could not begin to imagine or to understand, and whose connections with the once-distant and mythical land of Aylfenhame were inexplicably close. How had she contrived to hide all this from the placid, conventional social world of York? From her family?

Miss Tramble took her leave, tripping on the hem of her gown as she did so. This fazed her not at all, for she recovered herself in an instant and disappeared into the bright sun of the afternoon.

Sophy smiled after her. 'I find her humbling,' she said to Isabel. 'In England, you know, a young lady would spend hours agonising over precisely the right shade of lavender to complement her complexion. Miss Tramble, on the other hand, merely revels in the beauty of the fabrics, and thinks nothing of how she appears in them. I think she has no vanity at all.'

Isabel smiled in response, and went to kiss her friend. Sophy looked as she ever did, since her move to Grenlowe: cheerful, blooming with good health, and just a little untidy. Her blonde curls were escaping from beneath the wispy lace cap she wore, and her simple, unpretentious blue gown was covered in stray, clinging lengths of threads snipped from some creation of hers. 'She is a model for us all, perhaps,' Isabel agreed. 'Though she appears to have adopted one or two of the customs of England. Is she truly called Miss Tramble?'

Sophy laughed. 'She chooses to be. I do not know if it reflects her true name. She questioned me closely on the topic of English titles, and insisted upon begin given a suitable one of her own.'

'In that case,' said Isabel, laughing, 'I am surprised she did not choose something a little more prestigious. Why not Lady Tramble?'

'She was taken with it,' Sophy conceded, 'but when she understood its true meaning, she would not choose it. It would be unbecoming, to pretend to a station she does not possess. That is what she said.'

'A very honest goblin,' Isabel said gravely.

Sophy agreed to it. 'But come, let us settle you upstairs. You will want to rest, I should imagine, and perhaps arrange your dress?'

Isabel put a hand up to her hair, suddenly self-conscious. 'Oh dear, yes. I must look a fright. I am sure the winds have caused much disorder. Oh, but I have brought no luggage! I was not aware I was to travel, until the moment of departure.'

'The day has yet to come when you could manage to look a fright,' Sophy said with a warm smile. 'But you are, perhaps, slightly less beautifully turned-out than usual. You need not concern yourself about a lack of clothing, for I at least was given warning of your visit, and I have prepared a few things for you.'

Isabel allowed herself to be led upstairs, where a small but beautiful and comfortable room had been prepared for her. She had never before spent more than a few scant hours at Silverling, as the nature of travel between England and Aylfenhame did not allow for it. She took possession of the room with quiet satisfaction, delighted at the prospect of paying a longer visit to her dearest friend. Thoughts of the abandoned York assembly, of Mr. Thompson and her mother's expectations would intrude, but she pushed them away for the present. Her aunt had promised to manage all of these problems, and Isabel could no longer doubt her perfect capability to do so.

The wardrobe of garments Sophy had provided was delightful, of course, and she had displayed both a clear knowledge of Isabel's tastes and a desire to please her friend. There were three gowns hanging in her closet, together with two spencers and a pelisse, and matching shoes. All were fairly simple in style and without the fussy adornments which Isabel found repellent. They were also in her favourite shades of blue and green. Touched, Isabel thanked her friend sincerely, and received an affectionate smile in return.

Sophy left her to tend to her appearance, and to rest, but Isabel took advantage of only one of these offers. She was tired, but not terribly so, and other feelings took precedence over her desire to refresh herself with slumber or repose. She wished to see a great deal more of Sophy, without delay; and besides, her curiosity had yet to be assuaged. Within half an hour, she left her little room and made her way downstairs once more.

The shop was empty, so she stepped into the back. Sophy's workroom lay directly behind the shop-floor, and beyond lay the kitchens of Silverling. To her surprise, Isabel found both full of people. She could hear the voices of Mary and Thundigle coming from the kitchen, while Sophy had retired to her workroom. Isabel went into the latter, and found two others present: Sophy's husband, Aubranael, and the princess Lihyaen.

The two Aylir were remarkably similar in appearance; so much so that Isabel might assume them to be related, if she did not already know to the contrary. Aubranael was tall and lithe, with brown skin, long dark hair falling in a tumbled mess around his face, and brown eyes which typically twinkled with good humour. He had left off the wide-brimmed hat he used to wear indoors or out, which Isabel considered to be a good sign. His face was disfigured, an affliction which he had used to bear with considerable pain, and hid any way he could. Now he looked back at Isabel with no trace of self-consciousness, and smiled a genuine welcome.

Lihyaen was much shorter than he, though significantly taller than she had been upon Isabel's last visit. Her skin and hair were almost as dark as Aubranael's, though the latter curled delicately, and bore goldish streaks mixed in with the chocolate hue. Her eyes, though, were quite different: large and gold, a colour Isabel never saw in England. Her face was very pretty, and young. She looked to be perhaps eighteen years old, though Isabel knew her to be as old as Aubranael in truth. The lost princess of Aylfenhame, long supposed dead, Lihyaen had been a childhood companion of Aubranael's. She had been discovered, alive (if not entirely well), imprisoned in the Outwoods by a strange and unbreakable enchantment. Hidenory, witch of the Outwoods, had made the sacrifice of taking Lihyaen's place, and the princess had been free to resume her life.

Her growth, both mentally and physically, had been severely retarded during her long, long sojourn in the Outwoods. She had emerged with the appearance of a girl of perhaps fifteen, when she should have been of an age with Aubranael. Months of tranquillity and care had restored much of her shattered peace of mind, and she was growing and maturing very quickly. Still, Sophy thought she was often troubled, and suspected that the princess suffered much more in the aftermath of her ordeal than she would admit. These concerns had been confided to Isabel more than once, and she felt all the anxiety for Lihyaen's recovery that Sophy could do; the girl had suffered terribly under the curse, and the loss of her parents besides. But she appeared calm and content, and smiled readily at Isabel's appearance.

Aubranael and Lihyaen always welcomed Isabel in the kindest fashion, which gratified her exceedingly, for they were not very well acquainted with her. But Isabel herself had been one of the party which had ventured into Aylfenhame, a year ago, to bring back Sophy, and the excursion had resulted in Lihyaen's freedom as well. Neither had forgotten.

'Tell me, my dear,' said Sophy, drawing Isabel's arm through her own. 'That delicious creature presently occupying my shop counter. Has she aught to do with you?'

'Oh! Is Tafferty still there?' Isabel said, with a guilty flush. In her delight at seeing Sophy, she had forgotten about the catterdandy. 'Indeed, she came with me. She is my… my companion, she calls herself.'

'Ah!' said Sophy with apparent delight. 'Yes, I quite see. I received the kindest and most interesting letter from your aunt not two days ago, and she explained everything to me. My dear, I do congratulate you! Only to think! I had no notion that you bore such connections to Aylfenhame, nor such powers! Nor, I suppose, did you. I do hope you are not too much dismayed. It will require some adjustment, to be sure, but I do sincerely believe it will prove to be very much to your benefit.'

'Do you truly think so?' said Isabel, looking searchingly into Sophy's face. 'I know that you have settled very well here, but I cannot help wondering if it is sometimes painful to you, to be so far removed from England. And then, there is the question of how to reconcile this new aspect of myself with the rest! It is, you must own, wholly incompatible with the future I must be expected to have.'

'You are not to worry about any of that,' Sophy said firmly. 'Your aunt has given me the strictest instructions on this point, and I assure you I intend to carry them out! You shall not leave us until you are comfortable with this development, and at peace in your mind.'

'Peace!' said Aubranael, with a laugh. 'That is rather too much to expect, my love. When the foundations of one's world fall away and everything inverts itself, peace is not to be expected. But that is not wholly a bad thing. It is at such unsettling times that the most exciting and rewarding of developments can occur.' He gave Isabel an encouraging smile, which she could not manage to return.

Sophy nodded in agreement, and squeezed Isabel's arm. 'Never mind, Isa. All will be well.'

Lihyaen had not spoken before, choosing instead to listen with her usual quiet demeanour. Now she leaned towards Isabel a little, her golden eyes shining, and said: 'You were conveyed here by the Ferryman! Is it true? Was it indeed he?'

Isabel nodded. 'It was he, and he was a curious fellow. But how is it that you know of him? I understood that he has been gone from these parts for some time.'

'Oh, he has! But the Ferries of old are spoken of sometimes, in tales, and the last Ferryman as well.' Lihyaen's eyes sparkled with enthusiasm, for no reason Isabel could understand. 'They say he is very handsome. Is he so?'

Isabel hesitated, thinking of the Ferryman's long black hair and laughing eyes. 'Yes,' she said with a blush. 'Very handsome indeed.'

Lihyaen nodded with satisfaction. 'They also say that he is under a curse,' she said, her voice sinking. 'That he may never leave the Ferry, as long as he lives — and also that he shall never die.' Her enthusiasm had faded, replaced by a darkling glower and more than a hint of anxiety in her eyes. She was thinking of her own curse, Isabel surmised, and the pain she had suffered under it; of course she would feel for the plight of another. 'Is that also true?'

'He told me so,' Isabel said gently.

Lihyaen bit her lip. 'It is a terrible fate.'

Isabel nodded. 'I have promised him my aid.'

Lihyaen's eyes widened. 'Promised?' she repeated in a faint voice.

'Yes, of course I did. How could I have done otherwise?' Lihyaen said nothing, and Isabel continued, with a touch of pique, 'He seemed to think it a great deal, and I see that you agree, but I cannot think why! Tis a small thing indeed, and who could help offering their aid?'

Lihyaen gazed at Isabel with a mixture of admiration and concern. 'It is beyond kind in you,' she said. 'Sophy has told me you have the warmest heart in the world, and she is quite right! But I fear you do not understand what it is you've done. You have promised.'

Isabel nodded once, confused. 'Yes.'

'Such a promise is binding,' Lihyaen said. 'It must be performed.'

'I have every intention of carrying it out,' said Isabel.

'You must,' said Lihyaen simply.

'Oh dear,' said Sophy, squeezing Isabel's arm. 'I do hope there is not some penalty for failure, Lihyaen?'

'There may be,' said the princess. 'Though we cannot know what it will be.' Seeing Sophy's frown, Lihyaen hastily continued, 'It is the nature of such in Aylfenhame. Honesty is rewarded, but faith-breakers are held in low regard.'

'I shall be no faith-breaker,' Isabel said firmly, but her confidence faltered. 'It is only that I do not know how to go about it,' she confessed. Lihyaen's warnings were beginning to alarm her, and she felt an unpleasant degree of helplessness.

'We will help you,' said Lihyaen earnestly.

'Of course we shall,' said Sophy brightly, and Aubranael nodded.

Isabel felt a rush of gratitude. Sophy's sunny nature had always been a comfort. She never worried, the way Isabel was sometimes wont to do, and she was never gloomy. Her cheerful confidence had aided and supported Isabel before, and could not fail to do so now.

If Sophy possessed the spirit to assist and encourage Isabel, Aubranael and Lihyaen possessed the knowledge of Aylfenhame and its customs and magics that would aid her in finding her way. Her hopes revived, and she smiled. 'I thank you all,' she said. 'Truly, it was impulsive of me. I cannot think what possessed me to promise so readily, when I have no notion how I shall go about fulfilling it. But I do not mean to fail.'

Lihyaen eyed her with an unreadable expression, and exchanged a look with Aubranael. 'One of those things,' said Aubranael, and Lihyaen nodded.

'What things, dearest?' said Sophy, echoing Isabel's thoughts.

'Never mind.' He smiled at his wife. 'We are thinking there's more at work here than impulse, but cannot be sure.'

'Very well! Keep your secrets!' said Sophy cheerfully. 'Knowledge of Aylfenhame I may lack, compared to the two of you, but I do know a place to begin.'

Isabel looked an enquiry.

'Why, Mister Balligumph, of course!' said Sophy with a smile. 'He makes it his business to know a great deal about everything. If anybody can tell us where to begin, it is him.'

'But he is in Tilby,' Isabel protested.

'Most days of the year, he is,' agreed Sophy, 'but not all. Whenever he comes into Aylfenhame, he informs me of it, so that I may visit him. And this is one of those times.' She smiled at Isabel. 'I do not think it is a coincidence, for I received the impression that he has taken an interest in you. He wished to be close at hand, in case you should require his assistance in some way.'

'Has he indeed?' said Isabel, surprised. 'But we are not much acquainted!'

'That matters little to Balli,' said Sophy with a laugh. 'He would gladly be your friend, if you would let him. Especially now. There are not many witches in Tilby, after all.'

Isabel began at once to feel guilty, for she had made little effort to further her acquaintance with the toll-keeper; even knowing him to be a close acquaintance of Sophy's. 'That is very kind of him!' she said. 'I am sorry indeed that I did not know it before! Let us visit him at once.'

CHAPTER EIGHT

The visit to Balligumph was deferred until the following morning, as Sophy considered that Isabel's day had been eventful enough. Secretly, Isabel agreed, for she was feeling the effects of her day of unexpected adventures. But an unfamiliar, and not wholly unpleasant, note of excitement was dancing somewhere within her. When combined with the stronger and much more familiar note of concern that lived alongside it, she was eager to proceed with the task she had impulsively set for herself.

She consented to rest and recover first, however; and thus it was early on the following day that she set out with Sophy, Aubranael, Lihyaen and Tafferty to visit the bridge-keeper of Tilby.

On the edge of Grenlowe there stood surprisingly expansive stables, given the size of the village (though Isabel had been told before that Grenlowe was larger than it appeared, with a great many dwellings hidden underground — and hidden by other means besides). The stable was called, peculiarly, Lurrock's Leggy Beasts, and there it was possible to hire a host of different creatures for one's travelling requirements.

Aubranael procured four ponies. They were not precisely as one might expect, being unusually long in the leg (as the title of their establishment implied), and displaying highly unorthodox colours as well. Isabel's pony was a dainty, high-stepping mare whose gleaming coat was an enchanting, if odd, shade of pale lemon and whose braided mane and tail were dark gold. Lihyaen was mounted atop a slightly smaller, lavender pony; Sophy rode a white mare with a pearly coat; and Aubranael's taller gelding was deep blue. The whole party set off for the Outwoods at once, leaving Grenlowe by its southern gate and advancing into the forests at a comfortable trot.

Balligumph's dwelling was situated some way beyond the borders of Grenlowe, though not so very far. They travelled for less than an hour beneath the vastly tall, shady trees of the Outwoods before Sophy turned off the wide dirt road and plunged into the undergrowth. There was a path here, albeit a narrow one, and Isabel had to concentrate all of her attention on keeping to it — without permitting Tafferty, enthroned atop her mare's neck, to be swept off by a protruding branch. So engrossed was she in this task that she did not immediately notice when Sophy reined in her mount, and she almost walked hers into the back of Aubranael's horse.

'Ah!' came a great, booming voice from somewhere ahead — a voice she recognised as belonging to Balligumph. 'Visitors! An' me not fit to be seen. Hold yerselves steady fer just a second or two, an' I shall be at yer disposal.'

Isabel moved forward during this speech, and then regretted that she had, for she beheld two sights, one of them a little disconcerting.

The first was a large hillock rising from the ground immediately before her, surrounded on three sides by trees tall and wide of trunk, their bark ranging in hue from nut-brown to old gold. Fallen cinnamon-coloured leaves lay strewn all over the packed dirt of the ground. Into the side of this hillock, someone had built a house. Blocks of honey-coloured stone formed a front wall, into which a door easily eight feet tall had been set, along with two large windows of irregular shape. The top of the hillock formed the roof of the house, liberally grown over with velvety moss. It suited Balligumph well, Isabel thought, for it combined elements of his quirky character with a great deal of practicality.

In front of the house, and a little way to the side, there was a large pool of muddy-looking water. Isabel could readily suppose it to be deeper than it appeared, for Balligumph was immersed up to his neck, his pale blue hair slicked against his head and dripping water. As he spoke he began to lever himself up out of the pool, revealing an enormous torso liberally covered in hair. Shocked, Isabel averted her gaze and stared resolutely at the trees to the left of the house, listening as sounds of heavy splashing split the clearing.

Sophy was laughing. 'My goodness! We are terribly sorry to interrupt your bath, Mr. Balligumph. Is it the first one this year?'

'Tsh,' said Balligumph with a chuckle. 'I won't say as it is, an' I won't say as it isn't neither. Ye mind yer tongue, Miss Sophy.'

Isabel heard the door open and close as he disappeared into the house, and judged herself safe to turn back to the rest of her party.

Aubranael grinned at her. 'Balli takes a little getting used to,' he said, kindly enough, and Isabel nodded, aware that her cheeks were very warm.

Mr. Balligumph returned a few moments later, properly attired in the long trousers and boots, shirt, waistcoat and jacket he preferred, his hat crowning his still-damp locks. Isabel was always surprised anew at how enormous he was: vastly taller than she, and wider by far. He had tusks, too, on each side of his mouth, which ought to be fearsome. But his manner was so friendly, and his smile so congenial in spite of the tusks, that Isabel found it hard to be afraid of him.

'Come inside!' he invited, opening his door wide and beckoning with a vast sweep of his arm. 'I 'ave arranged fer tea an' somethin' sweet to please ye.'

Isabel dismounted carefully. There did not seem to be anywhere to tie up her mount, but this did not trouble any of her companions. She followed their lead in looping up the reins of her mare, and letting her wander.

Within a few moments she entered Balligumph's kitchen, a surprisingly spacious room built from stone, with a large round table in the centre. The chairs were all of different sizes: one was fully large enough to accommodate Balligumph himself, and it was upon this one that he seated himself in due course. The others varied: some were sized for human (or, more likely, Ayliri) guests while others were tiny, if very tall — just right to seat a brownie, perhaps, or a hob. Tafferty freely appropriated one of these, ignoring Isabel's invitation to sit by her.

Balligumph served tea in surprisingly delicate cups. These, too, were of different sizes: Isabel's was of normal proportions, albeit breathtakingly exquisite, while Balli's more nearly resembled a bucket. All were made from airy glass, as thin as a butterfly's wing, and swirled with iridescent colours. She picked up hers gingerly, certain that it would break the moment she lifted it from the table. It did not, however, bearing its load of pale green tea with ease. They were not at all what she would have expected the troll to possess; nor were the tiny, white-iced cakes which he soon afterwards served. They bore a fragility and a delicacy which seemed wholly at odds with the troll's pragmatic, down-to-earth manner and attire — not to mention his size.

'I bid ye welcome, Miss Isabel, t' Aylfenhame,' Mr. Balligumph said, handing her a plate of lacy biscuits with a wink. 'Tis a shock, no doubt, but I am certain in me own mind that ye'll adapt, and soon at that. Ye're a lively lass, an' wi' no small measure o' sense in yer brain.'

'Thank you, sir,' said Isabel, unsure what else to add. She was not required to speak much, for Balligumph went swiftly on.

'Sir!' he said delightedly. 'I like that! What a polite little miss ye are. Miss Sophy, there; she gave up on Sirrin' me long ago.' He twinkled at Sophy, who smiled in response. 'An' the princess, why, she don' like to be addressed as Her High-an'-Mightiness no matter how charmin' I am in sayin' it.'

Lihyaen paused with her mouth full of cake, and shook her head vigorously.

'There, now,' said Balligumph with a good-natured chuckle, 'I'll no' torment ye by doin' it. Anyhow. Tell me yer business in comin'.'

Sophy looked at Isabel. 'It is on Isabel's account that we are here, sir,' she said with a twinkle. 'She encountered the Ferryman, as I imagine you know.'

Balligumph grinned, displaying enormous pearly-white teeth. 'Ye're by no means slow on the uptake either, Miss Sophy! Aye, I did know. I was commissioned, ye may say, t' convey Miss Isabel t'

Aylfenhame by some means or other, an' word 'ad already reached me o' yon Ferryman's return. How did ye find the trip?' This last was directed at Isabel, his head turning to fix her with a golden-eyed stare.

Isabel swallowed a bite of cake, and set down her exquisite tea cup. 'It was remarkable, sir, as you may imagine,' she said. 'I never thought to fly! And in a boat, of all things! I enjoyed it very much.'

Balligumph nodded. 'Thas wonderful,' he said, beaming. 'But ye 'ave not come all this way to see me just to tell me that. Out wi' the rest, now.'

So Isabel told him everything about her conversation with the Ferryman, ending with her promise to find his name. Balligumph's eyebrows lifted near to his hair at her words, but instead of being shocked or alarmed, as Lihyaen and Aubranael had been, Balligumph broke into a vast, gusty laugh. 'Ye did not!' he bellowed. 'Ah! Tha' would've fair knocked the wind out o' his sails, I'll wager.'

'It did,' Isabel agreed. 'I do not think he believed me, quite.'

'Well he might not! Tha' a green young miss out of England should show up an' do what no one in Aylfenhame would've! Present company excepted,' he added, with a nod at the rest of his guests. 'An' wi' no more notion than a babe's o' what she's got her good self into! Well, well. I applaud ye fer it, Miss Isabel. Twas kindly done, an' brave.'

Isabel coloured. 'But I do not know how to find his name,' she said simply. 'Sophy thought that you might.'

Balligumph tugged on the curled end of one of his tusks, thinking deeply. Nobody spoke while he did so, for they understood that he was perusing his considerable mental catalogue of facts, a task which might take some time. Isabel applied herself to her tea, which was deliciously refreshing, and consumed a few of his pretty cakes and biscuits before he finally spoke.

'The Ferryman's name 'as been lost a long, long time,' he said. 'Even I cannot tell ye how long, exactly. So! If ye wish fer guidance, ye must consult someone a deal older'n me.

'The difficulty wi' that, though, is as follows: the Ferryman is not the only one o' the old folk to fade. It's 'appened to many since the Times o' Trial, as they call them Kostigern days. An' even more so since the loss o' the Royal folk.' He said this with a kindly nod at Lihyaen, who frowned and disappeared into her tea.

'But!' said Balligumph, brightening. 'The Ferryman isn't the only one to return, neither. Folk 'ave been wakin' up. Some good folk, some less so, but folk, an' so yer options are not so very limited as all that.' He paused to think for a little while longer, tugging again at his tusk and humming something low and tuneless to himself. 'I 'ave just the person,' he pronounced at last. 'Old as the hills, so they say, though I dunnot think he is quite so old as all that. Some few o' yer centuries, at any rate, an' he'll maybe 'ave a fair guess to make as to where else ye should go.'

Balligumph clapped one great hand down upon his hat, settling it more firmly upon his head, and stood up from the table. 'No time like instantly, an' without delay!' he declared, and strode to the door. Isabel hastened to follow, Tafferty close upon her heels.

'Get yer pretty ponies,' Balligumph called, already striding away into the forest. 'Ye'll never keep up wi' me elsewise!' He proved his point as he spoke, for his long legs ate up the pathway; already he was disappearing into the trees. Fortunately, turning the mounts loose had not been a mistake. They were gathered in a little group not far from the house, grazing placidly upon the sumptuous grass.

Isabel hurried to mount her pretty mare, struggling a little with the arrangement of her long skirt in the process. Aubranael assisted her aboard with kind care and an encouraging smile, for both of which she was grateful. Princess Lihyaen was quicker to mount, by virtue of the simpler, shorter gown she wore; Isabel felt a moment's envy for the girl's freedom in the matter of dress. Not for an instant could she, Miss Ellerby, consider adopting a more practical and convenient mode of apparel! Much as she loved the light muslins, narrow, draping skirts and flimsy shoes of the current English fashions, they were remarkably inconvenient whenever one wished to perform any particularly active task.

She urged her mount forwards and fell in behind the Princess, Sophy and Aubranael trailing behind. The whole party set off back into the Outwoods at some speed, obliged to ride at a fast trot to keep pace with their troll guide. Isabel could not tell whether Mr. Balligumph's speed stemmed merely from enthusiasm, or from some sense of urgency, but he maintained his rapid pace for fully half an hour, without slowing for so much as an instant.

The vast trees of the Outwoods provided ample shade, but the air was hot and dense, and Isabel grew unpleasantly warm and uncomfortable. Clouds of midges haunted the glades beneath the leaves, many of which she was obliged to ride through, holding her breath to keep from inhaling any of the wretched insects. As pleasant as the scenery may be, therefore, she was glad to see Balligumph come to a halt ahead of them, and to rein in her mare accordingly.

The troll had stopped abruptly, and not as though they had arrived at their destination. He stood very still, staring up into the canopy. One fat finger stroked absently along the length of one tusk, a gesture Isabel was beginning to understand meant that he was deep in thought.

'I reckon it is!' boomed the troll at last, a broad grin wreathing his face. 'It's ye, up there! That one, there, wi' the trailin' bits an' the frilly leaves. Ye always were a one fer the fancy fashions, Gunty!'

Isabel stared. Balligumph was talking to empty air, as far as Isabel could tell, for nobody stood before him. More than that, she could have sworn that he was addressing a tree. He had stopped in the midst of a neat ring of particularly tall trees, their trunks at least five feet wide. They towered so far overhead, Isabel felt a little dizzied when she looked up into their branches. What intrigued her the most was their colouring: there were seven of them in total, and each was decked in leaves and frondy vines of rainbow colours. The nearest to her was predominantly red, with crimson foliage and scarlet vines; its next neighbour was orange, saffron and cinnamon; and so on around the circle. The arrangement was attractive to the eye, but strange indeed, and Isabel could not imagine that they had grown naturally in such a state.

Balligumph's words died away, leaving nothing but silence. 'Come on!' he bellowed into the air. 'I know ye're there! Nappin', I shouldn't wonder, but ye've done more'n enough o' that, Sir! Wake yerself an' meet some very good folk. They 'ave come a long way to meet ye.'

Nothing happened. Isabel's mount grew restive, perhaps resenting the warmth and weight of Tafferty curled up upon her neck. Isabel devoted a moment or two to soothing her with gentle pats and soft words, and in so doing, missed whatever it was that encouraged Balligumph to shout with rousing delight: 'Thas the way! Good! Tis a matter o' some importance, ye collect, or I would leave ye be. Not tha' ye deserve it, ye old dog! Come on, now. A bit more o' that, an' ye'll be fit fer company.'

Isabel looked up from her mount and stared into the colourful circle of trees. Where all seven had previously been eerily still, now one of them displayed some slight movement. The green-hued tree was decked in velvet moss and sprouting pale green flowers; long, twisting vines hung from its higher branches, each one fabulously striped in jade and sage. The vines were swaying gently, and — did her eyes deceive her? — the star-shaped flowers were opening and closing, as though stretching themselves after a long sleep. As she watched, a strong shudder descended from the tree's branches to its trunk, raining bits of moss and leaves down upon Balligumph's head.

'Hah!' he barked, shaking himself. 'A pretty trick, but mayhap I 'ave deserved it. Come on, now. We 'aven't got all day.' He turned and winked at Isabel. 'He can be a mite sluggish, Miss, but he'll wake. It's because o' the long slumber. Tricky habit to shake off, that one.'

Isabel nodded, trying to look as though she possessed some faint inkling as to what he referred. She did not. As far as she could tell, Balligumph was talking to a tree and receiving some manner of response. How did that make any sense?

But the tree was shrinking, its distant boughs growing gradually but undeniably closer to the ground. Its bark smoothed and softened, branches shrank and faded away, and its trunk narrowed. The transformation was rapid, once begun: Isabel saw a vast, green-decked tree, and then she saw a giant.

He was bigger than Balligumph. Isabel judged his height at perhaps ten feet, with girth to match. In fact, he was only a giant on the top half, a great, mighty-looking man-like creature wearing green velvet and a soft, baggy hat. From the waist down, he was still a tree, his trunk firmly rooted into the ground.

Those velvets were odd to Isabel's eye, though not wholly unfamiliar. She had seen garb like it in old portraits, and sometimes in books. He was wearing a doublet, well-fitted, with long sleeves and a point at the hem. Whether it was indeed made from velvet, or whether he had taken the mosses which adorned his trunk and fashioned them into the semblance of clothing, she could not tell. It was liberally strewn with the same star-shaped flowers that decked the base of his trunk, and more of them covered the brim of his hat. The effect was flamboyant and rich — an effect he furthered in the next moment by performing a grave and surprisingly graceful bow to the company.

'Thou hast the manners of a swine,' the giant informed Balligumph. 'Motley-minded and a miscreant, troll! A reeky, knotty-

pated malt-worm!' He glared down at the troll, who was laughing uproariously at this barrage of insults, and added, 'I was but two instants from forming the most perfect leaf I have sculpt'd in all the long ages of my life.'

Balligumph swept off his hat and bowed low to the giant. 'My apologies, then! I am sure ye will make more.'

The giant's glare vanished, and abruptly he grinned. His eyes were jewel-green and they began, now, to twinkle; his leathery face wrinkled further as he grinned. 'Miscreant!' he repeated. 'Thou art a plague upon giant-kind.'

Balligumph nodded agreement. 'That I am, an' an honour it is to be so.'

The giant's gaze moved past Balligumph, and settled upon the rest of his party. 'A merry band of travellers! Wherefore hast thou conveyed such colourful folk hither?'

'Tis yer help we're after,' Balligumph said. He motioned the riders forward, and gestured for them to dismount. Isabel found herself standing almost upon the protruding roots of the violet-decked tree, and carefully avoided them, for what if they were all giants?

'This is Sir Guntifer,' Balligumph said, beaming. 'One o' my oldest friends, when he is not slumberin' like an old lazybones.'

'I am an old lazybones,' interjected Sir Guntifer.

'Well, an' I was bein' charitable,' said Balligumph. 'But if ye prefer, I will tell the truth. A more frippery fellow ye scarce 'ave met in yer lives, an' lazy to boot. But he is loyal, an' clever, an' he knows more about anythin' ye can think up than anyone.' His grin widened. 'Even me.'

Isabel's brows rose as Balligumph spoke of his friendship with the giant, for the insults they had hurled at each other were fresh in her mind. There was no mistaking the gleam of affection in Sir Guntifer's eyes, though, as he looked at the troll; nor the true geniality of Balligumph's smile.

The tree-giant's form began subtly to alter once more, and soon he stood a giant entire, his trunk gone in favour of stout legs in tall boots up to the knee and laced britches the colour of oak-tree bark. He carried a weapon like a rapier at his side. He took off his hat, from the brim of which sprang a cluster of tumbling vines finer than any feather, and swept them another bow. This was still more fluid and flamboyant than the first, displaying the grace and manners of a courtier. Isabel stared, astonished, and only belatedly remembered to curtsey in response.

'Fine folk,' pronounced Sir Guntifer, restoring his hat to his head. 'I am Sir Guntifer Winlowe! Once I was guard to the Royal Family of Aylfenhame, in lost and thrice-mourned Mirramay. Now, I am as you see me: slumbersome and adrift.'

'An' a trifle melancholy,' said Balligumph, patting Sir Guntifer gently on the back. 'But 'tis just because ye 'ave been asleep too long. Ye'll rouse. An' I have a task to help ye along.' He grinned and, with a swift glance at Lihyaen, added, 'Nigh on a century, no? P'raps more? A fine, long rest.'

Lihyaen had become visibly more alert at this mention of the Royal Family, and no wonder, for the possibility that he might have known her parents immediately presented itself. Perhaps he even knew what had become of her father — or the person who had taken Lihyaen herself! But at Balligumph's shrewd words these hopes faded and she settled once more. One hundred years and more was far too long ago; when the king had vanished and the queen had died, Sir Guntifer must have been asleep.

'Very well,' rumbled Sir Guntifer. His voice was very deep and rough, like tumbling rocks. 'Pray you, then: tell me of this errand.'

Balligumph took off his hat and scratched at his head, frowning. 'Did ye ever have cause to make use o' the ferries-as-was?' he said.

Sir Guntifer shook his head. 'Nay, I had nought to do with the Ferry-folk.'

'But ye'll remember Kostigern, I'll wager.'

Sir Guntifer's face darkened. 'Aye. That I do.'

'In the wake o' that, every one o' the Ferries was disbanded — all save one, an' its Keeper was cursed t' toil upon it forever. Can ye recall word o' such?'

'The Last Keeper.' Sir Guntifer peered at Balligumph. 'What is the nature of thy business with such as he, old friend?'

'It don't sound as ye like the fellow overmuch,' Balligumph commented.

Sir Guntifer shrugged his wide shoulders, sending puffs of moss and dirt into the air. 'Ne'r have I met the Keeper, but tidings of him reached me in ages past.' He paused, frowning. ''Tis his merited punishment, some say, for his support of the one called Kostigern in the Times of Trial.'

Isabel opened her mouth to object, but caught herself in time. Support of Kostigern, the traitor? Remembering the Ferryman's congenial manner, his kindness, and above all his loneliness, her heart cried out at the allegation. But good sense intervened before she could make a fool of herself. What did she know of the Ferryman, in truth? Little indeed. A mere hour's conversation with a man she found pleasant could not render him incapable of wrong-doing. But the thought troubled her.

'Aye,' Balligumph was saying. 'I 'ave come across such tales me own self. I dunnot know if there's a scrap o' truth in 'em.' He glanced at Isabel as he spoke, and she was warmed to detect a note of concern in his eyes — warmed and embarrassed, for had her liking for the Ferryman been so obvious?

'Ye don't know, then, how the curse came t' be bestowed, or by who?' Balligumph continued.

Sir Guntifer shook his head. 'That is not known to me.'

'An' therefore, ye don't know who he was before he was the Ferryman.'

Sir Guntifer shook his head again. 'I would that it were not so, for I see I am of no help to thee.'

Balligumph sighed, his shoulders slumping. 'I 'ad hopes,' he admitted. ''Tis said tha' to lift the curse his name 'as to be found. I was hopin' ye might know, old as ye are.'

The giant stuck a vine into his mouth and chewed upon it. 'Mm,' he said.

''Tis a thorny problem.'

'Verily.' The giant thought some more. 'Wherefore dost thou wish the Ferryman's freedom?' he enquired. 'He may be a foe, but if he is not that, he is certainly no friend.'

'The young lady,' said Balligumph with a slight cough and a gesture towards Isabel, 'is possessed of a heart o' gold, an' she has made somethin' along the lines of an unwise promise to the lad.'

Sir Guntifer's gaze settled upon Isabel, and she found herself surveyed with discomfiting keenness. 'Has she,' he said.

Isabel looked at her feet, colouring. Never had she felt so foolish as she felt now, speared by that intense, ancient gaze. She felt that every part of her folly was displayed to his discerning eye, without hope of respite. 'I felt...' she began, but her words died away.

'Ye felt?' prompted Balligumph. 'Come now, lass. Ye're among friends. Ye must tell us everythin', the better we'll be able to help ye.'

Isabel lifted her chin. 'I felt sympathy for his plight,' she said. 'No one deserves such a fate, and I do not care what he has done.'

'Some people do,' muttered Aubranael, and Lihyaen nodded. If they were thinking of the one who had taken Lihyaen, then she could not disagree; but the possibility that the Ferryman was capable of such villainy seemed, to her, utterly impossible.

To her relief, Sir Guntifer smiled upon her, and even patted her upon the head — crushing her bonnet entirely, she feared. 'A sweet maid,' he said. 'I hope for thy sake, little one, that he is worthy of thy belief in him.'

'Me too,' growled Balligumph.

Sir Guntifer stretched mightily, and shook himself. 'If it were some two centuries ago at this moment,' he said, 'I would say that the Chronicler is the person who would know. But thou art late indeed.'

Balligumph's eyes brightened. 'The Chronicler! I heard word o' him, once upon a time. Royal record-keeper, or some such, back in the golden days o' the Royals?'

'Aye,' said the giant. 'Every event of note went into his books, and he knew all. But he is gone. Gone since Kostigern.'

'Gone?' said Balligumph. 'Or destroyed?'

'That is not known.'

A wide smile split Balligumph's face. 'Ye were gone an awful long time,' he said to Sir Guntifer.

The giant raised a shaggy eyebrow.

'Come t' think of it, the Ferryman was also scarce fer the odd decade or two.'

'Aye,' said Sir Guntifer. 'Thou art thinking that, mayhap, the Chronicler has also returned.'

'There's a slim chance, do ye not think?'

'Slender indeed.'

'Thin an' feeble an' scarce worth the name o' hope, but a chance! Now, I'm thinkin'.' Balligumph tugged his hat from his head and began to turn it about in his hands, pulling at the brim and chewing upon his lips as he thought. 'Last seen in Mirramay, most like?' he said at last, looking at Sir Guntifer.

'Aye.'

'Then to Mirramay ye must go!' Balligumph stuck his hat back onto his head and tapped upon it with a pleased smile. 'Lots goin' on in me noggin,' he announced. 'The Missie, now. She's 'ere fer witch-trainin', ain't that the truth? Well, so. Send 'er to Mirramay wi' the right sort o' companions an' she'll get all the trainin' she'll need — an' a mite of perspective, like. Maybe she'll find the Chronicler there an' maybe she won't, but a great deal may happen on such a journey. A very great deal.'

Balligumph concluded this speech with a wise nod and a beaming smile at Isabel, who involuntarily stepped back a pace. 'Mirramay!' she said. 'Gracious me, I really... that is, I have not the smallest notion where that may be. Or what manner of place it is.'

'Not a worry!' said Balligumph promptly. 'Ye will have a guide. It is the largest an' finest city in all of Aylfenhame, an' the site o' the Royal Court.' His smile faded into a scowl, and he shrugged. 'Or it was. 'Tis all broken down, now, in the absence o' the Royal family.'

Isabel glanced uncertainly around at her companions, seeking signs of enthusiasm for this plan. They looked as blank as she, though Lihyaen wore an expression of intent interest. 'Is it very far away?' Isabel asked.

'Oh, a deal o' distance,' said Balligumph with unimpaired cheer.

'Then surely I cannot. I am here without my Mama's knowledge, and before long I must return to England.' She blushed with shame at owning such a piece of misconduct and deceit, though it had been embarked upon at her aunt's urging — and more than urging. But nobody looked shocked at such an admission. If anything, the sparkle in Sophy's eyes denoted approval.

'Yer Ma will manage without ye fer a week or two,' said Balligumph. 'An' ye may trust yer aunt to take care o' such matters as that.'

'She cannot conceal my absence forever!' Isabel protested. 'Nor explain it, once it is discovered! I must not place her in such a difficult position.'

Balligumph grinned. 'Seems to me yer aunt 'as more put ye in a difficult position, an' fer good reason. Don't ye worry yer 'ead about Eliza Grey. She is more than equal to the challenges, an' it was 'er own doin' at that.'

Isabel's mouth opened, but no further objections spilled forth. Not because she was disinclined to make any, but because she could think of no further reasons to refuse, besides her own deep reluctance to undertake any such journey. She ought to be paying morning calls with her aunt and attending York assemblies, not gadding about in Aylfenhame! Besides, how was she to manage such a journey? She was not so physically robust as Sophy, and it would surely be arduous.

'I will go with you,' Sophy said, her voice pitched low. It was typically considerate of her. Not for the world would she loudly push Isabel into any scheme she disliked, but she would always support her if her help was required. Isabel smiled gratefully at her.

'I thank you,' she said softly. 'But I… cannot.'

'You are afraid, I think?' said Sophy.

Isabel bit her lip, and nodded. 'I do not know how I am to manage,' she confessed. 'And it does not seem that we are likely to find this Chronicler in Mirramay.'

Sophy tucked her arm through Isabel's. 'It is remarkable what we can manage, when we are compelled to make the attempt,' she said. 'Or when we compel ourselves.'

Remembering Sophy's accounts of her own adventures in Aylfenhame, Isabel blushed. Sophy had been beset by trials of one sort or another, but she had weathered them all, and done so with cheerful good-humour. For Isabel herself to object to a mere bit of travelling seemed hopelessly feeble.

'Perhaps you will wish to take Lihyaen?' Isabel suggested, mindful of the princess's obvious interest in the plan.

Sophy shook her head. 'In time, but not now. She is… that is, we are still keeping her close. It is by no means certain that she could return to the Court without endangering herself.'

'Then may you safely leave her?' Isabel said — aware as she spoke that she was reaching for excuses, but unable to help herself.

'Yes,' said Sophy firmly. 'She will have Aubranael, and Mary, and Thundigle to keep her safe, and there are others set to watch over her. Balli makes sure of that.'

Isabel fell silent, her thoughts turned inwards. If she accepted her friends' rationale, was there any true reason why she could not go? She was easily tired, it was true, and the journey would be demanding; but tiredness could not harm her. The errand might prove futile, but nothing could be gained if she did not go at all.

Her mother would be disappointed in her. Her father… angry. These considerations weighed rather more with Isabel than any other, and she hesitated.

'Bah!' said Tafferty in disgust. Isabel looked down, startled, to find the catterdandy sitting close by her feet. Her companion butted her head against Isabel's legs, not ungently, and rubbed her thick-furred body against her gown. 'A lily-liver, an' a sorry one! Sit in thy fancy-fine chair all the days o' thy life, wilt thou, an' let thy Older Ones do all thy thinkin' for thee! Whose life is it, I ask thee?'

My father's, Isabel wanted to reply, for it often seemed as though his decisions ruled not only her own life but her mother's as well. But she did not, for Tafferty was right. She saw at last why her aunt had been so eager to convey her into Aylfenhame: it represented a chance for her to change the course of her life, and make choices of her own.

The prospect terrified her, for she had rarely in her life been permitted to make the smallest decision for herself — not even as to the colour of her gowns. But a glance at Sophy's serene, cheerful face calmed her nerves. Sophy had strayed far from the path of convention, and thrived upon it. Perhaps she would thrive, too.

'I will go,' she said, and managed to speak without a tell-tale tremor in her voice. 'Who will go with me?'

'I will!' said Lihyaen at once.

Sophy exchanged a look with Aubranael, but before either of them could speak, Balligumph drew the princess aside and began to speak in a voice pitched so low that Isabel could hear nothing of his speech.

Aubranael approached Isabel and Sophy. 'I will take care of her,' he said to Sophy, who nodded. Isabel marvelled at the degree of openness and understanding between the two: they had not needed to discuss what they would do or how it would be managed, each seeming to know the other's intentions and thoughts without asking. It was vastly different from the relationship between her mother and her father.

Sophy smiled and clasped her husband's hand in thanks. 'I think we will take Pinket,' she mused. 'And Pinch.'

'Pinch!' repeated Aubranael. 'Anyone but! You will have not an instant's peace.'

Sophy laughed. 'True, but I want Pinket with us very much, and you cannot believe that Pinch would consent to remain behind alone.'

Aubranael rolled his eyes and sighed. 'Take something soft with which to stuff up your ears,' he recommended.

Isabel smiled. She was not very much acquainted with Pinket and Pinch, but she knew them a little. Pinket was a will-o-the-wyke, a wisp of fae-light with more of a mind and personality than she would ever have thought possible. Pinch was a particularly diminutive pixie fae who sometimes took the form of a wisp — usually when he wanted to perform some manner of mischief. The two were staunch friends, and inseparable.

Balligumph's voice, raised above a murmur, reached Isabel's ears. 'Ye are a good lass,' he said in a kindly tone to Lihyaen. 'Yer time will come, mark my words, but ye've a deal o' growin' to be done yet. Aylfenhame cannot bear to lose ye a second time.'

Lihyaen sighed and drifted forlornly towards Sophy and Aubranael. 'I wish I could go with you,' she said to Isabel, with a hint of bitterness. 'This waiting is intolerable.'

Isabel sympathised. It was hard on the girl, but she saw the sense of Balligumph's words. Lihyaen was not yet ready to take the throne, and until she was, her survival and her location must remain a secret — for her own safety.

'I have a request,' said Lihyaen to Isabel. She hesitated, frowning. 'It is Hidenory,' she continued in a rush. 'My old nurse. The witch? You remember her?'

Isabel nodded.

'Mr. Balligumph says that she is gone from the tea-table,' said Lihyaen. 'But I can scarcely believe it to be true! I would like dearly to know, but I cannot bear to go near to the place…'

'We will look,' Isabel promised.

Lihyaen smiled with relief. 'Will you indeed? It is so kind of you! I know you will not be able to approach very nearly, but you may perhaps be able to tell whether she is still… there.' The last word was spoken doubtfully, and accompanied by a fierce frown. Hidenory had volunteered herself in Lihyaen's place, and had duly taken over as the hostess of the strange Teapot Society party. And there she must stay until someone else took her place — or until the enchantment was broken by some other means. If Hidenory was free, then someone else must be occupying the host's seat. Isabel did not welcome such a thought. If they arrived at the tea-table to find someone else doomed to such a fate, Isabel did not think she could again walk away and leave them there.

She could not but promise, and the promise was duly made.

'But who shall be yer guide?' said Balligumph with a twinkle. 'Let me think, now. Who could possibly know enough about the wilds, an' the Outwoods, an' Mirramay itself, to take ye safely there an' back?' His eyes strayed towards Sir Guntifer as he spoke, who reacted by drawing himself up to his full height and staring down upon the troll with strong disapproval.

'Methinks thou art insinuating something,' he said.

Balligumph beamed at him. 'Will ye, old friend? There's none better'n ye.'

Sir Guntifer shook himself mightily, sending a cloud of leaves flying into the air from — apparently — nowhere. 'Thou art a miscreant,' he informed Balligumph. 'There is naught of rest or slumber to be had with such friends as thee.'

'Aye,' agreed Balligumph. 'That's the idea.'

Sir Guntifer grumbled something inaudible. 'Very well. I will guide the maid and her band of friends.' He glared at Balligumph. 'But I shall do it because she is a fair maid, and kindly! Not because of thy meddling.'

'I don't care why ye do it, so long as ye do,' Balligumph said with a chuckle. 'Aye, very good! A fine day's work. Off wi' ye, then. The sooner ye get goin', the sooner ye may return.'

An' so it was tha' two fine English ladies set off to journey from Grenlowe to the city o' Mirramay, across many leagues o' the wilds of Aylfenhame, an' attended only by a wisp, a pixie an' a tree-giant. Mighty gumptious o' them, was it not, now? An' a merry adventure! I am proud to know the pair o' them. An' they managed very well wi' the demands o' the journey, ye'll no be surprised to hear. But it weren't entirely a smooth-like journey. Such a party as that cannot fail of attractin' a mite o' notice…

CHAPTER NINE

'The trick to it,' said Pinch, removing his pipe from his mouth, 'is to be a natural genius, like me. Then you will find everything easy.' He stuck the pipe back into his mouth, took a long drag upon it, and grinned.

Isabel eyed the little wretch, and wondered in the privacy of her own mind whether it would be acceptable for her to smack him. He sorely deserved it, and she felt tolerably certain that Sophy would agree. They had been two days upon the road, and Pinch had scarcely stopped talking — which would not be so very bad, had he been more amusing a companion. As it was, such self-aggrandising witticisms as he had just shared were all that could be expected from him.

'Pinch,' said Sophy gravely. 'If you cannot mind your tongue, there will be consequences.'

Pinch's grin merely grew wider. He was sitting on Sir Guntifer's shoulder, facing backwards so that he could see Sophy and Isabel riding behind. He looked the picture of comfort and contentment from this vantage point, and since his steed had long ago adopted the policy of ignoring everything that was going on behind him, he suffered no consequences for the crime of filling the tree-giant's ears with his nonsense. Isabel wondered whether Sir Guntifer had somehow arrived at a state where he genuinely did not hear the wretched little pixie, and envied him.

'Consequences!' carolled Pinch. 'The lady is severe! Pray, what could you find to do to me?'

'I will take your pipe.' Sophy's voice was deceptively serene. 'And then, Pinch, I will probably drop it. I will not be able to help myself. I am very clumsy, you know.'

Pinch's smile faded and his eyes grew wide. 'Aye, yes! Clumsiest wench I ever saw! That's a threat.' He sucked furiously upon the pipe as though to reassure himself.

Isabel privately thought it would be a shame to smash such a thing. The pipe appeared to be made from glass, though in all likelihood it was wrought from some Aylfish thing of a different character. It was a delicate object, too big for the pixie who carried it, and intriguingly coiled. A constant stream of smoke curled lazily through the long, twisting tube, and by some magic it ever changed its hue. As Isabel watched, somewhat mesmerised — a pursuit she had been engaging in a great deal in the past days — the smoke drifted from a sea-blue colour into a delicate violet.

'It is no empty threat, Mr. Pinch!' said Sophy. 'I am a danger to all delicately-made things, and I will not hesitate to exercise my talents upon your treasure!'

To Isabel's surprise, Pinch actually fell silent for a little while.

Tafferty shifted and turned about. She was enthroned once again on the neck of Isabel's mare, and had passed most of the journey so far in a sound sleep. Isabel envied that, too. But now the catterdandy woke and directed a considering look at Isabel.

'Happen it be time fer thy first lesson,' said Tafferty. Her voice was pitched so low, Isabel imagined no one heard it but herself. 'The pixie needs teachin', an' he is meant t' be teachin' thee. Happen thou must teach him a lesson first, an' then his mind will be brought t' a proper way o' thinkin'.'

Isabel nodded, for she was not at all averse to the notion of teaching the smug pixie a lesson. 'But what could I do? I do not share Sophy's talent for breaking things by chance, and I could not destroy such a pretty pipe deliberately.'

Tafferty's tail twitched. 'Thou takest a distressin' delight in bein' obtuse,' she said with deep dissatisfaction.

Isabel coloured. 'What, then, do you wish me to do?'

'Thou hast shown an extraordinary lack of interest in yer witchin' powers, up till now,' said Tafferty with a growl. 'A more lack-a-dais-i-cal apprentice I could scarce have asked fer.' She drew the word "lackadaisical" out long and thin, with great relish, and Isabel felt a twinge of guilt.

'I am sorry,' she said; aware, as she spoke, that those three words had passed her lips a great many times in the past few days of her life. 'So much has happened! I can scarce keep up. And besides that, I…' she fell silent as a wave of shame engulfed her.

'What?' Tafferty prompted.

'I am unsure if I… wish to be a witch at all,' said Isabel in a miserable half-whisper. 'It is very inconvenient. I do not at all think I will be able to be a witch in York, when I am married to Mr. Thompson — or someone else like him. It will not be thought respectable. And so I will have to hide it, as does my aunt Grey, and if that is all I am destined to do, there is little purpose in learning. Is there not?'

Tafferty's growl deepened. 'I will set tha' piece o' fatuosity firmly t' one side. What dost thou think thy aunt had in mind in sendin' thee here if not t' learn thee somethin' o' use? If thou wert a wittier bean o' humanity thou wouldst consider that thy aunt Grey maybe bears a regret or two in 'er mind.'

Isabel frowned, for that thought had not occurred to her. Mrs. Grey had existed in Isabel's life as a model of respectability and contentment. As such it had been a particular shock to her to discover her aunt's secret nature, and the little green companion of whom Isabel had never previously seen so much as a hair. She could not doubt that it had been a source of considerable strain to her aunt to conceal these things from York society; nor did she doubt the necessity. Household brownies may be common enough in some parts of England, and the people were by no means unfamiliar with the fae of Aylfenhame; but for a lady of quality to openly practice witchery, and keep with her such a peculiar animal as her aunt's Vershibat, could not be considered respectable. As tolerant as most folk were of the fae, there remained strict notions in most minds: the fae were other. It would not do for one of their own to become too deeply entangled with them.

If her aunt had discovered the peculiarities of her heritage at Isabel's own age, well, she had made the only choice Isabel would have expected her to consider: she had stayed in England, married suitably, and concealed her witchery. Isabel herself had consented — barely — to visiting Aylfenhame, but she had no expectation but that her visit would soon come to an end, home she would go, and proceed to follow much the same path in life as her aunt. What else could possibly make any sense?

But Tafferty spoke truly. Isabel remembered a passing comment of her aunt's, which had faded from her mind in the confusion that had followed: I have had my fill of duty.

Perhaps she did regret some part of her decision. But what did that mean for Isabel?

'What did you wish to teach me?' Isabel said at last.

Tafferty's growling stopped, and her tail flicked once — a gesture Isabel was learning to interpret as one of approval. 'Good. Thy aunt said thou would'st make a suitable choice, but I was beginnin' t' doubt.'

Isabel was momentarily tempted to protest that she had but asked a question, and had not intended to grant permission. But she held her peace. It could do her no harm to learn a little.

'Now then,' said Tafferty, settling herself comfortably before Isabel. 'A witch has a number o' Powers t' choose from. There's Glamour, the art o' Seemin', which we have talked of before. Thou mayst make any one thing seem like another — or hide it away entire. Watch.' Tafferty slowly disappeared from sight, bit by bit, until only her tail remained. Then she faded back into view — and changed, abruptly, into the semblance of an ordinary house cat, a fat creature with black fur and white patches.

'All manner o' fine uses fer that, but not what we need now,' she decided, changing back into herself.

Isabel thought, with an inward sigh, of her only previous lesson in witchery, and her utter failure to entice one fruit to resemble another. 'I have seen something of Glamour before,' Isabel offered. 'When I first met Aubranael, it was in England, and he was wearing the semblance of a human man. But it was not of his making.'

Tafferty licked her lips. 'Aye. Thou mayst impose a Glamour upon another, but I advise thee to do that only wi' their permission.'

Isabel flushed at the very idea of changing someone's appearance without their consent! 'Of course, I could not think of anything else.'

'The time may come,' said Tafferty cryptically. 'Anyroad, the second Power, which has no right-an'-proper name, may be called Craftin' fer our purposes. Wi' that, thou mayst concoct all manner o' useful odds an' ends. The most difficult an' rare o' these would be what thy folk call fairy ointment. Wi' such a magic in thy hands, thou mayst see through any form o' Glamour, on thy own self or others. But that… eh. Thou mayst live thy whole life through without discoverin' the secret o' that. Tis a rarity indeed.'

Isabel nodded, intrigued. Fairy ointment! She had heard of such a thing in stories, but had not previously imagined that it might exist in truth — nor that she might, someday, possess the power to make it.

'An' the third Power,' Tafferty continued, 'is what I will today call… Cursin'. Rightly Enchantin'. Bestowin' somethin' good or somethin' bad upon a person as 'as pleased or vexed thee, as thou wishest. Since today we are dealin' wi' a tiny bein' as 'as vexed us both, we are goin' t' start wi' a Curse.'

Isabel glanced at Pinch, troubled. Irritating he may be, but a Curse? She had experience of Curses. Lihyaen had been afflicted with a terrible one, and so was the Ferryman. Could she be responsible for laying such an appalling punishment upon Pinch — or any living thing? She opened her mouth to say some of this, but Tafferty forestalled her.

'I know what's goin' through thy mind,' she said with a touch of asperity. 'The Curses thou art thinkin' of are somethin' far out o' the ordinary way. Strong magics indeed, an' Evil. I very much doubt it is within thy power t' lay such a Curse, nor will it ever be — even if thou hadst the desire t' do so, which of course thou dost not. All we are thinkin' of today is a whisper of a Curse, easily laid and easily dispelled.'

Isabel nodded doubtfully. 'Very well. What must I do?'

'Fix thy attention upon yonder green-clad pigeon-egg an' think of somethin' bad thou would'st like t' see happen t' him.'

Isabel looked up at Pinch. He was still ensconced upon Sir Guntifer's shoulder, riding up there like a little king, and flatly ignoring the beauty of the tall trees on either side. His arms were crossed, his face set in a scowl, and his pipe stuck firmly in his mouth as he puffed madly upon it. The odd, spicy scent of the smoke drifted down to tease Isabel's nose.

'I cannot,' she said. 'Foolish he may be, and disruptive, but I could not wish ill upon him.'

Tafferty's tail lashed. 'Thou art thinkin' too big,' she said. 'Just a wee, tiny calamity will do.'

Isabel set her lips and shook her head. 'I wish calamities upon no one,' she said, mildly but firmly. 'No matter how minor it may be, nor how foolish the target.'

Tafferty growled. 'All right, I will do it.'

Isabel reached out to stop her, but Tafferty was too quick. As Isabel watched, the pipe flew out of Pinch's grip as though propelled by some unseen force, and — to her horror — something began sewing shut his mouth. Silken stitches blossomed rapidly around his lips, until his mouth was firmly closed and he could not possibly utter another word. Pinket, hovering near to Sir Guntifer's left ear, awoke and began weaving about in the air in a silent display of alarm.

'Now then,' Tafferty said in a placid tone, wholly unaffected by the desperate antics of the horrified pixie and wisp. 'A Curse must come wi' an out, see? As must an Enchantment — the positive kind. Thou canst not expect the target o' thy wishes or curses t' suffer under 'em forever, especially when they's the harmful sort o' kind. Hence the Ferryman: His freedom is won if the condition is met, that o' findin' his name. In this case, I 'ave imposed a simple condition fer a simple offence: Pinch must be sorry fer his irritatin' behaviour, an' then he may have his mouth back.'

'But,' Isabel cried in horror, 'how is he to express his contrition if he cannot speak?'

There was silence for a moment, then Tafferty said, 'Ah. Yes, I 'ave contrived this on purpose-like, so thou mayst see the importance o' thinkin' carefully through thy wishes an' curses.'

Isabel was by no means convinced it had been deliberate, and her heart ached for Pinch. The pixie was by turns furious and terrified, and his writhings and stampings finally attracted Sir Guntifer's attention. The tree-giant stopped, and stared with amazement at the gyrations of the previously placid pixie. 'What manner of trickery is this?' he said in his booming voice.

'Naught for thee t' worry thyself over, Gunty,' Tafferty said. 'Thy passenger is receivin' a lesson in courtesy, that is all.'

Sir Guntifer eyed Pinch and then Tafferty in turn, his mouth set in a grim line. 'I cannot blame thee, but I would beg thee to draw thy teaching to a close,' he said. 'Methinks he is moments from tumbling to the ground, and doing himself great harm.'

Tafferty grumbled to herself, then raised her voice to shout over the inarticulate noises Pinch was making in his distress. 'Pinch, thou reeky mammet! Stop thy yowlin' an' listen!'

Pinch subsided, staring at Tafferty with wide eyes.

'Art thou sorry fer thine infernal noise?'

Pinch nodded frantically.

'Truly? Thou must mean it.'

Pinch nodded so hard that his head flopped about on his neck, and he shook himself violently. As he did so, the stitches began to unwind themselves, and half a minute later they were gone. Pinch gulped in several huge breaths of air, staring at Tafferty in abject horror.

'That was the worst thing that's ever happened to me,' he said at last.

Tafferty curled up upon the mare's neck once more, tucking her tail around herself with an air of satisfaction. 'Very good,' she said, and closed her eyes.

Pinch exchanged a wide-eyed look with Isabel, before turning his back upon the company and facing forwards into the trees. His manner was unmistakeable: he would think twice before getting on Tafferty's bad side again.

So would Isabel. She swallowed, trying to calm the unsettled fluttering of her heart. Were these the powers she had gained? If so, she certainly did not want them!

The site of the Teapot Society proved to be less than a day's travel from Grenlowe, albeit only slightly less. Isabel was not used to riding for such long hours together, and by the time late afternoon drew in, she was feeling sore and deeply uncomfortable. Further, the beauty of the Outwoods delighted her only for a time; as the day wore on, the tall trees with the broad trunks, hanging vines and multi-coloured leaves began to be familiar, and as such lost her attention. A combination of discomfort and boredom led her to feel a sensation of relief when Sir Guntifer came to a halt at the head of their party, and held up a hand.

'Mark ye that clearing ahead?' he said. 'Methinks that is the Society.'

Sophy spurred her mount forward at once, though at a cautious pace. Isabel followed, feeling less confident than Sophy appeared to be. She had been caught in the Society's enchantment herself, for a short time, and she had not forgotten the experience: the burning and irresistible compulsion to consume as much as she could from the contents of the teapots set before her, and their accompanying delicacies. She well remembered how delicious they had been, and how very much she had enjoyed herself; so much so that she had not felt the smallest desire ever to leave. If it had not been for the presence of mind of Sophy and her friends, Isabel might still be there.

But she felt nothing but doubt upon drawing closer to the glade amidst the trees. There was the table, as she remembered. One end was visible, but the table was so long that its other end was lost somewhere amongst the trees. Tall-backed chairs were lined up along either side of it, and a particularly large, ornate chair stood at the head.

And that was all. The pristine white cloth that covered the table was bare; not a single teapot sat upon its surface. The chairs were all empty — even the one at the head of the table, the seat of the host or hostess. The glade should have been filled with the sounds of consumption and merriment; instead, it was silent.

Isabel exchanged an uncertain look with Sophy. 'Can this be the right place?' Isabel asked.

'I believe it must be,' Sophy said, albeit in a doubtful tone. 'I cannot imagine two such tables should happen to be arranged in just this fashion, and in the midst of the Outwoods. Besides, my own recollections suggest that we have been travelling in exactly the right direction to encounter it just here.'

Both ladies dismounted, and cautiously stepped closer. Not only was the table unoccupied, but it felt different to Isabel. Previously, the clearing had been so heavy with magic she had felt it as a prickling upon her skin. Now, there was nothing. It was only a table.

'Where, then, is Hidenory?' said Sophy at last. 'How can she have accomplished this?'

'I wonder if she knew, when she volunteered herself?' said Isabel. 'That she would be able to break the enchantment.'

'That is possible,' agreed Sophy.

Tafferty stretched and jumped down from the mare's back. 'Rightly she oughtn't t' have any such power,' she commented. 'Though the prodigious power o' Hidenory th' Witch is well-enough known in these parts. But this is an Everlasting Enchantment. There be ways t' free people from it, but not t' dissolve it altogether.' The catterdandy stalked closer to the table and sniffed at it, her tail twitching. 'An' it be dead as a proverbial.' Tafferty demonstrated this point by jumping onto one of the chairs and then onto the table. Isabel tensed, waiting for the table to suddenly set itself for tea, but nothing happened.

'Two ways t' manage it,' Tafferty announced. 'Either she 'as tricked it, or she 'as dissolved it 'erself because she were the one who 'ad set it in th' first place.'

Isabel glanced at Sophy. Her friend was clearly troubled by this latter notion; her usually sunny smile was absent, replaced by a deep frown. 'That would break Lihyaen's heart,' Sophy said softly. 'I cannot believe that Hidenory could have done such a thing.'

'I said she were the one who 'ad set up the table,' Tafferty said. 'Not that she also put thy girl here. The two may o' been different peoples altogether.'

Sophy looked a little relieved at this reflection. 'But surely, if somebody else had used her enchantment to entrap Lihyaen, she must have known of it? And she left the girl here for years.'

'She may not 'ave known,' Tafferty said. 'Then again, she may.'

The whole realm had believed the princess to have died, Isabel knew. When the princess had been taken, a stock had been left in her place — a kind of enchanted doll, which seemed to live for a little while, and then apparently died. The princess had been buried, and no one had known that she had instead been taken away and trapped within the Teapot Society. No one save for her abductor, of course.

If Hidenory had not been her abductor, perhaps she, too, had believed Lihyaen to have died. Supposing that she paid any attention to her creation at all, could she have realised that the girl at the head of the table was Lihyaen?

But perhaps she had not created the Teapot Society at all. Isabel knew little of Hidenory, but by Sophy's accounts she was fully wily enough to trick her way out of it.

'I wonder where she is,' Sophy said again, with a sigh. 'I should dearly like to ask her a question or two.'

Isabel agreed to it. 'I think it altogether unlikely that she had any hand in this,' she said to Sophy, hoping to soothe away the shadow of concern in her friend's eyes. 'Perhaps she was helped to escape.'

Sophy nodded. 'I wish she had informed Lihyaen of her escape, either way. The poor girl has been suffering a great deal over Hidenory's fate.'

'Perhaps she could not,' Isabel said reasonably.

Sophy smiled ruefully. 'It is impossible for us to know, and so it is useless to speculate. Let us go on.'

Sir Guntifer gallantly assisted the ladies to mount once more, and the party resumed its progress through the Outwoods.

Isabel had expected to encounter the discomfort of sleeping out-of-doors on her journey to Mirramay, but to her relief, she was obliged to endure no such ordeal. The Outwoods was a vast forest covering more space than she could easily imagine; they had travelled within it for two days without once stepping out from beneath the canopy of its over-arching trees, and they had but once passed anything which could be called a settlement. In spite of this, Isabel found that the way was clearly marked. Wide, well-tended roads wound through the trees, some of them paved with honey-coloured stone, and the way was sign-posted. Even better, the larger roads featured wayside inns at intervals, perfectly spaced to allow for one full day's travel in between. Thus, her adventure was of precisely the refined sort to appeal to her, for she slept in a proper bed each night, in a room of her own which bore, together with its other comforts, a lockable door. She dined very well upon the best of Aylfenhame's produce, and suffered no other trials save for a lamentable degree of saddle-soreness after so many hours of riding. Sir Guntifer stood guard outside her window and Sophy's, slumbering peacefully in his tree form, and Isabel knew few worries.

On the third day, the atmosphere began to change. Hitherto, the Outwoods had been airy, spacious and well-lit, in spite of the thick canopy. The leaves were vibrantly coloured, the floor carpeted in bright green, fragrant moss, and there were berries aplenty growing in bushes by every roadside.

As the morning wore on upon the third day, the light began, gradually but noticeably, to dim. The trees grew closer together, and the vegetation thicker. Pinket, who had adopted the role of scout for the party and sailed dreamily someway ahead, began to slow, and reduced the distance between itself and Sir Guntifer. It looked, to Isabel's mildly concerned eye, as though the wisp was uncomfortable and preferred to remain closer to the giant.

She could not blame Pinket, if so, for she began to feel less at ease herself. The road was growing narrower, and the trees crowded in ever closer on either side. The wind turned cool, and a chilling breeze plucked at the gown and spencer she had chosen for warm weather. She shivered, and tried not to turn her eyes upon the thickening undergrowth that lined the road. Too many shadows lurked there, and she began to wonder what else might be lurking besides.

How foolish, she reprimanded herself. Just because it had grown darker did not mean that monsters hid between the trees! She was behaving with all the absurdity of a child of five!

But even as she formed the thought, Sir Guntifer slowed his pace and finally stopped, his great head swivelling upon his mighty neck as he searched among the trees.

'What is it, Sir Guntifer?' asked Sophy, reining in her mount alongside the giant.

'This is not as it was,' he said tersely. 'I do not know what has chanced to happen here while I slumbered, but—' He broke off, holding up one large hand. 'Hark,' he said softly.

Isabel listened. At first she heard nothing at all, but after a few moments some faint sounds reached her ears. It was a kind of horn, she realised, and no pleasant sound either, though it seemed intended as a kind of music. The flaring notes were not without melody, though they were harsh sounds, and she resisted a temptation to cover her ears.

She could not tell where the music was coming from. She could swear that it was but a single instrument being played, but the notes seemed to emanate from everywhere around them all at once. The effect was disturbing, and Isabel shivered.

Sophy drew her pony up alongside and grasped the bridle of Isabel's pony, directing a smile at her friend which was perhaps intended to be reassuring. Isabel found the whole of her behaviour to be more alarming than comforting, and shivered harder.

'Do not be alarmed!' said Sophy. 'Something strange is afoot, but it will soon be sorted out. Sir Guntifer will know what is to be done, and you may perhaps see Pinch come into his own.'

Isabel nodded nervously. In spite of her discomfort, Sophy's words soothed her a little. Sophy had spent a year living in Aylfenhame, in addition to her prior adventures, and she must know of what she spoke.

'Pixie,' said Sir Guntifer, shrugging the huge shoulder upon which Pinch still reclined. 'Wisp. Methinks we have need of ye.'

Pinch sighed and clambered down to the ground, muttering

darkly. Isabel caught the word 'trow' in the midst of his grumblings, though it made little sense to her.

'What is a trow?' she whispered to Sophy.

'Darkling things,' said Sophy in response. 'They will try to cause mischief, but Pinch is a match for them. Pinket, too. Watch!'

Isabel watched. Pinch marched off into the trees, bristling with indignation. A stream of cinnamon-coloured smoke billowed out behind him, in the midst of which floated Pinket. The pair halted a few feet off the road, and Pinch adopted an uncompromising stance with his legs apart and hands upon his hips. Pinket hovered a few feet above his head and swelled in size, until the tiny bubble of light became as a small sun; so bright that Isabel was obliged to look away from him.

Dark figures approached through the trees, some of them as small as Pinch, others rather larger. At first they appeared as mere shadows, but as they grew closer Isabel discerned spindly frames with gnarled limbs and overlarge hands, feet and ears. They wore ragged clothing, shoes with pointed toes and black caps upon their heads, from underneath which their wispy hair protruded. They were odd creatures, gangly and ungainly, though not ugly; only the expressions of their faces deserved that term. They glared at the travellers with chilling malevolence, and more than one bore weapons: long, jagged knives and stout sticks. Isabel saw no piper among them, but nonetheless the music continued, growing in eeriness and volume as time passed.

'Ho!' shouted Pinch as the nearest came within earshot. 'Trow party, is it? We decline your kind invitation! Be off.'

These words had no effect upon the trows, but Pinch did not appear to be concerned. He made some kind of signal to Pinket, and then abruptly vanished. In his place hovered a second wisp, which grew in size and brilliance until two miniature suns hung there. Isabel blinked, sun-spots dancing before her eyes. She lost track of what happened next, so blinded was she by the dancing and weaving of the two wisps as they darted among the trows. She could not understand what they were doing, but its effects were clear. The trows halted, some of their truculence fading into confusion. Some few of them began to retreat, step by step, into the trees.

Then the wisps vanished. Pinch reappeared in his pixie form, his green jacket somewhat askew. In his hands he held a little golden pipe, which he began to play at a dizzying speed, the notes rippling over the glade like tumbling water.

To Isabel's surprise, he was not alone. Pinket had also disappeared. Where he had previously floated there now stood a second pixie, slightly shorter than Pinch, and dressed in a red jacket and trousers. This pixie — Pinket? — held a tiny fiddle, and this he began to play with a speed to match the pipe. The melody clashed horribly with that of the trows' horn, and Isabel winced and clapped her hands over her ears. This did little to exclude the sounds, and she gritted her teeth, waiting in intolerable discomfort as the fae's strange musical battle proceeded.

It did not seem to her at all likely that Pinch and Pinket could win, for they were sorely outnumbered. But that they were gaining ground against the trows soon became obvious, for the dark figures began to retreat further. At length, the horn faltered and fell silent, and the trows broke and fled.

Pinch and Pinket maintained their exhaustingly lively music for some minutes longer, and finally ceased only when every last hint of the trows' presence had faded. Even the light had returned to the forest, to some degree, though it remained shadowed, and darker than it had been before.

The pixies shook themselves mightily, and then packed away their instruments. They directed matching grins back at Isabel and Sophy, though Pinch's bore more of mischief; Pinket appeared simply pleased with himself. Then Pinket resumed his wisp shape, while Pinch swaggered over to Sir Guntifer and held up his arms to be lifted. 'Gunty!' he bellowed. 'I am tired!'

'Did you know he could do that?' Isabel asked of Sophy.

Sophy shook her head. 'Pinket! No, indeed. I thought he was a wisp only.'

Pinch cackled, restored now to his throne atop Sir Guntifer's shoulder. 'What's the use of secrets if you tell them to everyone?'

'A reasonable point, Pinch,' said Sophy drily.

'Are they brothers?' said Isabel, aghast. The two pixies had looked very much alike — too much so, for her comfort.

'A horrifying thought, is it not?' Sophy agreed. 'As if Pinch were not enough by himself!'

'Ungrateful!' said Pinch in a mournful voice. 'When we have but just saved both your skins from the most menacing band of trows I have seen in many a year! Tsk! But it is always that way with the ladies of England. You do them all kinds of favours and they only screech at you.'

'When I first met you,' Sophy said, 'the favour you were doing me was to lead me off an incline.'

'An incline of two feet!' Pinch protested. 'I would have been much surprised if you had done more than turn your ankle, and if you had suffered so much as that I should say it was due to your own clumsiness.'

'I hope your brother is more congenial than you are!' Sophy retorted.

Pinket answered this by shining a little brighter for an instant or two, which struck Isabel as rather like a smile — if wisps could be said to smile.

'A pitiful band of trows!' interjected Sir Guntifer. 'Insolent noise-makers only! Thou art a plague, pixie. Thou and thy brother hath dispatched the miscreants, indeed, and with skill. But do not imagine that I would have allowed any harm to come to the ladies of our party if ye had not! Ye will find that my protection is no small thing.'

Pinch rolled his eyes and collapsed backwards upon the giant's shoulder with an exaggerated display of exhaustion. 'Lecture me later,' he said, 'for I am all to pieces with weariness. Heroism! It is so exhausting!' With that, he began to snore.

Isabel could not help smiling a little. Pinch's manner could irritate, but at times he could also be an amusing companion.

'We must take more care,' said Sir Guntifer, and the smile faded from Isabel's face. 'I had not expected to find such creatures so near to Mirramay, and methinks they will not be the only loathsome band lurking in these parts.'

'What are "trows", Sir Guntifer?' asked Isabel.

'They are part of the Goblin King's Court,' the giant replied. 'Darkling beasts, full of mischief and noise, but no true threat to such as our party. However, worse may follow.' He glanced around at the dark trees that crowded close to the road, his twisting brows drawn together. 'I mislike the looks of this.'

Isabel guided her mount a little closer to Sophy's, who responded with an encouraging smile. 'All will be well,' she said to Isabel. 'Sir Guntifer will permit no harm to come to us, I am sure. Rarely have I encountered so impressive a gentleman in Aylfenhame!'

Sir Guntifer heard this, and Isabel judged by the softening of his mighty frown that he was pleased. 'Onward with us,' he rumbled. 'Keep a wary eye upon the trees, gentle ladies.

Isabel did so, shaken more than she cared to admit by the trows' unfriendly intentions and the oddity of their darkling music. As they rode, she could not shake the sensation that something — or someone — watched them still, even when they had ridden far from the spot where the trows had appeared. She thrice considered imparting her concerns to Sir Guntifer, and seeking his opinion. But neither he, nor any of the rest of her party, appeared to share her unease, and at last she put her unsettled feelings down to the effects of lingering alarm, and said nothing.

CHAPTER TEN

They stayed the next night at another wayside inn like the rest, though even this bore a changed character. The innkeepers — a pixie and a hobgoblin — were plainly uneasy, and when questioned, spoke of a lessening of such travellers as they were used to entertaining so close to Mirramay, and an increase of the troublesome kind. They stared in awe at Isabel and Sophy, and tended to their needs with alacrity.

On the following morning, the whole party set out for Mirramay. The sky was overcast and dull, and the atmosphere heavy with relentless heat. The conditions did nothing to raise Isabel's spirits, which were rather oppressed. She was feeling far out of her depth; not merely because of the strangeness of her surroundings, nor the unpromising character of the fae they were now encountering in this part of the Outwoods. She was also suffering grave doubts as to her part in this curious adventure. Tafferty's display of some of her witching powers had only increased her concerns, not assuaged them. To think that she, Isabel Ellerby, could ever even consider cursing a fellow being! She viewed the acquisition of such powers with dismay, and wished heartily that she could somehow separate herself from them.

But she could not, and never would. She rode towards Mirramay with a heavy heart, wishing fervently that she had never permitted her aunt to send her on such a journey.

Sophy sensed some of this, and in her typically kind way, she exerted herself to cheer Isabel. Stories of her customers at Silverling and the other people she had met in Grenlowe whiled away the hour's travel that lay between the inn and Mirramay, and went some little way towards lightening Isabel's heart — not least because Sophy's tales emphasised some of the other, less alarming powers that witches were said to possess.

Halfway through her third tale, Sophy fell suddenly silent. Following the direction of her gaze, Isabel could clearly see why.

The trees of the Outwoods finally ended some short distance ahead of them, and the grandest city Isabel had ever seen rose in their place. Mirramay was beautifully laid out and looked as though someone had simply imagined it into being (which, perhaps, they had: how was she to know?). The buildings were graceful and tall, with many towering spires. They were all constructed from smooth stone like marble, in pale colours; many white, others palest golden, ice-blue or pearly. The windows were set with panes of glass of a size Isabel had never seen, nor ever thought possible to create. Ornate carvings, columns and statues decorated every one, some of them gilded in gold — or something else, something that glistened with magical iridescence.

The sounds of running water reached Isabel's ears as they drew closer, suggesting the presence of several fountains not far away. Some delicious aroma teased at her senses, also: a mixture of the fresh scent of sea air, the perfume of summer flowers, exotic autumn spices and other things she could not name.

Truly, if she had set herself to imagine the most beautiful, magical city she was capable of dreaming, she would have fallen short of the magnificence of this place. She and Sophy rode under its vast main gate in utter silence, broken only by the ringing sounds their mounts' hooves made upon the wide, white-paved street that led into the heart of Mirramay.

'My goodness,' Isabel breathed at last.

'I had no idea,' Sophy whispered. 'Or I should have come here before now!'

Isabel merely nodded her agreement, struck briefly dumb by the sight of a breath-taking mosaic glimpsed through the gates of a mansion which rose to her left. So absorbed were she and Sophy in looking about themselves that they were falling behind; Sir Guntifer's long stride had carried him some way ahead. He had been here often enough that he was unfazed by its beauty, which amazed Isabel. She could not imagine ever growing tired of it.

Sir Guntifer was, if anything, walking faster. His head began to turn this way and that, as though he were searching for something in particular. Isabel and Sophy hastened to catch up, urging their mounts to walk a little faster in pursuit of the tree-giant.

Gradually it dawned on Isabel that something was amiss with the beauteous city. They had been riding for some minutes through its wide main thoroughfare, and they had yet to see a single other person. Nor were there sounds of activity elsewhere; the air was still and she could hear little save for the sounds they themselves made. Looking more closely at the houses, she realised something else: as beautiful as they were, they were not well-kept. In fact, many of them bore an air of decay. When they came upon a wall which had partially tumbled down through neglect, she realised that Mirramay was not only quiet but abandoned.

Sir Guntifer had stopped, and was waiting for them. 'Make haste, gentle ladies,' he said as they caught up with him. 'Fair Mirramay! Never did I think to see it thus!' He looked distressed, and Isabel's heart swelled with pity for him.

'Why is it empty?' she said, gently.

'I do not know,' Sir Guntifer said, in a grim tone. 'Balligumph warned me that it was not as I remember, but this...' He had taken off his moss-velvet hat and now twisted it around in his hands, his great emerald eyes sad as he stared at the abandoned buildings around him. 'The Royals are gone from Mirramay, and the city herself mourns Their loss.' He spoke of the monarchs with a reverence which surprised Isabel, for it seemed to her that it far exceeded the respect the people of England felt for theirs. Sir Guntifer shook his head in despair. ''Twas said of old that the King and the Queen were the heart of Aylfenhame. Were they ever to fall, the realm itself would fall into disrepair until They should be restored. Never did I wholly believe it, until now.'

'Do you mean that this—' Isabel indicated the silence and decay with a sweep of her arm — 'May happen to the rest of Aylfenhame as well?'

'Who is to say that it shall not?' replied Sir Guntifer. 'Proud Mirramay! Fairest city of all, and once the beating heart of the realm. To see it thus, it breaks my heart.'

Isabel began to wonder whether it would have been wiser to bring

Lihyaen after all, but the same thought had apparently occurred to Sophy. 'She is not ready,' Sophy said softly to Isabel alone. 'There is more afoot here than is apparent. It is not as simple as a person's sitting upon a throne. The land itself must accept a Queen — or a King.'

That Isabel might have guessed for herself, had she considered the matter. It could not be the case that no other person in the whole of Aylfenhame possessed sufficient Royal blood to assume the throne; so why had no one done so?

'Why did I sleep so long!' Sir Guntifer lamented. He was squeezing his hat so hard that his hands shook. 'The death of the Princess, and the Queen! The King lost! Some part of this I — we — could have prevented!'

Isabel gently disengaged Sir Guntifer's hat from his hands, and laid one of her own upon his arm. 'You could not have known,' she said softly. 'It is not your doing.'

Sir Guntifer took a huge, gusty breath and exhaled, expelling a cloud of tiny green shoots from his mouth as he did so. He shook his great head and sighed again, sending a flurry of fluffy white seeds sailing after, and carefully restored his hat to his head. 'We defeated the Kostigern,' he said sombrely. 'Never did I dream that a darker threat would follow, nor that another could carry out his foul intent when he had failed.' He shook himself, and looked around, blinking. 'Well, well. That is the past. 'Tis to the future we must look.'

It occurred to Isabel belatedly that Pinch and Pinket were absent. Even as this dawned upon her she spotted them approaching, both in wisp-shape, their lights burning low. They reached Sir Guntifer and settled upon him, one on each shoulder. Pinch resumed his pixie shape with a strong shudder, and gasped something inaudible.

'What manner of news have ye brought?' Sir Guntifer said with some urgency.

'Trows!' announced Pinch, his face dark with disgust. 'Goblins! Hobs! Redcaps and boggles, ogres, trolls — not the friendly Balligumph-a-like, you understand. They've even got a thrice-cursed wight down there.'

Pinket suddenly became a pixie, and said in a piping voice: 'Imps, too.'

Pinch growled. 'And those wretched dogs. Hill-hounds. The white ones, with the red eyes.' He gave another violent shudder and wrapped his arms around himself, hugging tightly as though to ward off these combined perils.

Sir Guntifer shook his head slowly. 'Twas once the case that all were welcome in Mirramay,' he said. 'Trows, goblins, ogres and all. These folk are not unwelcome here, even now.'

Pinch took off his hat and threw it down in disgust. 'That is not what I'm saying, Gunty! They are here in force. They're all over the city. There's not a single one of the fair folk to be seen, either — just the darkling things. And there are rats.'

'Rats everywhere,' said Pinket.

'And you've seen what's become of "fair Mirramay",' added Pinch darkly. 'It might be more rightly called Darkling Town by this time.'

Sir Guntifer rumbled something low and inarticulate, a sound reminiscent of crashing branches and fierce rain. 'Where are these foul folk?' he demanded.

Pinch waved a hand. 'That way,' he said vaguely.

'What are they doing, Pinch?' Sophy interjected. Her tone and expression implied that she found something amiss with Pinch's story.

'Taking over the city!' he said dramatically. 'They're mustering, or something.'

'All by themselves?' Sophy put her hands upon her hips and stared hard at Pinch. 'You know as well as I do that groups of darklings do not collectively decide to do anything whatsoever. In fact, persuading them to agree upon the smallest thing for more than five minutes together is bordering upon impossible.'

Pinch was silent.

'Was that not why the Kostigern was so fearsome?' she persisted. 'Because he alone could.'

'Say not that he hath returned!' said Sir Guntifer, recoiling in alarm. 'Pinch! It is not so?'

'It's not him,' said Pinch.

'So there is someone else involved,' said Sophy triumphantly. 'Tell us at once! Is it Hidenory?'

Isabel judged that Sophy was expecting an assent to her question — hoping for it, perhaps. But Pinch shook his head. 'Tall fellow,' he said. 'Looks like one of your types.' He nodded at Sophy and Isabel as he said so. 'Red hair,' he added as an afterthought.

Sophy blinked. 'A human?' she said. 'A human has brought the darklings here?'

Pinch cackled madly. 'Could be. Could be not.'

'Let us resolve this question once and for all,' Sophy said firmly. 'Take us to this human, Pinch.'

'Are you mad?' Pinch gasped. 'You cannot just walk into the middle of that lot! They'll eat you alive!'

'Tall, with red hair?' Sophy repeated. 'Pale sort of fellow? Bright green eyes?'

Pinch stared at her in awe. 'You are reading my mind,' he whispered.

Isabel caught on. 'Wild hair?' she suggested, gesturing with her hands to indicate a riotous arrangement. 'And he smokes a pipe with a long, thin stem.'

Pinch stared from Sophy to Isabel and back, and shook his head in wonder. 'I never knew,' he whispered. 'Do all the ladies of England read minds?'

Sophy made a shooing motion with her hands. 'We know this gentleman,' she said briskly. 'Take us to him.'

'It's my thought that he's dangerous,' said Pinch dubiously. 'I do not think you could know him.'

'Certainly he is! But not to us. Onward, Pinch. Let us not waste any more time.'

Pinch glanced at Isabel, who smiled reassuringly at him. 'It is all right,' she said. 'We do know him, indeed. He will not harm us.'

'He might not, but his foul little friends might,' muttered Pinch. As he spoke, he shifted to wisp shape with resentful slowness, and drifted off Sir Guntifer's shoulder. Pinket followed.

'Are ye certain, gentle ladies?' said Sir Guntifer. 'I mislike the scheme. Balligumph placed ye into my hands, and it falls to me to bring ye safely home.'

'All will be well, sir,' said Isabel, smiling upon him. She said it with conviction, for though Pinch's stories of darkling creatures had alarmed her at first, she had felt much reassured the moment she realised who had them in charge. Indeed, she was positively looking forward to seeing him! She had always found him congenial, and it had been some time since she had last encountered him.

'Very well, then,' said the giant gravely. 'Then we will follow the tricksy pixies.' He gestured them ahead in the wisps' wake and fell in behind them. Isabel felt further reassured by his presence behind; no malicious thing could creep up upon them while Sir Guntifer was there.

They wound their way through several long streets, turning so often that Isabel wondered how Pinch and Pinket could remember the way. As they rode, they saw increasing signs of habitation: some of the buildings were littered with rubbish, fires burned, and the smells of cooking rose into the morning air. Isabel began to glimpse movement here and there out of the corners of her eyes, though whenever she turned to look she saw nothing but an empty street, or an open gate swinging slightly in the breeze.

That changed, so abruptly as to draw a gasp from her. They turned a corner and found themselves riding into the midst of a crowd of fae creatures. Ogres even taller than Balligumph leaned against the walls, imps as tall as their kneecaps wandering around among them. Hobs and goblins fought over morsels of food and sparkling jewellery, and a troll sat by himself in a corner between two buildings, playing a horn which sounded eerily similar to the one the trows had used to lure their party into the trees. Over the crowd floated several wisps; Isabel could not tell if any of them were Pinch and Pinket.

In the middle of this ragged array of the fae there stood an enormous throne. Its seat was wide enough to accommodate four people sitting side-by-side, and its back was easily ten feet tall. The throne was made out of pure gold, or so it appeared; remembering Tafferty's comments about Glamour, Isabel wondered whether it might look altogether different somewhere underneath the illusion. An enormous, deliciously soft-looking cushion of purple velvet covered the seat, atop which sat the Goblin King.

He looked just as Isabel remembered him. He even still wore the clothes of a gentleman of England, though the precision of his attire had deteriorated somewhat: his coat was missing, his shirt-sleeves were rolled up in a most improper fashion, and he was hatless. But it was unmistakeably the same man: he who had called himself Mr. Green, and occupied Hyde Place near Tilby for several months. He had departed the neighbourhood only recently, to the dismay of its residents, for the persona he had adopted had borne all the virtues of good looks, wealth and charm; more than a few young ladies had fixed their hopes and their affections upon him. None save Sophy Landon and Isabel herself had known his true identity.

'Your Majesty,' said Isabel with a smile, and made him the best bow she could from atop her pony.

'Good morning, Grunewald,' said Sophy drily as she reined in her mount before him.

Grunewald stared at them both in horror. 'Just what do you think you are doing in Mirramay?' he demanded. 'It isn't safe for a party of ladies! I would think that Aubranael would die of shock if he knew!'

'How kind of you to feel concerned for our welfare!' said Isabel warmly. 'But I assure you, we have come very well-attended.'

'He is not serious!' said Sophy. 'Now, are you, Grunewald? What a mother-hen speech! You would not care if the worst imaginable fate were to befall the both of us.'

Grunewald grinned lazily. 'Miss Ellerby credits me with far too much attention, as always. But you, my dear Miss Landon, credit me with far too little. The truth lies somewhere in between, I assure you.' He rose from his oversized throne and solicitously helped both ladies down from their mounts. Isabel thought that he pressed her hand as he did so, and her cheeks coloured a little. 'But my question stands, you know. What are you doing in these parts? And without Aubranael!'

'I may very well direct the same enquiry at you,' retorted Sophy.

Grunewald's smile widened. 'Much as I appreciate Aubranael's company, I often travel without him.'

Sophy made an exasperated noise. 'You understand very well what I mean!'

Grunewald adopted a tragic air, looking around among his gathered followers for support. 'You see with what a lack of respect I am treated by the ladies of England! It is very shocking.'

Isabel thought that there was a dangerous look in his eye as he said this, however light-hearted his tone might have been. She suppressed an urge to caution her friend. Sophy had known Grunewald longer than she had; she knew how far she could presume upon his good nature.

'There are a number of things I could possibly be doing here,' Grunewald said in a more serious tone, though a glint of mischief sparkled in his eye. 'I might be here to investigate the lamentably ongoing absence of our glorious monarchs — with, I need hardly add, the most selfless of motives! I might simply be passing through, with my aides-de-camp.' He gestured carelessly at the ragtag band of darkling fae that surrounded his throne, his mouth twisting with self-mockery. 'Or I might be planning to move in. After all, no one has been using Mirramay in quite some years now.'

'Using it for what?' Sophy retorted. 'I can hardly imagine that Aubranael would approve of any such plan!'

Something between amusement and anger flickered across Grunewald's eyes. 'I note that you assume the worst, and with no conceivable reason to do so,' he retorted. 'Have I ever given cause to imagine I might be harbouring dreams of conquest?' With this said, he sprawled once more upon his glittering throne and cast his long legs over one arm.

Sophy considered the vision of Grunewald, the Goblin King, lounging lazily upon a gaudy and stupendously oversized throne and smiled. It was one of her special smiles, full of a mixture of mischief and amusement, and not unleavened with affection. 'I leave that to your own conscience to answer,' she said lightly.

To Isabel's surprise — and relief — Grunewald laughed at that. 'I would tell you that I care nothing for your Aubranael's good opinion, my dear Miss Landon, but to do so would be to wound you — perhaps past recovery. And I am far too much a gentleman.' He made an odd seated bow in Sophy's direction, somehow imbuing the gesture with a sinuous grace in spite of its awkwardness.

'You are not too much the gentleman to lie,' Sophy said with a laugh. 'You would prefer not to care for Aubranael's opinion, of that I have no doubt. Nonetheless, you do. He is your moral guide, of a sorts; now, is he not? Your own internal guide is a little broken, and you have made liberal use of his in the past.'

Grunewald grimaced. 'What a detestable idea.' Isabel noted with interest that he did not deny it. 'Now we return to the topic of your most unexpected appearance in these parts. My good Miss Landon, do not toy with my curiosity any further, I beg of you. I am positively expiring with the need to know how you come to be wandering in Fair Mirramay, and in such company.' His eyes flicked over Sir Guntifer, who drew himself up to his full, impressive height and eyed the Goblin King with distrust.

'It is Isabel's errand,' Sophy replied. Isabel hoped that her friend might go on to explain the rest, but she did not. She looked instead at Isabel herself, and informed her by way of an encouraging smile that she expected her to explain her own motive.

Isabel sighed inwardly. She had always felt a peculiar reticence in addressing Grunewald, for his station combined with his odd manners confused her. There was also the question of what he was, behind the Glamour that shrouded his form. Was he human indeed? Was he Aylir? Was he a goblin himself?

Furthermore, she had more than once suspected him of flirting with her. Given the circumstances, she could only view this as most impertinent, and rather uncomfortable.

And now she must contend with the additional obstacle of an audience; composed, too, of such an odd assortment of creatures! And so universally questionable in character! But speak she must. She thrust away the part of her mind that continued to marvel, disbelieving, at the situations she was lately finding herself in, and proceeded to relate her errand to the Goblin King. She spoke quietly, as ever, but it appeared that Grunewald's presence proved sufficient to quell the more mischievous impulses of his followers; no one interrupted her, or spoke over her. Grunewald himself paid her the courtesy of close attention, only the faintest hint of amusement lurking in his bright green eyes.

When she had finished, he shifted uncomfortably upon his throne — throwing himself into a still more indecorous posture in the process — and sighed. 'The Ferryman, eh?' he said moodily. 'I see how it is.' He glanced sharply at Isabel as he spoke, though as she could not fathom the direction of his thoughts nor the intended meaning of this remark, she failed to decipher his expression. 'I would tell you that he is no fit company for a pair of gentle English ladies, but if I did I would have to disqualify my own self from your fair company, and that would never do.' He smiled, just at Isabel, and to her annoyance she felt herself blush. This was exactly the worst of him! If only he would stop smiling at her in quite that way, she would be able to feel much more comfortable in his presence.

'Stop flirting, Grunewald,' Sophy said without ceremony. 'Poor Isabel does not know how to receive your attentions.'

Grunewald laughed, a disconcertingly wicked sound. 'But that is why it is so enjoyable. Such a pretty blush! It is a refreshing change.'

Sophy waved this away with an impatient gesture. 'The Chronicler!' she prompted. 'Have you seen anyone of that sort around Mirramay? I hardly dare hope that you might have, as it seems to be very much abandoned.'

'Oh, it is,' Grunewald agreed. 'Or was, until we arrived.' He accompanied this reflection with a wicked grin. 'However, there were some oddities about the Chronicler's Tower, if my memory does not betray me. If any part of the city has survived the decay of the rest, it might be the Chronicler's Library. It was protected, you know.'

Hope flickered to life in Isabel's heart. 'Indeed!' she cried. 'That is encouraging news. But if it is protected, I suppose it will not be easy to get inside?'

'Very good, Miss Ellerby,' said Grunewald, in the teasing tone he apparently reserved for her. 'It will not be easy at all.' The Goblin King smiled comfortably at Sir Guntifer. 'What of it, Tree-giant? Do you possess the means to pass the Chronicler's tests?'

'My purpose is to serve as guide and protector,' replied Sir Guntifer stiffly.

'In other words, no! I congratulate you all. A more ill-advised plan I have scarcely heard of, and to arrive ill-equipped for the challenges of the adventure as well! It is positively reckless! I had not thought it possible.' His delighted smile proclaimed that he spoke the truth, and Isabel frowned. Why should he applaud recklessness? To behave without due thought and caution could only be considered foolish, and she blushed with mortification to realise how correct he was in accusing them of it. The venture had been foolish indeed! But the fault was hers, in having acted impulsively to begin with. Was it allowable if she had done so out of a desire to help another?

Grunewald's laughter interrupted these reflections. 'I see I have disconcerted Miss Ellerby yet again, for how she blushes! But rest assured, my dear: a little recklessness is perfectly necessary, once in a great while. How are you to have any adventures, otherwise?'

'I did not seek to have adventures, sir, I assure you!' said Isabel with great indignation.

'I can well believe it. I might hazard a guess that your life has been a dull one, thus far? Excepting, of course, the temporary excitement of Miss Landon's adventure of last year.'

Isabel opened her mouth to protest against this characterisation of her life, but she was obliged to close it again without speaking. When she called to mind the pattern of her days, she remembered peace and tranquillity, which were by no means bad; common sense and responsibility, which were admirable traits; but she could not help remembering a great deal of dullness as well.

'You are too wise to deny it, I see,' said Grunewald. His mocking tone had gone; in its place was something that sounded almost sympathetic. 'These hide-bound Englishfolk! With your customs and your courtesies, your age-old habits and your etiquette! So stifling to the spirit! It amuses me greatly to play in your world from time to time, but only for the pleasure of turning all of your absurd customs upside-down. To watch the blossoming of a spirit, once it throws off the shackles of duty, expectation, and sound good sense! It is a liberating process. Miss Landon has discovered that for herself, to some degree, for here she stands: a proper young lady of England no more, but a citizen of Aylfenhame! A tradeswoman, a crafts-mistress, and (I would wager) happier by far than she would ever have been if she had married some dullard out of England.' He looked hard at Sophy as she said this, but his gaze soon returned to Isabel. 'How I wish you could be persuaded to attempt the same, Miss Ellerby! I see a dull future in store for you, and it pains me. To waste such a flower upon such a future would be the greatest of misfortunes.'

Neither Isabel nor Sophy had any reply to make to this wholly unexpected speech. Isabel could only stare at the Goblin King, lips parted upon a response which refused to form in her brain.

'I see I have been too precipitate,' Grunewald said with a wave of his hand. 'I will postpone the part where I invite you to join me in Mirramay and reign over the Goblin Kingdom as my Queen, and proceed post-haste to other matters.' His mocking tone was back, and the twinkle in his eyes more pronounced than ever. Isabel did not think that he made such a shocking offer with any intention of being taken seriously, but with Grunewald, one never knew.

'Such a wondrous adventure cannot be permitted to end in failure,' Grunewald continued gaily, and jumped up from his throne. 'I would see Miss Ellerby retained in Aylfenhame for as long as possible, and therefore, I take it upon myself to assist you.' He gave a sweeping, flamboyant bow, evidently expecting applause.

'Of course you will,' Sophy said instead. 'How could you be expected to resist the opportunity to further any kind of mischief?'

Grunewald laughed. 'I do believe Miss Landon is beginning to understand my character, and that is a lowering reflection. To become consistent and even, stars help me, predictable!' He gave a theatrical shudder. 'Palchis!' he called abruptly. 'Ertof! Yangveld! Instantly, I beg you.'

Three of the surrounding fae separated themselves from the crowd and presented themselves at Grunewald's feet. One was a trow, very like the ones that had accosted them upon the road: dark-skinned and small, with overlarge hat and shoes and an oddly-shaped horn carried in one hand. The second was a goblin, slightly taller than the trow and draped in silken garments. His skin was pale for a goblin, only faintly tinted with green.

The third — Yangveld? — was an ogre, and seemingly female. She was a foot shorter than Sir Guntifer, but still of an imposing size. She was fabulously coiffed and wore an entrancingly beautiful gown made from a rippling, watery green silk.

'Why, Yangveld!' Sophy cried delightedly. 'It has been some months, I think, since last I saw you at Silverling! I do hope you are still happy with your gowns?'

Yangveld grinned toothily, and nodded her great head, making her midnight-black locks bounce. 'Aye, ma'am, that I am,' she said in a deepish voice. ''Tis tricky keepin' the hems out o' the mud sometimes, but 'tis worth it for all o' that.'

'You have taken very good care of this one,' Sophy said, casting an approving eye over the pristine silk.

Yangveld smiled happily. 'I had Jenny Greenshoes put a Keep-Away charm on it,' she confided.

'A Keep-Away charm?' repeated Sophy.

'Aye! Keeps dirt away, an' other things.'

'Interesting,' said Sophy. 'Jenny Greenshoes, who is she?'

'She's the witch o' these parts. Handy with 'er charms.'

Sophy cast a speculative look at Isabel. 'A witch! Goodness. How wonderful it would be if I could have such a charm cast upon every gown I make! My customers would be very happy, I think.'

Tafferty, who had apparently slept through most of the past hour's events, stirred and said sleepily from the back of Isabel's pony: 'Oh, yes. Happen I might ha' forgot t' mention that t' thee. Charms an' the like! Little, useful bits an' pieces upon the whole; nothin' much worthy o' note. But mayhap thou wouldst find such trivial nonsense more t' thy taste than Cursin'.' She said this last with disgust, eyeing Isabel with strong disapproval. Upon completing her speech, she laid her tail over her eyes and spoke no more.

'I would very much like to learn it!' Isabel surprised herself by saying. 'Indeed, it would be of far greater use to me, and to my friends, than Curses.'

Grunewald fell to laughing at this, which offended and mortified Isabel in equal measure. 'You have yet to fully understand your new charge, I think,' said he to the catterdandy, who sniffed and refused to open her eyes.

'I do not see what is wrong with preferring to do good than to cause harm,' said Isabel, in the firmest tone she could muster in the face of Grunewald's mirth.

He smiled upon her in a generally kind fashion. 'Nothing at all, to be sure,' he replied. 'It is your companion who amuses me, not your own attitude. The catterdandy has never met your like before; of that I am certain.'

Isabel did not know what to say. Upon a moment's reflection, she said with at least the appearance of perfect composure: 'The Chronicler's Tower?'

Grunewald grinned at her. Isabel was mildly disconcerted to note that his teeth seemed a little sharper than she remembered. 'To the Palace!' he said.

There followed a flurry of activity as mounts were reclaimed and the party organised behind Grunewald. Isabel, feeling safe once more atop her pretty mare, took the opportunity to admire more of the remarkable city as she followed in the Goblin King's train. The Palace of Mirramay was easy to identify: Isabel rounded the corner of a narrow, twisting street paved with cobbles and there it was, a honey-coloured magnificence rising high above the elegant pale buildings of the rest of the city. It bore twin spires and corner towers; impossibly large, arched windows in which perfectly clear panes of glass twinkled in the morning sun; and graceful statues set into niches in the walls, depicting beauteous Ayliri and fae in striking poses. As she grew closer, Isabel saw that the Palace was more a complex of buildings than a single structure, all enclosed within high walls. The towering golden gates were open, and the party rode unimpeded into a deserted courtyard.

Isabel would have been content to linger here for a little while. On either side stretched twin pools of clear, calm waters, blue-green and roseate-lavender respectively; their surfaces were abloom with perfect white water flowers. The distance from the gates to the doors of the palace itself was marked by two rows of Elder trees, gold of bark and snow-white of leaf, and decked in flowers of heavenly aroma. Isabel marvelled at it all, but she had little opportunity to enjoy it, for Grunewald set a smart pace up to the great doors, where he reined in the curious green-skinned horse he was riding.

'There is the Chronicler's Tower,' he said, pointing to the southeasterly spire rising far above their heads. Isabel frowned, shading her eyes against the sun. It was difficult to be certain, for the tower was a long way above, but she thought that the windows were wide open. Did that suggest continued habitation, or the opposite?

Grunewald spun abruptly and strode away in the direction of the palace doors. Isabel and Sophy hurried to keep pace with him, though they could not quite keep up. As such, they were some steps back when Grunewald stopped abruptly in the doorway.

'What is it?' Sophy cried as they drew level with him.

He made no answer. Instead he drew himself up, seeming to gain three inches in moments as he drew in a great breath. Then he let forth a vast, bellowing cry which echoed off the walls of the palace. There were words contained therein, but in no language Isabel could understand. The words twisted and coiled oddly, simultaneously hissing and booming in the mouth of the Goblin King.

Isabel clapped her hands over her ears, hating the dark sounds. When Grunewald stepped forward and disappeared into the palace, she followed, but reluctantly. What manner of occurrence had prompted such a cry? She stepped over the threshold, and saw at once.

Darkling fae swarmed the grand hall of the palace. They had probably covered the floor, moments before, but it was as though the King's cry had physically blown them backwards, for they now clustered in a great, cringing horde at the rear of the hall. Trows and goblins they were, for the most part, with imps and hobs mingled in, and numerous others to which Isabel could put no name.

Grunewald did not hesitate, but strode away at once and passed rapidly beneath an enormous door in the wall. Isabel and Sophy followed. The corridors beyond were likewise swarming with fae, and Grunewald was obliged to repeat his terrible cry twice more as they wound their way through curving corridors and up spiralling stairs.

Isabel was out of breath by the time they finally stopped in a round-walled chamber far above the ground. Its great, heavy door had shut out the fae, but Grunewald had forced it open. The windows were indeed agape, but there was no sign of any living presence; dust lay thickly over the curving window-seats and the round table and chairs which occupied the centre of the room. Bookcases bore an air of neglect, as though their contents had lain untouched for many years.

The chamber was small; she and Sophy, Grunewald and his three fae followers barely all fit inside it together. She spared a moment's gratitude for Sir Guntifer's foresight in electing to remain below. He was just visible from the window, a great Elder oak stationed near to the main doors of the Palace. He bore the appearance of being on guard, which reassured Isabel to some degree. She did not know what the fae were doing in the palace in such numbers, nor whether they were a threat. But Grunewald appeared to be able to control them, and Sir Guntifer would keep others away.

'But this cannot be everything,' she said in confusion, for there were but few books and scrolls in evidence. Could this be the collected histories of all of Aylfenhame, these scant records?

'Why, no, my dearest child,' said Grunewald. 'Of course, it is not everything. One may not simply walk into the Chronicler's Tower and take from it as one pleases. Behold.' A curious glyph was inlaid into the centre of the table in silver; Grunewald leaned forward and laid his hand over it. At once an image flickered into being over the table: a beast, translucent and ethereal, clearly an imagining of some kind and not a real creature. It bore the shape of a wispy dragon, its hide glittering with white scales and its eyes gleaming bright blue.

'I seek entrance,' said Grunewald.

The dragon sniffed, sending wisps of ethereal smoke drifting forth from its nostrils. 'The Goblin King,' it said in a dusty voice. 'You are not permitted to access the Chronicles.' Having completed this laconic announcement, the dragon disappeared in a puff of mist.

Grunewald sighed and turned away. 'One would almost be tempted to think that Anthelaena didn't trust me.'

'I cannot think why,' said Sophy dryly. 'What possible reason could you have for accessing the Chronicles?'

'Oh,' said Grunewald softly, with a catlike smile. 'Perfectly unexceptionable, selfish, highly questionable reasons, of course.'

Sophy smiled. 'Quite so.'

Isabel stepped forward. 'I had better try,' she said, a trifle doubtfully. 'As it is my task.' She laid her hand over the glyph, and the dragon puffed back into being.

'I seek entrance,' said Isabel, smiling hesitantly at the dragon. Its expression had turned a little forbidding.

'Mister Grunewald,' said the dragon. 'I will not be granting you entrance to—' The dragon broke off abruptly as its eyes focused upon Isabel, and its forbidding air evaporated. 'Well, now!' it said, visibly brightening. 'This is most unusual. What are you? Aylir? Goblin? Something else? It is a very good Glamour.'

'Neither of those, sir,' said Isabel. 'I am human. It is no Glamour.'

The dragon blinked at her, then drifted down to examine her more closely. 'Why, so you are! And you have brought another. Two humans at once, in the Chronicler's Tower? My very goodness.' The dragon's gaze fell once more upon Grunewald and his darkling entourage, and a scowl crossed its ethereal features. 'And in company with His Most DisRespectable Majesty! Something very odd is afoot.'

'Are you the Chronicler?' Isabel asked.

The dragon appeared shocked by such a question. 'Certainly not! I am the Keeper.'

'I see. And… what is that?'

The dragon-Seeming swelled in size. 'Why, a fashioning of the Chronicler's! I am appointed to guard the entrance to his great creation.'

The Keeper spoke of the Chronicler in terms of such reverence, Isabel began to feel unnerved. Would she ever be permitted to access the records?

'Is… is he here?' she said.

The dragon appeared suddenly to wither, coils of mist shrinking in upon themselves. 'The Chronicler is not in residence,' it intoned, its voice odd and inflectionless — as though it had been given the line to speak.

'Will he return?'

The Keeper shrank a little further. 'Perhaps,' it said in a whisper.

Isabel thought for a moment. She had hoped to consult the Chronicler himself, for he must certainly know whether his collection contained the information she needed, and where it was to be found.

'I still seek entrance,' Isabel said firmly. She could not turn back without making any attempt, for the Ferryman relied upon her. Who else would help him?

The Keeper puffed itself back up to its former proportions, and

gazed at her. 'Who are you?'

'I am Miss Isabel Ellerby, of Ferndeane, in England.'

The Keeper mulled this over in silence for an instant, and then said simply: 'Why?'

'I seek information,' said Isabel guardedly. Should she reveal her full errand to this creature, or not? Would the Keeper approve, or would it share the doubtful opinion of the Ferryman she had heard from others?

'To what end?' replied the Keeper in ringing tones. 'Seek not the Chronicles for the exaltation of the Self, for it shall not be permitted. Is your errand for the good of Aylfenhame?'

'Do not try to lie,' Grunewald warned from behind Isabel. 'I tried that, the first time. It did not go well.' His tone was wry; Isabel could picture the deprecating smile that he often wore.

'I could not think of lying,' said Isabel with a touch of indignation. How like Grunewald to imagine that everyone thought and acted like him! But she suffered a moment's doubt. Her errand had nothing to do with exalting herself, but was it for the good of Aylfenhame? 'I seek to aid another,' she said at last. 'To gain his freedom.'

'Ah, Curse-breaking,' said the Keeper in a more normal tone of voice. 'Though it is unusual for any to venture here in the service of another.'

'I consider that unfortunate,' said Isabel, 'for are we not all in need of aid, from time to time?'

'Does this "other" propose to cause harm to Aylfenhame?' continued the dragon, as though Isabel had not spoken.

'I have no reason to believe that he does,' she replied, conscious all the while of how little she knew about the Ferryman. Was he the congenial soul she imagined him to be, or had he deserved the Curse laid upon him?'

The Keeper huffed a little, emitting another puff of mist from its mouth. 'The Test must be administered,' it pronounced, and swelled to a formidable size. 'You must answer one question, Isabel of Ferndeane, and you shall have but one attempt to answer correctly. Do you accept?'

Isabel mustered as much confidence as she could, and nodded. 'I accept.'

'Very well.' The Keeper swelled a little more, the mists comprising its draconic shape turning a sober shade of blue. It was now so big that its head hovered directly beneath the ceiling, and its misty coils had begun to spill out of the windows. 'The question is thus: If a faefly drifts a thousand leagues in Greyling and its wings turn cerulean, what colour is the Queen to wear on Beltane three summers ago?'

Isabel blinked. Her mouth opened, closed again, and she swallowed. 'Have you perhaps misspoken the question, sir?' she enquired. Something was gravely amiss with the latter part, for he had spoken of the Queen's attire on a future Beltane and then named it as three summers past. And that was merely the first point of confusion; for what was a faefly, or Greyling? What did it matter what colours its wings were, or how far it had travelled?

'Of course I did not,' said the Keeper. 'Will you hear it again?'

Isabel nodded, and waited in silence as the Keeper repeated the question. Nothing more occurred to her upon the second speaking than the first, and her heart sank.

'I cannot answer,' she said in shame.

'Of course you cannot, Isabel of England,' said the Keeper, shrinking down somewhat from its heights. 'You must seek aid. If those who Know are prepared to assist you, then I will consider your request.'

Isabel turned away from the table in despair. 'Who could possibly know the answer to such a question?' she sighed. No one answered her; the expressions upon the faces of Sophy, Grunewald, Yangveld, Palchis and Ertof were alike in their blank incomprehension.

Isabel felt hopelessly unequal to the task she had set herself. In order to find the Ferryman's name, she first had to find someone who knew what it had been. But in order to find the Chronicler — or at least, the books he had left behind — she now had to find someone else who could answer the strangest question she had ever heard in her life! And where was she to start?

A vision of the Ferryman passed through her thoughts, and she sighed inwardly once more. She had made him believe that she would help him; would she so easily give up?

'Tafferty?' she said softly.

The catterdandy was sitting by the door, with her tail wrapped neatly over her front paws. She had taken no part whatsoever in anything that had happened since they had discovered Grunewald's camp, and Isabel felt uncomfortable appealing to her. But she had sensed before that Tafferty's knowledge of Aylfenhame was broad, perhaps surprisingly so. Besides, she was Isabel's companion, whether she appreciated the idea or not.

Tafferty's head had been drooping towards the floor; perhaps she was asleep. But her head came up abruptly as Isabel spoke her name, and she opened her eyes wide. 'What?' she said.

'The Keeper's question,' Isabel prompted. 'Do you know who could answer?'

Tafferty's tail twitched and she glanced away. 'That Ferryman,' she said. 'He may help his own self! Thou art under no obligation t' assist him.'

'I do not see how he can!' Isabel cried. 'He cannot leave the boat.'

'Perhaps he may remember, if he tried a mite harder.'

'He has had many years to remember, and he has not. The Curse will make sure he does not, we may assume.'

Tafferty fixed her eyes on Isabel's face, and narrowed them. 'Why art thou so eager t' help the likes of him anyhow?'

'Would you like to find yourself in such a situation, Tafferty?' Isabel demanded. She was beginning to grow irritated with the catterdandy's ungenerous attitude. How anyone could consent to leave a fellow being languishing under such a Curse without even trying to help was beyond her comprehension!

'I would be far too wise an' clever t' get myself into such a mess in the first place!' retorted Tafferty. 'I would know better'n t' tangle meself up wi' the likes o' the Kostigern, too, an' the Ferryman is his creature entire.'

'Do you know that to be the truth? Or is it mere rumour? Oh! Do we not owe it to each other to be kind? How cruel it is, to condemn another on mere gossip alone!'

'And if it is not gossip?'

'If it is not, then he has been punished enough,' said Isabel firmly. 'If he has transgressed in the past, I am sure he is sorry for it now, and he ought to be given the chance to redeem himself.'

Tafferty made a noise of disgust. 'Thou art sure,' she said mockingly. 'Sure thou art, and basin' that opinion on what, exactly?'

'I feel it to be the truth,' said Isabel. 'If I am wrong…'

'If thou art mistaken, thou wilt unleash a liability upon Aylfenhame,' said Tafferty. 'The Keeper is right t' deny entrance t' thee.'

'Tafferty. Do you know the answer to the Keeper's question?'

Tafferty growled. 'I do.'

'Then I beg you, share it with me! If we are to be companions, then we must trust and help one another.'

'Thou art but an infant in the ways of Aylfenhame,' Tafferty retorted. ''Tis my duty t' keep thee from doin' thyself — or the rest of us — any harm.'

Isabel, speechless with indignation and dismay, could find no fitting response. Stubborn creature! Could she never be persuaded to give the Ferryman a chance? Her heart ached at the prospect of leaving her promise unfulfilled, and the Ferryman bound to his boat forever.

Her mind returned to the conversation she had had with him during her elongated journey to Grenlowe. She had liked him. It was difficult to decide precisely why she had liked him so much, but no mere rumour could dislodge her confidence in him! Her heart swelled with indignation at the very idea. If only he could speak to Tafferty himself — if only he could be given the opportunity to address these persistent and damaging rumours!

But he could. Isabel's mind flew to the parting gift he had given her — the whistle. She groped in her reticule, half in a panic lest she had mislaid it, but she had not; there it lay, safe at the bottom of the little bag. She drew it out.

'We will resolve this!' she said. 'Tafferty, please come with me.' She did not wait to allow her companion any opportunity to argue, but turned at once and left the tower. She was halfway down the stairs before she heard sounds of anyone following her.

'Isabel!' Sophy called. 'Do, please, take care!'

Isabel paused to reassure her friend, and as she did so Grunewald swept past, glancing sideways at her as he did so. 'Reckless, that,' he said with a twinkle, and not disapprovingly. 'Allow me!' He strode back down to the hallway, sending darkling fae scurrying out of his path with every step. Isabel, Sophy and Tafferty followed in his wake.

The moment Isabel stepped out into the warm morning air, she lifted the delicate whistle to her lips and blew. The sound that emerged was not the high-pitched, single note she had expected. A ripple of notes poured forth in a clear melody, which seemed to expand until it filled all the air around her. She waited, her heart pounding. Would he come?

She was not obliged to wait for very long. Two or three minutes passed, though it felt a great deal longer to Isabel, in her state of anticipation. Then a cloud rippled upon the horizon, puffing out a great cloud of mist, and the boat materialised in the centre of it. It sailed swiftly down to land in between the trees outside of the palace, hovering some little way above the ground. The Ferryman stood tall and straight in the prow.

He considered Isabel for a long moment, his expression unreadable. Then his eyes flicked to take in her odd assortment of companions, and the palace of Mirramay behind.

'I 'ad thought ye would use the whistle when ye were ready t' return t' England,' he said in a conversational tone. 'I 'ad not imagined I would find ye in Mirramay. Nor that ye'd be keepin' company wi' darklin's, an' one o' the tree-giants o' myth — not t' mention the Goblin King his own self.' The Ferryman made Grunewald a bow as he spoke this last, though the gesture was ironical.

Grunewald made a far more flamboyant bow in response, his mouth curling into a grin. 'Ah, the Ferryman. A fine figure of mystery, and how good of you to come. Something of a myth yourself, are you not?'

'Myths may live an' breathe, that I know.' He looked once again at Isabel, and raised one eyebrow. 'Is it passage ye seek? If so, I cannot fit ye all within, I fear. Yer human friend I may, an' His Majesty, if he so chooses. His Majesty's entourage, an' yer mounts — that's trickier. Yer giant friend? Not a chance, I do fear.'

'I do not seek to travel at this time, sir,' said Isabel. 'We have come here in search of your name, and have encountered an obstacle which only you can remove.'

Both of the Ferryman's brows went up at these words, and his mouth opened a little in shock. 'Ye came t' Mirramay in search o' my name?' he repeated. 'An' wi' the Goblin King?'

'Not precisely with Grunewald,' Isabel said cautiously. 'We discovered that he was already here, and he has been kind enough to assist us.'

The Ferryman's brows rose higher still at her use of the name Grunewald, and he turned outright incredulous at the rest of her sentence. 'Kind!' he said. 'He is not known fer kindness, His Majesty.'

'I have never known him to be anything other than kind!' Isabel retorted. 'He has been Miss Landon's acquaintance this past year, and has been everything of the kindest to her. And to me.'

The Ferryman surveyed Sophy, his expression markedly sceptical. 'I can see there is more t' ye than I guessed,' he said, returning his gaze to Isabel. 'Still, I would warn ye t' take some care wi' his Kingship. Tricky folk, goblins.'

'I might say the same of you,' said Grunewald smoothly. 'In fact, the catterdandy there is vehemently opposed to anybody's helping you at all.'

The Ferryman's face darkened with some unnameable emotion. 'She is right enough,' he said shortly.

'She is not,' Isabel protested. 'I cannot convince her of your worthiness, but you can! That is why I have summoned you. She possesses the answer to a question posed by the Keeper of the Chronicles, but she will not share it; and without it, I cannot get inside. Please, tell her that she is mistaken about you! There are rumours abroad, but they may be easily contradicted.'

The Ferryman merely looked at her. It struck her that he appeared wearied, if not in body then perhaps in spirit. His dark hair was a little disordered, coming loose from the ribbon he used to tie it back; his golden skin looked, she thought, a little paler than when she had seen him before; and his eyes were deeply shadowed. 'Whatever they are,' he said slowly, 'they are probably naught but the truth.'

'They cannot be,' Isabel said. 'They refer to — to —'

'T' the Kostigern?' he interrupted. 'An' ye, little innocent, cannot even say his name. Such a mind as ye possess could never fathom why any soul'd consent t' be one o' his, considerin' his actions. But yer mind is a place o' naught but light; ye cannot see the shadows in everyone else's.'

Isabel was speechless with surprise and dismay. She crept closer to Sophy, unconsciously seeking support. She was a little reassured when Sophy took her hand and gave it an encouraging squeeze.

'The rumours are true?' she said at last, in a voice barely above a whisper.

The Ferryman smiled sadly. 'Ye 'ave cast me in the role o' some kind o' prince in a tale, no? Afflicted wi' some dreadful Curse all undeservin', an' requirin' only a maid pure o' heart t' free me from my torment — be it wi' a name, or a spell, or a kiss. An' then all is well, an' everyone goes home dancin'. Is that how it is?'

Isabel coloured. The construction he had placed upon her reasoning sounded naive to the point of foolishness, and she could not even disclaim, for he was essentially correct. She had given him a shining character, and with no particular reason to do so. Was it because of his amiable attitude towards her? Was it his smile, or his handsome face? Or was it the cruelty of his fate, and the sadness she had detected in his eyes?

It did not matter which, for they were all foolish reasons. She bowed her head, wishing that her cheeks were not so aflame, and searching uselessly for something to say. Her mind reeled away from the vision she must now consider — the congenial Ferryman, willingly aiding such a character as the Kostigern! How could a person seem so charming and pleasant, and yet be so very other in character?

'Ye see, then,' the Ferryman continued, after a short pause. 'Yer catterdandy friend is more'n right t' distrust me, an' I will never be able t' convince her that I am worthy o' yer help. Because I am most assuredly not worthy.'

Isabel looked up, too sad and distressed to speak, to find that he was smiling at her. 'I am … touched, by yer faith in me,' he said. 'Misplaced as it may be. It's been many, many years since anyone believed in me at all.' He climbed down to capture Isabel's hands and laid a swift kiss upon each. 'Ye must abandon this quest o' yours,' he said softly. 'Find somethin' — someone — worthy o' yer time an' heart.' He gently pressed her hands and then released them, straightening. He stepped back into the Ferry, the mists swelled around the boat, and it began to rise. He was leaving, and Isabel merely stood, stupefied. In spite of his words, she did not want him to depart, did not want to abandon him. But she could think of nothing to say that would keep him with her, for he was right: if the worst Tafferty believed of him was true, then she would never help him. No one would. And perhaps — though it smote Isabel sorely to think it — perhaps she was right to refuse.

'Sir,' said Sophy abruptly. 'Miss Ellerby is unusually kind-hearted, it is true, and will never willingly think ill of anyone. I am not nearly so generous of spirit, but still I cannot help feeling that her faith in you may not be wholly misguided.' She hesitated, and added, 'Will you tell us why you were of the Kostigern's party in such a questionable business?'

The boat ceased to rise, though it did not descend either. The Ferryman looked down upon Sophy, and upon Isabel, with an unreadable expression. 'He was my Master,' he said. 'I wish I could give ye more of an answer'n that, but I cannot. 'Tis all I can remember o' those days.'

Tafferty made a disgusted noise, and then appeared — to Isabel's shock — to spit upon the ground.

'Tafferty,' she said, horrified. 'Please, try to have some compassion! How would you have fared, in such a situation?'

Tafferty rounded on Isabel, growling. 'His Master! That makes him an apprentice, no doubt in some manner o' sorcery-like arts. An' that means he was very likely oath-bound,' she said disgustedly. 'Which seemingly he was not plannin' t' mention hisself. But 'tis the way o' such things. Is it not, thou aggravatin', troublesome witherdandy o' nature?' This incomprehensible insult — for Isabel took it as such — was directed at the Ferryman, towards whom Tafferty now turned with a whirl of her tail. 'If thou wert bound in blood t' thy Master then thou wert powerless t' disobey. Why wouldst thou not happen t' mention that, hey?'

'I could,' said the Ferryman slowly, with an odd glint in his eye, 'have tried harder.'

Tafferty spat again and a strong shiver, apparently of revulsion, made its way from her head to the tip of her tail. 'Oh, ye make a fine, tragic pair, that ye do! Ach! An' now I must help thee after all, an' I was hopin' that Miss-there would get 'er head out o' the clouds an' settle t' some decent trainin' in 'er neglected powers o' witchery.'

The Ferryman blinked, apparently as bemused as Isabel felt. But then he smiled. 'I won't pretend that I won't accept yer aid, an' gladly,' he said. 'But yer point is fair. How about a bargain, then, betwixt the three of us?'

Tafferty sat up. 'Oh?'

'Ye help me, an' in return Miss Isabel will agree t' pay due an' proper attention t' the witchy trainin' ye're so eager t' give her. How's that?'

''Tis but half of a bargain,' Tafferty said promptly. 'Isabel has t' get somethin' out o' the deal, or 'tis hardly fair.'

'Why, she wins a friend!' replied the Ferryman, indicating with a bow that he meant himself. 'An' a truer-hearted friend she is scarce like t' find anywhere. Besides which, she learns t' be a most excellent witch, which may be o' great use t' her in future.'

Tafferty looked inquiringly up at Isabel. 'Thou art mighty quiet up there, Miss. What dost thou think o' this?'

Isabel had indeed been quiet, for she had failed to fully understand half of what had lately passed. Oath-bound, and in blood? Compelled to act? But the Ferryman should have mentioned that; why had he not? Did he truly take so much blame upon himself, in spite of so undeniable a defence? Her heart only warmed towards him more on account of it, which she knew to be absurd, but so it was.

The bargain he proposed had come when she was only halfway through this onslaught of reflections and ideas, and for an instant she merely stared at Tafferty as her brain worked to catch up. 'Of course I agree,' she said at last. 'I should agree whether there were no reward in the case at all! How could I think of refusing?'

The Ferryman smiled at her. 'Somehow, I had a thinkin' ye would say that.'

Isabel sighed inwardly, remembering her futile attempts to compel a strawberry to resemble a raspberry. Still, it was only effort that was required, and that she could freely give in exchange for a man's freedom.

'Makin' a note t' me own, fine self,' Tafferty growled. 'If I wishes Miss Isabel t' do sommat o' use in the future, all I need do is bribe her wi' the prospect o' doin' a good turn. Then she turns sweet an' tractable as a lamb.'

Isabel began upon an embarrassed, half-indignant response, but Tafferty touched her nose to Isabel's skirt in a gesture which seemed forgiving, even a little affectionate, and she allowed her words to die away.

'The answer to the Keeper's question,' Tafferty continued, 'is Celadon.'

Grunewald folded his arms and stared at the catterdandy. 'And how do you know that?' he enquired.

'Thou wert under the impression I was lyin' through my shiny-sharp teeth, eh?' said Tafferty in response, glaring up at the Goblin King with her tail lashing. 'Missy will test my knowledge any moment, an' prove it sound enough.'

'That does not precisely answer my question,' said Grunewald, his bright green eyes glinting.

Tafferty merely sniffed and looked up at Isabel. 'Wilt thou stand an' stare all day, or get on wi' the business?'

Isabel looked at the Ferryman. 'I may be able to return with your name, soon,' she said. 'So I hope! But I do not know how long it may take to find it in such a library. Will you wait?'

The Ferryman seated himself inside his boat, and touched his hat to her. 'Aye, I'll wait. Provided I am not summoned away while ye are busy.'

'You cannot ignore a summons?'

'Never. 'Tis a compulsion, an' I must obey it. But as I'm thinkin' I mentioned before, 'tis rare t' receive a summons, nowadays.'

'I shall make haste,' Isabel said, and with a curtsey, turned back to the palace.

A few minutes later, she once again entered the Chronicler's Tower. The Keeper had faded away; she summoned him once more with a palm to the glyph, and said without delay: 'The answer is Celadon, sir.'

The dragon smiled toothily at her. 'A resourceful English miss, and very quick work! Do you know why the answer is Celadon?'

'Why… no, I'm afraid I do not,' Isabel faltered. 'Oh, dear. Was that part of the test as well?'

'No, you have passed the test!' said the Keeper enthusiastically. 'But it is all very interesting! You see, Greyling is so-called because it is a colourless place; not in Aylfenhame, precisely, but Otherwhere. Seven colonies of faeflies live there — one for each of the Seven Shades, you understand. They are usually in hibernation, but one colony is woken from time to time in order that they might spin the finest and fairest of fibres for the Queen's gowns. Beings of purest magic, these! When their task is done they drift away, far and far, and their wings turn in hues related to the—'

'My good fellow,' came Grunewald's voice from behind Isabel. 'As interesting as all of this is, I believe the lady is in something of a hurry.'

Isabel resisted an urge to thank the Goblin King, for a sense of urgency was gnawing at her, but she did not like to interrupt the Keeper.

With good reason, for the Keeper swelled with disgust at Grunewald's words, and rose higher into the air. 'This is why you will never be permitted inside!' he said, his misty coils quivering with anger.

'Because I am impatient? Yes, yes. I dare say I shall go on living without the scintillating experience of an hour spent perusing your dusty scrolls. But do let the lady pass.'

The Keeper scowled upon Isabel, and huffed cloudily. Without uttering another word, the mist-dragon rushed at Isabel, engulfing her in a foggy haze, and an instant later she was elsewhere. The chamber resembled the Keeper's room, only it was much larger. The round walls went up and up, and the ceiling seemed impossibly distant. Those walls were lined with shelves, each containing a neat row of scrolls tied with ribbon. There were no ladders that Isabel could see; no way at all of reaching the upper shelves, in fact.

'Now, then,' said the Keeper crisply, in a tone markedly less friendly than before. 'You will want History, Fourth Era. Third shelf, Saffron.' The dragon sailed airily upwards towards a shelf of scrolls tied with saffron-coloured ribbons, which intrigued Isabel; shades and hues was an odd way to organise a library. She received the impression that colours were of some degree of importance to the royal family of Aylfenhame, though she could not conceive of how or why.

The Keeper hovered some way above Isabel's head for a few minutes, and Isabel watched as scrolls detached themselves from the shelves and began to hover alongside him. At last he seemed satisfied, and drifted back down to Isabel's level once more. The scrolls descended along with him.

'These are not to be removed from the library,' the Keeper said sternly, as the scrolls laid themselves in Isabel's hands. 'If the answer to your question is in my library at all, it will be found in these documents.'

Isabel thanked the Keeper-dragon with her best smile, hoping to soothe his irritated feelings with courtesy and congeniality. He did perhaps deflate a little, though his friendly demeanour did not return.

'You will find tables to your left,' the dragon said crisply. 'And—'

The Keeper broke off abruptly, staring hard at something over Isabel's shoulder. She turned, but could see nothing save for more shelves and tables. When she turned back to the Keeper, she discovered that he had swollen to five times his previous size and was still expanding. Worse, the mists that made up his ethereal form were turning dark, angry red.

'TRESPASS!' the Keeper bellowed. 'GUARDS!'

The library, so empty and tranquil before, was suddenly awash with dragons. More solid than the Keeper, these were coloured in various shades of red and orange and snarling with aggression. Isabel whirled, confused, as the whole pack of them streamed in the direction the Keeper had been staring.

The lead dragon's jaws snapped shut upon empty air — at least, so it appeared. But Isabel could see that it had captured something in its jaws — something fairly small and presumably solid, though invisible.

'SHOW YOURSELF AT ONCE!' bellowed the Keeper.

Nothing happened for a moment. Then, slowly, a figure materialised. It was less than three feet tall, dark of skin and hair, with an enormous hat and equally oversized shoes. It carried a horn in one hand.

A trow, Isabel realised, and an instant later: Palchis. One of Grunewald's entourage.

'The library will CLOSE!' screamed the Keeper. 'Instantly! Expelled, every one of you!'

CHAPTER ELEVEN

The Keeper began to spin in his rage, and within moments a fine whirlwind was sailing around the library, sending scrolls flying wildly through the air. Isabel barely ducked in time to avoid receiving two particularly large, heavy-looking scrolls in the face. Heart pounding, she clutched her saffron scrolls closely to her chest and looked around desperately for a way out. There was no door that she could see, nor any other means of egress. There wasn't even a window.

The Keeper howled something inarticulate, and a red fog enveloped Isabel. Panicking, she gripped her scrolls all the tighter and shut her eyes, gasping for breath as she was caught up in a swirling wind. It stopped abruptly moments later, and she opened her eyes to find herself restored to the Keeper's chamber.

Sophy was staring at her in amazed concern, but Grunewald, Ertof and Yangveld did not look at all surprised at her sudden reappearance.

'Are you well?' Sophy said, approaching with hands outstretched. Isabel could well imagine the picture she presented: her hair and bonnet disordered by the wild winds of the Keeper's fury, her face a mask of shock and dismay, her arms full of tumbled scrolls.

'Oh, Grunewald!' Isabel gasped, casting him a look of strong reproach. 'How could you!'

'Palchis?' was all that he said in response.

'Still inside,' Isabel said, and turned her back on him.

Grunewald cursed. He added as an aside, 'I am sorry, Miss Ellerby, but it is more important than you can know.'

Isabel made no answer. It had occurred to her that the Keeper, highly paranoid about unauthorised entrance to his precious library, would suspect a collaboration between the two English women and the Goblin King. 'We must depart at once,' she said to Sophy, and immediately darted towards the staircase. Tafferty bounded before her as she ran down the stairs, and she heard Sophy's footsteps behind.

To Isabel's relief, the Ferryman was still awaiting her outside the palace. Better still, he had possessed the forethought to lead her mount and Sophy's into the boat. 'Sir Guntifer!' Isabel called. 'To the boat, and quickly!' She looked behind herself, fervently praying not to see the Keeper streaming after her — or any of his frightening tower-guards. She was absconding with some of his precious scrolls! She could hardly believe it of herself, but after all the trouble of gaining access to the library, she could not bear to leave behind the information which might save the Ferryman. Particularly since Palchis's intrusion had not been either of her choice or her making!

She saw no sign of pursuit, but she did not slow her pace as she ran towards the boat. She tipped her armful of scrolls into the Ferryman's hands and stumbled aboard, drawing Sophy after her. Sir Guntifer was close behind, Pinch and Pinket streaming after him in matching wisp-shape. For a moment she was worried that the giant would not fit in the boat at all, and indeed, the Ferryman stared at him in open consternation. But Sir Guntifer turned himself into his giant's shape entirely, shedding his bark and branches, and somehow contrived to squeeze himself aboard.

'Go!' said Isabel breathlessly.

The Ferryman nodded, paused only to drop the scrolls into the bottom of the boat, and then set about the process of departure. Banks of cloud rolled in, quickly obscuring everything that lay outside the boat, and the craft began to rise.

'I take it,' said the Ferryman as he sat wearily down, 'that all did not proceed as ye had planned?'

Isabel realised that her knees were shaking, and quickly sat down herself. 'The Goblin King,' she said tightly, 'ruined our venture.' She recounted what had happened, and the Ferryman listened with arms folded.

'No doubt he has some purpose,' said the Ferryman once Isabel had finished.

'How wretched of him,' Sophy sighed. 'Tiresome man. But you retrieved something!' She bent down to the mass of ageing paper and saffron ribbons, and extracted the nearest scroll. 'It is very delicate,' she said, clearly changing her mind about unrolling it. 'They had better not be opened here, I think.'

'Aye, an' ye cannot leave them wi' me anyhow,' said the Ferryman. 'I have no place t' hide 'em.' He cocked his head at Isabel, and added, 'Fer that matter: where are we goin'?'

'To Grenlowe, I suppose.' Isabel felt as tired as the Ferryman looked, worn out by travel and care. Though she knew that the ruckus in the Tower had been none of her doing, and had come to pass without her advance knowledge, she felt a vague sense of guilt at having been the unwitting cause of the mess. She did not know why the Keeper had reacted so violently, but she supposed that the Tower must contain a great deal of important and sensitive information. What Grunewald precisely wanted, and whether it would pose any danger to anyone were he to acquire it, she could not say. But she knew that the Goblin King was not always the congenial, if sarcastic, gentleman she usually found him to be. Whatever his purpose was, it might be harmless — or it might be dark indeed.

'Yes, let us return home,' agreed Sophy. 'No more may be done abroad today, I think.'

The journey from Mirramay to Grenlowe was surprisingly short. Isabel was struck, and realised anew how lengthy was the delay the Ferryman had wilfully imposed upon her passage from England. He appeared to recollect it too, for he winked at her as the boat descended into the meadow on the edge of the town, and smiled. 'I 'ad a desire t' detain ye as before, but I must not, must I? Ye 'ave done enough fer me as it is, an' I must release ye t' yer business elsewhere.'

Isabel smiled, and blushed a little. How odd, that he should be so desirous of her company! For it did not seem that he felt the same temptation in Sophy's case. 'I wish I might stay, sir,' she said seriously. 'But I must not, indeed.'

He nodded gravely, his hands tucked into the pockets of his trousers, and heaved a great, exaggerated sigh. 'Aye, then, 'tis back t' my loneliness.'

Isabel winced, and attempted to conceal her distress by fidgeting with her reticule. 'I would stay if I could,' she said, without looking at him.

'Would ye?' said the Ferryman softly. 'An' why is that?'

'I do not like to think of you… of anyone, adrift in the world without companionship. And without the freedom to go in search of it, either.' She kept her gaze fixed upon the ribbon of her bag as she spoke, her fingers working to loosen a knot which had unaccountably become ensnarled within it. But a gentle touch upon her chin compelled her to raise her face, and she found the Ferryman looking closely at her.

'Ye are a mite unusual,' he said in a thoughtful tone, his gaze taking in every part of her face. 'Are all the ladies of England like ye?'

'They are not, sir,' said Sophy. Isabel could hear the smile in her voice. 'I can take it upon myself to assure you that Isabel is unique. There is no other heart like hers.'

The Ferryman glanced Sophy's way, then returned to his scrutiny of Isabel's face. She was growing uncomfortable with both his attention and his proximity, and took a step backwards. He smiled down at her. 'We are embarrassin' the lady wi' such talk. Fortunately, it is time t' expel ye all from my keepin', an' let ye go home.'

Isabel said nothing, torn between relief and disappointment. Moments later Isabel was being handed out, Sophy directly behind her. Sir Guntifer, silent and stoic, had already descended, the two pixies ensconced upon his shoulders. Both ladies curtseyed politely to the Ferryman, who doffed his hat in response. It seemed to Isabel that he smiled particularly at her before he turned away.

They watched as the boat rose into the skies and disappeared into a bank of clouds. Then Sophy took Isabel's arm and turned her in the direction of her home.

'Ye must stay safely behind me, ladies, I pray,' said Sir Guntifer.

'Aye!' cried Pinch. 'For we are in the wildest of wilds, you know, and there is no telling what catastrophes could befall us here!' He looked around at the serene meadow as he spoke, brandishing an imaginary rapier and twirling the feather of an imaginary hat.

'It is kind of you to escort us, Sir Guntifer,' said Sophy firmly, ignoring Pinch. 'You have performed your task kindly indeed; particularly so, considering that it was not of your choosing.'

Sir Guntifer bowed to her. 'Balligumph was a rogue to so force me from my sloth, but it was not misguided in him. I am truly awake, and it has been a century since I last swept the cobwebs from my eyes.'

'I am delighted if it has been of some service to you,' said Sophy with a smile. 'Never have I felt so safe as under your kind care! We will be glad of your escort to Silverling, and I hope you will accept some refreshment once we arrive.'

Sir Guntifer inclined his head with utmost politeness, but Pinch gave a horrified gasp. 'Refreshments!' he repeated. 'And not to be offered to us! For shame! We are hardly used indeed. And after we ran off the trows, too!' He shot a dark look at Pinket, who merely smiled gently back.

'How wretchedly rude!' Sophy protested. 'I had not forgotten the two of you, though I am minded to do so after such a speech as that.'

Pinch slumped down upon Sir Guntifer's shoulder and crossed his tiny arms, sullen. 'All right, I apologise.'

He was prevented from making any further comments as Sir Guntifer strode away, and at no inconsiderable pace. Isabel was left to the peace of Sophy's company, and immediately took her friend's arm.

Sophy smiled at her. 'I do believe you have impressed the good Ferryman,' she said conversationally as they walked towards Grenlowe.

'I imagine he is very lonely,' said Isabel.

'Undoubtedly, poor fellow. However, he has most assuredly not developed the same degree of interest in me. It might simply be because you are by far the prettier of the two of us, but I will do him the justice to assume that he has discerned the merits of your character.'

'Merits which you do not possess?' Isabel protested. 'The greatest nonsense, Sophy! You are the kindest person I know.'

'Besides your own self, you mean. And you are certainly the most modest. Consider! You no sooner meet him and hear his story than you are sorely afflicted with compassion for his plight, and promise to help him. That alone is far more than anyone else has ever done, I would wager. But that is not all! For it was no empty promise. You went as far as Mirramay in search of his name, faced down the mighty Keeper of the Chronicles and emerged with a promising armful of scrolls which you abstracted from right under that worthy's nose. Which, by the by, is the greatest transgression I have ever known you to make, and I am proud of you!' She squeezed Isabel's arm, and continued, 'I might even be inclined to conclude that the Ferryman has impressed you as well.'

Isabel suppressed a familiar urge to apologise for her conduct, and sought for a safe reply. 'I do feel for him, but I would feel the same pity for anyone in his situation. It is very hard.'

'It is a hard fate, indeed. Especially so, perhaps, when it befalls a gentleman who is both handsome and amiable, and who possess besides a great deal of wit to recommend him.'

'He is of the Ayliri, Sophy!'

'You have Aylir blood! Did you forget? And the powers of witchery besides. It is not so inconceivable a match.'

Isabel was silent. She had forgotten — or dismissed it from her mind. Lurking somewhere inside was a vague sense of trepidation as to what her mother and father would say when they learned the truth about their daughter — if they learned the truth. Should she tell them? Would Aunt Grey tell them? Perhaps she had already done so. Perhaps their reaction awaited her upon her return.

Her stomach clenched at the thought. They would be... angry. Perhaps. Hers had been a careful upbringing; they had sought to prepare her to take her position in society, and at a higher station than their own. At best, her witching powers were an intolerable distraction, at a time when all of her powers ought to be exerted to please Mr. Thompson — or another, still more eligible, suitor. At worst, her heritage may prove to be unattractive. The Ayliri were not hated in England, but they were poorly understood, and many people scarcely knew they existed. They were not loved, and not trusted. How would society view the intrusion of Ayliri blood into their own circles? Would she still be considered marriageable, when any children of hers would share that same heritage, and possibly inherit the powers that sometimes occurred along with it?

Isabel herself was frightened of these possibilities, though she had hesitated to name them to herself. She did so now, and quailed. If the path in life that had been so clearly marked out for her were to fail, what would she do? What could she do? For she had no option but marriage. No woman in her position could accept with equanimity the prospect of a celibate existence. Her fortune was not equal to it, and she lacked the extensive education necessary to seek a post as a governess — even supposing she could wish for such a life, which she could not. Marriage was the only choice she had.

'That cannot be, Sophy,' said Isabel. 'Even supposing you are right, and I am by no means certain that you are. I am not fitted for this world. I was made for other things.'

'I was not fitted for this world, either, but I have made myself a part of it. Your destiny is your own, Isa. It is not for anyone else to decide your future for you; not even your mother and father. Much as I respect them, I agree with your aunt. I cannot stand idly by and permit them, or anybody else, to dictate your choices.'

'Perhaps my choices are the same as theirs.'

Sophy stopped walking, and looked seriously at her friend. 'If they are, and sincerely so, then I will urge you no more.'

'They… they are,' said Isabel, rather without the certainty she had hoped to convey. 'I am not unhappy with my father's choice of husband for me, nor with my mother's expectations. Her life has been happy, I believe, and I have no reason to imagine mine will be less so.'

Sophy frowned as the words not unhappy passed Isabel's lips, and she indulged in a moment's silent thought before replying. 'It had not previously occurred to me to bless the circumstances that brought me here. My father's death, my lack of prospects — it was a frightening time for me. But it had one advantage, in that it compelled me to think differently about the world, and the alternatives that I had before me. Blessed as you are in wealth, comfort, beauty and all the prospects I did not have, you are unhappily circumstanced in that respect. You have nothing to force you to be brave.'

'I do not lack courage, Sophy!' Isabel protested, stung.

Sophy raised a brow at her. 'I would like you to be more than merely not unhappy,' she said. 'So would your aunt. So would all who care for your happiness.'

'My mother and father do care for my happiness.'

Sophy said no more. They walked in silence through the streets of Grenlowe, following in Sir Guntifer's wake, until they arrived at the door of Silverling. Sophy immediately disappeared inside, with a quiet word to Sir Guntifer as she passed him. She did not invite him in, simply because he was too big to fit into the little shop. But Pinch and Pinket clambered down from his shoulders and followed Sophy inside.

Isabel paused to make her own thanks to Sir Guntifer. He was a kind soul, and his courtly manners pleased her. His great green eyes twinkled down at her as she spoke, and he made her a bow.

'Tis a kindness in thee,' he said, 'thine efforts to extract the Ferryman from the confines of his miserable curse. I heard his speech to thee. It was correct of him to speak so, for few would do as thou hast done. I wish thee success upon thy quest.'

Isabel curtseyed, touched. There was not time for more, as Sophy re-emerged at that moment with a great platter in her two hands. The plate was heaped with delicacies; judging by their aroma, they were fresh from the oven. Isabel recognised the piles of cakes, tarts and tiny pies as the work of Mary and the brownie Thundigle, who between them produced treats as extraordinary in their way as were Sophy's gowns. It crossed Isabel's mind to wonder whether the giant, half-tree as he was, would be tempted by such viands as this. Apparently he was, for Sir Guntifer accepted the offering with a smile of pleasure.

'Isabel,' Sophy said next, turning to her. She put into her hands a letter, saying, 'This arrived but this morning. It appears it is urgent.'

The letter was an odd one. It was but a small piece of paper, and folded smaller still. The paper, meanwhile, was oddly translucent, and shimmered faintly. It opened easily the moment Isabel's fingers touched it; against her hands it felt as soft as silk. A few lines were written upon the letter in neat, elegant script.

My dear Isabel. It pains me to urge your return so soon, as I had hoped to allow you some two or three weeks in Aylfenhame. But alas, my resources are quite at an end! I cannot much longer conceal your whereabouts from your mother and father. I leave it to you, my dear, to decide upon an appropriate course of action. - E. G.

Isabel folded the letter and put it into her reticule. If she understood the missive correctly, she had little time in which to return home — if she wished to keep the secret of her adventure from her mother and father. She concluded from this that her aunt had not confided in her sister and brother-in-law regarding Isabel's heritage, and nor would she without Isabel's concurrence.

This relieved Isabel considerably, but it also heightened her sense of urgency. She must return at once, but how was she to do so? The Ferryman had only just departed. He would not wish to return for her so soon.

Isabel showed the note to Sophy, who read it quickly and then met Isabel's eyes with a questioning look.

'I will go,' said Isabel.

Sophy nodded. 'I am sorry for it, for I shall miss you! But I will see you on the next Solstice.'

'Yes.' Isabel frowned as she spoke the word, and hesitated. 'Sophy, it is possible that I shall be married by that time. And I do not know… that is, I am not sure if I shall have the same freedom to visit you, as I have before.' Freedom was a misleading term, as her mother and father had not precisely liked her venturing into Aylfenhame, even if it was to visit a person so well known to them as Sophy. But they had permitted it. Whether her husband would do so likewise was another question. Her heart sank a little at the thought, but she concealed her distress, and mustered a smile. 'I shall always do my best to see you.'

Sophy made no answer to this, merely looking at Isabel in silence. 'I have a gift for you,' she said at last, and beckoned Isabel inside.

Isabel paused to bid farewell to Sir Guntifer, who was still busily employed in the delectation of the treats Sophy had provided. She entered Sophy's shop, and was immediately presented with a wrapped package.

'Open it when you arrive at home,' Sophy said, putting the gift into Isabel's hands. 'Or it will take far too long to wrap it up again.'

Isabel stared at the parcel. It was a box, moderately sized, and wrapped up in paper as delicate and shimmery as a dragonfly's wing. 'May I know what it is?'

'I will leave it as a surprise, and only say this: It is in exchange for a kindness you once did me.' Mary entered as Sophy finished speaking, and gave to Isabel a large, prettily embroidered band-box. 'Take that away with you, my dear girl,' said Mary with a wink. 'All them fine, pretty bits are in it.'

'The dresses! But no, Sophy! You will perhaps wish to sell them.'

'I made them for you,' Sophy said, laughing. 'How like you to try to give them back! No, please. They were made with love, and fitted to precisely your measurements. I could not sell them even if I wished to.'

And so Isabel was obliged to depart, laden down with gifts, her heart overflowing with a mixture of gratitude and an obscure feeling of guilt for all the trouble her friends had gone to for her sake. Moreover, she was now obliged to summon the Ferryman once more, and so soon after his departure. She hoped he would not be angry with her, but what could she do? She had no other means of returning home, and he had said that he had been engaged to escort her home. And paid for it, too, though she could not imagine what he had been paid with. Did the Ferryman accept ordinary currency? Could he use it, in his condition?

She thought of the scrolls she had taken from the library, and hesitated. To leave Aylfenhame without the Ferryman's name, and with no prospects of a near return! It was a great shame, to be sure, but the urgency of her aunt's message swiftly banished any thoughts of studying the scrolls prior to her departure. She carefully unrolled one of them, thinking perhaps to breeze speedily through it in search of the relevant passages. But a glance dispelled that notion as well, for the scroll was so densely scribed, and written in such minute, and peculiar, characters, that nothing would serve to decipher its contents but a period of prolonged perusal. As near as she could imagine, it would take hours to read even a single one of the pile of scrolls she had acquired. The task would have to wait. She consoled herself with the reflection that she still possessed the whistle, and might summon the Ferryman to England the instant she learned his name.

This decision made, Isabel paused only long enough to make a final request of Sophy, as Sir Guntifer's obvious relish of his platter of delicacies inspired her with an idea. And then, with some regret, she turned away from Silverling, unsure when — or even if — she would be able to return.

Sophy walked with her back to the outskirts of Grenlowe, until they reached an open space where the boat might land. Isabel raised the whistle to her lips with more than a little trepidation, and blew. The ferry appeared in the skies almost at once; he had not been far away, then. She waited, her heart pounding unaccountably, as it sailed gracefully down from the skies and came to rest among the tall gold-and-green grasses of the Grenlowe meadows.

The Ferryman tipped his hat to her. 'Ye could not live without my company!' he said, with a wide smile. 'I admit, I 'ad suspected it might be the case.'

Isabel was so relieved, she laughed. 'I am so sorry! Only I received word as soon as I arrived, and my return is expected at once.'

He assumed a tragic air. 'Ah, so! Naught to do wi' me after all. My heart is fully broken.' He jumped down from the boat and extended his hand to Isabel, winking at Sophy as he helped Isabel aboard. 'So ye're t' lose yer friend already, Miss Sophy? A pity.'

'Indeed, I shall miss her very much,' Sophy said. 'But I am sure you will bear her good company on the journey home.'

'That I shall, to be sure.' The Ferryman bowed to Sophy, lifted Tafferty aboard and vaulted after, and soon they were away once more. Isabel watched, feeling more than a little forlorn, as Sophy's tall, wind-blown figure receded, and finally disappeared from sight.

CHAPTER TWELVE

'I have brought something for you,' Isabel said, and offered the Ferryman a small box. The contents had been her last-minute request of Sophy, and she hoped it would please.

His brows rose in surprise, and he quickly opened it. A delicious aroma of freshly-baked pastry drifted out.

'This… this is food,' said the Ferryman in a faint voice.

'Some of the best food,' Isabel agreed with a smile. 'Made by Mary and Thundigle, of Sophy's household. They are very talented.' Sophy and Isabel had packed the box themselves, cramming as much into it as they could manage to fit. There were iced berry pies, moonweed tarts with marzipan, pastries stuffed with rose apples and drizzled with syrup, and finally — Sophy's favourites — cheerful little sun cakes.

The Ferryman lifted out a tiny pie and stared at it in awe, then carried it to his nose and inhaled deeply. 'It is years since I ate,' he said.

Isabel stared at him in horror. 'Years! But how can you live without food?'

He shrugged. ''Tis part o' the curse. It holds me in a kind o' stasis, ye could say. I don't even sleep, in the true sense o' the word. More like a state of… blankness.' He took a moment to enjoy a bite of the pie, his eyes closing in ecstasy. 'I had forgotten.'

He had forgotten food?

'How long have you been under the curse?' Isabel asked.

'In terms ye would understand? I don't know. What year is it wi' ye?'

'In England, it is the year 1812.'

The Ferryman devoured the rest of the pie in one bite, and followed it with a pastry. 'Near enough a century, I reckon,' he said, in between bites. 'Give or take a decade or two.' He wolfed down a few more treats, then firmly closed the box and set it aside. 'I 'ad better slow down,' he said with a grin. 'Wouldn't do t' overdo it. Besides, t' eat before a lady when she is not eatin' likewise is no manner o' courtesy, so I understand. Will ye not share the goodies?'

Isabel smiled and declined. 'I think a hundred-year abstinence excuses you from ordinary etiquette.'

'Why, no!' he said. 'Nothin' excuses a gentleman from courtesy.' He gestured to the bag and band-box she had laid in the bottom of the boat. 'Those yer scrolls?'

'They are not precisely my scrolls, no. But they are the ones that I took.' She coloured as she said it, with guilt and shame.

The Ferryman did not look appalled, however. He looked at her with a glow of admiration. 'Ye 'ave thieved fer me!' he exclaimed in delight. 'An' ye look right ashamed o' yerself.'

'I am! Taking anything without permission can never be considered acceptable conduct, regardless of one's motive.'

'Then why did ye do it?'

Isabel paused to consider. 'I cannot answer you,' she said finally. 'I suppose I acted impulsively.'

'First time in yer life, eh?'

'Why, of course it is not. There must be some other occasion when I have acted without thinking.'

The Ferryman crossed his arms and made a show of waiting. 'Very well. I'll hold a moment while ye search yer memory.'

Isabel thought, and failed to think of a single occasion when she had ever done anything so rash. 'Oh, very well,' she said with a sigh. 'You are right. Aylfenhame is a strange place! I do not feel like myself here.'

'I like yer Aylfenhame self.'

'Even though I am a thief?'

'Especially because ye are a thief, an' on my miserable behalf.'

'I am no thief,' Isabel said, disliking the term in spite of the levity of the Ferryman's tone. 'I shall return the scrolls someday.'

He smiled at her. 'I 'ave not the smallest doubt of it. What will ye do when ye reach England?'

'I will return to my aunt's house.'

He nodded slowly. 'That tells me exactly nothin' at all. What do ye do at yer aunt's house?'

'Oh! Well, we will pay morning calls upon her friends, and attend dinners and evening parties. Perhaps we will walk a little in the city, when the weather is fine.'

'Sounds rivetin'.'

Isabel smiled. 'It is not as exciting as dashing around Aylfenhame stealing scrolls and travelling by flying boat, indeed. But it is my world.'

'Is there dancin', at least?'

'Sometimes there is. I do not know if there will be any dancing in York, before I return to Lincolnshire. It is not really the season for it.'

'Well, that's somethin'. An' how do ye dance, in England?'

'One dances with a partner, alongside many other couples. The steps are complicated, sometimes, but it is pleasant.'

'Ye 'ave just described virtually every form o' dancin' I ever heard of.'

Isabel laughed. 'I dare say I have, but I cannot describe it any better.'

'Then ye must show me.'

Isabel stared. 'But I cannot, by myself.'

The Ferryman took her hands and drew her to her feet. 'Indeed, ye cannot. So ye must teach me.'

'There... there is not space, here,' Isabel said, looking around in confusion.

'A moment, then.' The Ferryman waved a hand, and the boat shimmered and reformed itself, stretching wider by several feet. 'There, will that do?'

Isabel watched helplessly as her only viable excuse dissolved. 'I cannot, sir!' she said. 'It would hardly be proper.'

He smiled at her, his eyes twinkling. 'Oh, propriety! 'Tis hardly proper t' take scrolls from the Keeper's Library either, but so ye did. Would it be so very bad t' dance wi' me?'

Isabel bit her lip. Would it be? She had already committed a much greater transgression, and who would know, save her own self?

Tafferty, curled up near to Isabel's feet, nudged her ankle with her cool nose. 'Thou'rt inclined. Why dost thou not consent?'

'Very well,' Isabel said softly, and guided the Ferryman into place opposite her. 'We begin thus.'

The Ferryman proved to be an adept pupil, agile and light on his feet. The lesson progressed easily and well, and Isabel forgot all about York and her aunt for some considerable time.

At length, her breath grew short from exertion and her legs began to ache. These dual pains recalled her to herself, and she said with a gasp, 'We have been too long at work, I think!'

The Ferryman sighed, and stepped back. 'I was hopin' ye'd fail t' notice fer a while yet.'

'It has been a while.' Isabel smoothed her gown and patted her hair; finding, to her dismay, that the latter was indeed disordered.

'Ye look very well,' he said, sinking his hands into his pockets as he watched her. 'More'n well. I like ye a little less neat. It means ye've been doin' things of an amusin' sort o' nature.' He grinned, and she could not help smiling back.

'Perhaps it does. Though how I am to explain to my aunt how my hair came to be so blown-about, I do not know.'

'Yer passage in a flyin' boat isn't explanation enough?'

'Perhaps.' She looked around, observing that thick mists still entirely cloaked the boat. 'We are somewhere within the vicinity of England, I suppose?'

'Vaguely.' He sighed. 'Nay, it must be the truth. In point o' fact we are right above the spot where I first took ye up.'

'We have been here for some little time, I imagine?'

'Aye. Rather a while.'

Isabel attempted to look severe, but she could not muster the resolution, for it had been a very pleasant while. 'Will you let me down now?'

'I suppose that I must.' He looked at her in silence for a long moment. 'I've a question fer ye first.'

Isabel inclined her head. 'Very well.'

'Will ye come back?'

'To Aylfenhame?'

'Aye. To Aylfenhame… and t' me. Is this, in short, the last time I am t' expect t' see ye?'

'I should imagine not. I will be obliged to return once more, in order to deliver your name.'

'Obliged.' He nodded thoughtfully, then indicated her bag of scrolls with a jut of his chin. 'Ye're certain t' find it in there, then?'

'The Keeper knows his art, I am sure. If he believes I might find your name in there, then I have some hopes that he will be correct.'

'An' if he isn't?'

'I will search on.'

He smiled, but sadly, and half-hearted. 'Very well.'

'You think I will forget, or give up. But I will not! That I promise.'

The Ferryman took a step towards her, took both of her hands, and kissed each in turn. 'I will not blame ye if ye should,' he said seriously, looking into her eyes. 'Know that. Yer choices are yer own, an' I will not have ye bound t' assist me. I know well that yer life is very different from mine. What ye promise now, ye may not be able t' perform.'

Isabel returned the pressure of his fingers, briefly, before gently disengaging her hands. 'I will not forget, at the least. I could not forget you, I think.'

'Ye think.' His eyes gleamed with amusement.

'You must not tease me so badly,' she said, laughing. 'I think I could not forget so unusual a person as you. After all, you have a flying boat.'

He laughed, and touched his forehead in salute. 'Aye! True enough. Yer fine gentlemen of England, now. They'd have a hard time matchin' that.'

'They would indeed.'

'Though it isn't altogether right t' say that I 'ave a flyin' boat. More that it 'as me. But, it is home.'

'You do wish to be liberated?' Isabel said, with sudden concern.

'Oh, I do. I do.' The Ferryman eyed her for a moment. 'I am goin' t' do somethin' I should not.'

'We have already done a number of things we should not have.'

'Aye, but I can do worse yet.' He took her face in his hands and stroked his thumbs over her cheeks, very gently. Surprised, Isabel froze in his grip, and made no move to retreat; not even when he lowered his head to hers and kissed her.

He held her that way for some moments, before releasing her face with a sigh. 'Now, I would love t' know. Did ye let me get away wi' that because I took ye by surprise? Because ye did not wish t' offend me, wi' yer odd notions o' courtesy? Or because ye wanted me t' kiss ye?'

Isabel stepped back, her cheeks aflame, and said nothing. She could not even meet his eye. She had been surprised, but that had only been half of the reason why she had not prevented him. She could hardly admit that to him, however.

'Ye'll not answer. Aye, well. That's fair enough.'

'She will not, but I can.' Tafferty spoke from the corner into which she had tucked herself, surprising Isabel; to her shame, she had all but forgotten her companion's presence. The catterdandy rose and stretched luxuriously. 'She is adept at pretendin' not to think anythin' that might be considered inappropriate. But she'd have pushed thee away fast enough, if she were disinclined-like.'

Isabel scowled at Tafferty, who ignored her discontent with supreme indifference and began to wash. The Ferryman was looking at her again, enquiringly this time, but she could not answer him. She busied herself with collecting together her few possessions in preparation for departure.

The Ferryman turned away, and at the same moment Isabel became aware that the boat had begun its descent. Soon she could see the serene countryside of Yorkshire through the thinning mists.

'I am sorry,' she said softly. It did not begin to cover everything she wanted to say to him, but it was all she could muster.

'Nay, don't be sorry.' He flashed her a brief smile. 'I should not 'ave done that, an' I know it. I apologise.'

Isabel opened her mouth to reply, without having the smallest notion what she would say. But she was saved from having to speak, as the boat came to rest just off the York road. She was relieved to see her aunt's carriage awaiting her nearby.

She curtseyed to the Ferryman. 'I thank you for your kindness. You have been very patient with my various demands!'

'It had naught t' do wi' patience, as ye well know. But yer welcome.' He bowed to her, then helped her to gather her possessions. 'I'll bid ye farewell, then, an' hope t' see ye again someday. If I should not, though… I wish nothin' but happiness fer ye.'

'You will,' Isabel said simply. 'When I bring you your name.'

He tipped his hat to her, and helped her down from the boat. Mrs. Grey's footman opened the carriage door for her and assisted her inside. Isabel had time only to wave once from the window as the

Ferryman's boat soared away into the skies, and she was not even sure that he had seen.

She sat back with a sigh as the coachman spurred the horses into motion, and the carriage began to move. It was a relief to her to see familiar countryside around her, and to be on her way home. She felt comfortable and safe, two feelings she had not experienced since she had first boarded the Ferryman's boat.

But part of her heart was heavy, too. She had left Sophy behind, of course; that would be enough to dishearten her alone. She missed Sophy, very much.

The Ferryman had nothing at all to do with it. No matter that his laughing smile filled her mind at this moment, nor that she could not seem to help remembering his most reprehensible kiss. All that was mere nonsense, and would soon fade from her thoughts.

She tried to fix her mind upon Sophy, and sighed.

'Was I right?' said Tafferty, from her position upon the seat next to Isabel.

She did not need to ask what the catterdandy was referring to. 'I shall not answer that,' Isabel said with dignity.

'I thought so.' Tafferty licked her lips in a cat-like smile, then curled up against Isabel's hip.

Mrs. Grey greeted Isabel's return with rapturous enthusiasm, which was of some use in distracting her from her lowness of spirits.

'I could not precisely decide whether I wished for your speedy return, or not,' said Mrs. Grey as she kissed Isabel's cheek and handed her band-box to a maid. 'But I am happy to see you! A great many things have happened since your departure.'

'I hardly know how long I have been gone,' said Isabel, removing her bonnet and spencer with relief, for the morning was warm.

'Almost a week, my dearest love. And I am impatient to hear every detail of your adventures in that time! But first I must apprise you of how matters stand here, and at Tilby. You will be interested to know that you have been abed with a cold for several days, and your mama became insistent about coming here to nurse you. But you are quite recovered as of this morning, and perfectly fit to attend dinner at the Thompsons' this evening.'

'How tiresome an indisposition,' Isabel said, with a smile. 'And to keep me abed nearly a week!'

'Yes. How wretched for you to miss so much of your visit to your dear aunt! But you have the sweetest disposition, and suffered with perfect patience. I applaud you. Come into the parlour, there is tea ready.'

Isabel followed her aunt to the table, and partook of tea and other refreshments most gratefully.

'Now, my dear. You will remember that the matter of the piper was not to be spoken of, when last I saw you? Though I was so discourteous as to press you on the subject. That is all forgotten, for the piper and his merry group have been seen again! More than once!' She sat back, lifting her cup to her lips as she awaited Isabel's reaction.

'Again!' cried Isabel. 'But where? And how? What did they do?' She was as eager for information as her aunt could wish, for the interlopers at the Alford Assembly had intrigued her more than she cared to admit. The Ferryman had distracted her some long while, and driven recollections of the earlier incident from her mind; but she had not forgotten the piper's strange music, nor the way his intense eyes had, for a brief instant, stared into hers at the ball.

'There are reports that they were seen in Lincoln, just five days ago. At the Assembly Rooms! And it was just as it was in Alford. The orchestra was quite taken over, and the dancers as wild and enchanting as you described! And then again in Gainsborough, and at Wentworth Castle. And finally, just two days ago, at Sir Edward's private ball at Hayworth Lodge! There is no telling where they may appear next, and it is all anybody has talked of this past week.' She set down her tea cup, beaming at Isabel. 'Theirs appears to be a generally northward journey, does it not? I have high hopes that they may yet appear in York! And so, my love, I think we must steel ourselves to appear at as many evening parties, dinners and balls as we may, for they do not appear to be at all particular as to the nature of the occasions they attend.'

'You are excited to see them, are you, aunt?' Isabel sipped tea, and tried to appear composed as she thought over this news. Her heart had quickened a little, and she was conscious of a flutter of excitement. How very odd! For she had looked forward to a return to her peaceful world of quiet social engagements, country walks and evenings at home with her family. But the prospect of attending another event with the piper and his dancers thrilled her immeasurably.

'Very!' said Mrs. Grey. 'I confess I am! I had not thought ever to experience any part of Aylfenhame again, having given it up. Excepting Vershibat, of course.' She nodded towards her companion, who was supping vigorously from a tiny plate of fruit. A much larger platter sat adjacent to it, from which Tafferty was refreshing herself. They made a curious sight, Isabel reflected, looking upon them. A tiny green-furred, shrew-like creature and a cattish animal with the wildest colours, side-by-side and at peace, here in a perfectly ordinary English parlour. Brownies she was used to encountering in most households; the likes of these denizens of Aylfenhame, never at all.

'Do you miss it?' Isabel said.

Mrs. Grey nodded once. 'I do.'

Isabel did not enquire further. She did not need to. Aylfenhame had a way of capturing her interest, whether or not she wished it to. She thought back to something Sophy had said on Isabel's first visit to her at Silverling. Aylfenhame will catch at you, if you let it. And it can be… unwise, to eat or drink here. It changes you. Do you still wish to stay?

Isabel had agreed, for how could she do otherwise? To refuse was to give up Sophy. She had not really expected to be much changed by it, but perhaps she had. Perhaps Aylfenhame had been seeping into her soul ever since that first day.

It had certainly taken hold of her by now.

Soon it was Isabel's turn to talk, and that she did very willingly. It took some time to recount everything that had happened to her in Grenlowe and Mirramay, but she did not hurry, and left nothing out. It was a pleasure to her to share it with her aunt, knowing that she must conceal it from everyone as soon as she returned to Ferndeane.

'Are there a great many of these scrolls?' Mrs. Grey enquired when Isabel had finished.

'Some five or six, I believe, and they are not small. It will take me some little time to read through them.'

'I will take one or two, if you will permit me. We will work faster together.'

Isabel smiled at her aunt. 'I believe you are forming one of your soft spots for the Ferryman.'

'Without doubt! Quite as you did. Who could help feeling for him, poor man? We must certainly discover his name.'

Isabel felt obscurely better at this staunch support, for she had been feeling a little overwhelmed with the task, and the pressures it brought to bear upon her. For all the Ferryman's kind words to her on her departure, she fervently wished that she would not disappoint him.

She separated from her aunt soon afterwards, to rest before she was obliged to ready herself for her dinner engagement. She spared barely a thought for the prospect of meeting Mr. Thompson again; all her ideas were fixed upon the Ferryman, and the piper, and Mirramay.

Belatedly, she recollected the parcel Sophy had given her as she had left Silverling. It had been placed by the maid at the foot of her bed; she caught it up and quickly unwrapped it. She was not surprised when a gown emerged, though the garment itself caused her to catch her breath in wonder.

It was velvet, dyed in her favourite shade of blue: the serene, cool shade of twilight. The fabric was silk, though woven with something else; something fae, which felt cool against her hands, and caused the gown to ripple with the fluid shimmer of water. It was simple, as suited Isabel's taste, trimmed modestly at the neckline and sleeves with bunches of ribbons. An underskirt of darker blue silk peeped into view at the hem.

It was a ball gown, of course. Isabel had once given a gown of her own to Sophy, so that her friend might have something new to wear for a grand ball given in the neighbourhood. Sophy now returned that favour with a gown far, far more beautiful!

Isabel held it against herself, smiling delightedly. 'Tafferty! Is this not the loveliest thing you have ever seen?'

'No,' said the catterdandy, bestowing the briefest glance upon the gown. 'But it is pretty enough, I grant thee.'

'Fie upon that, for it is glorious. I only hope there will soon be a ball, so that I may wear it!' Her face fell as she recollected an obstacle. 'But I have nothing suitable to wear with it! Any ordinary accessories will fade into insignificance beside such loveliness.'

'That is a problem most easily fixed,' said Tafferty. 'An' thou didst promise me to work on thy Glamour.'

Isabel brightened. 'Do you think I might Glamour something to match? I had not thought to consider!'

Tafferty sighed, her head drooping. 'If I had known I need only promise thee somethin' extra pretty t' wear t' some ball, I need not 'ave wasted my time makin' complicated bargains with thee over the Ferryman.'

Isabel blushed, and laid aside the gown. 'Is it frivolous of me? I fear that it is! But I cannot help it. Such beauty is a delight to me, and I must make myself worthy of it in other respects as well.' She paused, and added more honestly, 'I believe I am growing accustomed to the idea, Tafferty. It has taken a little time, but my aunt's notion of sending me into Aylfenhame was a good one. I shall be happy to bring a little of it back with me.'

'I am delighted t' hear it.'

'Provided, of course, that my mother and father should not discover it.'

Tafferty flopped into a heap upon the carpet. 'Still some way t' go, then. No matter. Thou art makin' some feeble kind o' progress.'

Isabel went to her companion, and tentatively stroked one of her thickly-furred, gloriously tufted ears. 'I am sorry, Tafferty. I know I am a careful, shrinking creature, and it must be intolerable for someone as bold as you. But I am trying.'

Tafferty held herself rigid for a space, but finally softened, and leaned into Isabel's hand. 'Thy mother and father have somethin' t' answer for, I'll wager. They 'ave taught thee t' be dutiful, and by all accounts far too obedient. I must teach thee t' have confidence in thine own choices, an' t' think on things thy parents may not 'ave ever planned for thee.' She grinned up at Isabel, one long tooth showing around her top lip. 'I 'ave more than a little assistance from thine aunt, in that. An' she is a capable woman.'

CHAPTER THIRTEEN

Well, an' what a deal o' happenin's! I tell ye, I were never more surprised in the whole of me life. Oh, not about his Majesty, the Goblin King. I ought t' have known that he would be lurkin' in Mirramay, stickin' his tricky fingers in all manner o' business. Small wonder that he'd be kickin' up some kind o' lark thereabouts. But that Miss Isabel'd find the gumption t' carry on wi' her intended purpose regardless, an' steal away wi' a bundle o' scrolls! She felt a deal o' guilt, poor lass, but she was forgettin' somethin'. Scarce another person in the whole o' England could be better trusted wi' somethin' o' value — an' so I told the Keeper meself. She'd take 'em back in time, an' without so much as a scratch on 'em. That I knew.

Her powers, though. Thas another story. Tafferty 'ad a problem t' solve there, an' no mistake. How do ye persuade so reluctant a miss t' take a proper degree of interest in the arts t' which she was born? Well, that catterdandy's a wily one an' no mistake. The Ferryman, thas part of it; Miss Isa's one t' keep t' her word, an' stick t' bargain. But t'other part, thas real clever. Ye simply tell 'er 'bout all the many things she could be doin' t' make her life an' loves a mite simpler. An' prettier. An' if she can use 'er witchery t' do some kind o' good in the world, all the better.

That Ferryman, now. I'll admit, I 'ad an interest there. Good fellow, that, an' it irked me that I 'ad no more an idea what his deuced name was — beggin' yer pardon, fer my language — than anybody else. 'Tis a lapse, right enough! I, that prides meself on collectin' up all the choicest bits an' snippets of information! I 'ad t' do better. Not only that, mind. I also 'ad no notion what 'ad become o' the Chronicler. Two lapses, an' important business t' boot! Oh, I set all my very best folk t' work on that brace o' problems, ye can bet.

Isabel entered the drawing-room of the Thompsons' handsome York townhouse with a feeling of mild trepidation, and for two reasons: Firstly, because it was the first time she had been in Mr. Thompson's company since learning of her Aylir heritage, and she felt an obscure and irrational certainty that it would somehow show. Secondly, because Tafferty had persuaded her to embark upon her first proper Glamour in honour of the evening's events, and that most certainly did show.

She had not worn the beautiful gown of Sophy's creation. It was too fine for a dinner; it deserved to be kept for a ball. Instead, she had worn one of her own, fairly new, gowns and dressed it up for the occasion. But instead of adjusting its style and trim with a needle and thread and labour of her own, she had done so with Glamour.

And so she was clothed in an elegant, short-sleeved gown of ivory silk with an overdress of pale gold lace. The latter had originally been white, but she had altered its colour. She had also adjusted the shape of the neckline, and added bunches of ribbons at the sleeves in mimicry of Sophy's style. Her boldest — and favourite — alteration was the extremely life-like, gold-and-auburn butterflies which sat poised atop each shoulder. They looked as though they were perfectly real, which may prove to have been unwise. She berated herself for it as she entered the room, and watched as Mrs. Thompson's gaze went straight to the butterflies. They were so beautiful, though, that she had not been able to resist.

It was an oddity, Glamour. She knew well that underneath her witchery, the gown remained exactly the same as it had always been. But she had compelled it to portray an alternative appearance, weaving its new shapes and shades around it like a new cloak. It had been a long and difficult process, contriving to cast each little Glamour in a fashion both aesthetically consistent and stable, and it had tired her considerably. But she could not deny feeling a sense of accomplishment upon looking at her finished, re-wrought gown, together with a tinge of excitement. The effect was so convincing, even she was sorely pressed to remember that it was mere illusion.

To her mingled relief and dismay, she had enjoyed the process of adjusting her gown. She had been persuaded into acquiescing to Tafferty's demands against her will; it did not suit her to find that Tafferty had been, on some level, right to push her. It threatened to render her objections foolish, when to her they were as important as ever.

The butterflies drew the immediate attention of the three Misses Thompson, who at once pressed her to name the seamstress responsible for the creation. That they were interested in dress themselves was perfectly apparent. Isabel well remembered the gowns they had worn to the Alford Assembly: similar to each other in style but varied enough to differentiate each sister, and dyed in complementary shades. They had employed the same approach today. Miss Thompson wore palest pink; Miss Helena wore a darker shade of rose; and the youngest, Miss Matilda, wore fuchsia. Their glossy, curling hair was in shades of brown, too, from chestnut to auburn. Seated in a row upon a sofa, they resembled a neat little line of flowers in a cottage garden.

Isabel avoided their questions as to her gown as best she was able, with a little assistance from Mrs. Grey. She was grateful for more than one reason when their brother chastised them for their persistence.

'And when Miss Ellerby is but just risen from the sick-bed!' he said, with mild severity. 'Not a single enquiry as to her health have I heard!'

'It is remiss of us,' said Miss Thompson, with a gracious smile. Her air and composure were in better order than her sisters; Isabel received the impression that she took her role as the eldest sister seriously. 'Our apologies, Miss Ellerby. I hope you are fully recovered?'

'I am, thank you,' Isabel replied, blushing inwardly for the deception, and the lie. Why, she had never felt in better health in her life!

'You have missed a great deal of excitement!' said Miss Helena, with a bright, vivacious smile. 'None of us has yet encountered the Piper, or the Fiddler, or any of them! But we are living in hope, are we not, Matilda?'

Miss Matilda actually bounced a little in her seat with excitement. Isabel was bemused to note that volume of enthusiasm also appeared to run in a strict, inverse order from eldest to youngest. 'Oh, we are! It makes me wild with envy to think that my family and two of my dearest friends have actually seen the Piper, and I have not! It is too unfair!'

'Nor have I!' said Mrs. Grey with a laugh. 'It is vexing indeed. And I have been accepting all the invitations I have received, purely in the hope of catching a glimpse.' Her words were received with vigorous nods of agreement from Matilda and Helena, and a serene nod of assent from Miss Thompson. The sisters were united in their enthusiasm for the piper, and his dancers.

Isabel stared. Fresh in her mind was the totally opposite reaction to the Alford Assembly, which had taken place barely two weeks previously. The hushed silence on the topic had given way to excitement — not merely that, but chatter — and in so short a time! 'He is become a popular figure, then?' Isabel enquired.

'To be sure!' said Matilda. 'Everyone is wild to see him! And the Fiddler, too, and all the ladies and gentlemen. It is said they are very handsome.'

'And heavenly exotic,' added Helena.

'I scarcely noticed whether or not they are handsome,' Isabel said, truthfully enough. 'Their music is very… absorbing.' She could think of no better way to describe the curiously compelling melodies they had played, nor her reaction to them. 'It is generally true that the Ayliri are of a handsome order.'

All three girls stared at Isabel. 'Have you seen them?' gasped Matilda. 'Oh, but you are too, too lucky!'

'Tell us everything!' demanded Helena. 'Were they as exotic as everybody says? What were they like? Did you dance all night?'

'What were they wearing?' added Miss Thompson. 'Miss Jackson said their gowns were remarkable, and she has never seen the like! And that they have hair in strange colours. Is that so?'

Isabel, bemused, answered the onslaught of questions as best she could. It appeared that the Ayliri musicians and dancers had somehow become fashionable. She had never expected to find herself become a subject of envy for having been in their presence. Mr. Thompson and his father and mother listened to this conversation without contribution, but Isabel thought that they, too, were more interested in hearing the tales than they showed. Mr. Thompson caught Isabel's eye more than once as she spoke, and smiled at her in a manner both encouraging and faintly conspiratorial. He was laughing gently at his sisters' eagerness, but without being so discourteous as to openly show his amusement.

When Isabel's tale was finished, the reaction of her audience was still more amazement, eagerness and awe, followed by a renewed barrage of questions. 'To be sure,' said Mr. Thompson, laughing, 'it will be no longer be possible for any hostess to call her party a success unless the Rade should invite themselves to it! And as for the young men hereabouts, they will find themselves sadly out of luck. No young lady within seventy miles has eyes for any but an Aylir partner.'

'The Rade?' Isabel repeated.

'That is what they are now being called, The Faerie Rade. It is long since the folk of Aylfenhame rode in procession through England, and indeed, that is not precisely what they are doing. But it is close enough, perhaps.'

'They have never been seen riding, I believe,' said Miss Thompson. 'Or travelling at all. That is curious, is it not? For how should they contrive to appear at so many disparate occasions, and so far apart, if they did not travel between them?'

Isabel thought of the Ferryman. He had been summoned to bear the Rade from Aylfenhame to England in the first place; perhaps they also used him to convey them from town to town. Though if the boat had been seen flying about the skies of England, she could hardly suppose that it would not be talked of.

'Miss Jackson says that they have hidden ways,' said Helena.

'How I should like to go into Aylfenhame!' sighed Matilda. 'Everyone Ayliri, and each handsomer than the last! Like the Piper.' She sighed dreamily.

Mr. Thompson smiled at Isabel. 'I have heard it said that Miss Ellerby has ventured so far, some once or twice.'

Helena and Matilda gasped in unison. 'Oh, is it true?' said the latter.

Isabel could only own that it was. This prompted looks of such awe from all three ladies that she coloured with embarrassment. 'My friend, Miss Landon, now lives there,' she said, hoping to deflect attention from herself.

Matilda gaped. 'You mean that it is possible?' she said in a breathless whisper. 'To live there? Oh, Mama, may we go?'

'Certainly not,' said Mrs. Thompson coolly, though she smiled at Isabel as she spoke. 'You will give the oddest idea of yourself to Miss Ellerby, my love. We all enjoy the stories of the Piper and his dancers, of course, but it is quite another thing to talk of living in

Aylfenhame.'

'Though I am sure we wish Miss Landon every happiness in her life there,' added the elder Mr. Thompson, gravely, and with a glance at his wife.

'Of course,' said Mrs. Thompson.

'Is she going to marry an Aylir gentleman?' demanded Helena.

'She is married to an Aylir,' Isabel replied. 'His name is Aubranael.'

'Oh, but you called her Miss Landon!' said Miss Thompson. 'Surely she is Mrs, and with a terribly exotic Ayliri surname.'

'If she has such a name, I do not know it. Family names are not common in Aylfenhame, I believe.'

'How very odd.' Miss Thompson frowned as though the idea displeased her. It would not be altogether surprising if it did. Most women derived whatever status they enjoyed from their nearest male relative, or their husband, and marriage generally increased a woman's standing. The title of Mrs, then, together with a respectable (or in this case, exotic) surname was something in which women took pride. To marry and yet to be denied those advantages may well strike Miss Thompson as displeasing.

Isabel well understood those feelings, but for her own part she found every aspect of Sophy's life intriguing. Terrifying as well, for it was devoid of every single one of the usual rules and conventions — rules which Isabel found comforting in their familiarity. They marked a clear path through life, and all of its various events, great and small. It was difficult to go far wrong, if one kept an eye to the conventions and ordered one's doings according to the expectations of society. To manage without them all was to throw comfort and familiarity to the winds, and leave oneself exposed to untold vagaries. Isabel admired her friend's courage, but the prospect frightened her.

She was obscurely ashamed of herself for feeling so. Was it not cowardice?

These reflections had overtaken her while her companions talked on, sometimes about the Piper and then about various acquaintances of theirs, to whom Isabel was not known. But her thoughts were interrupted when dinner was announced. Young Mr. Thompson approached Isabel and offered his arm. 'May I escort you to the dining parlour?' he enquired, with a soft smile.

Isabel accepted, and was conducted thither at the head of the little procession. This was giving her distinction indeed, and she hardly knew how to understand it. Neither her standing nor her wealth were such as to explain any of the Thompson's apparent eagerness to honour her, or to promote her match with their son. What could be the reason for it?

Despite her confusion, she was flattered — and relieved. Her mother and father could not reproach her upon her return, for in spite of her absence, matters seemed to be progressing as they wished.

Dinner was a quiet affair. The young ladies seemed to have exhausted their effusions about the Piper — or perhaps they had finally obeyed the hints their mother and father had been attempting to give them for some time, and let the topic die. Conversation was kept up primarily between Mr. Thompson and Mrs. Grey, with occasional contributions by the elder Mr. Thompson, Mrs. Thompson and Isabel herself. Efforts were made to draw Isabel out more, and encourage her to talk, but she was not equal to it. Never a talkative woman by nature, she found the heavy atmosphere of the dining parlour stifling. She had preferred the earlier unreserve with which the young ladies of the house had talked. She ate quietly, listening to all that passed and attempting to persuade herself that she felt neither ill-at-ease nor bored.

Only once was she startled out of her quiet composure. When the first course was removed in favour of a second set of dishes, some mishap occurred. A young footman bent to set a platter of spiced beef in gravy near to Isabel's elbow. By some unlucky chance, he stumbled; the plate tipped; a measure of red wine sauce descended onto Isabel's gown. Seated and unable to move quickly enough to avoid it, she could only watch in dismay as the gravy left a dark stain over the beautiful gold silk of her overdress.

The footman was all apologies and consternation. Isabel did her best to reassure him, but unsuccessfully. His eyes repeatedly returned to Mrs. Thompson's face, and with each passing moment his panic seemed to grow. Isabel was puzzled and confused by such an overreaction to a simple accident — and more so when she noticed the storm brewing in Mrs. Thompson's face, for it belied the air of geniality she had hitherto displayed.

It was clear that the footman would not be lightly forgiven by his mistress. 'Oh, such a fine gown!' cried Miss Helena loudly. 'Shall it never be right again? I fear not, for wine, you know, can never be got out of silk. What a pity! How clumsy! And I am sure it was worth more than your year's wages.' This last was directed at the footman with a glower of strong disapproval, and the poor young man redoubled his apologies.

'It is but an accident,' said young Mr. Thompson in a mild tone, for which Isabel felt gratitude. But the weight of opinion was against him, and his attempts at restoring harmony went unheard.

Would the footman be turned off, merely for the accidental ruining of a mere frock? Isabel could not bear the prospect. Her eyes met her aunt's; Mrs. Grey winked at her, almost imperceptibly, and glanced pointedly at her gown.

Isabel took her meaning at once. Much of the gown's appearance was already naught but Glamour; could she, with a few moments' thought and effort, restore it to its former perfection?

She could. It was harder to focus, in the present chaos of the dining parlour, than it had been in the quiet and safety of her own bedchamber in her aunt's house, but it was soon done. The dark splash of sauce shimmered and vanished, leaving her gown unblemished once more.

Mrs. Thompson was in the process of making a grave apology to Isabel for the incompetence of her servants, and assuring her that the damage would be taken out of the footman's wages. Isabel heard this with quiet disapproval, and when she had finished, directly said:

'There can be no occasion for that, ma'am. It was but a small lapse, which may happen to anyone. And I assure you, my gown is perfectly unharmed. The sauce has narrowly missed me, it appears.'

Startled, the footman glanced down at her skirt. Here was the difficulty. He had certainly been able to observe the damage with his own eyes. How would he react to its sudden and inexplicable disappearance? She saw confusion flicker across his face, and he blinked.

'I am relieved to hear it,' Mrs. Thompson said regally. She was seated opposite to Isabel, and therefore had no opportunity to witness the fate of the gown with her own eyes. She dismissed the hapless footman, who whisked himself away — but not without a final, puzzled glance at Isabel.

Isabel sat quietly, suffering a tumult of emotions. She was relieved to have saved the poor footman, though she could by no means feel certain that she had. Her hostess's anger had seemed out of all proportion to the offence. Would she punish the poor boy anyway, for having embarrassed her? Even if Isabel's gown had, ostensibly at least, taken no damage?

And how would her little piece of Glamour be interpreted by the footman? Would he spread the story among the servants, and if he did, would it reach the ears of the family? Or was it too late to conceal what she had done, even if the footman kept silent? For Miss Matilda was seated next to Isabel, and she, too, had been close enough to witness everything that had passed. She looked upon the fine golden lace with a degree of puzzlement which dismayed Isabel. 'Why, how fortunate!' she said. 'For I could swear I saw a deal of damage! It is the poor light. Papa, there really must be more candles next time Miss Ellerby is invited.'

It was unlikely that the truth would be guessed, Isabel decided. Her venturing as far as Aylfenhame might be known, but no one would imagine that she herself bore any of the powers of the Ayliri or the fae. And she could not regret having done what she could to protect the young footman from the wrath of his mistress.

That wrath was another source of disquiet to Isabel. How could Mrs. Thompson appear so congenial to Isabel herself, and yet react with such disproportionate fury to the smallest lapse among her servants? It bespoke a wholly different personality hidden beneath the amiable exterior, and one which Isabel had no wish to further uncover. Miss Helena's comments had also been ill-judged and uncharitable, and no one had spoken up for the footman save for Isabel herself, and the younger Mr. Thompson. He had done better than the rest of his family, in making some effort to deflect his mother's anger from her servant. She respected him for that.

The subject passed after some minutes, and banal topics of conversation once again succeeded. The rest of the dinner passed in peace. When the ladies rose to remove to the drawing-room, Isabel found her gown scrutinised much more closely by all of the Thompson daughters. To her relief, they pronounced it unmarked, but the tight pinch to their mother's lips suggested that this did not pacify her.

Isabel was relieved, later in the evening, to take her leave and return home. Mrs. Grey felt as Isabel did, and did not conceal her distaste for Mrs. Thompson's behaviour.

'I do not think we will return to that house in any great haste,' she told her niece as they rode home in her carriage. 'Your mother's wishes notwithstanding.'

Isabel could only agree.

'But I congratulate you!' continued Mrs. Grey. 'You will be a fine Glamourist, I have no doubt. I could not have managed the gown any better myself. Such perfect beauty in these butterflies! And the stain upon it, so neatly hidden! I hope you are pleased with your own skill, for I am most impressed.'

Isabel's immediate reaction was denial. Of course she was not pleased! Her desire to reject the witch side of herself had not much diminished. But a moment's reflection showed her the folly of such thoughts. The beauty of her gown delighted her, however it had been arrived at; and she had been relieved to rescue the Thompsons' footman from the unmerited consequences of a minor accident. Today, then, she had learned two things about her powers: they may be used to add many a delight to her own life, and there were times where they could be of use to others. These were not insignificant advantages.

She retired to her bedchamber as soon as they arrived at Mrs. Grey's home, and retreated to her bed with a heavy heart. It was a relief to her to put the puzzling questions of the Thompsons out of her mind in favour of perusing the first of the scrolls she had taken from the Chronicler's Tower. She had given half of them to her aunt, as per Mrs. Grey's request, but several large and densely-scribed scrolls still remained.

The writing thereupon was tiny and difficult to read, and she suffered a pang of dismay. Good heavens, but at this rate it could take her two months to read everything upon these scrolls alone! For she must read closely and carefully, for fear of missing the very information she sought.

No matter. She must persevere, even if it took her six months together to find the Ferryman's name. She had promised, and he was waiting. She spared a thought for his merry dark eyes, fixed upon her with a glow of regard, and settled to read with renewed determination. She read far into the night, and did not close her eyes in slumber until her candle burned low, and at last flickered out.

CHAPTER FOURTEEN

Isabel soon mastered the trick of reading the scrolls' dense, crowded lettering and the sometimes curious phrasing and syntax the scribe had used. She and her aunt took to spending some part of their mornings together in the parlour, poring over a scroll each and conferring as to the contents. Isabel valued these hours, for they drew her ever closer to her aunt. Theirs had always been an amiable relationship, but Isabel felt that a real friendship was being forged through their shared endeavour.

Further, Mrs. Grey's enthusiasm — or Eliza's, as she began to insist upon being called — was contagious. Isabel had come to view her promise as rash and naive; how could she hope to discover something so small as a single name, long lost to time, and of a different world to her own? But Eliza was energetic and dauntless, and her optimism and motivation bolstered her niece's spirits and built her hopes.

Nonetheless, they were obliged to read a great deal of material which bore no relevance whatsoever to their quest. For three days, they read of the Kostigern and his attempts to master the realm of Aylfenhame. Or her. Isabel was frequently puzzled, for it seemed that a great deal about the traitor's identity was unknown. Sources differed as to the Kostigern's probable gender; even the Chronicler did not appear to be able to say for certain. Further, a question hung over his or her race. Was the Kostigern Aylir, goblin, or something else? Some even whispered that the he or she was human, or part human, and had come out of England to conquer Aylfenhame. The

Chronicler noted all such stories, whispers and tales without judgement, and Isabel was left mystified.

Nor was it apparent when this had occurred. The Aylfenhame way of marking time differed significantly from that of England. Isabel and Eliza spent more than an hour, one rainy morning, attempting to determine how the Chronicler's timelines related to their own, but without success. They were obliged to conclude merely that the conflict had taken place some long time ago, but that it was not ancient history. The Ferryman had estimated the time at approximately a century, but his reckoning had been vague — and besides, he had slept most of the time away, and Isabel knew not whether she could rely upon his judgement.

Of the Kostigern, the emerging picture was that of a traitor — a sorcerer — who had materialised from somewhere unknown, had rapidly mustered a formidable network of supporters among the fae and Ayliri of the realm, and had come perilously close to taking Mirramay and the throne. They had been defeated, but narrowly. Isabel was delighted to find Sir Guntifer mentioned by name, as a hero of the conflict. He and his fellow tree-giants had been instrumental in the defence of Mirramay. The Goblin King, however, had not been. To the confusion of all, he had been recorded as assisting both sides at different times. Isabel sighed over this, for it struck her as all too Grunewald.

While interesting, none of this was of relevance. It was the fourth day of such studies before Isabel encountered the first mention of the Ferry-folk. They had been among the first to be corrupted by the Kostigern, and for good reason; such powers of transport were highly advantageous. Some had answered the traitor's call, but some had not, and for a time battles had raged in the skies over Aylfenhame as ferry-boats from both sides encountered each other. Many of the boats had been outright destroyed.

But the Chronicler had recorded nothing more. Her heart had quickened as she read this, expecting at any moment to discover a list of the names of those who had assisted the Kostigern. But there was no such list. She sighed her disappointment, a sound which attracted her aunt's attention.

'It is a great shame,' Eliza agreed, upon hearing the tale. 'Perhaps the Chronicler did not know the names.'

'I dislike that notion excessively,' Isabel sighed, 'for if he does not, then who ever will?' She paused, as a notion struck her. 'I had not thought. The Ferryman talked of the Kostigern, and as a he. "He was my Master." And he implied that this apprenticeship of his lasted some years. How can it be that this information never reached the Chronicler?'

Eliza tapped a fingertip against her lips. 'That is curious indeed. But the Ferryman has not been at liberty to talk to anybody very much, has he? Have we yet discovered how he came to be cursed?'

'No, not yet. I imagine that is to come towards the end of these scrolls, for it must have followed the end of the conflict, I believe? But it is becoming clearer why he is the only Ferryman remaining.' She tapped the scroll spread before her. 'It is a terrible story, aunt. Many of them were slain, and their boats destroyed. They slew each other. I cannot help imagining our Ferryman caught up in such a war, forced to fight his own kind. Perhaps he killed some of them. Perhaps he was badly hurt himself. And all because he was oath-bound!'

Eliza's face clouded, and she nodded. 'I am curious as to how he became one of the Ferry-folk to begin with. I wonder if the Kostigern arranged it thus, in order to make use of him?'

'It seems all too likely,' Isabel agreed. The longer she read, the harder the task became, for to read of such terrible conflicts tore at her heart. The more so because she knew that her own friends had been closely involved. She regretted, now, that she had asked no further questions of the Ferryman, or of Sir Guntifer — and at the same time, she did not regret it. Could she bear to hear more, and from those who had been directly involved? But it was important that she persevered. She would have to muster her courage, and bear onward, in spite of the horrific images that formed in her mind with each new account that she read.

Of considerable interest, however, were the accounts of the Torpor that she soon afterwards discovered.

…and they whose treachery had so near brought the Betrayer to dominion over Aylfenhame were judged by Her Majesty, the Queen at Mirramay. In Her Mercy, She condemned them not to Death as her loyal subjects urged, but instead to the Torpor. Thus were many Lost to Time. And this marked the beginning of the Diminishing of Aylfenhame…

The Torpor. These words swiftly brought to Isabel's mind the

Ferryman's words regarding his long absence. Well, in Aylfenhame, those things which nobody wants or needs can… fade. That fading was the Torpor, a kind of enchanted slumber, though during the Torpor even the sleeper's body somehow faded from existence. The scroll advanced no information as to what the Torpor was, for that was not the nature of the discussion. It merely assumed that the reader knew of the phenomenon. Isabel hoped she was not incorrect to connect it with the Ferryman's words, but it made sense.

What she now learned was twofold: firstly that a denizen of Aylfenhame may voluntarily go into the Torpor, if they wished it, although they may also sink into the enchantment involuntarily.

But they may also be compelled to go into the Torpor. Most of the Kostigern's supporters had been pushed into the fading as punishment for their betrayal of the Crown. Had that been part of the Ferryman's fate? If so, why had he also been cursed? It hardly seemed useful to impose both sets of consequences upon him, for the curse which bound him to his ferry-boat meant little if he was in the Torpor anyway. Perhaps they had been separately applied. Isabel might guess that he had been compelled to fade along with the rest of the Kostigern's surviving supporters, but if so, who had cursed him?

These topics of conversation occupied Isabel and Eliza so completely that they began to resent the engagements which took them out of the house, and away from further study. Only the prospect of encountering the Piper's troupe could persuade Eliza to accept as many invitations as she did, though she was disappointed in that hope, for the Rade did not come to York. Isabel accompanied her aunt merely as a matter of duty. So absorbed was she by Aylfenhame, by its histories and mysteries and her promise to the Ferryman, that the quiet succession of entertainments which she would normally enjoy now wholly failed to interest her.

She did allow herself to be distracted, occasionally, by Tafferty. The wily catterdandy soon realised that Isabel's attention was unlikely to be brought to bear upon her witchery as Tafferty wished; not while so many scrolls remained unread, and so little information had been gleaned. So she began to find ways to encourage Isabel to use her witchery to support herself and her aunt in their task. It began one morning when the tea and cakes which were generally supplied for their refreshment ran out, and Eliza reached out to ring the bell and summon more.

'Stop a moment,' said Tafferty, waking and stretching luxuriously. 'Ye 'ave a teapot an' a plate. It may interest ye t' know that they may, by the smallest bit o' witchery, be encouraged t' refill their own selves.'

Isabel stared at her companion. 'I cannot imagine any such thing to be a mere trifle!'

'There's some as could never manage it,' Tafferty admitted. 'But I think thou hast the way of it. There's two ways, in point o' fact. Later, I will assist thee t' fashion a teapot o' yer own, of the enchanted variety. That manner o' thing will keep itself filled at all times, an' wi' whatever thou wishest t' find in it. But now, thou mayst simply coax yonder pot t' recall what was in it before. An' the plate, too.'

The ensuing lesson took up full two hours, time which Isabel sorely regretted losing. Particularly after the first hour, when her head ached and her thirst grew. But she was rewarded when the scent of fragrant citrus tea suddenly reached her nostrils. Lifting the lid of the elegant porcelain teapot, she discovered a steaming brew inside.

After that, it was the work of moments to encourage the plate to likewise restore its contents. Staring at the steaming pot and the small mound of delicate pastries upon the plate, Isabel was stunned — and delighted.

And also disturbed, for the exercise brought to mind the enchanted teapots and plates that she had supped from during the strange half-hour she had spent as a guest at the Teapot Society. The comparison chilled her a little, but it also enlightened her. Was this how the magical table had been contrived? Someone had woven enchantment into the very fabric of the table, constructing it, in all likelihood, for the purpose. And the pots and plates had likewise been carefully crafted: To react firstly to each new guest and fill themselves accordingly, and afterwards to keep themselves filled no matter how much their owners ate or drank.

She was awed, and a little frightened, by her own power. Tafferty observed her in silence as Isabel cautiously poured a cup of tea from the newly-enchanted teapot, and took a pastry.

'Thou art not at all likely t' turn thy hand t' the likes o' that,' the catterdandy said, and hoisted a pastry from the plate with her claws. 'I can see it in thy face. Thy fears. The Teapot Society, it is a corruption o' these kinds of arts. Now, why was it made? I cannot answer that, no more'n I know who it was that brought it into bein'.'

Isabel nodded, and bit into her pastry. It was perfect, crisp and still warm from the oven. There was nothing about it to suggest that someone had caused it to waft up out of a mere plate all by itself.

Eliza smiled at Isabel. 'Vershibat tried for years to teach me that art,' she said wistfully. 'Alas, it was beyond my skill.'

'Thou art more gifted at the Glamour side o' things,' said Tafferty, and Eliza nodded.

'Though it is long since I much employed the Glamour.' She frowned as she spoke, and her tone was dissatisfied. 'Ah, to leave such powers unused! It is a terrible waste.'

Isabel frowned and looked down at her scroll, unwilling to venture a reply. To waste her powers was precisely what she had wished to do. Indeed, some hidden corner of her heart still preferred the idea of slipping back into her old, familiar life, and forgetting the colour, the chaos and the confusion of Aylfenhame altogether.

When she looked up again, she discovered that her aunt had vanished. In her place sat another woman entirely: younger by twenty years at least, and dressed according to the fashions of Aylfenhame. Her hair was prettily bound up under a coronet of flowers, and she wore a shimmering, full-sleeved gown of rose-pink and gold velvet.

Isabel gasped, and stared wildly around the room. She had not heard her aunt leave, nor anybody else enter! Surprise clouded her thoughts, and some moments passed before the truth occurred to her.

The lady opposite was her aunt, only restored to youth. Youth, and something else. For her hair was no longer the familiar shade of brown threaded with grey, but had developed a coppery sheen. Stranger still, the hazel hue of her eyes had vanished in favour of a pale green colour, like polished jade. They were not quite human eyes.

'Is this… Glamour?' Isabel said in a faint voice.

Eliza laughed, and smoothed the front of her velvet gown with a loving hand. 'You see me as I was, when I last went into Aylfenhame.' Which did not precisely answer Isabel's question, but Eliza fell silent, pensive. At last she added in a quieter voice, 'As I was when I might have stayed.'

Eliza had been a beauty. This did not surprise Isabel, for she was a handsome woman in her middle years. What did surprise her was how well she suited the Ayliri garb she wore. She could almost be

Aylir herself. 'Why did you return to England?'

'Because I had already accepted a proposal of marriage from Mr. Grey, who loved me. The life he offered was laid before my feet, and I knew — I could predict — every step of it. But the life I might have led in Aylfenhame was by no means so clear. I had nowhere to go, no one to help me, and no notion as to how to keep myself.'

'Those were very sensible objections to the plan, aunt,' said Isabel gravely.

Eliza looked at her. 'Sensible,' she repeated. 'Yes, they were. And because I had so much good sense — and so little courage — I chose the simplest path, and turned my back on everything else.'

So little courage. Those words repeated in Isabel's mind. Did she lack courage? Was that why she clung to the familiarity of England, and tried so hard to reject everything that fitted poorly alongside it? She did not like to think so. She had always been praised for her good sense.

'Something occurs to me, my love,' said Eliza, disrupting Isabel's train of thought. 'In all my reading, I have not learnt what became of the Kostigern.'

Isabel blinked, and fought to turn her thoughts away from her aunt's surprising appearance and back to their shared study. 'Why, no. Nor have I. I had hoped to discover something of it in this passage, but there is nothing. It discusses what became of his followers, but says nothing of him. And now it has diverted into talk of the Royal Guards of Mirramay.' She tapped the scroll she held as she spoke, which had been unfurled almost to its fullest extent. Soon she would finish reading it. It was the last of the three she had studied, and Eliza had almost completed her share. Yet, so many questions remained unanswered, and they had not learned the Ferryman's name.

'It occurs to me,' continued Eliza, 'that there is one person who must remember the Ferryman's name.' She paused and regarded Isabel with a significant air, as though waiting for a similar idea to enter her niece's brain.

'Who do you mean?' Isabel was obliged to ask.

Eliza sat back in her chair, adjusting the floral coronet she still wore. 'Somebody laid the curse upon our poor friend, the Ferryman. I am inclined to agree with you: it is unlikely that this punishment was laid upon him by the Queen at Mirramay. For she had already dispensed her judgement, and sent all his compatriots into the Torpor — and very likely him, as well. Who, then, cursed him, and why?

'Let us speculate. We know that he had a Master, who bound him by oath to serve. The Ferryman, moreover, condemns himself for not having tried harder. He did not say that he did not even attempt to resist his Master.'

The pieces came together in Isabel's mind. 'Oh, no!' she cried. 'My dear aunt, you are not suggesting…?'

'I am. There are two who might remember what the Ferryman's name once was: his former Master, and the person who laid the curse upon him. It is my belief that these two are the same; that, in short, the Kostigern laid the curse upon his oath-bound apprentice. I think that our Ferryman attempted some manner of resistance.'

'But that means he was punished by both sides!' Isabel exclaimed, horrified. 'He was punished by the Queen for supporting the Kostigern when he could not help it, and cursed by the Kostigern for trying to support the Queen! That is a terrible fate.'

'It is. The Torpor appears to have released him, at long last, and we may be grateful for that. I believe we must to go all possible lengths to free him from the second, harsher punishment.'

'Without a doubt,' Isabel agreed. 'But… but, aunt. If you are correct, then — then we must —'

'Find the Kostigern. Yes.'

'Find the Kostigern. And somehow compel him to tell us what his former, despised apprentice's name was.'

Eliza nodded. 'It will be no easy task, that I know.'

'Can it even be possible? We have found no word of the Kostigern at all. We know that he was defeated, but not what became of him afterwards. Perhaps he was killed!'

'If he was known to be slain, I believe that would have been recorded.'

'Perhaps so, but what else may have become of him? If he was sent into the Torpor, like the rest, then there he probably remains. I do not have the first idea how to rouse him, and besides, I do not think we should! For once woken, do you not think that he would instantly revive his ambitions and take Mirramay? There is no one to oppose him!'

'Calm down, my love,' said Eliza in a soothing tone. Isabel became aware that she was growing upset, and endeavoured to do as her aunt bid, and calm herself. If the only way to fulfil her promise was to undertake so impossible, and ill-advised, a quest, then she did not know how to proceed — or whether she should. But she could not leave the Ferryman unaided!

'I do not propose that we attempt to find the Kostigern himself. You are perfectly right: to do so would be highly dangerous to more than ourselves, and at any rate I am convinced that it would not answer. He is unlikely to simply tell us his disgraced apprentice's name, after all.

'But he must have lived somewhere. There must have been some manner of — of headquarters, or something of the kind. Do you not think? And perhaps there we might find records of his apprentices. Contracts. I do not know how such things are managed in Aylfenhame, but I have some hopes that we may not be disappointed if we search there.'

Isabel nodded, turning the idea over in her mind. 'I think you are right, aunt, but how are we to proceed? We know nothing of the Kostigern's background, nor where he might have lived either during, or before, the conflict in Aylfenhame.' She frowned as another idea occurred to her, and added, 'Though I do not think that necessarily means that no one knows. Is such information likely to be written down, even by the Chronicler? The Tower may be guarded by the Keeper, but it is by no means inviolate.'

'I agree. I think the Chronicler knows a great deal more than he has recorded in these scrolls.'

'Then we must find him. He may, perhaps, know the Ferryman's name himself, in which case our task is complete. And if not…'

'If not,' said Eliza, 'then we must make him tell us where to seek the Kostigern. And then, my love, we must have courage enough to follow the trail. Have we, do you think?'

Isabel could not but hesitate. To return to Aylfenhame so soon, and with such a quest! To seek the Kostigern's domain must be to venture into the darkest, wildest and most dangerous parts of the realm, for she could hardly suppose such a person to have lived in a charming house in a town such as Grenlowe, or Avarindle.

'We must make the attempt,' she said, concealing her sinking heart as best she could. She was a little heartened by her aunt's manner of speaking, for she had said we.

Eliza beamed. 'Yes, I believe we must! I confess, I am ready for an adventure. I have had peace and tranquillity enough to last me full a lifetime.'

Isabel did not feel nearly so ready, but she left those thoughts unvoiced. Courage enough. She could have courage. The journey would not, in all likelihood, take very long.

'But my mother and father!' she cried, struck by a recollection of their inevitable disapproval of the plan. 'How may it be kept from them?'

Eliza looked strangely at her. 'Must it be?'

'They will be certain to forbid it.'

'I imagine it very likely.'

Isabel stared. 'You do not mean that I should directly disobey them?'

'Sometimes,' said Eliza with a strange smile, 'the very best things in life come about when one misbehaves. Just a very little.'

To leave her father's house without his approval, venture into the depths of Aylfenhame with no companion save her aunt and all in order to go in search of the greatest villain in the history of the fae realm did not strike Isabel as misbehaving a very little at all. She stared at her aunt in consternation. 'They will condemn me, utterly. Society will condemn me. My father may cast me out entirely.'

'He will not cast you out,' said Eliza scornfully. 'And some tale may be concocted to explain your absence as far as Society is concerned.' Isabel was not convinced. Her dismay must have been clearly visible upon her face, for her aunt continued, 'Will you permit two things?'

'What are they?'

'Firstly, to consult Mr. Balligumph. He is a person of information, and may be able to shed some light on the questions we are grappling with.'

Isabel inclined her head. 'I can have no objection to that.'

'Secondly, to talk to your mother and father about our venture.'

'Certainly not!'

Eliza reached across the table and grasped Isabel's hand. 'Truly, Isabel, you might trust me in this. They may surprise you. And I will support you in everything! Can you doubt it?'

'I do not doubt you at all,' Isabel said in confusion.

'I say again, your mother and father may surprise you.'

Isabel said nothing. Eliza released her hand, and sat back with a sigh. 'We may begin with Mr. Balligumph, regardless.'

Her manner was expressive of disappointment, and Isabel endured a stab of guilt — and shame, in herself. But her father! Eliza may choose to disdain a parental influence she would not feel, but Isabel could not lightly do so.

'I am always happy to see Mr. Balligumph,' she said quietly. 'Will you, then, accompany me home?'

Eliza grinned, and touched her coronet again. 'I believe I will.'

Isabel looked long at her aunt. She was astonished, not merely by the peculiarity of seeing a much younger woman seated opposite, but also by the perfection of the Glamour. Nothing was out of place, nothing amiss; Isabel could swear that the person sitting opposite was Eliza as she was meant to appear. Her powers of Glamour far outstripped Isabel's own! Her aptitude rivalled that of Hidenory and the Goblin King, both of whose Glamours had deceived Isabel in the past.

'Shall you come with me as your own self?'

Eliza raised an eyebrow. 'My real self? No. I do not think that I will.'

Isabel nodded, but with doubt. There was a glint in her aunt's eye which suggested some hidden meaning to her words. 'Aunt,' Isabel said slowly, as a strange thought occurred to her. 'Which one of these visions is your real self?'

Eliza laughed delightedly. 'You have a bright mind, my dearest girl. It is an intriguing question, is it not? Which of my utterly convincing selves is the true one?'

'Surely, it must be the one that I know.' Isabel hesitated. 'Otherwise —'

'Because the one that you know shows the appropriate signs of age? That would make the most sense, would it not?'

'Are… are the Ayliri particularly long-lived?'

Eliza smiled. 'Very good. Given everything that we have read, I believe we must assume that they are.'

'In that case —' Isabel could not finish her sentence, and left the rest unsaid.

'In that case, Aylir blood does have the effect of lengthening one's lifespan.' She smiled, and touched her lustrous, curling hair. 'We are nowhere near so long-lived as one of pure blood, naturally.'

Isabel stared.

'I was obliged to manufacture the process of aging,' Eliza continued. 'Or my youthfulness would certainly have aroused comment and speculation by now.'

'But then —'

'Yes, you too must expect to experience aging at an unusually slow rate.' Her amusement faded, and she leaned forward, speaking in an earnest tone. 'My dear Isabel. I have not been urging you out of an idle desire to see you succeed in Aylfenhame where I did not. There are aspects of your blood which will make it very difficult for you to lead a normal life in England. It may be done, through use of the Glamour and your other powers. But it will not be easy for you to conceal the fact that you do not age as you should — not from your husband, nor from your children.'

Isabel absorbed this news in silence. At first thought, the idea that her youth would be prolonged was delightful. Who truly wished to leave their liveliest years behind after a mere decade or two?

But she did not need her aunt to raise the idea of her future husband and children. Thither her thoughts had instantly flown. How long would she live? And how far would she outlive those she would love the most?

Eliza saw the pain in her face, and took her hand once more. 'I am sorry, Isa. I have been trying for weeks to find a gentle way to break it to you, and I think I have not succeeded. But it was important for you to know.'

Important to know before she accepted a proposal from Mr. Thompson. Yes. 'Did Mr. Grey never know?'

Eliza shook her head. 'I never told him. I wanted to, but he was… a creature of convention. He would not have understood.'

Isabel sighed. If she decided to marry, should she expect to tell her husband of her heritage, and its connotations? Or try to keep it a secret, as her aunt had done?

'I have given you much to think about,' Eliza said. 'Know this: If it is your decision to stay, and it is of all things most likely to make you happy, then it may be managed. I am proof of that. But you must bear in mind the difficulties.'

The difficulties worked both ways, Isabel thought with a little sourness. She was too long-lived for an English husband, and presumably too short-lived for an Aylir one. Her mind reeled. In mere weeks, she had gone from an Englishwoman of modest prosperity and prospects to a part-Aylir witch of unusually long life. Where was she now? Who was the real Isabel, in the midst of these mismatched things?

Eliza squeezed her hand and stood up. 'We are bidden to the Thompsons this evening. It is the last time we will encounter them here, but I believe it is your mother's intention to invite the family to a ball at Ferndeane soon.'

'Indeed, Mama wrote to me of it. Do we depart for Tilby tomorrow?'

'If that is agreeable to you.'

It was, and it was not. Isabel longed for the familiarity and the comforts of home, but it would be the first meeting with her parents since the whole truth of her heritage had burst upon her. She felt utterly, irrevocably changed. How would she contrive to behave as though she was the same Isabel she had been when last at Ferndeane?

CHAPTER FIFTEEN

While Miss Isabel was swannin' about in York an' hobnobbing wi' the Thompsons, I 'ad not been idle. When I need to know sommat fast, I can usually rustle up somethin' o' use sharpish-like. It ain't cheap, mind, but fer Miss Isabel — sweetest lass ye could wish to meet, an' a friend o' Miss Sophy's besides — there ain't much I wouldn't do.

I 'ad hoped that the Ferryman's name'd be one o' those things I could spirit out o' my very fine hat, but that weren't to be. Too many years 'ad passed, an' he was by no means a well-known person before he was packed off into the Torpor. But somethin' else turned up. Many an unlikely myth an' tall tale I 'ad to wade through, thas fer certain, before I came upon sommat o' use, but my network o' whisperers came up wi' the goods, an' pretty quick-like too! So when Miss Isa an' her aunt arrived to visit me good self, I 'ad a titbit or two o' news to share.

Isabel was relieved when her aunt resumed her real form in order to travel — or what Isabel persisted in thinking of as her real form, despite knowing that handsome, middle-aged Aunt Grey was a mere construct of Glamour. Mrs. Grey was familiar to Isabel, and therefore comfortable, but the Eliza she had come to know had abruptly become a stranger. With her impossibly youthful looks, her strange coppery hair and stranger eyes, the coronet in her hair and the lush otherness of her garb, she was a creature with whom Isabel could not be at ease.

Mr. Thompson called upon both ladies on the morning of their departure, though his visit was clearly intended for Isabel's benefit.

'I trust you will travel safely, rather than speedily,' he said after he had made his bows and accepted an offer of refreshment. His eyes captured Isabel's as he spoke, and his manner was significant. 'But I know I may trust Mrs. Grey to take the very best care of her niece.' His tone introduced a note of doubt in spite of the confidence of his words, to which Isabel took exception. Eliza, however, appeared to find him amusing.

'I shall contain my wild ways long enough to convey Miss Ellerby home in perfect safety,' she promised, her eyes glinting amusement over the rim of her cup as she sipped tea.

Isabel expected Mr. Thompson to laugh at this sally, but he appeared to take Mrs. Grey's words seriously. Isabel considered this unfair of him — though she could not but admit that her aunt had increasingly abandoned the appearance of sober respectability with which she had always cloaked herself, and had given rein to the more mischievous aspects of her personality. This troubled Isabel, for it was as though her aunt no longer cared what manner of figure she cut in society.

'I will be seeing you soon,' Mr. Thompson said to Isabel, without responding to her aunt's remark. 'I am charged to assure you that we will all be attending your mother's ball at Ferndeane. My mother has already written to accept the invitation. My sisters are especially eager for the treat, as you may imagine, but I am scarcely less so. I must have you run no risks and take no harm, for I should be sorry indeed to lose the pleasure of dancing with you there!'

Isabel smiled warmly. His manner may be over-protective and a little assuming, but it displayed a degree of regard for her well-being which she found touching. She murmured something assenting, and conversation progressed in a desultory fashion for some minutes. Mrs. Grey contributed little, choosing instead to observe Isabel and her suitor with a satirical eye. But Mr. Thompson was more than equal to carrying a conversation unaided, and required little from Isabel save a nod here and there and an occasional remark.

When he rose to leave, Isabel felt a flicker of alarm as he requested a private word with her. He did so with perfect civility, excusing both of them from her aunt's presence with faultless manners. Isabel found neither opportunity nor excuse to refuse, and moments later she was shut into the parlour with him. She waited in trepidation as he turned to her with a smile, and said: 'You cannot doubt what it is that I wish to ask you.'

Isabel opened her mouth, blinked, said something vague and hastily shut her mouth again.

He scarcely seemed to notice her confusion, for he merely smiled, took her hand and kissed it. 'You must allow me to claim the first two dances at Ferndeane,' he said.

Isabel blinked twice more, and took a breath. Oh. And swiftly afterwards, the words thank goodness drifted through her mind, rather to her confusion, for did she not find him a perfectly agreeable young man? And was not perfectly agreeable the height of felicity she could expect to encounter in a suitable marriage?

'I shall be delighted,' she said distantly, her heart pounding with the echoes of alarm. The moment had not yet come, then, but she felt that it would. Perhaps at the very ball he spoke of.

'I did not like to ask in front of your aunt,' he explained. She noticed that he had not yet released her hand. 'It did not seem quite the thing.'

'I am sure you are right,' she agreed, and risked the step of gently withdrawing her hand.

He took the hint, and bowed. Within two minutes he had conducted her back to her aunt, and left the house, together with profuse wishes for the safest of travels and a number of significant looks. Isabel did not quite like the faintly proprietorial air he assumed, but she had not time to consider its import nor how to discourage it, for her aunt demanded instant tidings of what had passed in the parlour.

'Did you accept him?' said Eliza. It struck Isabel that she spoke in a voice of forced calm.

'He merely wished to secure me for the first dances at Ferndeane.'

'Ah.' Eliza's very erect posture relaxed slightly in relief, but her eyes — hazel once more, at least for the present — remained fixed upon Isabel with a considering expression.

'It must be time for our departure, I think?' said Isabel, unwilling to face the question she read in her aunt's gaze.

'I believe it must be,' said Eliza, and rose from her chair. She followed Isabel out of the drawing-room without voicing any of her thoughts, and Isabel was grateful for the reprieve.

It had been agreed between them that they would visit Mr. Balligumph before returning to Ferndeane. The journey from York to Tilby was quiet, unattended by either interest or disaster, and they arrived at the toll-bridge late in the afternoon. Isabel, sleepy from boredom and inactivity, blinked in befuddled confusion at the empty bridge as they approached. The coachman stopped in the centre of it, as he had been instructed to do, and Isabel waited for the troll to appear. Moments passed, and he did not.

'Can he still be in Aylfenhame?' Isabel said with dismay. She opened the carriage door and stepped down. The moment her toes touched the smooth stones of the bridge, the sound of a great sneeze tore the air. So powerful was it that the bridge shook beneath her feet, and she caught hold of the carriage in alarm.

'Mr. Balligumph?' she called.

A second sneeze followed, and a third. Several moments passed in silence, and Isabel judged it safe to release the carriage and step forward. Still she saw no one. Tafferty jumped out of the carriage with a yowl of protest and stood in the middle of the bridge, shaking herself violently and cursing.

'I am comin'!' cried a deep, rumbling voice. 'Wait ye there jest a moment or two, an' I'll be wi' ye.'

Isabel frowned, for it sounded like Mr. Balligumph and yet not like him at all. She understood the reason why when at last he appeared, wrapped in a vast blanket and with a knitted cap upon his head in place of his usual tall hat. His nose was bluer than ever, and the smile he directed at Isabel was watery.

'Do ye know,' he said by way of greeting, 'in years past they used to think that to bathe in the winter time was a dangerous lark indeed! Why, ye could die from it! There's some as still believes it now. Mighty foolish, I used to say, but what do ye think has come to pass since my dip in the pool at home? I am sufferin' wi' the worst cold I can remember bein' burdened with in many a long year. An' if tha' can come to pass in the summer, what might be the consequence o' takin' a bath in the winter? I consider meself chastened, that I do.'

Isabel laughed, and expressed her sympathy in the kindest manner she was able. 'I do hope you are being well taken care of,' she added. 'Should you be living under the bridge in this condition?'

He winked at her, his great eyes twinkling. 'It's a deal snugger down below than ye'd think, Miss Isabel. But it is kind o' ye to think o' that.'

'I will send Lucy with a posset,' she promised. 'Just as soon as I reach home.'

Balligumph waved a huge hand dismissively. 'Nay, ye've no cause to go troublin' yer servants. I am well enough.'

'Then I will bring it myself.'

Balligumph smiled at her. 'I can see there's no refusin' ye. I will accept a posset, then, an' wi' thanks. But if ye aren't too tired from yer journey, I would first 'ave a word wi' ye.' He nodded to Eliza, who now joined them, and added, 'An' wi' yer good aunt, too.'

'We came in search of you,' Isabel replied. 'For we have a particular question to ask.'

'I'll tell ye straight off: I 'aven't the faintest notion what yer Ferryman's called.' He sighed, sniffling with cold. 'I did me best to learn it for ye, but wi' no success. I am sorry.'

'I did not know you had enquired! It is kind of you to try for it, and I am not at all cast down that you have not succeeded. Please, do not think yourself obliged to apologise.'

'Ye aren't?' Balligumph squinted at her. 'Ye've some plan in yer mind, then?'

'The beginnings of a plan, at least,' said Isabel, and glanced at her aunt.

'It is my plan, in truth,' Eliza said. 'And therefore, if you do not like it you must blame me entirely. Isabel has a great deal more good sense than I do.'

The troll narrowed his eyes at Eliza. 'By this I'm to collect that it's some manner o' mad plan, is that the case?'

Eliza smiled coolly. 'Perhaps a little.'

Tafferty hissed, her fur rising. 'A little, I very doubt it! Cracked in the brain, that thou art.' She bared her teeth, her tail lashing. 'An' do not be thinkin' I will stand idly by an' let thee haul my Isabel off into madness after thee!'

Balligumph sighed, and blew his nose upon an enormous handkerchief he retrieved from beneath the blanket he wore. 'Very well, I am braced fer somethin' truly hair-raisin'. On ye go.'

Eliza related her idea, briefly and with perfect composure in spite of Balligumph's lowering brows and Tafferty's bristling hackles. When she arrived at the part in which she and Isabel were to venture into Aylfenhame in search of the Kostigern's lair, he sat up in alarm and shook his head.

'Nay,' he said firmly. 'I'll not help ye wi' such madness as that.

Tafferty is right. Do ye have any notion what ye're fixin' to do?'

'We understand full well that it is dangerous.'

'I don't think ye do! Not if ye are plannin' to go wanderin' thataways wi' no more premonition o' disaster than a babe shovin' its hand into the fire! The Kostigern, an' all! He's a goner, but his little world is no less dangerous for all that. An' besides, we don't even know for sure that he is a goner. Not absolutely for sure. Nobody knows what became o' that one, an' nobody much wants to risk bringin' him back.'

Eliza began to argue, but Balligumph held up a hand. 'Tis ill-mannered o' me to cut ye off, an' I know it. But it is useless t' remonstrate wi' me on this. May I instead tell the two o' ye my news?'

'Please do!' Isabel interjected. 'We would very much like to hear it. Would we not, aunt?'

'It is of use to ye, that I promise. Ye'll have heard about the Piper's Rade, I'll wager?'

'Indeed, we have heard of little else,' said Isabel.

Balligumph nodded. 'Well, now. They used to ride through Aylfenhame an' England on the eve o' summer, many years ago, an' at other times as well. But after the antics o' the one we was just speakin' of, there came the Diminishin'. Thas what they call it. Many o' the fae-folk slipped off into the Torpor for one reason or another, or vanished into England an' were never seen in Aylfenhame again. It must be nigh on a century since the last Rade.

'An' now they are doin' it again, in a manner o' speakin'. Less o' the ridin', an' a deal more o' such merriments as dancin' an' music. They are makin' a deal o' noise, an' that's important. Pipes! Fiddles an' drums! Laughin' and dancin' and merry-makin' all over England. An' there's some as is doin' the same in Aylfenhame, since yer return.' Balli nodded at Isabel. 'It's spreadin'. An' I 'ave heard an interestin' theory as to why.' He paused expectantly. Evidently satisfied with the avid look Isabel was certain he would see upon her own face and her aunt's, he continued. 'They are wakin' people up. Draggin' them out o' the Torpor — kickin' an' screamin', if necessary. It's time fer the Diminishin' to be reversed, an' fer Aylfenhame to wake up!'

'That sounds like a wonderful thing!' said Isabel. She meant every word, for the prospect of Aylfenhame diminishing into silence was a terrible one. 'But why now? What can have caused the Rade to suddenly form up once more?'

'And why in England as well as Aylfenhame?' added Eliza. 'Are they seeking to draw back those who fled here after the Kostigern's war?'

'I reckon they are,' said Balligumph, nodding at Eliza. 'An' one other thing.' He transferred his blue gaze to Isabel and grinned, the tusks on either side of his mouth twitching with the gesture. 'That bein' ye, Miss Isabel.'

Isabel stared. 'Me?'

'Not ye personally. Folk such as ye, an' yer aunt as well. I think ye aren't the only people with Aylir heritage wanderin' about in England. Some, like Mrs. Grey here, are full aware of it an' choose not to pursue it. Some, like yer own self, know nothin' about it.

'In some o' that last group, well, they's too far entrenched in their Englishness to be drawn to their fae side. Yer mother'd be one, Miss Isa. She witnessed the Rade, same as ye, but not a flicker o' difference did it make to her.

'In some, though! That heritage can be woken up, so to speak, an' made lively-like. Ye bein' one particularly fine example.' He smiled at Isabel. ''Tis no coincidence that yer witchiness showed itself after the Rade began to travel in these parts. An' Tafferty arrived wi' ye soon after ye saw them in Alford.'

''Twas probably that very night I felt the call,' Tafferty confirmed. 'An' it were very unpleasant, I'll have thee know! Like an itchin' under my fur.' She shivered and shook all her fur out until it stood on end.

'As to why they are wakin' everyone up, an' why now, well. Thas harder t' answer.' He glanced around at the deserted bridge and equally empty road and fields around, and leaned towards Isabel and Eliza. 'The Diminishin'. It began after the Kostigern, but it worsened badly after They Majesties an' the Princess were lost. They're bound to the fabric of Aylfenhame in ways yer own monarchs are not. Wi' them gone, the realm drifts an' fades into slumber. But things change.' He winked, and straightened up once more.

Isabel understood. He would not say more for fear of being somehow overheard, but his meaning was plain. The Princess may not yet have set foot in Mirramay, but she was no longer lost; no longer enchanted, bound and disabled. Did the realm feel it, in some way? Did her presence begin to rouse those who slumbered, whether they understood the reason or not? Was that why the Ferryman had returned, and Sir Guntifer, and the Piper?

If so, she could only feel that Sophy had been wise to keep Lihyaen away from Mirramay. If the Princess's mere presence in any part of the realm, free and unimpeded, could have such a profound effect, what might occur once she finally returned to the royal city?

'Does Sophy know?' Isabel asked, for a disquieting thought had entered her mind. The folk of Aylfenhame must wonder why the Torpor was releasing those it had long held spell-bound and asleep. They must also be well aware of the connection between the Diminishing and the lost royals of Mirramay. Sooner or later, someone would begin to realise that one of that family walked the realm once more. Was Lihyaen safe? She was thought to have died, and few indeed knew of her true fate. But it was a danger, of which Sophy ought to be aware.

Balligumph nodded, and smiled upon Isabel with approval. 'Very good. Ye are thinkin' quickly. Yes, Sophy knows everythin' I am tellin' ye. I keep her well-informed.'

Isabel frowned, as her mind — ever to be relied upon for worrying ideas — continued to raise disturbing questions. The return from Torpor of Sir Guntifer and the Ferryman could only be considered desirable, but if they could be so released, did it not follow that other, less desirable folk might be released also? What of those who had been condemned to the Torpor for supporting the Kostigern — those whose hearts, unlike the Ferryman's, were truly black?

'I can practically see what ye're thinkin',' Balli said in a grim tone. 'Who else are we expectin' to see poppin' up out o' the long sleep? Tis a worrisome notion. But I 'ave many fine people keepin' their eyes well peeled fer trouble, don't ye worry.

'Which brings me to the rest o' my news. That Piper. Did ye never wonder how the Chronicler kept up wi' the news across Aylfenhame, well enough to write it all down an' save it in that fancy library o' his? He had folk such as I do: news-bringers, I call 'em. Folk what keep their eyes an' ears open an' bring back anythin' of interest. But the Chronicler didn't just record the happenin's of Aylfenhame. He spread 'em about, too — leastwise, those happenin's which pleased They Majesties t' have known. This Piper what's loose an' rattlin' around in yer merry old England? He is one o' the Chronicler's news-bringers an' news-bearers. Who better than a travellin' musician to collect all the tales, an' carry new ones about?'

Balligumph sat back, beaming, his demeanour expectant. Isabel lost no time in offering the rapture and praise he was waiting for.

'Why, Mr. Balligumph! That is wonderful news! For if he does not himself remember the story of the Ferryman, perhaps he may know of another who does? We will not need to go anywhere near the Kostigern!'

Balligumph nodded vigorously. 'Aye. Thas the way I like to hear ye talkin'. Forget yer ideas in that direction! Go ye t' the Piper an' see what he can tell ye.'

'That is easier said than done,' observed Eliza. 'You are a resourceful fellow, Mr. Balligumph, and this piece of news is encouraging indeed. We thank you for it! But we have just come from York, where half the city is agog for a glimpse of the Rade. And so far, they have been disappointed. Nobody can predict when or where they will next be seen, and merely showing up at every available ball or assembly in hopes of encountering them is a strategy which has benefited few. How are we to find him?'

Balligumph replied with a gusty sneeze, and a watery sniff. 'Sorry,' he muttered damply. 'They're in the Hills,' he added thickly as he groped for his handkerchief.

'The what?'

Balli blew his nose mightily, and took some time about mopping up afterwards. Isabel averted her gaze, slightly appalled at the sight of the mess pouring from the troll's nose. It was iridescent blue, and looked disturbingly pretty given its provenance.

'The Hills,' Balligumph said when at last he finished cleaning himself up. 'The Hollow Hills. Ye both know what I'm sayin'.'

Isabel exchanged a puzzled look with Eliza. 'Do we?'

Balligumph blinked at her in horror. 'Ye don't?' He looked up at the sunny sky in despair, and shook his head. 'Have the folk of England forgotten everythin'? Tafferty, I am done. Ye must explain fer me.'

Tafferty sat up and stretched languorously, her every movement expressive of disdain. 'The Hollow Hills,' she repeated. 'They was known as the Other, once upon a while. Not England an' not Aylfenhame. Somethin' in between, if ye believe the tales. In truth, I think no one knows where they fall. But if thou wert t' wander in the right direction, an' find thyself at just the right one o' yer English hills, thou mayst be so fortunate as t' find a door. An' beyond that door, there's the Other. The Hollows. Where many sleep, an' eat, an' dance, an' sometimes travel.' Her tail twitched and she shook herself. 'Some folk say that it is pretty well half an' half, under there. Fae an' humans mixin' themselves up all higgledy. But I cannot say. I 'ave ever been into them.'

Balligumph nodded along as Tafferty spoke, and shrugged when she reached the end of her speech. 'Nor 'ave I. But I'll wager ye anythin' ye like that the Piper an' his merry musicians are hidin' themselves in the Hollows. I'll go further: there's said t' be an entrance somewhere in the Wolds, an' given how they keeps appearin' in these parts, I'd say there's like t' be some truth t' that notion. If ye want t' find 'em, there ye must look.'

There was silence for a moment as Isabel turned this over in her mind, and her aunt perhaps did the same. They exchanged another long look, and Isabel saw her own thoughts reflected in her aunt's face. 'How would we know if we were wandering in the right direction?' she said. 'Or when we arrived at the right hill?'

'Good questions both,' said Balligumph cheerfully. 'There I cannot help ye, just at present. Tafferty?'

'I 'ave not a blinkin' notion,' said the catterdandy.

'Eh, well. I am workin' on it.'

Isabel smiled and thanked him, but absently, for her mind was busy. An idea had surfaced as he spoke. 'I think I may know someone who can help, but it requires a little thought.'

Balligumph looked enquiringly at her, but she shook her head. 'I will say nothing more at the moment, as I am unsure whether it will be of any use at all.'

'Intriguin',' said the troll, and grinned. 'Miss Ellerby has a secret! I am curiously impressed.'

Isabel blushed, for no reason she could understand. She looked away, annoyed with herself. Why should Balligumph's words make her feel guilty? There was no shame in sometimes keeping things to herself.

'I believe we must be going, my love,' said Eliza. 'Your mama has been expecting us this half-hour at least, I imagine.'

Isabel could not but admit the probability, and immediately made her curtsey to Balligumph. 'I will return with a posset for you,' she promised. 'Or if I cannot, I will send another. Pray do take care of yourself, Mr. Balligumph!'

The troll smiled genially in response and made her an awkward half-bow, still clutching the blanket around himself. 'Ye're a sweet thing, Miss. I'll await yer posset.'

The carriage conveyed Isabel, Eliza and Tafferty to Ferndeane within ten minutes, giving Isabel little time to absorb the information she had lately heard — let alone to prepare herself to meet her parents. When the carriage came to a stop outside of the front door of Isabel's home and the door was opened to permit her egress, she found she still had not decided what to tell her mother and father.

She was not immediately called upon to speak at all beyond the barest civilities. Eliza, as the guest, naturally dominated the majority of Mr. and Mrs. Ellerby's attention, and until she had been settled in the best guest room and partaken of the tea spread out in the parlour, there was no occasion for anybody to pay much heed to Isabel. She took the opportunity to order Balligumph's posset from Cook, and to give orders for its delivery to the bridge.

So occupied was Mrs. Ellerby in her role as hostess to her sister that she was long in noticing Tafferty. The catterdandy had refused to be concealed, in spite of Isabel's attempts to persuade her. She would not be sent around to the rear door and given her dinner in the kitchens. Nor would she consent to be wrapped up in Isabel's shawl and carried swiftly up to her chamber. She stalked into the house with her tail and her nose high in the air, and only Eliza's swift forethought in entering first prevented her being noticed immediately.

When the bustle of arrival was over and Mrs. Ellerby at last had leisure to look about herself, her eye soon fell upon Tafferty curled up upon one of the parlour chairs, and her dismay was immediate. 'Oh, Isabel! You have not brought that creature in with you! I have seen nothing of it these past weeks, and quite thought it had taken itself off.' She went to shoo the catterdandy off the chair, and encountered a dark stare from Tafferty together with an utter refusal to be moved.

Isabel sighed inwardly, her tremulous spirits sinking. 'Mama, there is no harm in her!' she said, in what she hoped was a firm but respectful tone. 'She is friendly, and a suitable pet for me. I have grown fond of her.' Tafferty's tail flicked with disdain at the word pet, but to Isabel's relief she did not speak.

'How can that be, my dear, when you have but just arrived from York?' said Mrs. Ellerby. 'Surely you did not take the animal along with you.'

Isabel cast about for a sensible response to make to this, and came up with nothing. How could she explain how she came to adopt Tafferty, without admitting the full truth — that Tafferty had, more rightly speaking, adopted her?

'Isabel was heart-sick at the poor creature's weariness and hunger,' Eliza interjected. 'You know her tenderness of heart, Harriet! She could not bear to leave her new friend behind. You may imagine my surprise when I received not only my niece, but also her cat, for a visit.'

Mrs. Ellerby sighed deeply, abandoning her attempts to move Tafferty off the chair. 'Is it a cat? I have never seen its like. It looks to me more like something fae. Now, does it not, Mr. Ellerby? It would be much more at home with the brownies, in the kitchen.'

Isabel winced, torn between annoyance at her mother's insistence on referring to Tafferty as "it" and dismay that she could relegate the brownies and Tafferty both to the kitchens, as though all things fae belonged in the servants' quarters.

'I would like Tafferty to stay with me, Mama, please,' she said, quietly but firmly. 'She is my friend.'

Mrs. Ellerby sighed again, and cast Isabel a look of pure annoyance. But she sat down, and made no further attempts to oppose her daughter's wishes. 'Truly, I think the whole of the neighbourhood has gone fae-mad!' she said instead. 'Chattering on about the Piper, and the Fiddler, and the dancers! The Rade, indeed! It is such nonsense. It had much better all be forgotten.' She regarded Isabel again, but her annoyance had given way to something else Isabel could not identify. Was there a tinge of concern? 'I have not seen the like since Miss Landon went away, and Isabel was drawn after. Do you remember, my dear? The things that befell you in Aylfenhame! I was never more alarmed. They had better keep to themselves, and stop pulling good English folk into their nonsense.' She nodded her head at her own self at the conclusion of this speech, well satisfied with her reasoning.

Isabel could not agree, but Eliza spoke first. 'But Miss Landon is as happy as can be in Aylfenhame, Harriet! Isabel brings me the liveliest tales of her. Truly, I think no better fate can have befallen her.'

Mrs. Ellerby looked askance at her sister, and clucked her tongue. 'You always were a little strange in your notions, Lizzy.'

Eliza smiled faintly, and said nothing.

'She is right, Mama!' said Isabel. 'Sophy was never happier in her life before. It is always a pleasure to visit her.'

'That is not saying a great deal, for I am sure she had little to please her before. I do wish you would stop visiting her, my dear, though I am sorry to have to say it! To be sure I always liked Sophia very well, but it gives me the greatest uneasiness to think of you travelling in such an odd place. It can hardly be safe. But I dare say you will not be persuaded, not even to please your poor Mama.'

'It would be the shabbiest thing to abandon her, and besides, I should miss her very much.'

Mrs. Ellerby eyed Tafferty with displeasure. 'I dare say you are right, only do please bring us no more of their odd creatures to Ferndeane.'

'I will do my best, Mama.'

Tafferty laid her tail over her eyes and grumbled something. Then she said, quite distinctly, 'Thou'rt a worryish bein'. That must be where thy daughter comes by 'er wibblishness.'

Mrs. Ellerby gaped at Tafferty, but before she could speak Eliza rose from her chair and set down her tea cup. 'I find I am tired after our journey, and I am sure you are likewise, Isabel. You will excuse us, Harriet? Mr. Ellerby? A little rest before dinner will refresh both of us marvellously.'

Isabel rose gratefully, and cast a significant look at Tafferty. The catterdandy refused to budge, however; indeed, her tail remained stubbornly wrapped over her eyes, and she probably had not seen Isabel's attempts to catch her attention.

'Tafferty, do come upstairs,' Isabel said, for it was hopeless now to pretend that she was any ordinary beast. 'It is much more comfortable upon the bed, if you are going to sleep.'

Tafferty's tail twitched upwards, and Isabel encountered a green stare. 'I am tired. Go upperty-stairsy I will not, lest thou'rt offerin' t' carry me.'

'I shall be happy to do so,' said Isabel, and scooped the catterdandy up in her arms. She curtseyed vaguely in her mother and father's direction and hastily made her exit.

Eliza followed her upstairs, barely troubling to conceal her laughter. 'Beautiful, Tafferty! I have not seen that look on my sister's face in many years.'

Isabel could not share her aunt's amusement. Her mother had relented with respect to Tafferty, but that was before she knew that the catterdandy spoke — and moreover, was possessed of strong opinions and a tart tongue. But she would fight that battle later, if fight she must. Her aunt was correct: she was tired.

But she was not yet to rest. Eliza followed her to her room and closed the door behind her, first ensuring that they were alone. 'I have something else I must tell you,' she said, and her demeanour puzzled Isabel. She appeared to experience some difficulty in meeting Isabel's gaze, and her manner spoke of some measure of... guilt?

Isabel deposited Tafferty gently upon the bed, and found her a shawl to sleep upon. 'What is it, aunt?'

Eliza looked at her hands. 'When I told you of your Aylir heritage, you scarcely believed me at first. I had told you of distinctive features and colouring, and you had them not. Commonplace, you called yourself. Do you remember?'

She looked up at she spoke, and fixed Isabel with an intense, unnerving stare. Isabel felt a sense of deep foreboding, and had to swallow her unease before she could reply. 'I remember.' Eliza had also said that Ayliri features had not manifested in her either, but that had not proved to be true, for the ordinary, human appearance she wore was but a Glamour. Her aunt's appearance was distinctly other, her fae heritage stamped clearly upon her features.

But she had hidden that truth from everyone — even those who knew her best. Because she was a mistress of the art of Glamour.

Isabel's breath stopped.

'I see you have anticipated me,' said Eliza with a faint, crooked smile. Her cloaking Glamour melted away in an instant, leaving her youthful and obviously Aylir once more.

'Oh, no...' whispered Isabel. She rushed to the mirror and stared hard into it, examining every inch of the features which were so familiar to her. Her dark eyes, a little large but perfectly ordinary. Her hair, a comfortable brown shade, curling a little. Her features were attractive enough, but not arresting. It was her face. 'Is this... is this not...?'

Eliza sighed. 'I had to do it,' she said. 'You heard your mother downstairs. She has never had much time for anything fae — excepting, of course, the brownies who obligingly keep clean her house. Many agree with her. My mother used the Glamour more and more as she grew older, muting and fading her more remarkable features until she was able to blend in with those around her. And she camouflaged me. Harriet would not recognise me as I am now.'

Isabel clutched at her own face, as though she could retain it by force of will alone. 'No. This is me.'

But as she spoke, her reflection rippled like water and changed. Her hair was not commonplace brown at all, but as rich in hue as chocolate and threaded with gold. Her eyes were burnished jade. Her features were more regular, and somehow more distinct; her cheekbones sharper; her lips more finely sculpted, her nose straighter, her lashes longer. As she stared at heself, Isabel detected a hundred tiny signs, impossible to describe, that these were not human features.

She did not know when she began to cry; she only became aware that her cheeks were wet and tears were dripping from her jaw. 'This is not me,' she said indistinctly. 'Tell me this is a Glamour.'

Eliza came up behind her and laid a hand on her shoulder. 'I am sorry. I have wanted to tell you for so many years, but I did not know how you would react. I did not know if you had inherited Harriet's opinions about the fae. For a long time, it seemed that you had. All you wanted was an English life! The same life, the same concerns, as all your neighbours.'

'That is still what I want!' said Isabel fiercely. She turned away from the mirror, dabbing angrily at her tears with the edge of her shawl. 'When did you begin this charade?'

'Soon after you were born. Your eyes, and your hair! Your Mama noticed. So did your father, and others. They were uneasy. I watched your mother withdraw from you, unsure what she had given birth to; unsure whether she could love you. When I altered those things, fractionally only, they were able to believe that it was but a brief and passing thing, or perhaps some trick of the light. And they accepted you, and loved you as the child they had wanted. Was I wrong to do it?'

Isabel could not answer that question; not now. 'Is there nothing of me that is real? Who am I, aunt?'

'You are still Isabel,' said Eliza quietly. 'You are who you have always been.'

'I do not know who that is. It seems I have never known.'

Eliza bowed her head. 'I will leave you to grow accustomed. Would you prefer it if I were to restore the Glamour?'

Isabel shook her head blindly. 'I do not know. It can be of no consequence now.'

Eliza nodded, and quietly withdrew. Isabel paced the room for some time, gripping her shawl so tightly that her fingers hurt. Nothing that she had ever known of herself was the truth! Nothing, nothing. Not even her face was her own. She could not bear to look again in the mirror, for she saw a stranger.

At length she yielded to the impulse of weariness, and lay down upon the bed. To her surprise, Tafferty uncurled herself and lay down by Isabel's side. She was warm, and a rumbling purr vibrated her small body. 'Aye, an' thou'rt bound t' struggle wi' the lot of it fer a time. Yer aunt acted wi' the best o' wishes fer thee, but I could wish she 'ad told thee before now. 'Tis a shock fer thee.'

Her companion had never before been so understanding, and her kindness soothed Isabel a little. She tangled her fingers in Tafferty's fur and closed her eyes, curling up around her catterdandy. 'I do not know who I am,' she said in a hollow voice. 'Miss Ellerby has been naught but a lie.'

'Miss Ellerby, perhaps,' said Tafferty. 'But Isabel, now. Thou'rt still she.'

'I do not know who Isabel is, either.'

'Thou wilt,' said Tafferty simply. 'In time.'

CHAPTER SIXTEEN

Isabel did not again trouble her aunt to restore the Glamour of her human face. With Tafferty's assistance, she was able to restore it for herself. She wept as she did so, recognising the artifice that lay in every line of her familiar features. But once the Isabel she knew looked back at her from the looking glass, she dried her tears and returned to Miss Ellerby's world.

She was more disturbed than she cared to admit by her aunt's story. What would have become of her had Eliza not modified her face, when she was newborn? Would her mother have grown accustomed to her daughter's differences, and accepted her as she was? Or would she have rejected the child? And if so, what would that have meant for Isabel's life?

She could hardly imagine that Tilby society — and, even moreso, beyond — would have accepted so obviously fae a child as one of their own. Isabel might have grown up as an outcast, and her family forever looked at askance, as not quite right. So far, at least, she could understand both her mother's feelings and her aunt's actions.

But her heart still cried out with pain and confusion at the extent of the trickery that had been played upon her. That sense of self, so important to the peace of any young woman, had been built upon a lie and was now torn from her entirely.

Was I wrong to do it? Isabel did not know if her aunt had done the right thing. Perhaps no one would ever be able to say for certain. But the question that weighed upon her mind was: How would her mother react if she were to learn the truth? If she had not been able to accept the real Isabel at her birth, would she be able to do so now?

Should she, in short, tell her mother and father — and the rest of the world — the truth, or should Eliza's Glamour conceal the true Miss Ellerby forever?

No answers to these questions presented themselves, and Isabel's head began to ache with the effort of puzzling her way through the possible consequences of exposure versus concealment. It proved difficult for her to focus upon the conversation in the parlour that morning, which ought to have been reassuring in its ordinary simplicity. At length she excused herself, ignoring her aunt's attempts to catch her eye, and collected her bonnet and shawl. The day was fine, and not too hot, and she intended to partake of the refreshment of a walk in Tilton Wood.

Her going thither also served another purpose. She walked for half an hour, turning her steps in the direction she had taken a mere few weeks previously — before she had learned of the peculiarity of her heritage; before she had become something so other than Miss Ellerby of Ferndeane. On that day, she had been so absent in her mind that she had lost herself, and encountered unexpected aid.

When she judged that she had arrived in roughly the same part of the wood, she stopped. The exertion of rapid walking had overheated her, and she took off her bonnet, looping the ribbon over her arm. The breeze felt refreshing as it ruffled her hair, and she unwound her shawl from her shoulders as well. 'Tiltager!' she called softly. 'Tiltager, I would speak with you.'

No response reached her ears, and she knew disappointment. Had she found the right place? The woods looked familiar to her, but perhaps she misremembered. She wandered a little, her bonnet swinging upon its coloured ribbons, and called Tiltager's name from time to time. At length, just as she was preparing to abandon the project and return home, she heard a faint little voice hailing her from somewhere in the vicinity of her knees. 'Goodest of mornings, Mistress!'

Isabel looked down, and smiled. The little fae looked unchanged, gnarled as a bundle of twigs and wispy as a dried leaf; only the tattered brown dress that she had worn had been replaced with a merrier garment of faded violet rags, and she wore a bundle of moss for a hat. She bowed as she had before, and held up for Isabel's interest a cluster of daisies.

'Thank you,' Isabel said, and carefully took the flowers. 'Tell me, Tiltager. Why is it that you call me "Mistress"?'

'My line has served yours for centuries, Mistress,' said Tiltager happily. 'Did you not know?'

'I did not know that I was of any line at all, save for that of the Ellerby family.' Isabel tucked the daisies into the sash of her gown and smiled at the little fae. 'Nor that there was any such arrangement as you describe.'

Tiltager bowed again. 'My granny trained your great-grandsire's companion,' she said proudly. 'May I be of help to you?' She quivered with enthusiasm at the prospect, which made Isabel smile, though it puzzled her a little.

'Someday I would like you to tell me more of my forebears,' she said, 'since you appear to know far more than I. But today, I have a particular question to put to you.'

Tiltager adopted a listening pose so exaggerated that Isabel laughed. 'It will be my pleasure to answer any question you may have, Mistress!'

'I pray you, do not call me Mistress! For though I shall be glad of your help, I do not consider you as a servant.'

Tiltager tilted her head at the word servant. 'What is it that you speak of?'

Isabel attempted to explain the concept of servitude, but Tiltager could not understand her. 'I am here to help,' she simply repeated, and grew injured by Isabel's efforts to assure her that she was in no way bound to do so. At length Isabel abandoned the discussion, reassuring Tiltager as best she could that she had meant no offence — for she saw that she had inadvertently hurt her.

'I am very much in need of your help,' she assured the fae, 'for I have a difficult task to fulfil. Do you know a way into the Hollow Hills?'

Tiltager's eyes widened, and she shook her head, sending her knotted curls flying. 'Oh, Mistress! You do not wish to go there, no indeed!'

'Isabel, please. I do not wish to go there, precisely, but I must urgently speak with someone who I believe to be residing there.'

Tiltager continued to protest, but Isabel was firm. At last the little fae sighed deeply, and flopped onto her back among the moss. 'I know a way,' she said.

'Will you take me, and one other?'

'If I must,' said Tiltager unhappily.

'Why is it so ill-advised?'

'Because the folk of England, they wander in and then they do not always wander out!' said Tiltager. 'They are lost, and forever!' She sat up suddenly, and jumped to her feet. 'But you are not wholly of the folk of England, you! Perhaps it will be all right.' She smiled, and added helpfully, 'But I hope you are not particularly attached to this other person that you intend for me to guide.'

'She is my aunt, and of the same line.'

Tiltager brightened further. 'Then we shall make a merry party of it, yes! And perhaps there is a small chance that we will all come out again.'

Isabel tried not to feel too alarmed.

'It will be best to go at night,' continued Tiltager. 'For that is when they are dancing! And most of them will be too busy and merry to notice you and your aunt. I think it will be much better.'

'It will not be easy for us to be abroad at night. Shall it be so very ill-advised to go in the daytime?'

Tiltager looked grave. 'If you wish it especially, then of course we will go in the daytime.'

'But you think it unwise.'

'Most unwise! Most very much unwise.'

Eliza would not shy from such an adventure, Isabel knew that well enough. Nor, precisely, did she. Only it would be difficult indeed to escape Ferndeane at night without waking anyone. 'Where is the way into the Hills?'

Tiltager looked surprised. 'Why, we are close upon it now. It is at yonder edge of the Wood.' She pointed unerringly behind herself, without making the smallest effort to orient herself first.

'Are there many ways into the Hills, Tiltager?'

'None, that I know. Not for many miles.'

Isabel was surprised, too, though after a moment's reflection she felt that she should not be. Tilby was not precisely usual in the generality of English towns and villages. There were, on average, more household brownies in residence across Tilby than in other places, and no other town that she had ever seen or heard of had a troll for a bridge-keeper. And it was, perhaps, no coincidence that her own Aylir ancestor, whoever it had been, had come here, and left a child behind. What it was about Tilby that drew such interest from the denizens of Aylfenhame, she did not know.

'I shall find you here this evening,' Isabel said. 'At a late hour, once the moon is up. Will you be waiting?'

'I shall be waiting!' said Tiltager, and bowed.

Isabel took her leave soon afterwards, aware that she had been gone some little time already. She did not wish to excite comment or suspicion at home; not when she was to so far transgress as to leave Ferndeane in the late hours and wander abroad at night. If she were to be caught leaving or returning, it would be as well to avoid compounding those problems with some earlier misdemeanour; her mother's temper would not be quick to recover.

On returning home, she found an early opportunity to speak to her aunt alone, and availed herself of it at once. Eliza, predictably, was excited by the prospect, and eager to accompany Isabel. She appeared to wish to take her niece's request of company as a sign that her meddling had been forgiven, but Isabel could not fully assure her of that. She did not precisely know how she felt about Eliza's actions; only that she was more than sensible of the folly of venturing into the Hills alone, and none but her aunt could or would follow her there. The arrangement was made, to creep from the house at midnight, once all had sought their beds. Thus they parted, conspirators in Isabel's second secret undertaking in a month, to while away the intervening hours with all the innocent and mundane activities of a normal day at Ferndeane.

Isabel was unused to subterfuge. It was not easy for her to undergo the rituals of dinner, and subsequently supper, with her family while betraying none of the unease and guilt she felt inside. Her brother engaged her in conversation about her visit to her aunt in York, and she was obliged to conceal from him the truth of her sojourn in Aylfenhame as well as disguising her discomfort about her upcoming venture behind a facade of normality. The strain resulted in a headache before dinner was over, and weariness threatened to dissuade her from attempting the Hills at all.

Eliza sensed her difficulties, and exerted herself to deflect attention from her niece wherever possible. She chattered in the liveliest fashion about the calls they had paid upon her acquaintance, and the dinners and evening parties they had attended; she made light of Isabel's supposed bout of illness, while still contriving to present it as full reason enough to explain Isabel's absence from York society for near upon a week; and she entered into the interminable discussions of Charles's upcoming wedding with sufficient enthusiasm to disguise her niece's lack of liveliness on the subject. Isabel was grateful to her, and endeavoured to remonstrate with the part of her soul which blamed Eliza for the masquerade she had imposed upon Isabel's life. She felt plagued with guilt; guilt that she had deceived her parents, and would do so again; guilt that she could resent her aunt, when Eliza had probably displayed a truer and deeper concern for her happiness than any other member of her family; guilt that she could not welcome the heritage which Eliza gloried in.

When at last she was permitted to retire to her room, she wished deeply that she could tuck herself into bed with Tafferty beside her, and sleep away the tumult of emotions she had suffered throughout the day, and the weariness they had left behind. But she grimly pushed such impulses aside, and forced herself through the motions of changing her evening attire for more practical walking dress. She whiled away the ensuing hour with a book, though her mind refused to focus more than passingly upon the text. Her thoughts drifted back to the Ferryman, and the way he had laughed with her, danced with her, welcomed her and accepted her. She held his smiling image firmly in mind, reminding herself of the irreproachable reasons behind her departure from propriety, obedience and — so her mother would certainly say — good sense. A voice at the back of her mind persisted in wondering: How would he feel about her true appearance? Would he be pleased? Would he be dismayed? What if it was her very Englishness that had appealed to him? How would he react to the truth of her heritage, her face, her nature?

This voice went steadfastly ignored.

At last she heard a faint tap upon the door, and put away her book. When Eliza entered moments later, Isabel stood ready to accept the bonnet and shawl which her aunt brought with her. They donned their outdoor attire in silence, and crept unshod through the house with Tafferty padding along at their heels. The hour was early enough that some one or two servants were still awake and at work; Isabel trusted that any faint sounds she and her aunt made would be put down to such a source, but still she did not breathe easily until they had successfully traversed the great staircase and slipped out of the front door. The house would be locked up for the night upon their return, so she made sure to take the spare door key from its regular spot in the porch and tuck it into her reticule.

They paused upon the threshold to don stout walking shoes, and then slipped away into the darkness. Isabel's heart pounded alarmingly as they crept down the driveway and out into the fields, for she had never before been afoot in the full dark of night, and so far beyond the shrubbery of Ferndeane as they now ventured.

The moon was bright, but its silvery light availed them little once they stepped beneath the trees of Tilton Wood. Eliza had had sufficient forethought to acquire a lamp, however, and she held it high, lighting the path some few feet ahead of them. Tafferty took the lead, navigating the uneven pathways of Tilton more successfully, with her sensitive night eyes, than either Eliza or Isabel could have done alone. The half-hour it took to reach Tiltager's part of the wood passed with agonising slowness to Isabel's mind, as it seemed that their passage beneath the trees stretched interminably. They had woven Glamours behind themselves, maintaining the illusion that both she and Eliza lay peacefully asleep, in case anybody should take it into their heads to go into either of those rooms. But every moment, Isabel imagined some unlucky chance undoing all of their careful plans, and exposing her absence to the household. She could not be calm, not even with her aunt's confident reassurance.

When they at last found Tiltager these concerns rapidly faded from Isabel's mind, for she was faced with the very near prospect of entering the Hollow Hills, and without the permission or invitation of any of those who lived within. Tiltager bowed and chattered as she led them through the Wood towards the Hollow Way, and Isabel's courage threatened to fail her more than once as she pictured all the possible catastrophes that might befall them once within. She was obliged to summon the Ferryman's image to her mind and hold fast to it, in order to go on, and nothing but the recollection of his wit and his smile and the tragedy of his unearned plight could keep her from abandoning all thought of pursuing the elusive Piper.

She missed him. His company cheered and enlivened her in ways she experienced with no one else. In his presence, she was able to do and be as she pleased, with regard neither for the propriety of her behaviour, nor for the opprobrium of society. She had taught him to dance, and she had danced and laughed herself with a degree of merriment, of contentment and happiness she had rarely ever felt before; for she had, at last, ceased to think of the behaviour expected of her, and simply done as she wished. It had been a heady experience, and one she had scarcely allowed herself to think of before, for it cast the rest of her life into a stark, and unflattering, contrast.

Now she allowed those thoughts and memories to overtake her entirely, for they strengthened her resolve and kept her hurrying into the darkness ahead. She did not know how long she and Eliza followed Tiltager and Tafferty through the night, but at length they came to a halt in some part of Tilton Wood which Isabel had never before seen. The trees grew thick and close, their trunks wide and gnarled with age. The ground was no longer flat here: ahead of them rose a tall hill, its sides covered with clusters of dark, aged trees gleaming silvery-grey under the moon.

'Here we are, strange ladies!' said Tiltager brightly. 'Onwards, do you still wish to go?'

'That we do,' said Eliza firmly. 'But first, my dear Isabel, I do advise relinquishing the Glamour. In the Hills, I think it will be advisable to allow our own true selves to show.'

Isabel could not but admit the sense of this, but still she hesitated. She did not think she could restore the Glamour of her face without the benefit of a mirror, and so she would have to travel home and slip back into her bed with her Aylir face on full display. What if they were to encounter someone on the way, or upon their return to the house?

No matter. Her aunt was correct, and she had no time now to concern herself with the possibility of trouble later. She allowed her painstakingly-assembled Glamour to fade, suffering a small pang of regret as she did so, and nodded to her aunt. 'I am ready.'

Tiltager waited until Eliza had likewise prepared herself, and then turned away from them. She stared up into the trees ahead, motionless and silent, and Isabel could not discern what she was attempting to do. But within moments a light began to shine, a light as pale as the moon but growing ever stronger. At last the brightness swelled to such proportions that Isabel could scarcely bear to look at it a moment longer.

'Here's off!' cried Tiltager, and she jumped forward into the light.

Tafferty sprang after her, tail lashing.

Isabel exchanged a look with Eliza, and accepted the hand her aunt held out to her. They moved forward together, shading their eyes against the light until it engulfed them. The glow extinguished abruptly, and Isabel tumbled into darkness.

The first thing Isabel became aware of was the strong scents of flowers and honey in the air, a combination she found both heady and tantalising.

The second was faint strains of music, echoing as they reached her ears. Some oddity in the arrangement of the melody, and the strangeness of the tones, struck her as familiar. She had heard such music once before.

'The Piper,' Isabel said softly, reaching for her aunt in the near-darkness. 'That is his music. He was first seen at Alford, because his regular home is here.'

'Excellent,' said her aunt, with strong satisfaction, and such a pragmatic manner that Isabel recollected herself. The passage had disoriented her, and she had to force herself to focus upon her surroundings.

She could see little, initially, for they stood in near darkness. But the ground was soft beneath her feet and she detected the springy texture of grass, or perhaps moss. Looming shadows implied the presence of trees, and she heard the soft sounds of leaves rustling in a cool breeze, and of scurrying animals somewhere close by. In the near distance, soft lights glowed. Tiltager and Tafferty set forth in the direction of the lights, and Eliza and Isabel followed.

The music grew gradually louder as they ventured on, and the lights grew brighter. Stepping carefully, Isabel walked on through dark, whispering trees until the ground dipped beneath her feet and she all but fell.

'There be the dancers,' whispered Tiltager, startling Isabel. She had stopped, too, and her tiny form had been all but hidden in the darkness.

They stood on the edge of a valley ringed with tall, gnarled trees. Lanterns hung from the branches, softly illuminating the revelry underway below. One of the trees was no tree at all, Isabel realised with delight; she was a tree-giant like Sir Guntifer, her trunk firmly planted on one side of the valley and lanterns in her hair as she swayed to the music. Abundant flowers and fragrant foliage ringed the glade — the source, no doubt, of the delicious aromas which teased Isabel's nose.

In the centre, a clear space served as the dancing-floor for a great many Ayliri couples. The dance they performed resembled a lively cotillion, though the steps were as nothing Isabel had ever seen before. They danced with abandon, laughing and whirling with unabashed enjoyment; Isabel felt an instant, inexplicable but strong desire to join them. Judging from the tightening of Eliza's hand upon hers, her aunt suffered from a similar compulsion. Even Tiltager was beginning to sway in time to the music.

Isabel gasped, as the piercing notes of a pipe rose above the music. She could not see the Piper, but that must be him. 'Tiltager!' she said softly.

The little fae bobbed one of her funny bows to Isabel. 'Mistress?'

'That pipe! The one who plays it is the one I seek.'

Tiltager brightened. 'Oh, Lyrriant! Probably he will not be angry. Wait here.'

Isabel winced inwardly at that probably. She watched as Tiltager trotted away in the direction of the dancers, Tafferty following at her heels.

Eliza sighed softly, and began to sway back and forth. 'It is very hard, to be obliged to wait.'

Isabel nodded her agreement. Somehow she knew every note of the melody, though she was sure she had never heard the tune before. It hummed through her bones, urging her to abandon caution and her errand both, and join herself with the music at once. She gripped her aunt's arm, fighting hard to resist the allure of the dance.

Then the elegant, soaring notes of a fiddle reached her ears, emanating from somewhere close by. She jumped, and instinctively stepped backwards and further into the shadows of the trees. A man passed them only a few feet away; Isabel realised with a start that she recognised him. He was tall and broad of shoulder, his skin pallid and his hair even paler. He wore a flamboyant full-sleeved shirt and knee-breeches, with strangely curled shoes. He played haunting notes upon a violin with a slender, pearly bow; the instrument seemed to her wondering eye to be made from spun glass, and mist curled in its depths.

'The Fiddler,' she whispered to her aunt. 'I saw him at the

Assembly.'

The Fiddler disappeared into the throng of dancers and musicians. Isabel soon lost sight of him, though she could hear the strains of the music he played. She could not see Tiltager either, nor Tafferty.

'Aunt, do you think we should—' she began, but she came to an abrupt halt as the Fiddler appeared directly in front of them. He bowed to them, his bow still drawing a lively melody from the strings of his violin, and smiled graciously upon them both. But his smile held a hint of something far less than congenial, as he said, 'Tis a rudeness to spectate, and without an invitation! Some might call it spying.'

Isabel curtseyed at once and curtseyed low, her heart pounding. 'Our apologies, sir! We had no intent to spy. We are here to speak with one of your own — the one who plays the pipe.'

The Fiddler smiled a little wider, his pale eyes glinting with all the warmth of ice. 'Lyrriant is occupied at present. Perhaps you will permit me to entertain you.' He turned his head slightly, and at this minor gesture two Aylir gentlemen instantly left the dance and approached. One was as slender and graceful as any woman, his hair tumbling in silver-grey curls around a pale, elegant face. The other was dark of skin, his hair a contrastingly pallid cloud, his black eyes wide-set above high, sharp cheekbones. They were both attired in an approximation of the court dress of England, at least that which had been fashionable in the past century: Silken knee-breeches and stockings, shirts as light as gossamer and as pale as moonlight; their waistcoats patterned with cobwebs and leaves; their coats sewn from mist-grey and twilight velvet, and richly decorated with lace. The two gentlemen bowed to Eliza and Isabel, and each extended a hand.

'But—' Isabel tried to say. The rest of the words she had intended to speak would not come, for the Fiddler raised one ice-white eyebrow and played three swift, sharp notes upon the violin. All thought of anything save the music, the dance and her partner left Isabel's head in an instant. Instead of darting away in search of the Piper, or Tiltager, or Tafferty, she found herself curtseying low to the gentleman with the silvery curls and accepting his proffered hand. Moments later she was deep in the dance, tripping lightly through the steps of the strange cotillion as though she had danced it all her life. She saw Eliza whirling close by, laughing with delight, her eyes bright with merriment and her cheeks pink with exertion.

A stray wisp of thought intruded itself upon Isabel's happiness: She saw Tiltager in her mind's eye, and the Piper as he had been at the Alford Assembly, his attention fixed upon her for one brief, intense moment. Her last thought was of the Ferryman, laughing as she taught him to dance.

Then the music engulfed her, and everything else faded.

A short, sharp, piercing pain abruptly jolted Isabel out of her merry reverie some immeasurable time later. She gasped, stumbled and almost fell, for the pain came from her left ankle, and a weight hung there, dragging her off-balance. She blinked, brought suddenly back to her own mind. The cotillion whirled on around her, but she was no longer absorbed by it.

She knew a pang of regret, which she quickly smothered. Looking down, she was not surprised to see Tafferty hanging off her leg, the catterdandy's jaws clamped tight around her ankle.

'I thank you,' she gasped. 'But I beg you will release me.'

Tafferty relaxed the grip of her sharp teeth, growling in her throat. 'Thou may'st apologise t' me later,' she grumbled. 'Which part o' stay there was confusin' t' thee?'

'Oh, we did! But we were observed, I must assume, and the Fiddler came, and somehow I lost my senses.' Isabel looked wildly around for Eliza, but did not see her.

'Aye,' muttered Tafferty. 'Music went straight t' thy bubblish head, an' away thou didst wander. An' thy aunt, the same! A precious pair ye do make. Make haste. Tiltager 'as got the Piperish one in speech, an' she requires thee.'

'I am coming this moment, only I cannot find my aunt.'

'I will attend t' that. Off with thee. Thataway.' Tafferty pointed her nose off to her left, and then dashed away.

To her dismay, Isabel realised that her bonnet and shawl were lost and her hair had come loose from its bindings. Stranger still, her walking-dress had changed. In place of her staid, practical garments she now wore an airy dress of gossamer silk bedecked with ribbons. The fabric was so light as to be near translucent. In this disreputable state of dress she was obliged to remain, for there could be no hope of restoring herself to respectability.

She began to walk, tentatively, in the direction that Tafferty had indicated. Soon she was able to abandon her care and move with greater speed and confidence, for the dancers around her did not seem to notice her at all, though they moved in such a way as to avoid colliding with her. In a moment, Isabel came upon a dais secreted behind the dancers, and there the Piper — Lyrriant — was seated.

He reclined upon a chair which appeared to have grown from the stump of an old tree. His indigo hair was swept back from his brow, and his pale goldish skin shimmered in the lantern-light. His eyes were fixed upon Tiltager, who stood upon the arm of his chair in a gown made from rose petals. At first her words were impossible to discern amidst the tumult of the music, but as Isabel neared the dais she could hear something of the speech the little fae was making to Lyrriant.

'…and Miss Isabel, she cries, I shall not rest until I have freed thee, brave Ferryman, from thy torment! And the Ferryman, he was smitten with her upon the instant, for she is the most beauteous of ladies as well as the truest of heart!' These astonishing proclamations were accompanied by extravagant gestures and mimes; Tiltager appeared to enjoy a strong talent for the dramatic. 'Ever since that day, my good and kind mistress has striven to fulfil her promise to the beleaguered Ferryman, and release him from his cruel fate! And now her quest has brought her here, into the heart of the Hollow Hills, for you see she is courage itself, and shrinks at nothing! It is to your court that she has come, seeking aid for one who cannot aid himself.' Tiltager bowed deeply, her efforts rewarded with hearty applause from Lyrriant.

'A lively tale!' he said in a light voice. 'But I scarcely believe in the heroine of the story! A lady in possession of quite so many merits can hardly be a living creature.' His eyes flicked to Isabel as he spoke, and his smile widened. 'This, I perceive, must be the lady. Is it she?'

Tiltager turned to regard Isabel, beaming. 'It is she! Mistress, I have told to kind Lyrriant every part of the tale, and you see he will not be able to refuse to assist you now that he has heard it all, and seen you for himself!'

Isabel paused to wonder how Tiltager had come by the story at all, though she could find no immediate answer. 'I fear you have embellished a little, Tiltager, though I thank you for your efforts. The gentleman is perfectly right. I am not nearly so sparkling a creature as you have described. Why, I shrink at many things, and I have no doubt there are ladies far truer of heart, and far more beautiful, than I!'

Lyrriant's eyes pinned and held her, their expression considering. She quailed a little under such scrutiny, for she felt, oddly, as though every part of her character was laid bare. 'Beauty she has, though in no extraordinary degree,' he mused. 'And she is correct: she shrinks at many things. But there is heart there, and plenty.'

Isabel coloured, and looked down at the ground, unsure how to respond to such frank appraisal. She felt both shamed and flattered, and in such equal degree that she knew not where to look.

Lyrriant's eyes narrowed. 'I know you,' he said. 'Do I not? I have seen you dance before. Though the face has altered, I know the spirit that lies beneath.'

Isabel inclined her head. 'You played at an assembly in England, some weeks ago. I was also in attendance.'

Lyrriant smiled, his lips quirking in an odd way. 'I have played at many English assemblies, these past weeks! I remember you, for you caught my eye. But you are not now as you were then.'

'No, sir. I have undergone changes aplenty since we encountered each other last.'

'I see that you have.' Lyrriant watched her with a meditative air, playing idly with the curled pipe he held in his hands. 'I cannot help you,' he finally said. 'If I knew the name, I might consent to share it, for it is an affecting tale. But I do not, and it is unlikely that any here will have the information you seek. A mere Ferryman, and long in Torpor! His will not be a known name.'

Isabel had scarcely been aware of the degree of hope she had nurtured, until these words abruptly extinguished it. She stood speechless, momentarily bereft of ideas. If Lyrriant did not know, nor could he direct them to anyone who could... where could she turn? All that remained was Eliza's terrifying idea about—

'The Kostigern,' said Eliza, speaking loudly and clearly to be heard over the music. 'Do you know where he came from?

Isabel looked up. Eliza stood a few feet away, Tafferty sitting at her feet. Like Isabel, she had been somehow divested of the simpler dress she had worn earlier in the evening. Instead she wore a gauzy ball gown of sea-foam silk and lace; her abundant hair was swept up in an elaborate arrangement, and secured with jewelled combs. No trace of Mrs. Grey was discernible in any part of her appearance, her

posture or her manner. Gone was Isabel's congenial aunt in all her neat respectability; in her place stood a proud, strong and uncompromising woman, certain of her right to be here in this place that was not England. She looked every inch an Aylir.

Isabel wondered, for a fleeting instant, whether her own appearance was in any way comparable to her aunt's. In her borrowed wisps of fae-silk and her jewels, her gold-threaded hair wild and loose and her colour high, was she not also a different creature from Miss Ellerby of Ferndeane? For the first time, she began to feel that her transformation was not wholly a lamentable one. She may feel out of place here in the Hollow Hills, but perhaps she was not. And she could be every bit as strong as Eliza. She stood a little straighter, lifted her chin, and awaited Lyrriant's response with a firmer resolve.

Lyrriant was not so impressed with Eliza as Isabel was. As the word Kostigern left her mouth, he sat up straighter on his curious throne, his brow darkening in a foreboding frown. 'That name should never be mentioned here, madam.'

'Then I will not mention it again,' said Eliza with a smile, and a slight, apologetic inclination of her head. 'But my question stands.'

Lyrriant stood. At his full height, his was an imposing figure; all the more so given that he stood upon a dais before them. He towered above the two supplicant ladies, and his manner was not conciliatory. 'And why,' he said in a dangerously quiet voice, 'would you ask such a thing?'

Isabel became abruptly aware that the music had stopped. Only the violin continued to play, and that soon petered out, leaving the company in a hushed silence.

Eliza was not cowed. Isabel would not be, either. 'If anyone is like to remember the Ferryman's name, it must be his former master and the one who laid the curse,' she said. 'We hope to find some record that will give us the information we seek.'

Lyrriant stared down at her, icily cold where he had been congenial enough moments before. 'You do not know what you ask. I will not help you venture into the heart of that one's territory. Nor will any of mine. Such things should be left undisturbed, for none can know the consequences of meddling.'

'Please,' Isabel said, beginning to feel desperate. 'It is so small a thing we seek!'

'Great and terrible consequences may come of the smallest of actions. I will not help you, and you should not have come here.'

The atmosphere in the starlit vale had changed, all merriment vanished in favour of a subtle, but growing, menace. Lyrriant's displeasure spelled the end of their welcome, such as it had been. The Fiddler appeared upon the dais before them, and made a mocking bow to Isabel and her aunt.

'Allow me to escort you out,' he said. His pale eyes glinted with a cruel light, and Isabel knew that the seeming courtesy of his offer disguised an uncompromising intent.

She exchanged a despairing look with her aunt, who had no more idea of how to proceed than Isabel did. They could do nothing but curtsey to Lyrriant, and follow the Fiddler away from the dais. The crowd of dancers parted smoothly to allow him passage, and he strode through without a backward glance, his posture erect with anger and disdain.

Isabel paused only long enough to ensure that Tafferty and Tiltager were safe and following along. The journey from the dais back to the trees from which they had emerged was short, but it felt long indeed. She was conscious every moment of the anger of the Ayliri behind her, and the threat they posed should any of them decide to express their disapprobation by more direct means. She walked with her head high, unwilling to permit them to see how her skin prickled under their hostile gaze — or how her heart quailed in the knowledge of her own helplessness, should such a company of Ayliri choose to be overtly hostile.

No one did, though the heavy silence which attended their departure was terrible enough, contrasted as it was with the lively merriment which had prevailed only moments before. The Fiddler stopped when he reached the knot of trees at the edge of the valley, and stood staring coldly at Isabel and Eliza until they caught up with him. He smiled with all the warmth of a frozen lake and whispered something which Isabel barely heard. 'Whishawist.'

Isabel was conscious of an abrupt, sickening sensation and dizzying, intolerably rapid movement. Bile rose in her throat and she retched, falling to her hands and knees and then onto the earth. When she opened her eyes some time later, she saw the familiar trees of Tilton Wood swaying peacefully in the breeze above her, and beyond them, a night sky glittering with stars that she knew.

'Eliza?' she gasped. 'Tafferty and Tiltager?'

'I am here,' said Eliza, in a voice as strained as Isabel's own. Tafferty growled and spat, then pressed herself up against Isabel's side. She was shivering violently, and Isabel tried as best she could to comfort her companion.

'Tiltager?' she repeated, when moments passed with no response from the tiny fae.

'He was not supposed to be angry,' said Tiltager forlornly. 'I told him he should not be.'

Isabel sighed, and picked herself up off the ground. Her legs shook, and for a moment she felt a strong desire to be ill for the second time. She gritted her teeth and waited until the feeling passed. 'It is none of your doing,' she said to Tiltager, when she was certain she could speak without embarrassing herself. 'And we are grateful to you for guiding us, however unsatisfactory the result.'

Tiltager peeped miserably by way of reply. Isabel caught but a brief glimpse of her in the moonlight, head bowed, before she faded into the darkness and disappeared.

'If we hurry,' said Eliza, 'We may contrive to arrive at Ferndeane before the sun rises.'

Startled, Isabel glanced at the eastern sky. A pale glow was indeed beginning to glimmer somewhere behind the clouds, and she sighed. 'Then let us hurry.'

CHAPTER SEVENTEEN

I'll admit, I was surprised at Lyrriant. 'Twasn't like him t' be so unhelpful-like, 'specially to a pair o' pretty young ladies. But the Kostigern, thas a thorny topic. Gets people mighty worked up.

I 'ad all my best folk out lookin' fer some way to help Miss Isabel, as ye may readily imagine. Nobody remembered the poor Ferryman, let alone his name, an' no one knew where to go lookin' fer the Kostigern's hidey-hole neither. Aye well, he was always well tucked away, that one. But wi' the Ferryman rememberin' next to nothin' himself, the Chronicler missin' an' Lyrriant unwillin' to speak, where did that leave us? Wi' a mighty ole mess.

It worried Miss Isabel, I'll no deny. But somethin' odd came to pass soon after — an' in the midst of a grand ball, at that! 'Twas a confusin' day fer our young lady, an' she 'ad some hard decisions to make...

The failure of the expedition into the Hollows left Isabel at a loss to know where next to direct her attention. Nor was she much at leisure to consider the question, for the ball at Ferndeane was almost upon them, and the house descended into all the flurry and chaos of the preparations her mother deemed necessary before her friends and neighbours could be permitted to cross the threshold. Isabel quickly saw that her mother's aspirations had outpaced her resources; the house was by no means large enough to accommodate everyone to whom she had extended an invitation. There was no ballroom at Ferndeane, either, and they were obliged to throw open the doors in between two other rooms in order to create a makeshift dancing space.

The Thompson family were to be the guests of honour, of course, and it fell to Isabel to ensure that their stay at Ferndeane would be perfect in every conceivable way. All her mother's anxious care of Isabel's appearance, largely forgotten since the Alford Assembly, returned as well. In the midst of these various and burdensome demands on her time, Isabel found barely a moment to reflect on the problem of the Ferryman, or indeed to think of anything else at all. Eliza gave as much assistance as she could, but Tafferty's notion of helping was more of a hindrance.

'Thou couldst enchant their closets,' she suggested, wandering along behind as Isabel surveyed the room that was to be assigned to Miss Thompson. 'A self-tidyin' closet, where nothin' is ever creased an' messy. Or thou couldst encourage it t' change all the colours o' their gowns.' Tafferty snickered under her breath as she pronounced this second suggestion, and Isabel could not help smiling a little, too, as she pictured Miss Thompson's confusion upon opening her closet to dress for the ball.

'I will do no such thing,' she chided, but gently. 'I cannot deny that a self-tidying closet would prove useful, but it would be impossible to explain. And besides, how can one expect a closet to appreciate precisely the way in which one would like one's gown's arranged?'

'Then yonder chamber-pot. Tell it t' keep itself empty, no matter what may be put into it.'

Isabel blinked, strongly tempted by the notion. 'How convenient that would be, to be sure! But again, I do not know how I could explain it to our guests.'

Tafferty sighed. 'Thou'rt too gullible. In truth, I am not certain any o' those things would be possible. But would it not be entertainin' t' try?'

'Perhaps, but now is not the time.' Isabel spoke firmly, and Tafferty sighed and slunk away. Isabel did not see her for the remainder of the day.

The ball was set for the morrow. Isabel retired to bed late, and was obliged to rise early, for nothing would do for Mama but to spend half the day fussing over Isabel's hair, and her gown, and all the rest. She had received favourable reports from her sister regarding their interactions with the Thompsons while in York, and her hopes were high indeed.

Isabel could not care about any of it; not when her failure of the Ferryman weighed so heavily upon her conscience. She was content to permit her mother to determine everything just as she liked — with one exception. She would not consent to wear anything other than the beautiful gown Sophy had made for her, and no remonstrance of her mother's could detract in the smallest degree from her resolve. Mrs. Ellerby was obliged, though with ill grace, to relent. Her distaste for the gown puzzled Isabel, until it struck her how unmistakeably fae the garment looked. But her accounts of the Misses Thompson's eagerness for all things Aylfenhame did nothing to mollify her mother's doubts as to its probable appeal for that family. Mrs. Ellerby had always disapproved of Isabel's occasional excursions to Grenlowe to visit Sophy, though she had not outright forbidden her daughter's going. Her clear dislike for Isabel's bringing any part of it back with her brought all Eliza's words to mind, and Isabel was saddened. Why was difference so easily equated with inferiority, or danger?

The Thompson family arrived before two o' clock. All was a whirl of noise and obligation as they were settled at Ferndeane, and subsequently entertained, until the hour to dress arrived. Isabel retreated to her own room with a sense of relief, for the Misses Thompson were a little overpowering when encountered all together. Furthermore, she had been showered with more attention from young Mr. Thompson than she had expected, and the meaningful looks exchanged between her parents and his were unwelcome to her. She closed her door upon all of this with a sigh, and submitted to the efforts of her mother's abigail in dressing her hair.

Eliza entered when this process was almost complete, and stayed to assist Isabel into her gown. She contrived, with a few deft touches of Glamour, to enhance the otherness of the garment. Fully dressed, Isabel seemed garbed in magic itself. Her gown was woven twilight, her ribbons shining like moonlight upon water. The simple necklace at her throat was no longer a sapphire; instead a living butterfly, or its semblance, had alighted at the hollow of her throat as though she were a flower in summer. Fireflies dreamed amongst the coils of her hair.

Isabel gazed at this magnificence, torn between wonder and dread.

'But shall not—' she began.

Eliza cut her off. 'If you are going to say that your mother will be displeased, then I beg you not to speak at all. Harriet wishes for her daughter to look her best, and so you do. It is not for anybody to dictate how you choose to appear.'

It occurred to Isabel that her aunt had not sought her permission before transforming her simple jewellery and hair ornaments into the marvels they now appeared to be, but she held her peace. If she was becoming some manner of battleground in the ongoing conflict between her mother and her mother's sister, this could not please her. But the butterfly did, very much.

Her remaining qualm related to the other young ladies due to attend the ball. They could not like being outshone by such arts as were available to her, and it was perhaps unfair of Isabel to employ them. Further, she would be no less at a loss to explain the magical beauty of her garments and jewellery now than she had been before. Would the three Thompson girls permit her to evade their questions yet again?

She opened her mouth to give voice to some of this, but a glance at her aunt's raised eyebrow silenced her.

'It is well,' said Eliza firmly. 'You appear as you should — and as you have every right to be seen.'

But not necessarily the desire, Isabel thought. She swiftly packed that thought away, for it was not strictly the truth. It wasn't that she didn't wish to make her appearance in such attire; merely that she feared the possible consequences of doing so. And that, she could now recognise as a fear inherited from her mother.

Upon descending the stairs, she swiftly found herself subjected to all the close questioning and enthusiastic examination that she expected, most of it from the Misses Thompson — though their mother was more forward in her interest than she had ever been before. Eliza was of assistance in deflecting some of these, though Isabel did not feel that they were fooling anybody. She caught Mrs. Thompson's eye more than once, and found that lady's gaze fixed upon her with an air of consideration.

Mr. Thompson had already claimed her hand for the first dances, and Isabel knew it was her mother's wish that they should open the ball together. She performed this duty with her colour high, for she was conscious that the attention of all those guests who were not dancing was fixed upon her — or rather, upon her gown, and the ornaments in her hair. Such scrutiny might please some women, but it could not please her, and she was by no means used to it. Afterwards she was much sought after as a partner, and was not obliged to sit down for any of the dances. This was more than merely flattering. It reduced the opportunities her mother's guests could find to comment upon her appearance, or question her about the provenance of her gown.

Her Mama was clearly delighted with the attention she was attracting. Isabel thought she was far too inclined to attribute it to her daughter's beauty, rather than to the remarkable nature of her garments. But she trusted it went some way to reconciling her to the choice of attire, which she had still never approved.

There had been much speculation, prior to the beginning of the ball, as to whether the Piper and his dancers might be disposed to make an appearance. Considering the outcome of her venture into the Hills, Isabel thought it to be, of all things, the most unlikely. She could hardly explain that to her mother's guests, however. As such, hopes ran high, unimpeded by mundane probability. Every time the strains of a violin became particularly prominent in the music, or some unexplained bustle occurred in some part of the room, there was a collective sense of excitement, as though it must surely presage the event they all hoped for. But it never did.

Isabel was glad of it. Such an occurrence could appear to her mother in no other light than that of a catastrophe, and she would still be complaining of it a decade hence.

One source of discomfort proved both distressingly persistent and sadly troublesome to Isabel. Mr. Thompson was not contented with opening the ball with her; he would seek her hand for further dances throughout the evening, in spite of the clear impropriety of her standing up with the same gentleman more than twice. Only a forthcoming engagement could make such particularity respectable, and the significant manner he thought it appropriate to adopt whenever he interacted with her led her to feel that a proposal was imminent. The conspiratorial air she detected whenever her mother stood talking with Mrs. Thompson only seemed to confirm it.

Her reaction to the idea puzzled her, for why should she not welcome it? She had long since determined that she was not at all ill-disposed to encourage Mr. Thompson's suit. Well might her mother expect him to offer, and her to accept, for she had never expressed any disapprobation for the idea. Not out loud, and not even to her own self. She wanted a home of her own, respectability, and a family. All of these, Mr. Thompson could surely provide.

Where, then, had her disinclination come from? She was surprised at herself, and vexed; for to decide only at the last moment that she did not wish for a proposal of marriage was poor timing indeed. And she had encouraged him — or at least, she had not actively discouraged him, which amounted to the same thing.

The moment came. In between one dance and the next, Mr. Thompson approached, smiling in a manner both familiar and affectionate. He took her hand and bowed over it.

'May I request the favour of a moment's audience with you?' he said in a soft voice.

Isabel sighed inwardly, unable to think of a reason to decline. She murmured her assent, and he led her to an alcove and took a seat beside her.

The proposal was quietly and properly made, for which she gave him all due credit; at least he had not postured and made wild professions of love. But his manner was so collected that her puzzlement increased, and at first she made no reply at all, merely examining his face for some sign as to his intent. She saw none.

'Why is it that you wish to marry me?' she said at last. The question emerged in a blunter fashion than she had intended, and she coloured a little, but she lifted her chin and awaited his response in silence.

His smile turned quizzical. 'Any man would wish to marry you,' he said, with more gallantry than truth. 'You are a young woman of sense, intelligence and beauty, and of a good family—'

'The real reason, if you please,' she said, cutting him off without compunction. 'I understand perfectly why my mother and father are in favour of the match, but I do not at all comprehend why yours should be. Or why you would consent to go along with the plan. Your family is far beyond mine, in terms of fortune and connections; and for all your compliments just now, you are not in love with me.'

He winced at her uncompromising speech, but she did not care. It was a relief to her to speak nothing but the plain truth, at long last.

To his credit, he made no further attempts to persuade her of affection he clearly did not feel. Instead, to her confusion, he gestured at her gown. 'I had thought that your appearance this evening indicated your perfect understanding of the case.'

Isabel glanced down at her gown in surprise. 'I am afraid it does not, sir. I have no notion as to what you are referring.'

His brows went up. 'Do not you? Is it not true that your family bears some hereditary connection to the Ayliri of Aylfenhame?'

Isabel stared at him, for some moments unable to speak for surprise. 'I beg your pardon?' she managed at last.

'Our mothers were at school together, were not they? And your mother once confided as much to mine.'

'Nothing would surprise me more! For Mama has always viewed those connections as deplorable.'

Mr. Thompson spread his hands in a helpless gesture. 'That I cannot explain. I gather only that there was some family trouble occurring because of it at that time, and she found some comfort in talking to my mother.'

Perhaps he referred to some action of Eliza's. She had no time to give the matter further consideration, as he hurried on. 'I take it that it is indeed the truth! Then you can require no other explanation.'

'I am afraid I do, sir! Can you truly be seeking my Ayliri connections? Why would you do so?' The idea puzzled her exceedingly, accustomed as she was to her mother's mild but persistent distaste for all things Aylfenhame — and Eliza's long habit of concealing all trace of it, both in herself and Isabel.

By way of answer, Mr. Thompson reached out and gently touched the fragile wings of the butterfly at Isabel's throat. 'Because of marvels such as this. Who would not wish to have such wonders at their disposal?'

Isabel was silenced. The sheer strangeness of being sought out because of her Ayliri heritage, instead of being shunned for it, left her with nothing to say. Not least because she could not immediately decide how she felt about it. Was it somehow worse to be sought for her witch heritage, than for her inheritance or her beauty? Many a marriage had been arranged because of the desirable, preferably noble, family lineage of one or both parties; it was merely unusual for Ayliri lineage to be considered worth chasing.

Nonetheless, she felt peculiarly displeased. Perhaps her illusions of good sense had been baseless after all; she had been foolish enough to imagine that some part of his family's interest in her had been on more personal grounds. Perhaps she had even hoped that he himself sought her for reasons particular to herself as an individual, whether he was in love with her or not. It was pleasant, in some ways, for the heritage she had viewed with such suspicion to be sought after and revered, rather than condemned. But overall she felt reduced by his explanation; reduced to naught but an accident of birth.

She also felt not the smallest desire to accept his proposal — however congenial he may be, and however respectable and luxurious was the home he could offer her. To her surprise and dismay, visions of the delights of life as Mrs. Thompson faded rapidly in favour of the Ferryman's face, and he was all she could think of.

She was prevented from answering, as she wished promptly to do, by some commotion spreading rapidly through the room. A buzz of excitement began with it, and for a shocked instant Isabel wondered — feared? — that Lyrriant had chosen to attend the ball at Ferndeane after all. But an instant's reflection reassured her on that point, for the music was unchanged, and soon it stopped altogether.

She stood up, murmuring some abstracted courtesy to Mr. Thompson as she did so. It was the work of a minute or two to weave through the chattering crowds. The scene that met her wondering eyes brought her to an instant halt, and she stared.

The Ferndeane Ball had indeed received a number of uninvited guests, but they were not Lyrriant and his companions. Isabel was astonished to perceive Mr. Balligumph ducking his head to fit through the doorway. He had abandoned the blanket and cap he had been wearing last time Isabel had seen him, and was attired once more in his usual trousers, waistcoat, boots and tall hat. On one shoulder he carried Tafferty; ensconced upon the other was Tiltager.

'I am lookin' fer Miss Ellerby,' he bellowed, causing an immediate stir as everybody in the room tried to point out her probable location at once. In their eagerness to assist — and perhaps to get the noisy troll out of their ball room again — they impeded Isabel's attempts to present herself, and she found herself engulfed in a wave of humanity which must utterly conceal her from Balligumph. To her surprise, she found her arm taken by Mr. Thompson, who pushed his way to the front of the room without the compunction Isabel would have felt in doing so, and drew her after him.

'Here she is,' he said, with a bow. 'I imagine there must be some

important matter at hand?'

Balligumph tipped his hat to Isabel, but before he could say another word Tiltager spoke up, clearly agitated. 'Mistress! They are going to the place to do bad things to it!'

Isabel smiled up at Tiltager in a manner she hoped was calming. 'Who are going, Tiltager, and where?'

'Lyrriant!' she proclaimed.

'They are plannin' t' burn it,' added Tafferty.

'Best make haste, my lass, if ye wish to search it before they has chance to destroy the lot,' said Balligumph.

Putting these disparate pieces of information together, Isabel arrived at the conclusion that Lyrriant's people had decided to go to the Kostigern's former residence after all — with the express intention of ensuring that no one else ever would again. 'How is it that you know?' she said quickly.

'I went back,' said Tiltager. 'They did not see Small Me! And I heard. And then I came back.'

'She knew not where to find ye, but she found me quick enough.' Balligumph's face was unusually grim as he spoke, with no trace of his amiable smile. 'Ye've still time to catch up wi' them, if ye can be fast.'

'I am coming this moment,' said Isabel at once.

'And I shall also go,' said Eliza. She came up beside Isabel, and together they all but ran from the room and out of the front door of Ferndeane. None tried to impede them, and their progress was as rapid even as Isabel could wish. She was aware, however, that more than a few of the ball guests followed along behind.

It was only once she was outside in the driveway that she realised she did not have her reticule with her. She was obliged to turn about, but the crowd had closed in behind her. 'Pray excuse me!' she cried, exasperated and half-despairing.

'MOVE yerselves out o' the way, my fine ladies an' gents,' hollered Balligumph. 'Tis a matter o' grave importance to the young lady! There we go! Very good, now.' The mighty troll did not stop at words; he used his great arms and hands to push people aside, gently but firmly, in order to clear a path. Isabel instantly took advantage of it, caring nothing either for the grumbles of discontent or the excited speculation that she heard taking place among those she passed. She darted upstairs to her bedroom, where she snatched up her reticule.

Abandoning propriety and dignity both, she picked up her skirts in her hands, drawing them out of the way of her feet, and ran downstairs.

'Here,' she said, breathless, as she reached the driveway once more. She took the little whistle from her reticule, thrusting the latter heedlessly at Eliza, and blew a quick, sharp blast upon it.

'Oh, dear. I hope he is not far away!' She could only wait and pace and hope as the moments passed, expecting any second to see some sign that the Ferryman approached, and fearing that he could not arrive in time.

But there. The light of a lantern blossomed in the sky and swiftly drew closer. She felt a familiar rush of wind as the boat approached, though she could see little of it in the dark night sky.

'Ferryman!' she cried as soon as she judged the vessel had drawn close enough. 'I beg you, make haste!'

'I am here,' he replied, though his voice was still a little distant. Then the boat landed. A great, shining lantern hung at its prow, illuminating the Ferryman's tall figure standing beneath the main sail. He stood still for a moment, and Isabel realised he was startled. And well he might be! For she stood in her evening finery with Eliza at hand, Balligumph nearby and a host of ball attendees at her back, all of whom must inevitably be staring at him.

He soon recovered himself. 'Up, then, an' fast,' he said. A gangplank came down and Isabel hastened up it, accepting the Ferryman's hand and assistance as soon as she was close enough to do so. Eliza followed directly behind, carrying Tiltager, and with Tafferty close on her heels.

Some few of the assembled ball-guests surged forward, and Isabel realised the more curious among them intended to follow her. 'Do not let any others embark!' Isabel cautioned.

The Ferryman smiled down upon his audience, and quickly withdrew the gangplank. The boat rose up at the same instant, and at speed. The crowd of people below rapidly dwindled into miniature as Isabel soared upwards, a high summer wind whipping at her hair. She was left with an impression of Mr. Thompson's face as he watched his hoped-for bride vanish into the night skies, and then an influx of cloaking mists obscured everything below.

'Where is it that we're goin'?' said the Ferryman.

Isabel explained, as best she could, but it fell to Tiltager to recount the tale in more detail. Isabel was relieved to find that she was able to do so, as the little fae's communications could sometimes lack clarity.

'But if you did not take Lyrriant's folk into Aylfenhame, how came they there?' she thought to ask.

'I did take them,' the Ferryman replied. 'And now I will take ye all t' exactly the point where I left 'em.'

'Oh! That is very convenient, to be sure. You arrived so promptly that I thought you could not have also conveyed them.'

The Ferryman looked, remarkably, a little embarrassed. 'Aye, well. I 'ave been in the habit of stayin' in yer vicinity, fer the most part. I was already on my way back t' the environs o' Tilby when I heard yer call.'

Isabel could find no words to frame the questions aroused by this remark, but her face must have spoken for her, for he added, 'In case ye should need me fer somethin'.'

'Thank you,' she said, which was inadequate, but she had not time for more.

'Ye'd best hang on,' he said. 'Time bein' a little short, we are goin' to speed up more'n a little.'

Isabel quickly sat down and tucked herself against the side of the boat, gripping her seat as best she could. And not an instant too soon, for the boat surged forward, and the circling winds strengthened accordingly. She clung to her perch as the howling currents tore at the bindings of her hair, amazed and a little sickened by the unaccustomed sensation of violent speed. Abruptly the alarming pace slackened, and the boat began to descend.

'An' we are here. Not far from Mirramay, ye'll be interested t' know.' He looked at Isabel, his brow darkening with a frown. 'I don't strictly like the notion o' ye fine ladies dashin' into such a place on my account, an' wi' naught but a leafling an' a catterdandy t' attend ye.'

'There is no time for such qualms, sir!' Isabel cried. 'The attempt must be made, or I fear you will never be set at liberty.'

'Ye put me in a difficult quandry.'

'Not at all, for it is not your decision to make.'

He bowed his head at that. The boat settled onto solid land, and the gangplank materialised. Eliza hastened to disembark at once, but the Ferryman briefly detained Isabel. 'If ye're in luck, ye should find Sir Guntifer somewhere below. He 'as been standin' watch around

Mirramay these past several days, an' the instant I dropped that likely lot below I sent fer 'im. Seemed t' me that someone should be keepin' an eye on them.' The moment he had completed this speech, he lifted a small bone-wrought horn to his lips and blew upon it.

'Ho, the Ferryman!' came Sir Guntifer's great voice from below.

'An' now I need not worry so much for ye ladies,' said the Ferryman with a smile.

Isabel did not wait for more. She followed her friends down the gangplank to the ground below, unsure what she would encounter when she arrived there. The ferry-boat's lantern illuminated a patch of open grassland, at the edges of which she detected the dark, looming shadows suggestive of trees.

One of those shadows stepped forward, and bowed to her. 'Gentle lady, an it please thee, I will serve as thy guide.'

'I would be honoured, Sir Guntifer.' Isabel curtseyed in return, hoping privately that the exchange of courtesies would not be excessively drawn out.

'Then let us away,' said the tree-giant, pausing only to bow to Eliza before he turned. 'I know well wither they have gone,' he said grimly, as he shed the bark of his tree shape and became a giant complete. 'Friends aloft have marked their passage well.'

Isabel did not immediately reply, for a strange — but not unfamiliar — sensation afflicted her at that instant. She felt, in some obscure fashion, that the close attention of some hidden being lay heavily upon her; that she was observed by someone, or something, that she could not see. She had felt it before, after her encounter with the trows as she had travelled to Mirramay with Sophy. She looked about, but in the darkness she could detect nothing that might explain the feeling.

She had not time to dwell upon it, for her errand was too urgent. She must trust to Sir Guntifer's care to keep her safe, if indeed a menace lurked in the shadows. 'Can he have dwelt so close to Mirramay?' Isabel asked, as she hastened to keep pace with the giant.

'It is strange indeed, but it doth appear so. Where better, in sooth, to prey upon Their Majesties than from close by? If a man hath the nerve for such effrontery, and such risk, then much may be won by it.'

Isabel was doubtful, not least because it did not appear possible to her that the Kostigern's dwelling-place could have been so well-hidden if it lay within such a short distance of Mirramay. She did not know how far from that city they were, precisely, for everything seemed strange to her in the dark; she did not even know if she had passed this way before. They arrived at a road, and followed it for a few scant minutes. An occasional lantern hung by the wayside, casting a bright light over the road, but everything upon either side of it remained shrouded in darkness.

Sir Guntifer swerved abruptly left, and Isabel hurried to follow. A narrow path led away from the main thoroughfare and into a small wood. They left the lights of the road-lanterns behind, and for a few suffocating moments all was darkness. But Sir Guntifer whistled a lively little melody, and motes of golden light began to wink into being over her head. Fireflies, she realised.

Their aid was not long required, for soon the silence of the wood was broken by the sounds of raised voices coming from somewhere up ahead. Lights bobbed among the trees, growing larger and brighter as Isabel drew nearer. They came from lamps held in Ayliri hands, she soon realised, as she discerned the shadowy figures of tall, graceful forms darting amongst the trees ahead.

Then a stronger light blazed into being; not white and clear like the lanterns, but fierce and orange.

Fire.

'We are too late!' she cried in dismay.

'Stay a moment,' cautioned Sir Guntifer, as they came to the edge of a clearing amongst the trees. Isabel could barely make out the looming shape of a house up ahead. She could discern little of its details in the darkness, but it did not appear to her that it was a dwelling much out of the ordinary. It was not especially large, and perhaps only three storeys high. It bore an air of neglect, but it was neither an interesting ruin nor a building of unusual character. This, then, was how the Kostigern had contrived to live within such easy reach of the Royal City: He had hidden himself in ordinariness.

The orange light of the fire shone through one of the windows upon the ground floor. As Isabel watched, the fire spread; soon two, and then three and four windows blazed with the fierce light.

She was seized by a sudden wild urge to run forward; to find a way into those parts of the building left unburned, and somehow wrest from it the secret of the Ferryman's name. But she was not so mad. She did not require the restraining influence of her aunt's hand laid upon her arm.

'It is a great pity, indeed,' said Eliza, 'but you must not endanger yourself! The Ferryman could not wish it of you.'

Isabel could not answer. Her own helplessness choked her, and a sense of despair robbed her of words. She had no other means of determining his name. Every endeavour had failed, and where could she now turn? She felt a surge of anger at Lyrriant and all his folk, they who flitted here and there in the night, burning away the last hope she had of setting her friend at liberty.

Then Lyrriant appeared out of the darkness. His hair was a wild mess, and his face was smudged with something that could have been soot. 'You need not have come,' he said. His tone lacked warmth, though it also lacked the anger Isabel might have expected him to feel upon finding her there. 'I have searched this foul place. No trace of the name you seek did I find.'

'Did you?' Isabel demanded. She did not know that she could trust him to search at all, or to search thoroughly if he had. What, after all, was the Ferryman's fate to him?

'I did,' he said, a hint of ice creeping into his tone. 'I have no love for the Ferryman, but nor do I bear him any ill-will. If his name had been here, I would have discovered it.' He did not pause to hear her reply, but melted away into the night.

Tears pricked at Isabel's eyes. The Ferryman's manner had been calm enough, but she did not think she had imagined the sense of contained excitement — and hope — that she had sensed from him. Now she must return to him with the news that she had once again failed.

Then the sensation of close scrutiny deepened, and she knew she was watched indeed — she had not imagined it. A presence materialised at her back, so silently that she had heard no one approach. A voice whispered in her ear, or perhaps in her mind. *I admire your perseverance, my lady.*

Isabel whirled around, and saw no one. 'Who is that?' she demanded.

She was answered by a soft chuckle. *I have been watching you.*

Isabel's skin prickled, and her heart beat faster. Someone had been following her? 'Who are you?' she demanded.

I know the name you seek.

She took two seconds to absorb that statement, her heart beating quicker still with excitement and hope — and fear. 'I do not know who you are,' she said warily. 'But if you can help me, I beg that you will.'

Why should I do so?

Eliza was staring at her, as was Sir Guntifer. Could they, then, not hear the words that sounded so clearly in Isabel's ears? She had not time to explain. 'Oh, because the Ferryman's fate is so cruel!' she said desperately. 'Any who know him must know that he suffers unfairly! And he has suffered long indeed!'

Are you so certain that he has not merited his punishment?

'Yes,' said Isabel, without an instant's hesitation. 'I am certain of it. And I will not rest until I have freed him.'

Silence, stretching so long that Isabel began to fear that the presence, whoever it was, had gone away. Her heart pounded so hard, she feared it might break within her.

There must be some payment.

'Yes!' Isabel said, willing to grasp at anything so long as she received the information she sought. 'Payment will be made, in any form that you could wish.'

I will require a favour in return, said the voice. *Do you promise it, when I should come to claim it?*

'I promise it!'

A name was whispered to her. It was a long name, and ornate, but she felt that it fitted the Ferryman somehow.

Then the presence was gone.

'Isa? What is it?'

Isabel realised that Eliza had been attempting to gain her attention for some time.

'I do not know how it has come about,' said Isabel slowly, 'but I have the name.'

The Ferryman waited in the moonlit glade where he had deposited them so short a time before. The boat had not quite come to rest upon the ground; its hull, shrouded in roiling mist, floated some few feet above the grass. The light of its lanterns illuminated the figure of the Ferryman, pacing about beneath the grand sail.

He looked up as they approached, his eyes skimming over Eliza, Sir Guntifer, Tafferty and Tiltager before coming to rest upon Isabel herself. She read a painful degree of hope in the imploring look he gave her, and her heart twisted.

The gangplank came down, and Isabel went up it at once. 'I have your name,' she said, hoping that she spoke truly. For the possibility that her unnamed and unknowable source had lied was prominent in her mind. To first raise the Ferryman's hopes and then dash them would be far crueller, she felt, than if she had never endeavoured to help him at all.

Worse, she had promised her aid to the mysterious presence, whose identity and purpose she could only guess at — and her guesses were dark indeed. If the information she had gained was sufficient to free the Ferryman, then it was worth it; she felt that instinctively.

But if not...

The Ferryman seized her hands and kissed each one in turn. 'Ye miraculous thing,' he said fervently. He took a deep breath, his fingers tightening on hers to an almost painful degree. 'Let's 'ave it, then.'

Isabel drew in a deep breath, too, momentarily afraid to speak the name in case it proved to be the wrong one. 'You are Talthimandar.'

She waited, watching for some sign that the curse had been dispelled — a sound of some kind, a change in the air, anything. But nothing happened.

The Ferryman stared back at her with stark fear in his eyes. 'Did it work?' he whispered. 'I cannot tell. I feel... I feel the same.'

Isabel's apprehension turned into heart-pounding panic. 'Oh, no. Do you not recognise it? I am so sorry.' She walked up and down a little, trying to breathe slowly. Perhaps she had misheard the name? It had been whispered to her in the midst of a great deal of noise and activity. She concentrated, trying to remember more clearly the precise contours of the name as it had reached her ears.

'It is not familiar t' me,' said the Ferryman in frustration. But his eye fell upon the gangplank, still let down to the grass below, and in a sudden motion which startled Isabel he leapt for it. 'Only one way t' be sure,' he said grimly, as he strode down to the ground. 'In the ordinary way o' things, I cannot step more'n nine paces from the boat. I 'ave tried, many times.' He began to walk, watched by Isabel from the boat above him and Eliza, Sir Guntifer, Tafferty and Tiltager from below. He counted each step out loud as he walked, and Isabel could tell from his posture and the high carriage of his head that he held himself under strict control. 'Eight…' he said loudly, and then more quietly, 'Nine.' He paused, took a breath, and then extended his leg for a tenth step. His outstretched foot came down into the grass, and the other followed. 'Ten.'

He stood, rigid with surprise. Then he took another step. 'Eleven.' He took three more, then began to run. All of Isabel's fear left her in an instant, and she laughed with delight and relief as she watched Talthimandar run with wild abandon far away from the ferry-boat Mirisane.

He turned at last and began to run back. He tore off his three-cornered hat and threw it high; it did not float, but flew up and then came down in a rush. Talthimandar left it lying in the grass. He threw himself onto his hands and flew about in a circle, landing neatly upon his feet once more. This manoeuvre he repeated over and over again until at last he fell in a heap in the grass, and lay there laughing.

Isabel had by this time descended to the ground herself, and she approached Talthimandar's prone form with an unexpected sensation of shyness. Ought she to interrupt his raptures? But Eliza had no such qualms, nor did her other friends. They gathered around him, offering tumultuous congratulation, and barely noticed Isabel's approach.

Until Sir Guntifer turned to her, and offered a courtly bow. 'Thou art true in heart, gentle Isabel. It is a pleasure to know thee.'

'Aye, that it is,' said the Ferryman, as he bounded to his feet. Isabel had not time to respond to either gentleman, for she was swept up that moment in a vast embrace and swung about thrice in a circle. Talthimandar kissed her soundly before setting her back upon her feet, and then he bowed to her. 'I should not 'ave done that, o' course,' he said merrily, 'but I am unrepentant. Ye 'ave earned ten thousand more such.'

'I beg you will not attempt to bestow them all at once,' said Isabel, laughing to cover her embarrassment. 'And some few ought to be given to my dear aunt, for she has been quite as much involved in the business as I, I assure you.'

Talthimandar turned to Eliza, who laughed and backed two steps away. 'That will be unnecessary, sir,' she said with a smile.

He satisfied himself with a bow, his eyes twinkling with merriment as he straightened. 'I'll attempt t' contain my exuberance, ma'am.'

'Talthimandar,' said Isabel, upon which he turned his attention back to her.

'Ye must call me Tal, I believe,' he said promptly. ''Tis a mighty mouthful o' sounds, is it not now?'

Isabel smiled. She could not consent to such an informal mode of address, but time enough to argue that point later. 'Have you... that is, do you recall yourself? Have you remembered?'

The merriment faded from his face, and he shook his head. 'Nothin' has changed, in that respect.'

Isabel was disappointed. 'Perhaps your memory will return in time?' she said hopefully.

'Perhaps.' He took one of her hands, raised it to his lips and kissed it. 'But I will not repine if I am not t' regain any o' that. Ye 'ave given me freedom, an' that is enough. More than enough.'

Isabel basked in Talthimandar's joy, radiant with the happiness she had helped to win for him. But in the quiet of her mind, her fears remained. Just who had she promised to help, and in what way would she be required to assist? She decided at once, that unless compelled, she would never dim Talthimandar's joy by telling him of the perilous bargain she had made. It was a burden she had willingly shouldered for his sake, and the knowledge of it must be hers alone.

EPILOGUE

The story of Miss Ellerby and the flying boat proved a persistent one in Tilby. It was talked of everywhere, and as is often the way with stories, with each telling its proportions grew larger and more fantastic. After a week, Isabel's companions expanded to include not just Mr. Balligumph, a leafling fae and a strange cat, but also a gaggle of pixies, a trow fiddler and all the brownies of Ferndeane. It later began to be said that the Piper's Rade had swept her away; even that Miss Ellerby had been a part of the Piper's band from the beginning, for had she not been present for their first appearance?

Isabel herself tried, with all the power of modest dignity and unassuming manners at her disposal, to divert the wildest of the stories, and steadfastly denied every part that did not perfectly coincide with the truth. But she was universally credited with more modesty, humility or perhaps secrecy than she possessed, and the stories continued to circulate unimpeded.

Mr. and Mrs. Ellerby knew not what to think of their daughter's fame. It was Charles's opinion that the gossip would rather enhance, than harm, his sister's reputation both in Tilby and beyond. With this theory Mrs. Ellerby could only vehemently disagree, and she was by no means reticent with the expression of her vast disapproval for all of Isabel's actions.

In truth, perhaps they were both right. There were some who considered Miss Ellerby's behaviour to be, at best, highly improper, and ceased to consider her as a proper associate. Others sought her acquaintance much more assiduously than they ever had before;

attracted, perhaps, by the romanticism of her supposed exploits.

Isabel was pained by the former attitude and embarrassed by the latter. Worse, she could not disagree with her mother's view that she had acted with gross impropriety, for she had. The only point of real disagreement between them was upon the topic of whether or not her behaviour had been either justified, or worth the outcome. Isabel sometimes doubted whether it had; but whenever she remembered Talthimandar's excessive joy at his freedom, and reflected that he was now free at last to pursue the life he wanted, she could not repent.

She often wondered what kind of life that might prove to be. He had returned her to England aboard the Mirisane, though she believed it had cost him sorely to climb back aboard his prison so soon after his release. Once he had set her down, she had watched him fly away back to Aylfenhame, unwilling to admit to herself the extent of her regret at his departure. She would not be drawn on the subject by anybody else — neither the curious gossips of Tilby who wished to know all about the handsome Aylir with whom she had flown away, nor even her aunt Eliza, who might more reasonably expect to be taken into her niece's confidence. It was a topic upon which Isabel resolved to remain silent.

It appeared for some days that the Thompsons, at least, had ceased to consider Miss Ellerby or her family as deserving of their acquaintance, for they departed Ferndeane upon the day following the ball and nothing more was heard of them for almost a week. But at the end of that period, the younger Mr. Thompson arrived at Ferndeane in person, to beg the family's pardon for their silence and to seek an audience with Isabel.

'I come bearing an invitation to you all to visit us at Ashford,' he said as he made his bow to Mrs. Ellerby. 'It was my mother's intention to send it sooner, but an illness in the family unhappily prevented her from thinking of it until now.'

Mrs. Ellerby was profuse in both her thanks and her evident relief at such an explanation. She was likewise prompt in accepting his request for a private interview with Isabel, without seeking her daughter's approval. Isabel sighed inwardly, unwilling to commit so direct an act of rebellion as to refuse, but privately wishing that the gossip had been as effective in lowering Mr. Thompson's opinion of her as it appeared to have been elsewhere.

That realisation surprised her a little, for on the topic of his proposal she had been as silent as the subject of Talthimandar — with herself, as well as her family. She had not told her mother of his offer, and she had scarcely thought about it. Her disinclination, mild as it had been at the time of the ball, had grown since, in spite of her refusal to contemplate the idea.

It was not, she thought, that she disliked him. There was nothing about him to dislike, in particular. He led her to the parlour, all quiet courtesy and neatness of dress, and she thought that she might have grown to like him very well, had her attention not been so diverted these past weeks. Eliza's plan had been successful: though Isabel remained uncomfortable with her Ayliri heritage, she could no longer envisage herself as an English squire's wife either — even if that squire was as supportive of her unusual ancestry as Mr. Thompson appeared to be. It was hard for her to move forward, but she could never go back to the person she had been.

Mr. Thompson watched her as she quietly took a seat. His expression was quizzical, and his air uncertain; it took him some few moments to gather his thoughts and begin. 'If I judge your manner correctly, I believe I may draw my own conclusions as to your answer to my offer.'

'I am sorry,' said Isabel simply. 'I do not think we would suit.'

He bowed his head. 'May I enquire as to your reasons?'

Isabel paused to consider. She could not precisely say why her interest in him had cooled. In every respect he was perfectly eligible and amiable, and if a little dullness was his worst flaw, Isabel would be considered a lucky woman indeed. Was it because his attitude towards her Aylir ancestry was not so much supportive, as eager — even grasping? Did she wish to be sought merely for the traits she might pass on to her children? That, she reminded herself, was no worse than being sought for her wealth or her beauty — both of which were common motives for marriage.

Talthimandar's image flitted briefly through her mind, but she ignored it.

'You do not love me,' she said at last. 'Nor am I in love with you.'

'You are a romantic,' he said, and she could not tell from his manner whether he approved or condemned such an attitude. 'It is not unusual for couples to marry without love, I think? It is to be hoped that we would in time come to feel all the affection for one another that we might wish. For my part—' and he smiled at her in a way which, she could not deny, conveyed more than a little fondness '—I do not think I would find it difficult at all.'

Isabel found herself with nothing to say. He was correct, but the truth of his argument made little impression upon her. She was unmoved.

'Will you at least grant me a little time?' he said. 'Say not that this is a final, and irrevocable, refusal. I have been precipitate, perhaps. If we come to know one another better, perhaps you may feel differently.'

Isabel did not wish to consent to his request, but she struggled to find a graceful way to decline, for there was nothing unreasonable in it. Besides, perhaps he was right; she might come to appreciate his qualities more, the closer her acquaintance with him.

She opened her mouth to give her consent, however grudging, but she was prevented by the curious sight of the door suddenly opening, and Tafferty appearing in the doorway. How the little catterdandy had contrived to open it herself she could not imagine, but there did not appear to be anybody else with her.

'Thou'rt wanted,' said Tafferty abruptly. 'I recommend a mite o' haste.' She looked at Mr. Thompson, sniffed, and whisked away again.

'Isabel?' said Mr. Thompson, with a note of urgency.

Looking at him, Isabel realised she did not even know his first name. 'Please excuse me,' she said, and rose at once before he could further detain her.

She found Tafferty in the hall, together with Mr. and Mrs. Ellerby, her brother Charles, her aunt Eliza, two of the brownies of Ferndeane and Tiltager. They were gathered around a stranger who had, she surmised, but this moment arrived. There appeared to be some manner of disagreement in progress, for voices were raised, and she detected more than one symptom of grave disapprobation in her parents' posture and manner.

'Tafferty?' she said quietly, making her way to her companion's side. 'How am I wanted?'

'Yonder caller is fer thee. Thy mother did not wish fer thee t' be disturbed.'

Well she might not. Picturing her mother's disappointment at her refusal of Mr. Thompson's offer, Isabel sighed. But that was to be borne later. She moved forward, saying, 'I am here. Who is it that calls upon me?'

'I am sorry you have been interrupted, Isabel!' cried Mrs. Ellerby. 'Go back to the parlour with Mr. Thompson, my dear. This gentleman can have nothing to say to you.'

Charles, however, caught hold of his sister's arm and drew her into the knot of people. She came face-to-face with the strange gentleman, who stared back at her in dismay.

He was elegantly dressed in sand-coloured trousers, a pale waistcoat, and an elegant blue coat, all of the best quality and of the highest fashion. His boots were polished to a mirror shine, and he held a tall black hat tucked under his arm. But his black hair was not at all fashionable, for he wore it long and tied back with a length of red ribbon. His golden skin and bronze-hued eyes were likewise at odds with his attire. She felt a surge of pure joy as she recognised him, and in that moment she understood why she could never marry Mr. Thompson.

Talthimandar. His eyes widened as he saw her, and he bowed, but his face did not lose its stricken expression.

'Miss Isabel,' he said. 'It seems I must apologise t' ye. I wanted t' see ye, but I… did not realise how unwelcome such a visit must be t' ye. An' yer family.'

Isabel felt a flicker of anger ignite. 'I do not know who has told you that you are unwelcome to me, but it is not the truth. Nor are you unwelcome in my home.' She offered him her hand, and he took it, though with an air of confusion.

'My dear!' said Mrs. Ellerby. 'Mr. Talthimandar ought to know that he may not freely call upon a household where he has never been introduced.' Nor ever will be, her tone seemed to say.

'He is very welcome to me, Mama.' Isabel spoke quietly and with dignity, but her anger was growing.

Mr. Thompson appeared next to Isabel, and made the Ferryman a cold bow. Talthimandar's eyes flicked to that gentleman, and he released Isabel's hand. 'I also did not know that ye 'ad a gentleman caller already,' he said in a quieter voice. Isabel could see that he imagined matters between herself and Mr. Thompson to have progressed further than they truly had, and she wondered what her mother had said to him.

'May I offer you some refreshment, Mr. Talthimandar?' she said. 'I will ask Lucy to bring tea to the drawing-room.'

Talthimandar said nothing. His gaze travelled from Isabel to Mrs. Ellerby to Mr. Thompson and back to Isabel, and her heart sank at the trapped look in his eyes. 'No, I thank ye. I will take my leave,' he said, his voice barely more than a whisper. He bowed to Isabel, clutching his new hat too tightly.

'Please,' she said softly. 'Do stay.'

He straightened up slowly, and directed a searching look at Isabel. 'If ye wish me t' stay, then I will.' A smile returned to his face. It was tentative and weak, but it held.

Isabel smiled back.

'Isabel!' exploded Mrs. Ellerby. 'I must insist upon this gentleman's leaving at once!'

Isabel turned to her mother, her brow creasing in a frown. 'Why must you, Mama?' she said softly, but making no attempt to conceal the simmering anger she felt. 'May I not welcome my friends to my home?'

'That depends very much upon the friend, I would say!' Mrs. Ellerby swelled with indignation.

'I should say so, indeed!' said Mr. Ellerby, standing directly behind his wife.

'Why should Mr. Talthimandar be considered so objectionable?' Isabel directed the question at both of her parents. She was conscious of her aunt Eliza moving to stand behind her, offering the same kind of support — albeit silent — that Mr. Ellerby provided for his wife.

'Honestly, Isabel!' said Mrs. Ellerby crossly. 'A gentleman of no birth, no family, no connections! And though he is very well turned-out I should think it unlikely that he is a man of any property. Indeed, he is not even of your own world, let alone your own society. A fit connection for an Ellerby of Ferndeane! I should say not.'

Mrs. Ellerby spoke brusquely, but Isabel detected a note of fear in her eyes. Mr. Ellerby, a vision of cold disapproval, said nothing, but he, too, betrayed signs of anxiety.

Isabel understood. If she married Mr. Thompson, she was — in their eyes — safe. He was a person they could understand. His family and connections were well-known and conventional, and his property was nearby. But Talthimandar, or anybody like him, was wholly unknown. They saw that his intentions towards Isabel tended towards more than friendship, as she saw it herself. How could they entrust her safety and her happiness to one such as him? And how could they bear to relinquish the prospects of greater importance that came with her prospective marriage to Mr. Thompson, besides?

In preferring Talthimandar, she knew she was dashing those hopes, and forever. No child of theirs would improve the Ellerby's social standing through marriage; neither their son nor their daughter would bring an increase of either wealth or status through connection to a family of importance. These were not goals with which Isabel could sympathise herself, but she understood that they were of great importance to others — not least her mother and father. As such, it cost her a pang to disoblige them; but disoblige them she must. She gathered herself to resist these arguments, searching her mind for the best way to represent Talthimandar's worth to her parents — but she was forestalled by Talthimandar himself.

'Actually,' he said, 'Cursed I may've been, but I never said I was destitute.'

There was a speechless silence for several moments, which was broken at last by Mr. Ellerby. 'You are a man of property?' he said in pure disbelief.

'Not rightly speakin', no,' said Talthimandar. 'In no way as t' impress ye fine folk, fer certain. But I 'ad some thoughts t' purchasin' somethin' in the way of a dwellin' in these parts.'

'You are going to live in Tilby?' said Isabel, feeling suddenly breathless.

He smiled faintly upon her. 'That depends, a bit, on whether I could expect t' find a welcome here.'

'And a bride?' said Mr. Thompson, somewhat acidly.

Talthimandar looked at him in silence. 'I appear to ye as a threat t' yer hopes, an' ye would like t' despise me for it. That I can understand, fer I'm minded t' think the same o' ye. But the choice lies wi' the lady, now, does it not?'

'When the lady is an Aylir witch as much as she is English, it is hard to compete with a sorcerer who possesses a flying boat.' Mr. Thompson spoke wryly, but he was certainly disappointed. Whether he was so because he regretted Isabel herself or merely the prospect of an Aylfenhame alliance, Isabel could not tell.

'I may be missin' the mark in sayin' so, but it does not seem t' me that Miss Isabel is likely t' be so much impressed wi' that kind o' thing.'

'Indeed, I am not,' said Isabel, feeling more than a little indignant at the notion that she would be so influenced.

Mrs. Ellerby spoke at the same time. 'An Aylir witch?' she said faintly. 'But no! That is by no means true!'

'Now, Harriet,' said Eliza. 'Take a moment to consider, I beg you.'

'Lizzy?' said Mrs. Ellerby, her voice growing fainter still. 'What can you mean?' Realisation began to dawn on her, and she stared first at her sister, and then at her daughter, in growing horror. 'Isabel?'

Isabel went to her mother and took both of her hands, squeezing them in an attempt to comfort her. 'It is the truth, Mama,' she said, and as she spoke she allowed the Glamour which camouflaged her appearance to gradually fade. 'As you can see.'

Mrs. Ellerby could only stare at her daughter's changed face, speechless with dismay.

'Is it so very bad?' said Isabel. 'I am different, as you see. But must it be deplored?'

'Oh, Isabel,' whispered her mother. 'You do not understand! Society will never accept you! Not with those eyes, and that hair. My mother...' she faltered, glanced at Eliza, and continued, 'My mother was talked about. Whispers and gossip and chatter, until she could bear it no longer! And she hid herself, until the people who had shunned her began to treat her with at least the appearance of civility. But the whispers never wholly died away! She was not trusted, and in the best houses, never fully welcomed.' She tilted her head towards Isabel, and said in a lower voice, 'There may be nothing wrong with the Ayliri, my dear, but they are not as we are. It would be like having someone foreign for a husband.'

Isabel knew that when she said foreign, she meant someone with differently coloured skin. 'I cannot consider that something to be ashamed of in either case, Mama. Mr. Talthimandar is a good man, and I am your daughter — even if I am also an Aylir witch.'

Mrs. Ellerby's eyes filled, and tears spilled down her cheeks. She pulled her hands out of Isabel's grasp and allowed herself to be supported by her husband. Isabel noted that her father looked no more convinced of her arguments than did her mother, and sighed.

Talthimandar spoke up. 'It is true that I came t' seek yer permission t' court yer daughter,' he said quietly. 'As I understand is the convention in these parts. If ye will give me a chance an' get t' know me, ye may find I am not so different as ye think. Nor so objectionable.' He looked at Isabel, and added, 'That is, if Miss Isabel will permit me.' He smiled at her with obvious appreciation, and spoke directly to her. 'Fer my part, I think yer real face is every bit as charmin' as t'other.'

Looking at Talthimandar, Isabel felt all of the delight and anticipation at the prospect of his courtship that had been so lacking in her dealings with Mr. Thompson. It was the liveliness of his spirit that enchanted her so, perhaps; the quickness of his mind and his wit; the peculiar gallantry of his manners, and the fascinating eccentricity of his behaviour. It was the dignity he had shown under the burden of the curse which had bound him to his boat; his refusal to descend into self-pity, or to blame another for his actions — even when he had clear enough cause to do so. It was his unabashed exuberance in being freed from the curse, and the unbridled joy he had shown — so far from the stiff, respectable, sensible behaviour that she had been used to show herself, and to experience in others.

And it was in the reasons why he sought Isabel. It could have nothing to do with the respectability of her family or the inheritance she one day expected to receive; he could know nothing of such things, nor was he likely to care. And she felt fully persuaded that it had nothing to do with her looks, for even in the heights of her beauty she was to the Ayliri of Aylfenhame as a candle to the sun.

She might have hoped that Mr. Thompson sought her for her own self, but in Talthimandar's case she was certain of it. 'I do permit it,' she said to him, smiling for the first time that day. 'And Mama and Papa will not forbid it.' She looked at her parents as she spoke, allowing all of her hope and fear to show in her face.

'You really ought to allow it, father,' said Charles unexpectedly, who had hitherto kept his thoughts to himself. 'It is perfectly obvious that Isa's happiness is at stake here. She ought to be trusted to decide for herself where it is most likely to lie, should she not? You have always said that she has a good head on her shoulders, and has never been given to wild flights of fancy.'

Isabel cast her brother a grateful look, and received a wink in return. His words did not appear to operate upon their father as he might have hoped, for Mr. Ellerby's frown deepened, and she could see that he was working himself into one of his fits of disapproval. He would burst forth any moment in an angry tirade, and none of the opinions or judgements he expressed would be at all to Talthimandar's taste — or her own. She braced herself for the onslaught, biting her lip to hold back the tears of frustration and dismay which began to approach.

Talthimandar's hand crept into her own, and she gently squeezed his fingers, attempting to offer all the silent comfort in her power.

But her father's indignation seemed abruptly to dissipate. He said nothing at all for some time, except to direct some soothing comment to his wife. When at last Mrs. Ellerby had composed herself, he said brusquely to Talthimandar: 'Which property were you planning to purchase?'

Talthimandar blinked. 'I… had not yet proceeded so far with my plans.'

Mr. Ellerby sighed, and beckoned to the erstwhile Ferryman. 'You may speak with me in my study.' He turned and left the hallway the moment these words were spoken, and did not wait to see whether Talthimandar followed.

'Mr. Ellerby!' wailed his wife. Her remonstrance failed to stop him, and she was left to the comfort of her sister's embrace. Eliza winked at Isabel as she led Harriet away, and smiled her dazzling approbation of her niece's choice. Tafferty followed them, pausing only to press her nose against Isabel's leg by way of farewell.

Mr. Thompson, Isabel that moment realised, had quietly withdrawn at some point during the discussion, and Tiltager was also nowhere in evidence. Her brother now also took his leave, pausing to bestow an affectionate kiss upon Isabel and a cordial handshake upon Talthimandar. 'Father will come around,' he said. 'Mother will take longer, I'm afraid. She has many years of ingrained prejudice to overcome.' He departed, leaving Isabel alone with the Ferryman.

Talthimandar looked at Isabel. 'D' ye really wish me t' proceed?' he said softly. 'Ye need say but a single word, if'n ye don't, an' I shall go away at once.'

Isabel could not help contrasting this deference to her choices with Mr. Thompson's reluctance to accept her refusal, and liking Talthimandar the better for it. She gave him her hands, and smiled up at him with unreserved approval. 'I do not wish for you to go away,' she said. 'Not ever.'

He squeezed her hands, and kissed them. 'Then I will speak wi' yer father.' He touched her gold-streaked hair, very gently, and kissed her cheek.

Alleny, one of Ferndeane's brownies, tapped his knee. 'I will take you to the Master's study,' she said in her soft voice.

'Thankin' ye,' said Talthimandar, and gestured for her to lead on. Isabel watched as her Ferryman left the hall in the wake of the tiny brownie, her heart swelling with love and joy and relief until she felt in danger of bursting with so much felicity.

Well, now! We 'ave reached the end o' my tale, which I think to be somethin' of a shame. I 'ave right enjoyed talkin' to ye. An odd bundle o' happenin's, were they not? Strange things come to pass when the worlds of England an' Aylfenhame 'appen to collide, an' no mistake.

Talthimandar did settle in England, if ye were wonderin'. He got hisself a nice little place 'bout two miles from Tilby, an' there he an' Miss Isabel went to live straight after they was married. Oh, but Mrs. Aylfendeane, I should say! An odd name, perhaps, but it were chosen to satisfy the requirements o' society, an' to reflect both his heritage an' hers. Fer my part, I think it rather fine.

I am sorry to say tha' Mrs. Ellerby was not wholly wrong in her doomin' an' gloomin'. There's talk about the Aylfendeanes o' Somerdale, an' some as will 'ave nowt to do wi' them. But Mrs. Isabel cares nothin' fer that. An' why should she? Them as matters 'ave grown used to her face, an' accepted her husband, an' thas all she wanted.

They's often in Aylfenhame, as ye may imagine. There's a new Keeper o' the Ferry Boat Mirisane, now, an' the lass is often seen around Somerdale, pickin' up the Aylfendeanes or droppin' them back home. I'm happy to say tha' Miss Landon an' Aubranael are often visitin' at Somerdale, too, now tha' travellin' betwixt their realm an' this is a mite easier. Some say tha' freer passage is to be a growin' thing, now, an' I did hear word tha' there's a new ferry-boat bein' built. Not news to please all, I'll wager, but I think it a mighty fine thing indeed.

There's just one disquietin' matter on my mind, which I'll share wi' ye before ye go. Who was it that gave Talthimandar's name to Miss Isabel? It were none o' Lyrriant's folk, or so he says. I mislike tha' it was done so clandestine-like, an' on the Kostigern's own property besides. There's more to that than meets the eye, mark my words, an' I mislike my Isabel bein' beholden t' whoever-he-be.

An' what o' tha' tricksy Grunewald? His Majesty the Goblin King, if ye please? I don't rightly know what he was gettin' hisself up to wi' meddlin' at the Chronicler's Library, but he 'ad a purpose. No doubt about it. What that might ha' been, though? Yer guess is as good as mine.

If ye should happen to pass this way again in the future, stop a while wi' me. Mayhap I'll have more to tell ye. Fer now, though, I wish ye a good journey! Mind the road towards Toynton, now. It's dry enough at this time o' year, but there's a stretch as'll do yer carriage-wheels no good if'n ye go too fast. I'll 'ave a quick word wi' yer coachman.

243

there's a stretch as'll do yer carriage-wheels no good if'n ye go too fast. I'll 'ave a quick word wi' yer coachman.

Other Titles By Charlotte E. English:

Tales of Aylfenhame:
Miss Landon and Aubranael
Miss Ellerby and the Ferryman

The Draykon Series:
Draykon
Lokant
Orlind

The Lokant Libraries:
Seven Dreams

The Drifting Isle Chronicles:
Black Mercury

The Malykant Mysteries:
The Rostikov Legacy
The Ivanov Diamond
Myrrolen's Ghost Circus
Ghostspeaker